What people are saying about
The ForeverFactor . . .

"In a blend of science and human drama, this novel captures the journey of a visionary inventor driven by personal tragedy to transform a ground-breaking scientific discovery into a life-saving medicine."

–SANGEETA BHATIA, MD, PhD Professor, Director, Marble Center for Cancer Nanomedicine, MIT

"Hogan and Iles have taken our obsession with longevity and weaved in the intrigue of the Silicon Valley startups and the wonder of scientific discovery."

–JAGESH SHAH
SVP, Head of Platform at Stealth Flagship Pioneering Startup
Assoc. Professor of Systems Biology, Harvard Medical School

"A riveting suspense novel that takes the reader into the workings of Silicon Valley and the startup culture that changed the world of business and how we live."

–JIM GOETZ, PARTNER, Sequoia Capital

"Finally. Someone has written a novel that captures the startup culture that makes Silicon Valley so unique. *The Forever Factor* is an inside baseball look at the workings and challenges of daily life in the startup world of Silicon Valley."

–ASHEEM CHANDNA, Partner, Greylock Capital

"While serving up its heady mix of Silicon Valley-style competition, conspiracy, and coding, *The Forever Factor* also draws us into a crucial ethical debate: Who should own and control access to the life-saving and life-extending technologies emerging from 21st century science?"

–JAMES DECKER, PhD in Philosophy

"In this smart, fast-paced story, the Silicon Valley dream of radically extending the human life span is tantalizingly in reach for Petra Alexander. Will she succeed? Or will the obstacles, subterfuge, and competing interests prove insurmountable? More than just a suspenseful read, *The Forever Factor* tackles the unexpectedly thorny issues that surround this techno- scientific quest."

–LINELL CADY, Professor Emerita of religious studies,
Arizona State University

THE
FOREVER
FACTOR

THE
FOREVER
FACTOR

LAUGHING DOG PUBLISHING • AUSTIN, TEXAS

Dedication

TH: To Pamela, Rachel and Maya
AI: To Jim, the one and only

The Forever Factor
Tom Hogan and Amanda Iles
Copyright ©2025 by Tom Hogan

ISBN: 978-1-7369436-6-3 Paperback
ISBN: 978-1-7369436-7-0 eBook
Library of Congress Control Number: 2024921940

Published by
Laughing Dog Publishing LLC

For bulk orders or permission to make copies of any part of the work email your request to Tom Hogan: Tom@CrowdedOcean.com

Cover + Interior design by Bob Schramm, Bookends Design
www.BookendsDesign.com

First Edition
Printed in the United States of America

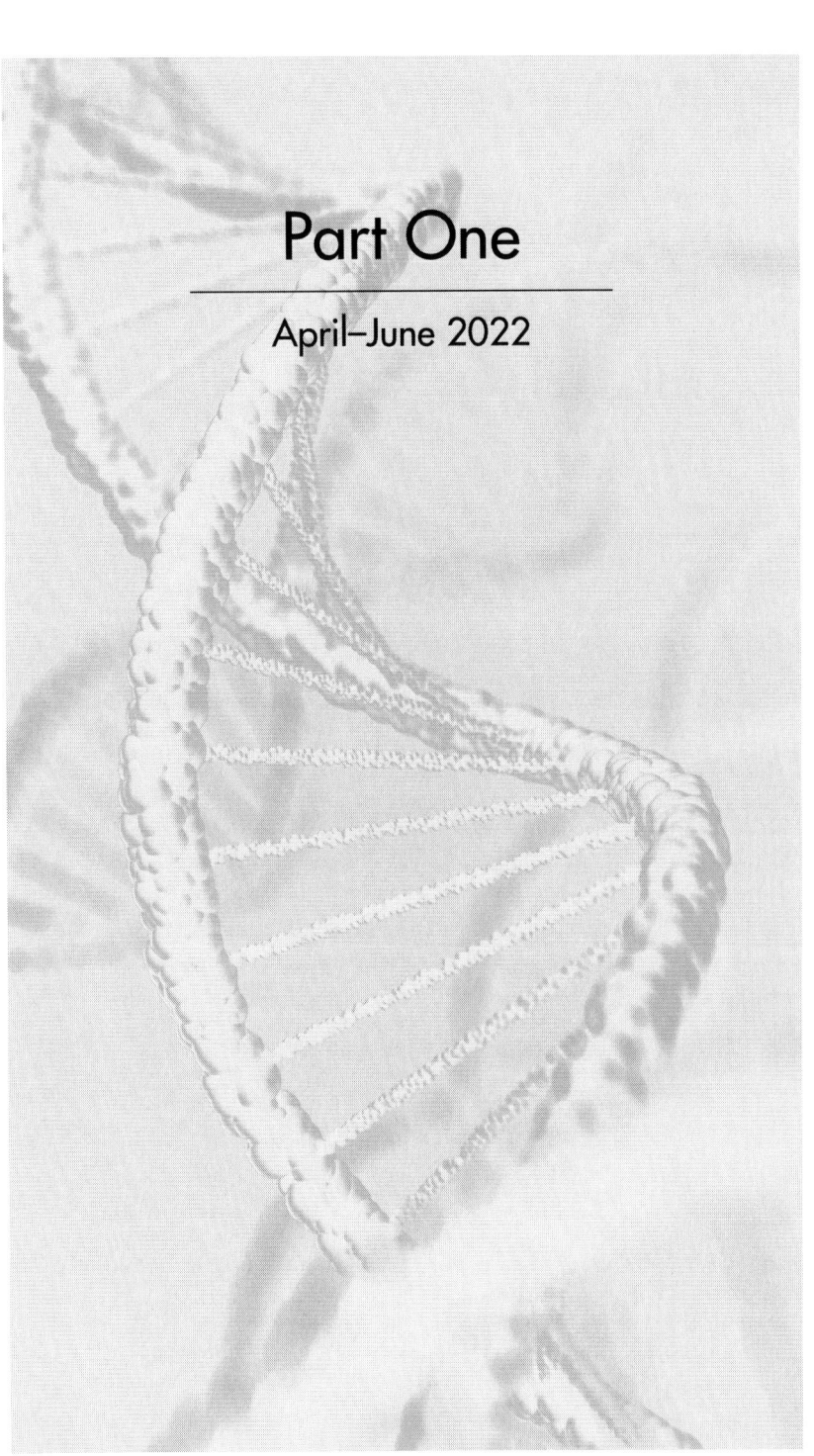

Part One

April–June 2022

Prologue

"DON'T LISTEN TO VINOD," Trina says to Zac, the new guy. "When it comes to biohacking, he's our resident Luddite. I'll bet he's still drinking his own piss."

"Filtered or unfiltered, Vinnie?" asks Maksym, who everyone calls Max. His English, learned in Ukraine, is more precise and bookish than casual, but it also has a confusing southern drawl, a remnant of his four years at the University of Alabama.

"Unfiltered, but with a twist." Vinod stands up unsteadily and gyrates his hips. "Shaken, not stirred." Even though Vinod's been in the U.S. for over a dozen years, his accent still betrays his upbringing in India. With the distinctive intonations and rise and fall, it's an accent that Valley folk think they can mimic but can't.

The table issues a collective forced laugh. Trina says *sotto voce* to Zac, "We have to laugh at Vinnie's jokes. Now that he's sold his latest startup for four billion, he's the biggest of the Big Swinging Dicks. Or Dick of the Moment. Take your pick."

"I thought Freddy hates that name. He told me in my interview to always refer to the group as the Hydras, not the Big Swinging Dicks. No one told me why."

"Why Freddy hates the name, or why the Hydras?"

"Both."

"On the BSD front, he says why rub the public's nose in our success. Also, he thinks I'm offended by the term, though I'm not. I know the other boys call me 'Strap-On' behind my back." Seeing

Zac's surprise, Trina says, "Hey, they're assholes. I'm not going to change that. Plus, I'm an asshole, too. Just a higher-class one."

"And hydra? What's up with that?"

"The hydra is the only animal whose stem cells are in a state of constant renewal, making it the only creature that can seemingly live forever. It makes sense for us and what we're trying to do here." She takes a sip of wine and smiles. "Plus it's always fun to see which name a reporter uses."

The Dicks are an eclectic group of Silicon Valley legends, brought together by their shared interest in biohacking and longevity. As Max put it in an interview, "We are our own guinea pigs. We experiment on our own bodies, trying to live forever." A pause and a small smile. "Or die trying."

The group is gathered on Eric's yacht, currently parked offshore of the island he owns and is developing in the Caribbean. In the world of yachts, mega-yachts, and now super-yachts, the *First In* is testimony to its owner's contrarian streak, one that has served him exceptionally well in the world of venture capital. Instead of trying to keep up with Larry Ellison and the rest of the boys, who continually one-up each other over who's got the biggest one, Eric has opted for style over length.

To celebrate his newly minted billionaire status in 2014, he bought a 200-foot yacht, gutted everything except the supporting structures, and turned it over to the team that designed his favorite Manhattan boutique hotel, one so unique and private that it has no name out front. His only guidance was to make his floating treasure unique, modern, and comfortable, something to come home to, not to show off. The result is a spectacular and startling combination of glass—tons of it—distressed steel, and concrete with modern but comfortable furniture. "A cross between an aquarium and a Tribeca warehouse loft," is how Trina describes it.

The group is assembled around a dining room table that mirrors the yacht's overall design: nothing flashy but everything distinctive. Black steel flatware, hand-formed dinnerware, and Venetian-blown goblets, no two the same. The table is set formally for the first time this weekend, signaling the end of a productive three-day gathering, with the group hearing from a dozen biohacking and longevity startups. They're now awaiting both their host, who is 15 minutes late—a rarity for him—and Chef Andre, flown in especially for the occasion.

"Where the hell is Eric, anyway?" Max asks, looking past the rest of the group and down the hall. "He's never late. I have this image of Chef Andre getting impatient and spitting into our appetizers." Max is the most technical of the group. Known as "The Coder's Coder," he has developed a number of technologies, including some of the earliest versions of artificial intelligence, which virtually every software company now licenses and uses.

Two years into its history, the group still has no idea whether Max is the nerdiest rich guy they know or is having them on with his style choices. Take tonight's attire. Max has come to dinner in madras shorts, sandals with socks, and a white short-sleeved collared shirt. With his favorite heavy-rimmed black glasses, the bridge often held together with black electrical tape, all that's missing is the pocket protector.

The question about their host is directed at the group's leader, Jason Fredericks, known in the industry as 'Freddy.' The Managing Director of Headwaters, the leading VC firm in Silicon Valley, he's the only Dick with a full-time job these days, now that Vinod has ostensibly retired. Freddy is the poster child for the VC world. With a brush cut of graying hair, always just the right length, swept back from a chiseled face, and a tan physique reflecting his raft of challenging outdoor activities, he has every right to be an arrogant asshole, like most of his VC compatriots. Instead, he's soft-spoken and thoughtful, directing Headwaters collegially, mentoring his startups with the same soft touch. His uniform for nearly every occasion is creased khakis, boat shoes, and a starched white collared shirt. The only way to tell he's on a BSD outing is he leaves his socks at home.

"While we're waiting for our host, let's hear from our resident grinder," Freddy says, inclining his chin toward Zac. "Any new implants to report, Zac?"

As the newest Dick, Zac is presenting to the group for the first time. His hair spiked, and clad in a black T-shirt and ripped jeans, he comes off initially as trying too hard. Think early Brad Pitt, with gel but minus the abs. It's a look he's cultivated for years: The trust-fund kid with more money than sense, the loud-voiced amateur waiting to be fleeced by his betters. It's also a look that has taken him from Wall Street curiosity to a grudgingly acknowledged master investor with a better track record than any of his vocal critics.

Zac's heard the stories of would-be founders fleeing this table in tears or in immediate need of the boat's restroom. But today's meeting is comfortable and collegial. After all, the Dicks are on his turf, biohacking, and his invitation to join the group is based on his own experience as well as his investments in the field. That and the fact that he's grown his trust fund from $1 billion to $3 billion in six years, surpassing his parents' net worth. Which he brings up in every interview and which makes for awkward family gatherings.

"You guys think *I'm* a grinder," he says, his voice lacking the gravitas of age but rich in confidence, "you should meet my pal, Jesse. Magnets in his fingers to open doors and direct his computer, chips in his arms to monitor his health, and implants in his ears for both music and phone calls. His brain's next."

"Maybe we should have invited this Jesse to join the group instead of you," Max says.

"Jesse's broke," Zac continues. "Every cent goes into his hacks. I can have him here tomorrow, though, if you'd like. One caution—I'd advise against shaking hands. He started experimenting with fecal transplants last week."

The faces around the table display a mixture of curiosity and disgust. "Is that what I think it is?" Trina asks.

Zac nods. "Think blood doping, but with excrement. Young, vibrant shit replacing your old, tired shit, with the goal being to reset your internal clock to a younger state." He looks around the table. "I'm looking a little better to you guys, aren't I?"

"A little," Vinod says. "But notice none of us has transplanted any of *your* blood into our bodies. Given your history of experimenting with 'alternative chemicals,' I'm petrified my kids would come out with ears growing out of the middle of their foreheads."

Zac takes a sip of cucumber-infused water and does what he always does in these high-pressure meets. He looks around the table, meeting each person's gaze, gauging their interest in the subject as well as their attitude toward him. It's an exercise that calms him, and at times puts his audience on the defensive. Not tonight, though. This is the Dicks' game, and he'll have to validate his place at the table.

The first gaze he returns is Vinod's, this weekend's star. Vinnie is what Trina calls "high-school handsome." The looks are there, but his newest incarnation is better suited for a younger man—hair a tad too long, the earring a little too precious, the clothes a bit too hip. Trina has expressed her hopes that one of his "savor the good life" promises will be to engage a good personal stylist.

Trina is the opposite of Vinod, stylish without trying. The most successful woman CEO in Silicon Valley history, she's a healthy thin—not that gaunt East Coast socialite look. She always arrives elegantly dressed down for any occasion. Today, for example, her stylish long bob is pulled back into a casual ponytail, in deference to the steady Caribbean breeze. A wide-brimmed straw hat with a rusty orange Pucci scarf sits on the chair next to her. No jewelry. A white bikini halter top shows under a crisp white linen slip top, with practical drawstring linen shorts and Tory Burch sandals under the table. In a movie, she'd be played by Julianne Moore.

Freddy's the Dick Zac wants to impress the most. He knows Freddy had initially resisted bringing him into the group, saying he reminded him of the rich kid in high school who lorded his wealth over you, and who hired football players to stuff anyone who crossed him into trash cans. But, as Max pointed out, the rest of the Hydras are about the same age and have come up through Silicon Valley and the tech world in roughly the same ways. For their new fund, one populated entirely with their own money, they need a broader perspective, generationally and experientially. Zac knows more about biohacking than the rest of the group combined. And he's willing to put his money, as well as his body, behind his research, making him the guinea-est of the guinea pigs, enthusiastically sharing his research, as well as the results of his personal biohacking experiments, with anyone who asks.

Zac has prepared a formal presentation about biohacking, but that will wait for Eric. Instead, he talks about his own program and solicits questions and updates from the other Dicks. After 10 minutes, with the subject exhausted, Max stands up on unsteady feet. "I'll go get Eric."

Trina rests a hand on his and motions for him to sit down. "A couple more minutes. Then Freddy or I will go roust him."

"I bet the SOB is on the phone with the last presenters, trying to cut us out of the deal," Max says, winking at Zac as he takes his seat.

Freddy says to Zac, "The team that just left. This was their second time presenting to us, but your first time with them. What was your take?"

"As far as their formulas go, I'll defer to Max. But as Vinod —Vinnie—noted, I'm acquainted with some of their chemicals. And the ones they're using are volatile as fuck."

Freddy checks his watch and sighs. He stands and heads down the hall to fetch Eric. Vinod turns to Zac. "Did you get your Kiwi package yet?"

"It's stalled. My agent there says the government will be more amenable to my application if I up my investment in the New Zealand Tech Fund to 15 mil."

"That's bullshit," Vinnie says. "I got the whole package— passport, land, plans for the bunker, preferential landing at the airport in case of a shutdown—all for ten."

Zac is the last of the BSDs to purchase the "Kiwi Apocalyptic Package." The package had its genesis when some UK university deemed New Zealand the optimal place on the planet to ride out the 'imminent global collapse.' Peter Thiel, the political and social Silicon Valley contrarian, saw the article and petitioned New Zealand for citizenship. Despite having spent a total of 12 days in the country in his life, he was approved immediately. New passport in hand, Thiel bought a big chunk of land, with plans for building an apocalyptic Shangri-la for himself and a select group of his pals. A number of tech, finance, and Hollywood uber-rich followed suit, until international coverage and local objections shamed the government into publicly outlawing the practice. But with the right connections and the right contributions to New Zealand's tech industry, the opportunity is still there.

"Which package did you wind up going with?" Zac asks Trina.

"The Gradual," Trina says. "I can't afford the 'Sudden,' neither the money nor the time. And to be honest, I kinda don't want to be around if the Sudden happens."

"I'm with Trina," Vinod says. "Eric's the only one I know with the Sudden package. I looked into it, and the preparation and maintenance left me exhausted."

There are, as Vinod explained to Zac at their last meeting, three different packages. The Core consists of New Zealand citizenship, a remote plot of land, and blueprints for a survival bunker. The Gradual is a step up and is for those who believe the Apocalypse will be foreseeable, something sparked by social unrest or a pandemic, allowing for preparation before migration. The Gradual package comes with citizenship, a built and fully stocked bunker, and landing rights for your jet, even in the case of a nationwide shutdown. Most of the Dicks have the Gradual.

The Sudden package is for those who believe the collapse of society will be due to a major natural disaster or nuclear attack, giving little to no warning. As Vinod explained to Zac, "Eric keeps a go-bag with him at all times. Because the roads will be blocked or collapsed, he's got a motorcycle fueled and ready to get to the airport, where his jet is always ready. But remember, someone needs to fly the jet, which means he has to pay for his pilot to have the same package, including citizenship, the motorcycle, and everything else. I get tired just thinking about all that."

"Besides," Max adds, "with the Sudden package, the only ones who are going to survive are the sheep, some New Zealanders I've never met, and a few rich assholes like us, all thinking they should be in charge of this new world. If that's what survival looks like, I'd rather just have a nice glass of scotch, toast the mushroom cloud, and kiss my ass goodbye."

• • •

Freddy reaches the sleeping level at the bottom of the stairs. Even though he's working on his third scotch, his gait is steady and relaxed. Each room he passes has the door open, allowing a glimpse inside. One room looks like Al Gore's stylist got there first, all earth tones, but in gentle blends and textures that pull everything together. The next is all black and white and grey, with enough metal accents to evoke either an East Coast diner or a heavy-metal rocker's wardrobe.

The end of the hall holds the boat's masterpiece. Built into the prow of the yacht are full-length windows that hover just above the waterline. At night, with the prow lights on, you have a view of the stars as well as an aquarium, the light drawing inquisitive fish of all sizes and types.

Reaching Eric's stateroom at the end of the hall, Freddy knocks and waits. When he doesn't get an answer, he puts an ear to the door. Hearing nothing, he tries the handle, expecting it to be locked. But it turns. Frowning, he stays in the hallway for a few moments, giving Eric a chance to tell him to get the hell out, that he's coming already. It's the continuing silence that finally impels him to ease the door wide open and step inside.

Eric is splayed on his bed, a dab of foam drying on his mouth like toothpaste. His empty blue eyes are fixed on the ceiling. Freddy steps back into the hall and in a cracking voice calls to the crew to summon the Virgin Islands harbor patrol and a water ambulance.

He approaches Eric's bedside and feels for a pulse but has no idea if he's doing it right. Cleaning the foam from Eric's mouth with a finger, he inclines his ear until it touches Eric's lips. There's no sound, no breath, no motion of any sort. He puts a hand to Eric's forehead, but recoils at the clammy feel.

He looks around the room quickly. It would be like Eric to have one of those heart-jumper kits nearby. Finding nothing, his eyes land on the bedside table, which holds three small plastic bags. Each bag is open, with a sliver of aluminum foil next to it. Each piece of foil harbors a residue of blue powder.

"You dumb sonofabitch," Freddy whispers to his friend. "What part of 'volatile' did you not understand?"

The captain of the yacht bursts into the room, followed closely by his lieutenant. Freddy gestures with a resigned wave at the corpse, rises unsteadily, and leaves the stateroom. He returns to the dining table to break the news to the rest of the BSDs and wait for the harbor police and the coroner. He wonders what the official cause of death will be. And what the startup providing the samples will do with that information.

1

In the Hole

PETRA WAKES BEFORE THE ALARM GOES OFF. She sits up straight, her posture alert and relaxed—no stumbling into the day, no yawning or pawing for the alarm. Her eyes slide to the clock, though she knows what it'll say: 5:40. Clad in yoga pants and a sleeveless stretchy black T-shirt, she slings her feet over the side of the bed and pads out of the bedroom.

Knuckling her hair, she walks down the hall toward the second bedroom, which is bedless but full of workout equipment. The walls hold two framed Ansel Adams prints, one of El Capitan, the other of Half Dome, the famed photographer's use of shadow and sunlight articulating the ledges, veins, and cracks on the rock faces she's so familiar with. It's time to start her day.

• • •

In her first meeting with her financial advisor, Jeff Overstreet, he had asked her to define herself in a few words. She had chosen "practical" and "functional." When he'd remarked that the two words were similar, she added a third: "Subaru." When he looked puzzled, she said, "I don't make statements with what I drive, what I wear, or where I live. I pick a car for its ability to hold my climbing gear and get me safely to my destination. I choose where I live based on proximity to work and its ability to hold all my equipment. I dress for warmth and comfort"—a slight smile—"and to avoid being arrested for public nudity. Does that help?"

"Absolutely," Overstreet said. "I wish all my clients were that clear." He held up a finger for a minute as he made some notes. Petra nodded and waited. She liked both his attitude and his office trappings, which reminded her of her Salvana office. His furnishings fell somewhere between basic and tired. She couldn't tell if the desk was solid wood or laminate. The plants, including the standing palm in the corner, were fake. A high-end fake, to be sure, but nothing that required watering. His suit looked off the rack.

More importantly, he had started the meeting by asking her about herself, rather than thumping his chest and highlighting his financial acumen and results he'd achieved for other clients. "Let's talk discretionary income," he said. "Your profile lists some exotic locations over the past five years. How does that square with ..."

"They weren't chosen because they're exotic," Petra interrupted, "but because they're locations of the rock faces my partner and I climb. Though once the climbing is over, we do enjoy doing normal traveler things, like exploring the local landscape and culture and talking with people."

"Got it. Risk, then. I'm assuming, based on your hobbies, that you're pretty comfortable with it."

She shook her head. "Climbing isn't risky. Planned and executed right, it's far safer than driving to this meeting. When it comes to my finances, I'm risk averse." She nodded at the folder on the table, which held a printout of all her assets. "I know conventional wisdom says that at age 32 I should have 80 percent or more of my assets in the market. But I want no more than 50 percent there." Before he could object, she pulled out an envelope and slid it across the table. "This is a discretionary account, from my poker winnings, which I keep separate. I regard it as found money, so take as much risk with it as you like. Just explain it to me first."

· · ·

She strides straight to the incline table, an elaborate contraption that took the better part of a day to assemble. She shackles her ankles in and tilts back until she's completely inverted, the soles of her bare feet conversing with the ceiling. The initial light-headedness, with the blood draining south, gives way to calm as her meditation breathing takes over. Reaching over and touch-ing a large button atop a small square box on the floor next to her head, she relaxes fully as the room fills with the sound of small waves splashing the shore. Though she's most comfortable in the mountains, the sound of the ocean always soothes. For 15 minutes, she lies there, suspended, restrained, at rest, until a barely audible gong silences the waves' chorus. Petra hoists her-self into a half sit-up, her back parallel to the floor, and holds the position for a full minute, her stomach quivering at the end, her forehead beading.

She rights herself and clips out, then walks over to the Pilates Reformer, an impressive assemblage of wood, straps, and springs that looks like something designed by Torquemada. She uses all the machine's components to put her body through its paces. Though someone peering in at her from the doorway might think the exercises look comfortable, 10 minutes at her pace leaves her bathed in sweat. Lying on her back, feet in straps and using different springs to alter the resistance, she brings her legs back over her head.

Switching to a kneeling position, she moves through a variety of upper body moves. Next, standing alongside the machine, she pushes on a wooden bar, as if starting a bobsled run, then holds the posture until her hamstrings quiver. After 30 minutes, her shirt collar and underarms are a deeper black. Wiping her glistening face with her sleeve and feeling pleasantly worked over from head to toe, she heads for the kitchen.

Synchronized with her alarm clock, her coffee machine has a cup of her favorite brew waiting. Into the blender next to the coffee maker, she pours small bags of pre-measured strawberries, blueberries, and powders, adding oat milk and ice from the refrigerator. The blender comes to life, grinding then whirring its jumbled ingredients into a froth. She shuts it off and pours the bluish-pink concoction into a go-cup, placing it next to the gym bag and briefcase standing by the front door. Sipping her coffee, she goes back to her bathroom, puts her toothbrush, toothpaste, and deodorant in a small plastic bag, and heads out the front door.

Even in the pressurized world of Silicon Valley, most garages and carports are still full at this hour, and the one at Petra's apartment complex is no exception. Over the years, she has determined that the Valley wakes up in shifts. Shift one is the Type A's, the ones standing in line at gyms when they open at 5:30. The bulk of these are VCs, CEOs, or wannabes trying to impress the first two groups, all determined to get their mile swim or trainer-supervised workout out of the way before the day has a chance to get away from them. Some are driven by a desire to be at their desks before 7, their wet hair testimonial to their work ethic. For Petra, her early, damp-haired arrival at work has nothing to do with impressing anyone. She does it to prepare her body for the next major climb and for the kickstart that the morning ritual brings to her research.

The second shift is the standard business crowd, on the road by 7:30, hoping there's no line at the Starbucks drive-through, shooting for an 8:30 arrival at work. Though that's dependent on the traffic, which rivals that of Los Angeles for congestion and delays.

As the morning rush eases, the rock stars of the valley, the engineers—both hardware and software—start their days, rolling in between 10 and noon. No one begrudges them this schedule, knowing that, fueled by company-provided dinner and unlimited espresso and Red Bull caffeine fixes, they often work into and even through the night.

Petra exits her nondescript apartment complex, just one of the many that pepper the various communities that combine to make up Silicon Valley. From San Jose up to San Francisco, the Valley is one interconnected sprawl. Cupertino, Santa Clara, and Sunnyvale blend with Mt. View, which bleeds north into Palo Alto, then into Menlo Park, where Petra lives, the destination chosen not for its great restaurants or upscale neighborhoods, but for its proximity to Salvana. And to The Ascent.

It's a 10-minute drive to The Ascent, a route she can do in her sleep. As usual, Petra's is the only car in the parking lot when she arrives. A converted warehouse in one of the few industrial pockets left in the Valley, The Ascent contains two large climbing walls, a bouldering cave, and a social area for the climbers and watchful parents of young budding rock-jocks.

Petra lets herself into the gym with her own key, given to her long ago by Spyder, the owner. She opens her gym bag and removes a pair of climbing shoes, which look like the result of slippers mating with running shoes. She tugs them on, the fit intentionally tight, allowing for a better feel for the rock. Walking over to the bouldering area, she eyes the large, low-ceilinged room with padded floors and walls and a ceiling that looks like something out of a spelunker's wet dream. Plastic rocks of every shape and color are affixed to all the surfaces, except the floor. The climbers call them "holds" and, depending on their size and shape, they can be further delineated as jugs, slopes, pockets, pinches, or crimps. Routes are outlined for those who want or need them, but most of the climbers make up their own challenges.

Petra grabs two small ceiling holds and hoists herself up, swinging her feet until they find purchase on the ceiling, wedging between some of the larger holds. Suspended upside-down, bug-like, she rests for a moment, gathering herself physically, then hoists herself up and grabs two different holds. She releases her left hand to grasp a plastic rock two feet to her left, then stretches her right hand toward a hold that seems beyond her reach. But by contorting her shoulders and changing the position of her feet, she's able to grab it. Her arms are a coordinated chorus of straining, articulated muscle and tendon.

As she contemplates her next move, physics and fatigue prevail. Petra falls to the heavily padded floor, slapping it with her forearm to absorb some of the impact. She wills her breath to settle, then gets to her feet and hoists herself up to a new ceiling position and a fresh set of moves.

Twenty minutes later, her calves and forearms burning and shivering in an early sign of cramping, she takes a break, ducking as she exits the bouldering room. Facing the main room's climbing wall, she slides down with her back against the room's wall until her butt's on the floor, her knees up by her shoulders. Then she stares intently at the edifice in front of her.

The main climbing wall is the gym's town square, where everyone congregates to climb, belay, or simply watch. The wall, to the uninitiated, looks like a slab of cement decorated by a horde of crazed kindergartners. Seemingly random placements of plastic rocks and ledges, some of them less than a fingertip in width, form an intimidating blend of colors and routes that makes sense only with time and effort. When the wall isn't in use, the ropes hang limply from the ceiling, like uncoiled snakes.

Every afternoon the wall comes alive. Its congregants, their waists slack with rope, move with deliberation and determination, their eyes fixed on their next move, calling down at times to their belayers for confirmation or encouragement. It's a tight community, where standing is determined solely on how a climber interacts with the wall. The ultimate accolade to the beginner is ringing the bell at the top of the wall. More serious climbers settle for a nod from another climber when they pull off a difficult move.

Petra has been climbing since her university days in Chicago. She was originally drawn to team sports, especially soccer and volleyball. But two deaths in her early life caused major adjustments in both her personality and choice of sports. She became more withdrawn, then began chafing at the sports where she had to rely on others to succeed. Previously enthusiastic and supportive, she became increasingly demanding of her teammates and of herself, until everyone was glad when she quit.

She migrated to individual sports, trying tennis, running, and cycling until she found climbing at a local rock gym. With her slim but strong upper body and muscular legs, she had the makings of a promising beginner. Applying her analytical mathematical prowess and iron will to the study of routes, she moved quickly up the gym's hierarchy. By the end of her first year, the gym's owners told her that she had more promise than any other climber in their experience.

In Boston, due to the weather and as a release from her graduate studies, she began competitive indoor climbing. With her climbing skills still developing, she relied on her mental game to level the playing field. Before any contest she would stare intently at the wall for minutes at a time, memorizing all the possible routes and options. Then she would close her eyes, slide into a semi-trance, and envision herself on each route, rejecting all but one. Only then did she open her eyes and step toward the wall.

The inclusion of sport climbing in the 2016 Olympics presented Petra with a decision. Her coaches told her that if she took a year off and devoted herself full-time to the sport, she was a lock for the U.S. team, with a good chance at medaling. MIT was all in favor of the plan, the PR department saying it would help counter the image of the school as just a bunch of lightbulbs with legs. But Petra couldn't justify the time away from her research. It was something she owed her sister, as well as herself.

It wasn't until she arrived in Silicon Valley that she got into outside climbing. Once she began with The Ascent and Spyder, she knew she'd found her gym and her coach. Spyder, who had more first ascents than anyone else in the area, coached her, but only when asked and then offering just the minimum, allowing her to develop her own style at her own pace.

Eventually he introduced her to Zoe as a possible climbing partner. The two bonded quickly, belaying and encouraging each other indoors and eventually moving outside. They frequented the Santa Cruz mountains' abundance of training areas until they felt ready for Yosemite. After mastering routes on Half Dome, El Cap, and a number of Yosemite's lesser known but equally difficult granite rock faces, Spyder directed the two to increasingly difficult climbs in Europe, the Andes, and Southeast Asia.

While both women are strong climbers on their own, their contrasts make for an even stronger team. Petra is the better technical climber but the more cautious of the two. Zoe is the one who pushes, arguing for difficult routes that test their physical limits. In choosing each route, they meet with Spyder to review their options. Zoe then chooses the destination, while Petra handles the research and planning.

Sitting on the floor of The Ascent, Petra rubs her hair—brownish black, worn short, with little sense of style. She would wear it even shorter for convenience, maybe even a buzz cut, but doesn't want to answer questions about her sexual orientation or whether she has cancer.

Her skin is unlined and almond-colored, a reflection of her Greek and Anglo origins. Her nose is thin-lined and strong-boned, with a slight bump in the middle, the remnant of a fall in Yosemite a few years back, where the belaying rope halted her descent and swung her, face-first, into the wall. Petra reset it herself and was fine with the result.

Her appearance is often a topic of discussion, one that Petra's good friend and former lover Izaak is accustomed to fielding. "She shouldn't be attractive," said a friend of Izaak's, upon meeting her, "but she is. You know?" When Izaak didn't reply, his friend went on. "Maybe it's her intensity, the way she seems so sure of herself. Is she seeing anyone?"

It's a question Izaak gets more often than he'd like, from both men and women. He and Petra first met at the University of Chicago, where he majored in computer science while Petra started in math but then transferred to biological chemistry. They were drawn to each other, intellectually and physically, leading Izaak into his first encounter with "the Petra wall." As Petra explained to him on one of their earlier dates, she wasn't interested in romance. Friendship, yes. Sex, absolutely. But sex more as a sport and a form of release, not a route to deepening intimacy. And showing the practicality and logic that's her constant guide, she saw no reason to limit that sexual expression to just one person, let alone one gender.

Izaak and Petra had enjoyed the sex tremendously, but even though Petra never talked about other sexual partners, he knew they existed, and it brought out a jealous, almost possessive side that he didn't like. Petra also didn't like that version of Izaak and curtailed the sexual side of things, saying that friends were more important to her—as well as harder to find—than sexual partners.

Izaak preceded Petra to Silicon Valley, landing the plum assignment of overseeing all of Stanford's IT needs. He became her guide to the Valley and the Bay Area in general. They initially tried to renew the sexual side of things, but this time it was Izaak who suggested they go the platonic route, a decision Petra had no problem with.

She faced a similar decision with Zoe. On their first trip together to Yosemite, it was clear by their second night in the tent that both were open to exploring the sexual side of their relationship. The sex continued for the remaining three days of the trip, but on the way home, they agreed that a climbing partnership was already complicated enough without the additional layer. Still, every now and then, when they were in some tent thousands of miles from the Bay Area, they would renew the recreational sex, ending it by unspoken but mutual agreement on the flight back to the Bay Area.

Their first year as climbing partners, Zoe invited Petra to a Thanksgiving celebration she hosted. Also at the dinner was Zoe's sister, Viv. A casting agent in Hollywood, Viv took a great interest in Petra. The attraction was professional, or at least Zoe hoped so. At the end of the evening, after Petra had gone home, Viv had offered her professional opinion of Petra's looks and overall package.

"She's what we in the business call a 'Sophia.' After Sophia Loren. You take any of Sophia's features by themselves and they're wrong, even off-putting. Same with your friend. Her eyes are slightly froggy—not bug-eyes, more like Susan Sarandon. She's got Joni Mitchell teeth, and her nose has got that bump. But put them all together and you've got something that indie directors would definitely be interested in. If I were putting her in my files, the key search terms would be 'edgy' and 'compelling.'"

"What about him?" Zoe teased, gesturing at Izaak, who sat in an armchair in front of the fire, a scotch in his hands.

"Go ahead," Izaak said. "Don't hold back. Growing up half-Jewish, half-black, and inheriting the worst physical characteristics of both, there's nothing I haven't heard. So have at me."

"You're not leading man material," Viv said, "I'll grant you that. But you're comfortable with yourself and audiences can sense that. I'd cast you as the best friend, the one everyone likes, the one everyone depends on. The guy with the heart of gold that the audience will relate to immediately."

"That's the nicest letdown I've ever received," he said. "I'm touched by the thought that went into it."

· · ·

Petra continues to stare at the climbing wall, her eyes flitting from one brightly colored rock to the next. The color coding traces routes of a particular difficulty. Climbers can use any of the rocks on the wall, but achieving a desired level of difficulty means sticking to a single color.

Petra's route is lime green. Spyder designed it especially for her after she had conquered every other route on the wall, some in record time. He told her when he unveiled the route that it was the toughest he'd ever designed. He also cautioned her that the way to the top was as much mental as it was physical.

She's so fixated on the wall and on the small ledge that has her stumped that she doesn't hear the key in the door. It isn't until Spyder slides down next to her that she realizes she's no longer alone. Short and rail-thin with longish hair that floats around his face, he is all angles—in his face, his climbing, his conversations. He motions at her hands, the fingertips white from the chalk. "Working on fingertip strength again?"

When she doesn't answer, he nods at the wall and the lime-green tape and rocks. "I keep telling you, it's not a muscle move. And yet, as they say, 'She persists.' What would your pal Einstein say about doing the same thing over and over and expecting different results?"

Petra doesn't smile. "One try, and then I have to go to work." She harnesses up while Spyder stands, clips in, and leans back slightly into a belaying posture. She clicks the carabiner onto her climbing belt. "On belay?"

"Belay on."

"Climbing." She clambers up the wall as if it were horizontal, rather than vertical. She comes to the spot that has stumped her the past two weeks. Spyder cinches his rope a little tighter, then waits and watches.

Petra stays dead still on the wall, her toes on two small ledges, her eyes fixed on a spot just above her head and to the left. Then she gathers herself, coils and leaps dramatically, both feet and hands coming off the wall. Her hands find new homes about 12 inches above her head. Hanging there for a moment, she then swings her legs, seeking a rock that will give her safe harbor before her next move. She finds purchase with her left foot. The move holds for a moment, then Petra feels her arms vibrate with fatigue as she comes off the wall. Spyder swings his arm across his chest, bringing her fall to a halt after only a 2-foot drop.

"Okay. Bring me down," she says. Once she's on the floor she clicks out and stands next to him. "Alright. I'm convinced. No more muscle moves. What am I missing, mentally?"

Spyder takes her elbow and leads her from the climbing wall over to his counter, where glass shelves hold an array of climbing ropes, carabiners, cams, chalk, and other climbing equipment. Behind the counter, looming over the retail area, is a large, framed photo of an imposing granite wall. There's no artsy or enhancing elements such as clouds. This is a photo taken by a climber for other climbers, shot from a perspective and time of day that will expose the face most starkly, bringing out all the facets of the rock and the challenges they pose.

"This is that face in Peru I told you about, the one I climbed two years ago. I tried it four different times and each time, just like you are now, I wound up stuck in the same spot. Each time I tried to muscle my way up, and each time I came off the wall."

His eyes narrow on the photo, his thoughts back in Peru. "But coming off the wall was what helped me solve it. Hanging there at two thousand feet, instead of looking up, which is what I'd done each time I'd come off, this time I looked to the side and saw that 50 meters to my left and down about 30 degrees was a ledge you couldn't see from the valley floor. It took me an hour to get over there, but once I did, the route to the top was clear. I summited later that afternoon."

Petra gestures back over her head at the climbing wall. "And you're telling me this why?"

"Your thinking is always vertical, about gaining the summit," he says. "It's what makes you such a strong competitive climber, this fixation on getting to the top cleanly and quickly. When it's just you and a wall and a timer, there's no one I'd put my money on ahead of you." He gestures at the Peru face. "But that's what true climbing is about. And to conquer that face, and others that I'll suggest to you and Zoe in the future, will require more than vertical thinking."

"So mentally, what do I need to add to my game?"

"Two things. You need to be able to adapt. You and I could have sat at the bottom of that Peru face for days and never seen that ledge. You get up on a wall, you'll find that there are things that just aren't visible from the ground."

"What's the other thing?"

"I don't want to sound like Yoda, but sometimes the best way up is to go down. Or sideways. Both will give you new options."

"You're saying I'm too linear in my approach."

"I'm just saying there's nothing wrong with lateral thinking now and again."

2

Early Position

PETRA STANDS IN THE DOORWAY of her office, a cup of coffee cradled in her hands, and surveys the Salvana lab. Clad in yoga pants and a grey silk V-neck, she's anxious to close the door and get to work, but she's heeding Jerry's advice and showing her face, now a part of her morning ritual.

"You're a mystery to them, Kid," Jerry told her after her first year at Salvana. "They know you're important, but they don't know why. They're curious, but too intimidated to ask. And your closed door and less-than-welcoming persona don't help. Ed and I like to run a friendly, collegial lab, so come out now and again, ask them what they're working on, even if you don't give a shit."

Jerry Martin is Salvana's Chief Scientist. He has a laidback style of speaking and of managing, a holdover from his days following The Grateful Dead. Forty-five, with a grey ponytail that meanders halfway down his spinal column, he has a pear-shaped body that has never seen the inside of a gym. Married to Alice, the love of his life and fellow Deadhead, his attire hasn't changed a bit from his first day at Salvana, 11 years ago. Every morning he dons a pair of Levi's—no Wranglers or any other of those impostors—Birkenstocks, and a T-shirt featuring either a rock group or concert he's attended. He owns more than 300, enough to wear a different shirt to the lab every day for a year, which his team tracks, hoping to catch him in a repeat. The contest has been going on for six years and Jerry has yet to slip up. Today's shirt is from The Who's Quadrophenia tour.

Surveying the lab, Petra sees three scientists clustered around Jerry's work area, where they're taking turns looking through a high-powered microscope. He could be showing them one of his own developments, but more likely is looking at one of theirs. If he sticks to form, he'll discuss the development with the group, praising the owner and asking them to give the background. Then Jerry will make a suggestion or two—or raise a what-if question—and stand back and let the discussions and insights happen organically. This leadership style, coupled with his impressive list of patents and discoveries, have made him not only the Chief Scientist but a figure of reverence among the scientists and technicians under him and throughout the company.

Petra shifts her gaze to the other end of the lab, where Ed Hutchens, the lab manager and Jerry's right-hand man, is laying out this week's schedule. A scientist with his own array of patents, Ed now runs the lab, working with Biz Dev and Product Marketing to turn pure science into marketable technology. He's that rare combination of a basic research scientist with a business brain, able to appreciate both the intricacies of product development and the usage of the products the team develops.

Though she maintains her distance and usually works behind a closed door, Petra feels at home in the lab. Its tidy lineups of instruments, bright lights bathing sleek surfaces, and array of colorful liquids in flasks radiate calm and efficiency, as do the researchers and technicians busy pipetting solutions to and from culture trays. Monitors scattered around the lab display graphs, 3D molecular structures, or more mundane-looking article drafts in progress.

Even the sounds and smells are calming. The soft humming of incubators, periodic whirring of centrifuges, soft clicking of keyboards, and muted conversations, punctuated by occasional beeps signaling a piece of equipment is ready for some human intervention. And despite the various chemical agents at work, the lab has a surprisingly neutral smell.

Having shown her face for the requisite number of minutes, Petra steps back into her office and closes the door behind her. She walks over to the Keurig, grabs another pod of espresso, and continues the steady intake of caffeine that will carry her through the day, alternating the Keurig with cans of diet Coke.

The walls of her office, at her request, have been painted with whiteboard material, allowing her to surround herself with everything from complex formulas to random thoughts and reminders. One wall is filled with drawings of molecular structures and experimental data, using a color code known only to her.

Another wall is dedicated to a six-by-six grid and a boxed set of three sentences, with "Do Not Erase" and "No Borre, Por Favor" written above and below the two rectangles. Either Jerry or Ed—she's not sure which one—has written "Petra's Manifesto" over the boxed text. In the spirit of lab fellowship, she has let it stay. On her bookshelf, which is jammed with science journals, rest the only other items of any personal note. There's a framed photo of 12-year-old Petra with her mother and sister, and a battered hacky sack that she's never explained to anyone, not even Jerry.

She works for the next hour in a deep, concentrated silence, rising from her desk and laptop to either scribble a note on one of the walls, or input data into the workstation that shares a table with a printer/scanner/copier machine. She keys in various commands, looks intently at the screen, then keys in more data.

The computer program she's running is a modified, AI-enhanced version of a mathematical model she developed as an undergrad at the University of Chicago. That model, which predicted the rate of cellular replication under certain conditions, allowed her to co-author a paper published in the journal *Cell* and present her findings in a poster session at the annual Cell Bio meeting.

That notoriety impressed MIT, which offered her a full ride in their Biological Sciences PhD program. For her thesis, Petra developed a series of cellular breakthroughs, showing new ways cells communicate with each other as they grow, develop, and age. Her analysis of how and when older cells stop dividing was featured in the prestigious *Nature* journal. It was her doctoral research's direct pertinence to aging research and development that caught the attention of Salvana, which recruited her to head up their longevity initiative.

At the moment, though, Petra isn't thinking about any of her past successes. All her focus is on the simulation model running on her workstation. As she watches the screen, her face lights up. She's about to go share the good news with Ed and Jerry when the numbers quit scrolling. Petra frowns and looks closely at the screen, then double checks the figures on her laptop. Standing up, she throws her marker at the wall.

Out in the lab, Ed walks over to Jerry. The two look at the clock on the wall, then Ed takes out his wallet, extracts a single dollar, and hands it to Jerry. "I thought, it being Monday and all, she'd make it to noon. Same bet tomorrow?"

Jerry nods as he pockets the money and heads to Petra's office. He knocks gently and enters without waiting for a response. He looks at her for a moment, gauging her mood, then says, "Let me guess. Nanos a no-go?" He encourages her to smile at the joke, but her face stays tight, angry.

She walks over to the grid on the far wall. The six boxes in the grid are labeled: MOLECULAR; CELLULAR; GENOMIC;

EPIGENETICS; STEM CELLS; IMMUNOLOGY. Each is marked with a red X except 'IMMUNOLOGY,' which she now X's out. She taps the middle of the board. "I'm 0 for six on major categories. Which means I now have to test each combination, square by square. We could be talking years here." She looks around the office as if it were a prison cell.

"And what's wrong with that?" He squints at the grid. "From where I sit, that's three to five years of a steady paycheck and interesting work. Not to mention that much more time enjoying my company." Seeing the impatience on her face, he turns serious. "Okay, then why not ask the company for more resources? Put a team on it."

"And become what? A manager?" She says the words as if they've got a stink. She also sees the hurt register on Jerry's face. "I work best alone, Jer. You know that."

Jerry looks at the grid again. "Then why not join a startup?" He points to the grid. "You've already done your due diligence. Pick the leader in the most promising category on your grid and bring your work with you. They'd let you work alone, I'll bet."

"The problem is," Petra says, "they're all wedded to their one approach. And I've just spent the past four years proving that no single approach holds the answer. No one is going to want me coming in and telling them, however helpfully, that they're wasting their time and investors' money."

"Then start your own company. You know more about this field now than most of the players out there, maybe all of them. You shouldn't have any trouble raising funds."

She shakes her head. "If I'm not a manager, I'm certainly not a CEO. My social skills, as you like to point out, are limited. I'd suck at interacting with the board and kissing up to investors." She looks away. "And then there's my own family history. So no, no startup for me."

"You're not your father, Petra."

"Maybe not. But I've got his genes. And genes, as you and I prove every day, are the basis of our future." Her eyes bore in on Jerry. "So, no. If I'm going to ruin someone's life, it'll be my own."

Jerry holds up his hands. "Last time I'll bring it up. But if you're going to be here for the long term, get some plants in here. This place is depressing as hell."

Through the window, he and Petra see Ed showing a woman around the lab. She's not dressed in lab garb, more like an executive dressing casual for the visit. There's a deference in Ed's mannerisms that Petra hasn't seen before.

"Who's that?" she asks.

"Cheryl Aynesworth, new VP of Biz Dev. They introduced her at the last all-hands meeting. Which you'd know if you ever attended them or read your company emails."

"What's she doing here? In the lab?"

"It's her first official day. Also, I think she's here to meet you. From what I gather, she's your new boss."

Petra gazes at the visitor with new interest. She sees a woman in her forties, dressed and coiffed casually, though with style. Her face is strong-boned—high cheeks, small, blunt nose, and firm chin. Even through the glass, she exudes confidence as she listens to Ed, nodding occasionally, her eyes taking in the lab as they walk.

Petra turns back to Jerry. "I've never had a boss."

"Well, I think those days are…"

There's a brief knock at the door, then Ed opens it, ushering the woman in. He motions to Jerry. "You remember Jerry, our Chief Scientist." The woman nods and shakes Jerry's hand. Then she turns to face Petra. Ed continues the introductions.

"Petra, this is Cheryl Aynesworth, new VP of Business Development. This is Petra Alexander, our ... I never know how to describe what Petra does."

Cheryl takes a step forward and extends her hand. "I do. She's creating the blueprint for Salvana's future. I'm looking forward to hearing about your work, Doctor Alexander."

"Petra."

"Then call me Cheryl. Let's get together next week. I'll have my AA schedule something." She nods at both of them and leaves, Ed holding the door for her.

"What the hell just happened?" Petra says to Jerry.

"I think summer vacation just ended, Kid."

3

Railbirds

"C'MON, GIRL," ALICE URGES ZOE. "Your Oracle stories are the highlights of my Wednesdays, if not my week. No new sexual harassment charges?"

"No," Zoe says, "but the week's young." She thinks for a minute. "Okay. Here's a chestnut I heard this week. Years back, there was a reggae band at one of the company celebrations and an employee who'd had a few asked Larry if it bothered him that there were more blacks in that band than in the entire company. Larry said, no, that Oracle was nine percent black. When the employee scoffed at the figure, Larry explained that HR counted our Indian employees as black. True story."

"They must love your ass, then," says Jerry. "A real-live black woman, complete with tats, piercings, and street slang. They still think you're gay, right?"

"I prefer the term 'fluid,'" Zoe says. "All those photos of Petra and me on our climbing trips don't hurt." She looks at Izaak. "Oh, and I went into my files and updated my identification to 'biracial.'"

"I can't believe this," Izaak says. "Petra's the fluid one. And I'm the one who's biracial. You're just a poacher."

"My mom's Ethiopian and my dad's from Detroit," Zoe says. "I'd say that qualifies me as biracial." She turns her attention to the leather cup and the dice it holds. "Seven sixes," she says, without looking under her cup, then smiles sweetly at Izaak.

"Seven sixes in the blind?" Izaak says, his voice hovering between disbelief and admiration.

"They're there," Zoe says confidently. "Raise or call, Slick."

It's Wednesday night, which means The Speak Easy, the group's bar of choice after a six-month search. It started with Izaak and Petra taking Wednesdays as a time to reconnect after her move out to the Valley. It then expanded to include Zoe, once she and Petra started climbing together. In search of an 'our place,' the group visited a new bar each week, assessing it afterward for atmosphere, price of drinks, appetizers, and bartender knowledge. They rated the establishments by briefcases, with five briefcases the best and a handle the worst. Once the search was declared over and a winner selected, Petra asked the other two if she could invite Jerry and Ed, who had been following the contest avidly. Jerry's wife, Alice, had attended one night, since she and Jerry were heading to a movie afterward. She fit in so well that night that no one had to issue an invitation to her for the following Wednesday or any thereafter.

At first glance, it's not clear why The Speak Easy emerged as their bar of choice. The exterior is nothing remarkable, just a step up from a strip mall dive, with neon signs embellishing the three windows. But once inside, the atmosphere and staff make up for the humble exterior. The bar dominates the room and is the highlight, purchased for a song at an auction from a faux British pub that went out of business. L-shaped and richly wooded, it's usually populated by opinionated and vocal blue-collar types, a vanishing species on the peninsula. A bay window holds a bench and two mismatched couches around a low table. That was where the three original members congregated, but when Ed, Jerry, and Alice joined the group, they migrated to a round table that could hold six tall chairs. It's where the owners place a Reserved sign at 4 every Wednesday afternoon.

An initial game of Liar's Dice determines who pays for the first round. Six leather cups are hoisted and slammed down at the same time, trapping 30 dice. The last one to arrive states how many dice of a certain domination—say, deuces—there are under the cups, aces being wild. After that it's what Izaak calls "binary." You either raise the previous bet—if the call to you, for example, is six fives, you either go six sixes or seven of something—or you call, and everyone turns over their cups and counts. If you're right, the person you called loses a die and buys the first round. If you're wrong, you lose a die. The last person with a die wins and collects the pool of single dollar bills on the table. The first person out buys the first round, the second person out owns the second round. There is rarely a third, and if there is, each person pays for their own drink.

Petra smiles at the audacity of Zoe's opening bet but recognizes its genius. It's just high enough that the betting won't get back to her and just low enough that Izaak probably won't snap-call her. Sitting to Zoe's right, Petra is confident the betting won't even get to her. Which is why, when possible, she tries to snag Zoe's right side on Wednesday nights.

Besides being Petra's climbing partner and BFF, Zoe is an HR rep at Oracle and a constant source of gossip and outlandish stories. With her tattoos, piercings, and vibrantly tinted hair, she's the last person in the bar you'd pick as corporate material. But over her five-plus years at the company, she's continued to add to her visual eccentricity, creating a persona that she says the company is uncomfortable with, but that renders her untouchable when it comes to layoffs. Of Ethiopian heritage, she is slender all the way around, physically and facially. Her narrow face has high cheeks and a fine-boned nose. Tonight she's sporting a tight sleeveless black top, revealing toned arms that are a match for

Petra's. Her hair is a compact Afro that she teases at times, this evening with a streak of teal running through it.

Zoe is also why the group has a reserved table for Wednesday evenings. She comes to every get-together with an order for an exotic new drink, hoping to stump the bartenders. In return, she has persuaded the group to be guinea pigs for the bartenders' newest concoctions. Tonight she ordered a Midnight Monkey, for which Ray, their server, demanded proof of existence. Zoe produced the magazine where she found it, along with a small plastic bag containing matcha, the only Midnight Monkey ingredient the bar doesn't carry. The group is awaiting the return of Leo, the bartender, with the drink before they place their orders. He always brings one for Zoe and one for the table. It's rare that they order the night's mystery drink, given Zoe's exotic tastes, but they always give it a chance.

As Izaak looks back under his cup and considers whether to call or raise, the pager on his belt buzzes. As the head of Stanford's major IT facility and a consultant to the other computer labs on campus, he has to be reachable 24 hours a day. He takes the pager off his belt, looks at it for a moment, keys in a response, and brings his attention back to the dice game. The product of a Berkeley couple—mother, black; father, Jewish—Izaak maintains that he got the worst of both gene pools. "I'm shitty with numbers and sports, with the exception of Ultimate Frisbee. And I've got a nose that looks like a hood ornament."

"And yet women find you devastatingly handsome," Zoe says. "At least the women around this table do."

"Thank you for that, my sister," Izaak purrs. He looks under his cup a final time. "Eight fours," he says, turning his head to Alice, who is next in line.

"I was going to say that *I'd* do you," Alice says, "but not after that call." A marriage and family counselor, Alice is equal parts

Earth Mother and no-excuses therapist. The one person in the group not a scientist or techie, she has a habit of throwing out questions that reflect the human side of the projects they're working on. Petra's explorations in longevity are ripe for Alice's queries, but she knows she has to frame them in the most non-judgmental terms possible.

She's also the group's cheerleader, of sorts. "You guys are too close to your projects to see their larger ramifications," she'd said in one of her early meetings with the gang. She'd looked at Izaak. "I don't know what you do at Stanford, only that they'd have a hard time getting along without you. But we're all living through an amazing time in human history. I just hope we can appreciate it. All of us."

"Tell them your Renaissance analogy," Jerry said.

Alice looked at him to see if he was teasing, but he seemed serious. "All I said to my beloved man the other night was that I don't think Michelangelo and da Vinci got together in a tavern like this in Florence and said, 'Isn't it great to be living during the Renaissance?'" She sees the smiles forming, so continues. "I'm saying that when they write our history, I'll bet Steve Jobs is going to rank up there with Edison. And Tim Berners-Lee and the internet are going to be equal to Gutenberg and the printing press. Perhaps above them."

"Eight sixes," she says, almost apologetically, to her husband, who is next in line.

"I met my new boss today," Petra says, preempting Jerry's call. The entire table stops talking and looks at her. Petra is normally the quiet one at their Wednesday night gatherings, listening far more than she contributes. And she never interrupts.

"I thought you didn't have a boss," Zoe says. "That's part of what I find so attractive about you."

"Well, I do now."

"You're the poker player," Alice says. "What's your initial read?"

"She's a tough one. Friendly, but on her terms. Casual in her style and speech, which is odd for Salvana, which is pretty buttoned-up. But she's clearly in charge. If she sat down at my poker table, I'd probably watch her play at least a dozen hands before taking her on." She turns to Ed. "You spent more time with her today. What's your take?"

"She's got an agenda, this major reworking of Salvana's product line, and I wouldn't want to be someone who's not on board with her plans or is standing in the way. I can see her being a strong advocate, though, once you and she get on the same page."

"By the way," Izaak chimes in. "What happened to your immunology experiment? You seemed pretty optimistic last time we talked." He sees her face tighten, then looks at Jerry and Ed, both of whom are shaking their heads slightly. "Okay, sorry I asked," he says. "And no more work talk." He looks at the table and the six cups of dice. "I believe it's eight sixes to you, Jerry."

4

Long Odds

"COME ON, YOU GUYS," Max says. "I can't be the only one who sees the irony in all this."

"In what?" Zac asks.

"Eric killing himself trying to live forever."

"You're not the only one to *see* it," Freddy says. "Just the only one to say it out loud. Thanks for not sharing your insight at the funeral."

The Dicks, minus Eric, are assembled on his yacht for what was initially intended to be a final salute to their friend. It's been a rocky two months since his death and the first time the team has come together since the funeral. Vinod, who was Eric's closest friend, took his death hardest and initially suggested the Hydras disband. The deciding vote, surprisingly, came from Shauna, Eric's wife. She told the group that the Hydras and their longevity project held a special place in Eric's heart. In his will he stipulated that the Hydras have full use of the yacht for the next five years, encouraging them to use it for meetings, trainings, and as a longevity library and lab. At the end of that five-year period, the Hydras could either buy the boat from Shauna with their earnings or return it to her.

"I hope to god it's Option 1," Shauna told them at the wake. "That boat is all Eric, not me. I've always hated that fucking thing. I could never get over the whole look-at-me vibe it puts out. Don't get me wrong, I love being on it once I'm there—who wouldn't?—because then I'm inside looking out. And the scenery's always fantastic. But driving up to it—or being ferried out to it—I could never get over the cost, to build, of course, but especially to maintain."

She also polled the group to see if they, or anyone in their circles, wanted to buy Eric's Kiwi Apocalypse package. "Same thing. Eric, not me. What the hell am I going to do, now that Eric's gone? Bunker down in New Zealand with our pilot and his family? Speaking of which, I'm selling the jet as well, in case any of you are interested."

The Hydra meetings are modeled on their VC Monday-morning meetings, where the group dedicates its morning—if not its entire day—to hearing pitches. Kerry, the group's assistant, fields all requests from startups or researchers for access to the group, vets them with one or more of the Dicks, then creates an agenda for the offsite, working with whoever's hosting the event to handle the logistics.

The schedule is always the same: no more than three presenters each session; 30 minutes for the actual presentation, 15 minutes for a demo or technical/scientific drill down; and 15 minutes for Q&A. At one hour, unless one of the BSDs gives a signal that they'd like to extend the time, Freddy thanks them and Kerry sees them to their cars. Or boats, in this weekend's case. Kerry always schedules an hour between meetings for internal discussion, calls, and email.

For today's relaunch of the Hydra offsites, Freddy has directed Kerry not to schedule any new presentations. By unanimous agreement, the group decided to pass on the company whose technology killed Eric.

Today is all about restarting the Hydras, reviewing their investments to date, resetting expectations, if necessary, and laying out a plan for the coming year.

The group has convened at the yacht's mooring in San Francisco. With the open sea a bit rough, the captain suggests a gentle cruise around the bay. Or they can stay at the mooring. They opt for the cruise. As they glide past Alcatraz, the meeting comes to order, beginning with updates on their individual bio-hacking efforts and progress. Each of them has a personal trainer versed in biohacking, so Zac, as the resident extreme biohacker, has volunteered to act both as recorder—creating a spreadsheet to track and contrast their progress— and assistant coach, if needed. Vinnie talks about his recent fast, which the others listen to with little interest. When they see the need for a purging, they opt for juice cleanses. All are taking multiple supplements, so they give Zac their type, dosage, and frequency to enter into his records.

Finished with the updates, Zac turns the conversation to sleep, a subject he feels is an overlooked, or underappreciated, component of a healthy life. "Currently, I'm focusing on two things," he says. "The first is how to maximize melatonin intake, both through my environment and with supplements. The second probably won't sit well with you guys and your Type A personalities." He looks around the table, but no one seems offended. "How many of you are proud of how little sleep you need?" No hands go up, but there are some sheepish looks.

"I'm too new to this group to feel comfortable calling you guys liars," he says, "but I've been in this valley too long to believe you. Freddy, I've got you pegged as one of those Masters swimmers who's in the pool at six in the morning. Tell me if I'm wrong and I'll apologize."

"No, you got me. On both the swimming and the hours of sleep. Five, max."

"Who else here is six or less? Hours of sleep?" Zac asks, surveying the table. All the hands go up.

"My preferred sleep schedule is nine hours," Zac continues. "Eight is more normal, though. Right now I'm experimenting with magnetic beds and thermal regulation. See me on the break if you want more info. Now let's review our biohacking portfolio."

He passes around the folders and lets everyone read for a few minutes. "The good news is that 80 percent of our hacking investments are either making money or about to. The bad news is that, as I stated in the last review, they're all singles and doubles, and I know we're looking for a home run."

Having been coached by the captain on the lounge's internal workings, Zac presses a button. The wooden panels on the far wall part, allowing a view of the 86-inch screen. A second button triggers the drop of light grey curtains that eliminate any glare on the screen but still allow a view outside. He opens his laptop and an agenda pops up on the screen. It lists five major categories:

- Diet
- Sleep
- Blood
- Implants
- Brain

"All of our biohacking investments fall into one of these categories. Any other area we should be considering?"

"What about psychedelics?" Vinod asks. "I'm microdosing with LSD, and I think most of this table is as well." A number of nods validate him.

Zac nods. "I'm playing around with ketamine as well, but it's early days. But as far as a field to invest in, I think we're too late to the dance."

"Any of these categories have the potential of a home run?" asks Max.

"Definitely the brain. But it's also the riskiest. Currently the focus is on which parts of the brain control which activities and whether chemicals or electrical stimulation is the best way to boost performance. Most of these are in their infancy, with experiments barely starting on mice. Dogs and monkeys are a ways off. Off the record, I'm in touch with a number of grinders who are messing with chip implants, trying to rewire the brain's currencies."

"I hope you're not one of them," Trina says.

Zac shakes his head. "I have a worst-case scenario. In my nightmare, I do everything right on the physical front and am on track to live to a hundred and fifty. Unfortunately, one of my brain experiments goes wrong and I spend those last hundred years as a vegetable. I think I'll wait a while for the brain studies to mature before I do anything to my upstairs."

"On that cheery note," Freddy says, "let's shift our focus to longevity. Max?"

Max hands out the package Kerry has prepared, a one-pager summarizing finances and activities for each of the longevity startups the Hydras have funded. He lets them read for five minutes, then says, "Reactions?"

Vinod closes his file. "This is embarrassing. When did we get so dumb?"

"I'm glad you said it," Trina says. "It always sounds nicer, more elegant, with your Indian boarding school accent."

Vinnie smiles. "Thank you, my Trina." He gestures at the numbers. "But seriously, guys ..."

"Before we start beating ourselves up," Max says, "this market is only now starting to take baby steps. No one's making money in it."

"That's about to change," Freddy says. "Two years ago, when we started the Hydras, we had the field to ourselves. But these days all the major VCs, including my firm, have forever fever. And they've got the time and money to bet on a number of horses. We don't."

"What's our best course of action, then?" Trina asks.

"We have neither the resources nor the bandwidth to invest in and develop multiple companies. We just don't. I suggest we take the next three months to examine the market and candidates with fresh eyes. Then we select the most promising candidate—the Steve Jobs of longevity—and we put all our resources behind him."

"Or her," Trina says.

"Or her."

As the group closes their longevity folders, Trina speaks up.

"Before we break for dinner, there's something I want to discuss with the group. So if you need to freshen your drinks, now's the time." When no one stands up, she starts in. "I know we've done our due diligence on the longevity market—the Gartner reports, the industry-by-industry projections, all that. But there's this nagging feeling I have that we might be giving a party that not that many people want to attend."

Zac cocks his head. "I'm missing something here. Who wouldn't want to live longer?"

"My husband, Jeff, for one," Trina says. To Zac: "He's a doctor. An internist, to be precise. The other night, after I caught him up on what we're doing, he hit me with two things. One's a joke, sort of. The other bothered me enough to bring it here today."

"Start with the joke," Max says.

"Okay. Do you know which parts of the human body grow the fastest as we age?"

"I should know this," Zac says. "Fingernails?"

Trina shakes her head. "Nose and ears. Jeff said that if his nose and ears grow at their current rate, by the time he's a hundred and twenty his nose will be below his chin and his ears will be resting on his shoulders. He says that if we're smart, we'll start a second fund to invest in plastic surgery centers. That and Botox, for all the turkey necks that vain women like me will be doing anything to get rid of."

"I always like Jeff's input," Freddy says. "What was the serious thing?"

"That if you knew the human body the way he does, you wouldn't want to live to a hundred and twenty. He says he wants to check out of this hotel at eighty, eighty-five max."

She holds her hand up, even though no one is saying anything. "I know. A focus group of one means nothing. But it got me thinking. We may be guilty of the same sin as many of our founders—falling in love with the challenge and the concept without researching whether there's a market for it."

"She's right," Vinnie says to the table. "We should be doing more research, even though we all know how tough that is to do in an untapped market. We all agree that a longevity solution along the lines of what we're looking to fund is inevitable, and picking the right horse or approach to bet on is critical. But after that—before that, even—we're going to need to educate the market on extended longevity and its benefits. We're playing the long game here."

"Jeff said something the other night that dovetails with Zac's nightmare about living to 150 but as a vegetable. If he were advising us, he'd tell us to have two arms to our investment strategy. The first is what we're doing now, the physical part. No changes to our approach. Find the right person or solution that moves the needle from 85 to 120 or beyond. The other arm focuses on mental solutions that will either keep pace with the physical or lead the way. Which means ..." She lets it hang there.

"We're looking for two Steve Jobs," Freddy says.

"Right. I gave it a little thought once Jeff went to sleep. If we find this second Jobs—which is a long shot in itself—we keep the two companies as separate entities, but we cross-pollinate their work so that people like Jeff are at least open to the idea of living past a hundred. And people who have never thought about it before are now comfortable with the prospect of growing old, as long as they stay in control of their minds and bodies."

5

Opening Positions

"THIS IS A FIRST FOR ME. A detective in the HR department."

"Welcome to biotech, ma'am, where paranoia is a way of life. And with cause. You're now part of a multi-billion-dollar industry that runs on intellectual property and lawsuits. I know you've spent most of your professional life in the nonprofit arena, so let me assure you that most of the companies in Salvana's space have someone like me on staff or retainer."

Cheryl is sitting behind her desk, which holds only her laptop and a single file folder. The walls are empty—no diplomas, no vanity photos with bigwigs. Also, no photos of family or children's artwork. Seated on the other side of the desk, wearing a tight-fitting suit, his hair military-short on top, whitewalls around the ears, is Detective Mike Perkins.

"Good to know. But I simply asked for background on one of my employees. How did that merit your involvement?"

"Your Ms. Alexander is a high-profile employee, a designation that triggers an alert whenever someone wants a background check, especially when that request comes from another high-profile employee." He inclines his head towards Cheryl.

"So did you vet Petra?" she asks.

"No. She was before my time. My predecessor did. I've only been here two years. I vetted you, though." He stops. "I'm sorry about your husband." Cheryl raises her eyebrows slightly, then nods her thanks. "At any rate, HR thought it better if I staffed this meeting, in case some of your questions wandered into areas a standard HR rep couldn't answer."

"I doubt that. I just wanted some background on her, prior to our initial one-on-one. She'll be here in 15 minutes, so give me the basics of what I need to know about her. Especially what isn't in her file."

Perkins opens his laptop and spins it around so it's facing Cheryl. A photo of a man in his forties appears on the screen. He's handsome in a rakish way—hair a bit too long for someone his age, though he pulls it off. His grin is almost a smirk, but there's something in his eyes that invites others to share in the joke.

"This is her father," Perkins begins. "He was one of those…"

"Do we have to go back that far? Fifteen minutes, remember?"

"Actually, we do. It's why she's at Salvana and not running her own startup. Her dad was this charismatic big-idea guy who sank all the family money—plus that of his friends and in-laws—into a venture that failed. He committed suicide, but made it look like an accident for the insurance. Petra discovered the body. She was 12."

"Jesus. That's the same age as Rachel, my oldest."

"As a result, Petra is phobic about the world of business and risk. She loves the safety of a big company like Salvana. My guess is she'll be at Salvana for the next 20 years."

He touches a key and Petra's father is replaced by a photo of a woman in her twenties. She bears a physical resemblance to Petra's father and channels his charisma, in her smile and her eyes.

"This is her older sister, Thea. Outgoing, a talented actor, the youngest member of Second City. Headed for big things."

"But…"

"She developed a variation of Werner Syndrome. It's where young people age prematurely and die young. In Thea's case,

23. Though to be precise, cancer got her a decade or so before the Werner would have killed her. But still."

"Jesus, that family can't catch a break."

"Thea dies when Petra is at University of Chicago, causing Petra to switch her major from math to biological chemistry," Perkins reads from his notes, "where she develops a mathematical model to predict the rate of cellular replication. She co-authors a paper on her model, a big deal for an undergrad."

He pauses for questions or a response, but Cheryl motions for him to go on. "That article catches the attention of a prominent professor at MIT, who personally shepherds her into their Biological Sciences PhD program. She excels there as well, developing ..." He consults his notes again. "I can read you what I downloaded, but it'll probably make your head spin the way it did mine. Unless you know what ..." He peers closely. "... Cellular senescence is." Cheryl shrugs and shakes her head. "Let's just say she came up with a new method for identifying how cells communicate and age. That research was published in *Nature*, another big deal."

As Cheryl starts to speak, he hurries along. "I'm almost done. She finishes her doctoral program, which normally takes six years, in just three and a half. Her research in aging leads to Salvana hiring her to head up its longevity program."

Perkins closes his laptop. "Anything else I need to know?" Cheryl asks.

"Just that she can't let her sister's death go. Evenings and weekends she works on a cure for Werner and related premature aging diseases. That's not in Salvana's area, so I haven't dug any deeper into that. Also, I don't know if it matters, but she's a card shark."

"How so?"

"You remember those MIT kids who took the casinos for all that money?"

"I do. It had to do with card-counting in blackjack, right? Didn't they make a movie out of it?"

"Yeah. Turns out our Ms. Alexander idolized those previous MIT card counters. She can hold the odds for up to six decks of cards in her head, whereas you or I might be lucky to do that for a single deck. At MIT she met and joined some of the original team and a few current students who quietly continued the tradition, on a much smaller scale. Now she plays poker, both online and tournaments."

"This is just what I needed, Detective."

"Mike."

"Mike, then." She looks at her watch. "Now I have to ask you to leave, since she'll be here any minute."

* * *

Five minutes later, Cheryl is wrapping up a phone call when Petra enters without knocking. Petra points at the chair in front of Cheryl's desk, then at the small table and its four chairs, holding up her hands in a where-do-you-want-me gesture. Cheryl motions at the table. She finishes the call, grabs her pen, pulls out a yellow notepad from a desk drawer, and walks over as Petra takes a seat.

"Thanks for meeting on short notice. I know you aren't due to present to management for another two months, but I'm eager to get up to speed on your longevity research."

"No problem," Petra replies. "I always keep a core presentation updated, just for requests like this." She opens her laptop. "How much do you know about what I do? And how much do you want to know?"

"To the first question, not much. To the second, as much as I need to. One caution. When it comes to your area of expertise, I'm a simpleton, so treat me like one."

Petra smiles slightly, knowing that Cheryl is blowing smoke up her ass, deferring to her while at the same time reminding them both who the boss is. As Texas Dolly Brunson, every poker player's guru, says, you don't play the cards, you play the player. In this case, Cheryl seems to be genuinely warm and direct, with a casual style that's both natural and practiced. Petra reminds herself that the key words here are "seems to be." It's going to take a while to get an accurate read on her new boss.

"Management at Salvana, as you know, believes that the future of our industry is longevity. My position here is to discover and assess the different companies and approaches working to extend life expectancy to a hundred and fifty." Petra gives Cheryl a sidelong glance. "If PR were in this meeting, they'd remind me to always put the word 'healthily' in there. To help people live *healthily* to a hundred and fifty years."

Cheryl scribbles something on her writing pad. "Noted. As long as we're talking terminology, I'd like to add the word 'recommend' to your job description. My understanding is that you've spent the last four years assessing all the different methodologies and approaches to aging and longevity, both academic and commercial. I want you to tell us what to do. Don't give us options. Take a stand and then educate us on why it's the right course of action. Understood?"

"Understood."

"Good. Please continue."

Petra hits a key and the grid from her office wall appears, with the major categories highlighted in yellow. "These are the six major technologies or approaches to longevity I've been studying and experimenting with these last four years. Do you want a summary of each one?"

"Just send me a one-pager on each and I promise to be up to speed the next time we meet." Nodding at the grid, "You think the answer is there in one of those six categories?"

"I believe it's in there, but not in any specific square on the grid. I've assessed all six categories individually, and to use your term, there's not one company or single approach I would recommend to you and the management team. They each have potential, but I believe the answer lies in a combination of two or more of those technologies."

"Ed tells me that you've got a manifesto that guides you in your research. Care to elaborate?"

Petra frowns to herself. She'll have to talk to Ed about being careful until they've got a read on her new boss. "Manifesto is a bit strong. It's just some guidelines."

"Nevertheless, I'd like to hear them."

"It consists of three statements. The first is: Aging is not inevitable; it's a disease that hasn't been cured yet."

"Interesting. And the second?"

"Since the causes of aging are multi-factored, the solution will also be multi-factored." Petra touches her keyboard, bringing up a cursor. She points it to the middle of the grid. "I believe the answer will be in a combination of two or more of these technologies."

Cheryl nods, then rolls her hand at Petra. "And the third?"

"We *reverse* aging by starting from death and moving backwards. We *prevent* aging by starting at birth and moving forward. Most of the startups and technologies out there are going with the reversal process. I'm suggesting the opposite, that we should start from the cradle and establish a broad definition of aging. Then identify, isolate, and treat each symptom as it occurs, even if it's in infancy, rather than waiting for it to materialize later in life."

"Interesting. In other words, kill aging in the cradle."

"Not a term I'd use, but yes. Kill it in the cradle."

6

Misdeal

FRIDAY NIGHT IS ONE OF RITUAL FOR PETRA. When she arrives home from Salvana, a package marked "Across the Pond" is waiting in the oversized box in the apartment mailroom. Across the Pond, affectionately called ATP, is the name that Not Your Mom But Close, Petra's go-to meal service, has given the British standard, fish and chips.

Regular meal deliveries are part of Silicon Valley culture, at least as Jerry has relayed it to Petra over the years. Jerry's friends, many of whom are computer nerds, have told him about the Valley's culture and customs. Dinner is a prime example.

In the early days, the idea of a company catering dinner was unheard of. The best they could hope for was a microwave in the break area, which employees used to heat up their Hungry Man or Lean Cuisine entrees. But as non-nerds began to join the start-ups—or as the original nerds had families and became more exercise and health-conscious—a raft of companies like Not Your Mom popped up, servicing those who work late, as well as those too tired or lazy to cook.

Petra has Not Your Mom's healthy fare four evenings a week. On the other evenings she makes a salad or an omelet or brings in Chipotle. As she does every Friday, she wonders if ATP is a holdover salute to the Catholic tradition of no meat on Fridays, which still holds sway in many ethnic enclaves on the East Coast and in the Midwest. Whatever the answer, the preparation is simple and delicious, with just the right touch of vinegar. If you want ketchup or tartar sauce, you have to ask for it, which marks you as both American and someone without discernment.

Tonight she's perched on her couch watching PBS NewsHour, which she grew up with back in the days of MacNeil and Lehrer. Her father had been the political and socially conscious parent, but after his death her mother had made NewsHour required viewing for both her daughters. These Fridays, Petra misses Mark Shields and his perpetually positive outlook, and thinks David Brooks has grown stiffer in Mark's absence, though Jonathan Capehart is growing on her.

She nurses a glass of Primitivo, her new favorite red wine, as she catches up on the world's goings-on. She keeps all news feeds off while at work, and her commute is so short that she rarely turns on the radio. So she depends on the PBS crew to keep her abreast of the world's events and their significance.

With the news and dinner both concluded, she clears her environmentally correct sturdy cardboard plate and spends a few minutes tidying the kitchen. Wine in hand, she returns to the living room, where a stand-up workstation occupies a corner nook. The workstation, an AI-powered serious upgrade from her laptop, holds all her research on Werner Syndrome and its variants, including her research from MIT.

What began as an attempt to acquaint herself with the condition that was stealing her sister from her, morphed over the years into an obsession. It was during her time at MIT, as she investigated the genetic underpinnings of certain diseases, that she started to believe a cure for WS was possible. As a result, a portion of each evening, as well as each weekend she isn't off climbing, goes to reading medical and scientific journals and devising her own tests and theories.

Ed has repeatedly offered her the services of the lab to facilitate or accelerate her WS work, but Petra is determined to keep things separate. Although she foresees herself being at Salvana for years to come, she doesn't want any confusion about who owns what when it comes to any progress—or solution—she might achieve on the Werner front.

The ancient sound of a dial-up modem breaks the silence. It's the customized tone she's given to incoming calls from her mother. Petra hits a key on her laptop and the workstation screen fills with her mother's face.

Eleni Alexander is a handsome woman in her late fifties, her rich black hair shot with gray. Zoe's sister, the casting agent, raves about Eleni's looks and has urged her to take acting lessons. "She's like those Greek actresses of the Sixties—Melina Mercouri and Irene Pappas. There's this deep sadness to their eyes and this mature sexuality that American women just don't seem to possess. These are not women to be trifled with." Eleni's face has kept pace with her hair, the lines beginning to deepen, but in a way that accentuates all the features that Zoe's sister finds so attractive.

"*Yiasoo*, Mamá. How was your weekend? Another date with Jeff?"

"Dinner and a stroll around North Beach. How about you? Are you seeing anyone special these days?"

Petra smiles at the "anyone special." Over the years Eleni has come to grips with her daughter's bisexuality, though they speak of it only in glancing terms. Eleni's one concession in this area is that, over time, her opening question has changed from "Are you seeing any nice man?" to "any nice person" to "anyone." Petra spars with her occasionally, telling Eleni all about whomever she's seeing, telling her everything except their gender.

"You'll be the first to know."

"Do me one favor," Eleni says. "Don't get involved with any-one who's—what's the phrase, 'in transition?' I'm still getting used to you talking about your girlfriends."

"Not a problem. At least, not these days. But if I do ..."

Eleni smiles. "I'll be the first to know."

• • •

When her husband died, Eleni initially sought the solace and support of Chicago's large Greek population, even though some of them had been fleeced by her husband's venture. She sleep-walked through her first year of widowhood, dressing all in black and staying away from most social situations. It wasn't a period of reflection as much as a numb recognition of the basics of life, with no sense of options or forward movement. Her family closed ranks to help raise Thea and Petra while Eleni retreated into herself and into the new apartment, her husband having lost the house in the last gasp of his enterprise.

By her own admission, Eleni would have probably ghosted her way through the rest of her days had Thea not gotten sick. In the face of the Greek Orthodox priests bemoaning Thea's fate as 'God's will' and urging her to integrate this newest catas-trophe into her black-clad life, she rejected a life of increased passivity in favor of one of advocacy, of learning as much as possible about Werner Syndrome and pushing the few Werner experts to attempt the experimental techniques she was reading about.

Thea's death meant the end of Eleni's faith, as well as her pas-sivity and acceptance of her lot in life. She shed the all-black garb, did an inventory of what few assets remained, and started looking for a job, both for income and mental stimulation. Always good with numbers —a trait she'd passed on to both her daughters— Eleni found a job as an accountant in a neighborhood factory.

The owner initially rejected her as unqualified, given her lack of a degree, but when she had him read off 20 numbers and then recited them back to him flawlessly, the job was hers on a trial basis.

She spent the next four years managing first the books, then the entire company. Two evenings a week she was at a local community college, studying accounting. Degree in hand, she opened her own agency, answering the phone with the perky tones of a receptionist, then passing the call over to herself. The support of the Greek community gave her initial success, but it was word of mouth, especially among what Eleni called "the Gentiles," that grew the business, until she had three offices bearing her name.

She continued to expand her business while Petra was away at MIT, but when Salvana made its offer and Petra changed coasts, Eleni decided that the next, if not last, chapter of her life was about to begin. And it wasn't going to be in Chicago.

Once she was sure that Petra's invitation to move out to the Bay Area was genuine, she sold her business and retired. Given Silicon Valley's reputation as the new center of the universe, she looked there first. But, with the possible exception of Palo Alto, which she couldn't afford, she found the Valley lacking the richness of culture and tradition of Chicago. When her search exhausted the towns and neighborhoods that made up the Valley, she broadened it to include San Francisco. There she found a one-bedroom apartment in the Mission, which, though heavily Hispanic, reminded her of the Greek neighborhoods back in Chicago. She could see herself living there the rest of her days.

Not so Silicon Valley. "How can you two live down here?" she asked Petra and Zoe one night over dinner. "Where's your culture? Where's your art? Where do you go to hear music?"

"Don't get her started," Petra advised Zoe.

"I'm with Leni on this one," Zoe answered. "In HR, part of our job is selling the families of people we want to hire on life here in the Valley. I wind up looking at it through their eyes, and the biggest thing I find the Valley has to offer them is proximity. To the snow, to the ocean, to San Francisco. But if they're looking for tradition, or heritage, or a sense of belonging, it'll be a long wait."

"You know what I'm missing when I'm out here?" Eleni ventured. "Not just a sense of community, but a sense of pride. You two get that from where you work and what you create, and that's great for you. But what of your families?" She looked over at Petra. "I know I sound like a broken record, but you go up and down this peninsula and all you find is taquerias and ... what do you call them, the theaters bunched together?"

"Cineplexes."

"Cineplexes. What kind of culture is built on cineplexes?"

Zoe smiled, not at Eleni's rant—which she'd heard almost as many times as Petra—but at its accuracy. "As Oracle has grown, we find we're no longer the pretty girl at the dance, the place everyone wants to work. If a prospect likes our size and stability, Google, Facebook, and Apple are newer and prettier. And then there's the startups. We can't compete with them on equity or, to be honest, job satisfaction. When we started doing focus groups at Oracle, to find out what drew them to us and why they stay, the number one reason was 'stability.' We've become the IBM of Silicon Valley."

"What's wrong with being IBM?" Eleni asked. "Aren't they one of the most admired companies in the world?"

"Not in Silicon Valley," Zoe said. "Out here they're your father's Oldsmobile. I do a lot of informal interviewing of Oracle employees, focusing on building a pitch—about both the company and the Valley—that we can sell to candidates. The first is how to keep Oracle fresh and relevant, not an easy task given the competition. The second has to do with building a sense of community, and how we can contribute to it. Anything that will get them to put down roots here. And hopefully stay with us."

"What's the most interesting thing you've found?" Petra asked.

"I did an exit interview the other day with Oracle employee number 40. It was like he was reading from Eleni's list of grievances. He's staying with Oracle but moving to Boston. He wants his kids to be from somewhere they feel a part of. He's surprised, and somewhat disappointed, that Oracle hasn't gotten more involved in the different Silicon Valley communities. He's big on community involvement and charitable work, and back in Boston—in any number of places not called Silicon Valley—getting involved is a way of life. For people and companies alike."

Eleni nodded. "Chicago's the same way."

"Then he said something that really stuck with me," Zoe said, nodding at Elena's input. "He said: 'This valley was built on what I call the James Dean ethic: Live fast, die young, leave a pretty corpse.' Our version of that was: 'Come out here, make your millions, and go back home.' If we thought we'd still be working and living here 20 years on, we'd have invested in schools, streets, and community projects. But we didn't, and now it feels too late."

"Jerry puts it another way," Petra said. "'If we'd known we'd be setting down roots here, we would have planted trees for the shade. Now, we just invent new and better sunscreen every few years.'"

* * *

As mother and daughter finish updating each other on their lives, Eleni pauses. Petra knows what's coming next.

"You know what next Thursday is, right?"

"I do. And no, I won't be joining you at her grave, just like the last few anniversaries."

"You know how disappointed I'll be." It's somewhere between a question and statement.

"I do. But Thea won't be. She'd agree that my taking the day off and working full-time on a cure is the best way to spend that day. That's how I honor Thea."

There is a long pause, but an expected one. When it comes to discussing Thea, Petra has learned how to outlast her mother in terms of guilt and expectations. Eleni lets the silence grow to over 30 seconds, but she eventually gives in. "Okay, then. I'll tell her the flowers are from both of us."

Petra nods into the camera. This is normally the spot in the phone call where Eleni would ring off, ending on a note of guilt. But she stays on. "Speaking of Thea, I think there's something odd going on with me. In fact, if I didn't know Werner only strikes young people, I'd be worried."

Petra is immediately on full alert. "What's going on? Specifically."

"It's probably nothing. But my skin feels different. Not tighter or stretched-out like with Werner, but saggy. Older. Maybe it's my imagination, but my hair feels a little thinner, too. Brittle. Maybe it's the weather, or with the anniversary coming up, maybe I'm just more ..."

"No, no. I'm glad you said something. You're right, there might be any number of contributing factors. But let's do this. Come into the lab this week. I'll draw a blood sample and take a look at it."

"Okay. But you draw a sample, too. If this is anything, I want to make sure it isn't hereditary."

• • •

It's 11:15 when Petra calls it a night. She saves her data from that night's work in the appropriate files, then powers down the work-station.

Ten minutes later she's in bed, two pillows propping her into a sitting position. She takes out her laptop and places it on her blanketed thighs. Three clicks and her screen morphs into the home screen for Poker Parlor.

She logs in and a series of windows opens. The bank vault shows $4,000 on hand and available for withdrawal. Another window shows "Winnings to date: $78,425." Petra removes $250 from her account and settles in. A conversation bubble pops up: 'Welcome back, Petra.' Within the next 30 seconds, three of the players, recognizing her screen name, cash in and call it a night. Petra smiles, antes five dollars, and joins the game in progress. A few minutes later, up $45, she's talking to the screen, where two players are taking the full 30 seconds with every bet, even the most obvious ones. Petra mutters at this lack of etiquette and opens a second window. She plays both hands and chats with players in the sidebars. An hour later, up $300, she calls it a night.

7

In the Dark

THE FOLLOWING MONDAY, Eleni meets Petra at Salvana at around 11 am, saying she wanted to let the morning commute subside. But Petra suspects she's timed it so that she and Petra, perhaps with Jerry or Ed in tow, could have lunch at the Salvana cafeteria, with its impressive menu and dirt-low prices.

As she always does, she tells Petra how lucky she is to work for such a generous company, but Petra is having none of it. "Generosity has nothing to do with it, Mamá. It's all about two things, finding and keeping employees, and boosting their productivity while they're here. The hiring market these days is brutal. A strong candidate probably has three or four offers, so a free or discounted lunch is just table stakes. Large companies, like Salvana or Oracle, can't compete with startups in terms of equity, so they heavy up on salary and perks, like a gym, dry cleaning, even onsite day care. There's even talk these days of the major companies providing housing—including a path to ownership—for its employees."

"Don't be so cynical, *kardia mou*," Eleni says. "I can't imagine anything like this back in Chicago. When I visit and they ask about you, they nod politely when I try to explain what you're working on. But when I talk about all the different benefits you have out here, they think I'm exaggerating or lying."

"That's because Chicago is the opposite of Silicon Valley, at least for most of the employee base. Many of the businesses there are just struggling to survive. And the employees, at least the blue-collar ones, are grateful to have a job. That's not the deal out here."

"Zoe was telling me that each floor at Oracle has its own coffee area," Eleni marvels, "with one of those espresso machines and snacks. And that's on top of their café and all the other great things they provide."

"Those coffee areas have to do with the other element I was talking about, productivity. These employees have no timecards, no standard hours. The best thing you can do for productivity is to not give them a reason to be away from their desk. Or office. Ask Zoe about the numbers Oracle came up with when they were considering the café. Just take one employee—me, for instance—and do the math. Before the café, I'd head down to my car, drive to the nearest café or restaurant, wait in line, maybe eat or drink there, then come back."

Eleni starts to speak, but Petra holds up a finger. "But after the café was up and running, the people measuring productivity found that many times an employee would go down to the café for coffee, meet up with a friend, and stay around talking, sometimes for up to an hour. So to compete with its own café, and keep people closer to their desks, Oracle put coffee stations in each area."

* * *

After lunch, Petra and Eleni stay in the café, nursing their cappuccinos. With the lunch crowd gone and all the stations cleaned, the café is elegantly cavernous. The light from the floor-to-ceiling windows bathes the room in a quiet warmth and the empty glass tables sparkle, as do the metallic chair legs. The walls display the offerings of local artists, some of them Salvana employees, their prices available by scanning the QR code.

A handful of tables are occupied, but everyone is speaking in low tones, as if in a library. Petra and Eleni cradle their cappuccinos, the inside of their elbows sporting the clump of cotton held down by flesh-colored tape from where Jerry drew their blood. "Be honest with me, honey. Skin and hair. How do they look to you?"

Petra examines her mom with a clinical eye. When Eleni first moved to the Bay Area, she looked older than her actual age. Whether it was the harsh Chicago winters or the demands of running a business, she wore her years heavily. But once she settled in San Francisco, with its hills and marine weather, her clock seemed to move backwards.

To celebrate Eleni's first birthday in the Bay Area, Petra gave her a makeover. Initially resistant to the concept, once she saw the results, Eleni became an active user of the makeup, moisturizers, exfoliants, and other tools of the trade, giving her cheeks a smooth youthfulness. Jerome, a hairdresser recommended by Zoe, and the first openly gay man Eleni had ever met, cut and shaped her long, jet-black hair into a shoulder-length modern statement, tinting it with a touch of burgundy that, in just the right sunlight, gives her a defiant look, someone not to be messed with.

Now, as Petra's eyes move about Eleni's face and hair, she sees what her mother is talking about. The hair is indeed slightly brittle, which is new. And the skin is sagging noticeably, looking thinner than she remembers. She hopes that Eleni is right, that it's a stress response to the upcoming anniversary of Thea's death. But this is the fourth anniversary out here, and she's never shown any of these symptoms before.

"You're right, Mamá. It looks like there's something going on. Jerry will run the tests on our blood once the lab clears out. I'll compare your results with those of studies I've conducted in the past and let you know what I find."

* * *

It's early evening the next night. Petra is working from home. Standing in front of her workstation, she's experimenting with new data that her former colleagues from MIT are sharing with her, running it through the custom generative AI tool she developed specifically for her Werner research. Though the figures have to do with aging in general, Petra is trying to identify any patterns in the data that could apply specifically to Werner.

At about 7 pm, Petra gets a call from Jerry, his face coming up in a corner of her screen. He doesn't waste time with greetings. "Here are the results," he says, as his face disappears and is replaced by a screen full of numbers. Petra hits two keys and her printer comes to life, delivering the screen's contents to paper.

"Werner Syndrome: negative," he says. "Given her age, that's to be expected. I ran some additional tests, but nothing stands out. I don't know if that's good or bad news."

"Looking at her today brought me back to the early days with Thea," Petra says, "right before the diagnosis, when we started noticing changes in her skin and hair. I figured it wasn't Werner because of her age, and my mom's skin changes don't look the same as Thea's, but I'm wondering if this isn't a mutant strain, either of Werner or something else we don't know about."

"So how do we test for something we're not sure even exists?" Jerry asks.

"Can you run a full genomic analysis on my mom's blood when you get a chance? Do me and Thea, while you're at it. Her blood samples are in a vial on the right side of the second shelf in my refrigerator, along with mine."

"Will do. I'll let you know when the tests are done."

8

Shifting Odds

TWO DAYS LATER, Jerry calls Petra at eight in the morning. Without even a good morning or hello he plunges in. "I'm sending you the genomic data on you, your mom, and Thea."

"Anything stand out?"

"You'll need to do a full AI analysis, but there are definitely anomalies there that we'll need to look into more."

Petra starts to object to Jerry's use of "we." She's growing increasingly concerned about him using Salvana time and equipment for her private crusade. But he stops her. "Don't be silly. I can give any number of legitimate Salvana-based excuses for what I'm doing. And now you've got me seriously curious. At this point, I'm doing this for me as much as you."

Camped in her living room, Petra loads Jerry's test figures into her customized AI system and spends the rest of the morning playing with different angles, some of them generated by her work on the longevity grid. She works through lunch but is interrupted in the early afternoon by a call from Zoe.

"Hey, Zoe."

"What's up, partner?"

"Doing some work with Jerry."

"We missed you last night," Zoe says with a slight chastening tone.

Petra looks at the calendar in her screen's left corner. It's Thursday. She missed the Wednesday evening drinks for the first time she can remember. "Oh, shit. I'm sorry. Lost track of the days. Everyone else show?"

"Jerry wasn't there, though Alice came. She apologized for the two of you, said you were working on some major stuff. Ed backed her up, said Jerry oscillated between excited and dejected all day long. Changing subjects—or maybe not—I was over at The Ascent last night. Spyder says you haven't been in for a while. Should I be worried? Or looking for a new climbing partner?"

"No. It's just that work's a bit more intense these days, with the new boss. And then this thing with my mom."

"Any progress on that front?"

"A little. It doesn't look like Werner precisely, given her age, but there's definitely something wrong. Maybe a variant or mutation. It would be exciting if there weren't so much riding on what we find out. For now, at least, I'm stumped."

"Do you think this might be one of those cases of lateral thinking Spyder was suggesting?"

Petra's lips tighten. "Meaning?" A slightly peeved tone colors her voice.

"Quit obsessing on a direct route to the top. Go back to the base of the mountain and clear your head. Forget about what hasn't worked. See if you can find a different route. We've done it before on our climbs. Why not apply the same logic here? Think sideways, not just up and down."

After hanging up with Zoe, Petra sits on the living room floor, her back to the couch, laptop across her knees. But the laptop is closed and serves only to prop up the notes she's making on a yellow legal pad. Two hours later, she's still in the same place, same posture, but she's surrounded by balled-up sheets of yellow paper. A notebook on the floor next to her is open, revealing a series of scribbles and formulas.

Petra gets up from the floor, walks to the computer, and calls Jerry. With a key click he appears on the screen.

"I have an idea. Can you run a proteomic analysis on the three samples?"

"Sure, but why?"

"Because I think we've been so busy looking for a genetic answer, we've ignored proteins and some different cellular components. Can you do that?"

"Will do. You on to something?"

She ignores the question. "Also, can you include samples of yours and Ed's blood, to rule out a hereditary link? You got any blood on hand?"

"Mine? Always. If we don't have Ed's, I'll draw some. He's five feet away."

"Thanks. Have I told you lately how much I appreciate you?"

"You don't need to. But it's nice to hear, anyway."

• • •

At work the following Monday, Jerry ambles into Petra's office. "How about we meet at your place tonight, around seven? We're going to need your AI engine."

"Sounds mysterious. Anything to do with today's T-shirt?"

Jerry looks at his chest, confused. He forgot that he's wearing a shirt sporting Pink Floyd's "A Saucerful of Secrets" album.

"No, but nice catch. I'll have the proteomic data for you to pump into your AI system. I thought I might watch while you do your magic, see what I can learn."

"Sounds good. I'll supply dinner. When you call Alice, apologize for me for keeping you out late, and tell her you're bringing home some Chinese."

• • •

Later that afternoon the phone alert sounds. It's Zoe. "Just checking in. Making sure you haven't jumped off your balcony."

A slight smile from Petra. "I live on the second floor. You know that."

"That's what would make it so pathetic. How's it going?"

"I hate to admit it, but I took your advice. For three hours I did nothing but look at everything with fresh eyes. No pre-suppositions. No I-tried-that-already negativism. And I did it not just with my Werner work. I revisited my MIT work on fatal diseases as well. I expanded my possible areas of investigation to include the microbiome, mitochondria, even DNA mismatch repair."

"Should I be taking notes here, so I can Google later?"

"Don't worry. None of them panned out. But the fresh thinking and the options it created made me feel like I was using an underused part of my brain. I rewound to the biology basics: cells, proteins, and genes, and how your genes contain instructions that code for various amino acids, which combine to make proteins. Are you with me?"

"So far."

"Since Werner is hereditary, I've been focused on looking at gene sequences pretty exclusively. I ignored the proteins for the most part. The better way of saying it was that I took proteins for granted. I totally overlooked them."

"What a moron," Zoe says. "I'm embarrassed to know you. Now give it to me in English—what did my sage advice lead to?"

"Proteins are often described as 'building blocks' of the body because they play a crucial role in constructing and maintaining tissues, organs, and cells. They also have other important functions, including acting as enzymes, hormones, and antibodies. Anyway, that got me thinking about those condos in places like Florida that fall down, even though their own building blocks passed all the initial tests for quality and stability. There was an inherent flaw in their composition that wasn't detected in the earlier tests, so no one thought to test again. Not until the buildings came down. Which made me wonder if that had any implications physiologically at the protein level. What if there was some kind of change in the structure or function of a core protein over time? And that the results of this change accumulated, but slowly, leading to issues later on? But because we're not looking at the proteins, we don't notice the change."

"I'm following you so far. Now what's that got to do with your mom?"

"In my mom's case, maybe a mutation or environmental stressor or other factor is affecting a Werner-related protein and changing the protein's function, to the point that either Werner symptoms are no longer appearing only in young people, or we have a new disease that is Werner-related. Which is what Jerry and I are working on from different angles. So thanks again for the kickstart."

"No problem," Zoe says with a smile. "You guys need any more advice, you know where to find me."

9

Inside Straight

THE UPPER CORNER of the workstation in Petra's home office reads 7:20 pm. Flimsy white and red containers from a nearby Chinese restaurant are open and perched on her kitchen counter. Petra and Jerry are huddled around her workstation.

Petra nods at her screen. "There's a protein there that doesn't show up anywhere else in my system. Whether it's a splice variant or an entirely new protein, I can't say at this point. It's going to require more analysis. But I'm wondering if this is a protein that's ever been seen before. By anyone."

"And it was in all the samples?" Jerry asks.

"Yeah. But at different levels. Mine's at a little over 1, my mom's at 3 on a 1-5 scale. Thea's last reading was 4.5."

"So it's hereditary. Maybe ..."

"But then I looked at your and Ed's blood, and you both tested positive, too, though at much lower levels, less than 1. So whatever my family's got, you've got it, too."

The two sit there, both frowning. The silence grows for over five minutes, their eyes glued to the screen. "It can't be environmental," Petra says, "because Thea never made it out here. Maybe it's ..."

She stands and walks around the apartment. Picks up a half-empty takeout container and stirs its contents idly with the chopsticks as she continues to pace. She tries to clear her mind, but a rising sense of frustration holds her back. "The variance in the levels indicates it's disease-related, but ..." She stops and puts the container back on the counter, next to the refrigerator. Seeing the refrigerator, she has a thought.

"Can you do one more huge favor? In the mini refrigerator in my office are vials of blood from the six grid categories I was testing. They've got absolutely nothing in common. Can you run back to the lab and test for this mystery protein in those samples? While you're doing that, I'll do a quick check to see if it's shown up anywhere else."

"I'll load the test tonight, on my way home," Jerry says, as he heads out the door, carrying the remainder of the Chinese to drop off for Alice. "Now that we know what we're looking for, I should have the results by tomorrow evening."

"While you're doing that, I'll keep checking the scientific literature to see if our mystery protein shows up anywhere else."

The next evening, Petra and Jerry meet in the lab as the last of the grid tests finish running. While they wait, she tells him about Zoe's contribution to their discovery. Jerry is dutifully impressed.

"Keep going like that and you can write off all your climbing expenses as work-related. By the way, what's your guys' next destination?"

"It's on hold for now. I don't think Salvana would look too kindly on me taking three weeks off. Especially to climb one of the most dangerous faces out there. But that won't stop Zoe from picking a great location and then shaming me for not being able to go. All I know about the destination is that it's one of the Stans." At Jerry's confused frown, she explains. "Kazakhstan, Kurdistan. I think there's a Turkmenistan as well."

"I hope Afghanistan is off the list."

"Yeah, it is. How about you? What do you and Alice have planned for the summer?"

"You know what a baseball freak she is. She's put together this amazing two-week agenda that involves catching games at eight minor-league parks." He smiles. "Then, to throw me a bone, she's worked in a Phish concert and one of Dead and Company." In response to her confused look he adds, "The remnants of the Grateful Dead."

Petra returns the smile. "That woman's a jewel."

"Tell me about it." He hoists himself to his feet. "Tests should be finished."

When he returns, printouts in hand, his face is flushed. With his free hand he's twisting the end of his ponytail, a gesture that Petra knows he uses only when he's stumped.

"The mystery just deepened. Every sample from the grid shows positive for our mysterious friend, all at low levels, except for two that are elevated." He looks at the data and shakes his head.

"Do we know anything about those that had high levels?"

"Not without doing some digging," he says. These are all anonymized samples." He tosses the papers on the table. "Two days ago, this protein didn't exist. Now it's everywhere. If it's disease-related, which still seems the most likely scenario, what kind of disease has this kind of scope?"

Petra is staring at the office wall, more as a calming activity than a search for answers. But then her eyes latch onto her mantra. She stands and walks over to the whiteboard, stopping next to her boxed sentences. She taps the first sentence. "What about this?"

Jerry reads: "Aging is a disease that hasn't been cured yet." His eyes shift from the wall to the printouts. Then he walks over to Petra's desk and picks up the various results. His eyes go from one to the other and then to the most recent set. Then he looks up at her with wide eyes.

"Holy shit," he whispers.

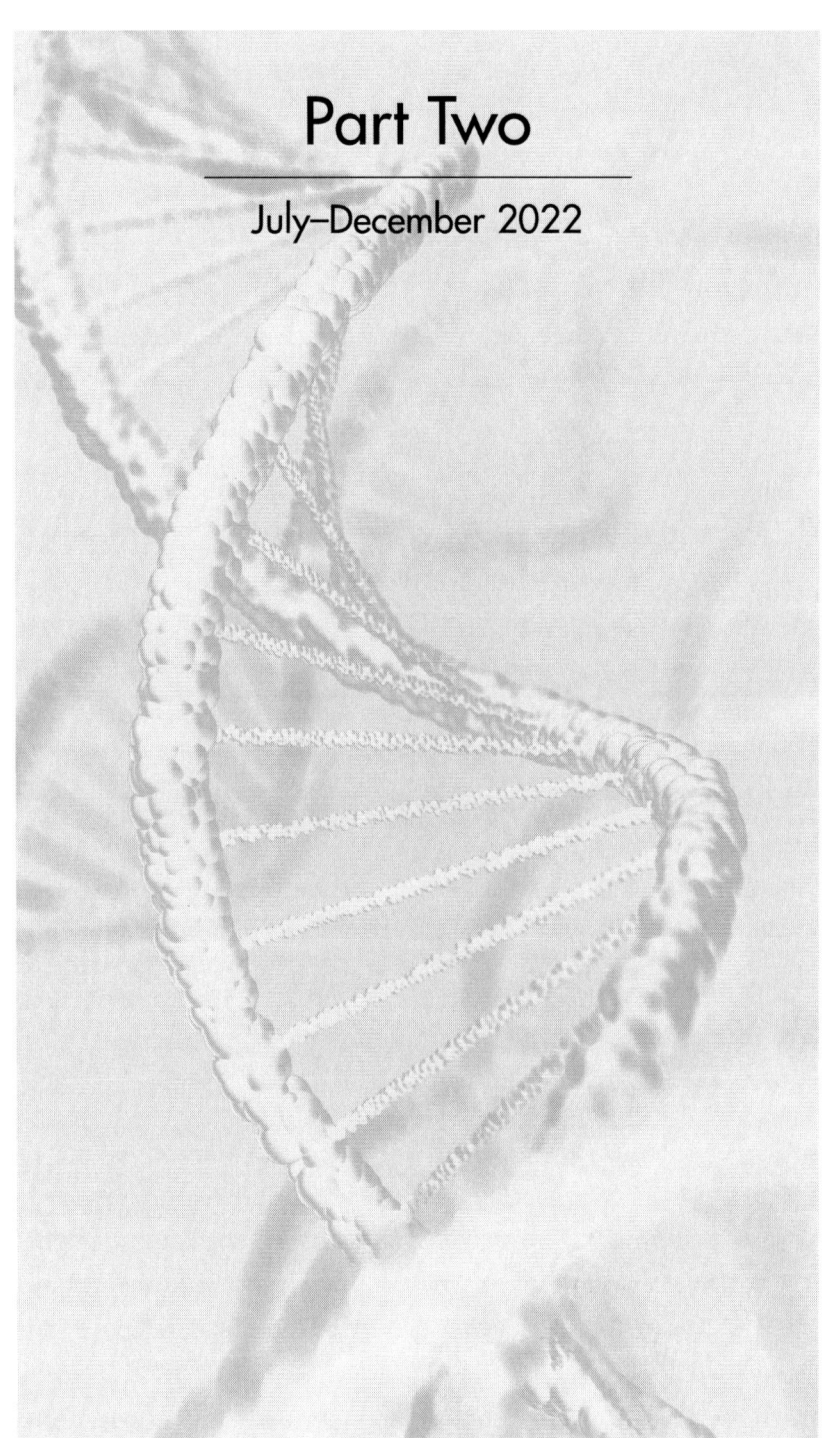

Part Two

July–December 2022

10

Table Talk

"I DIDN'T GET MUCH SLEEP LAST NIGHT. You?"

"Same."

It's Wednesday evening, and Petra and Jerry are at the Speak Easy. They've arrived ahead of the regular Wednesday crowd so they can process the discovery of what they're calling "the mystery protein."

After yesterday, both of them realized that the moment was too large to absorb, that they needed to take a beat—more than a beat, actually—to determine what they had and what its ramifications are.

"Let's meet up an hour early at The Speak Easy and kick around what we've got here," Jerry had texted her that morning.

Petra had replied with a thumbs-up emoji.

• • •

Petra stayed home that day, intent on exploring whether this mystery protein held the key to her mother's situation, whatever that was, or for Werner. She spent a good part of the day revising prompts and running new tests using her AI toolkit, checking and rechecking her findings with everything known about Werner and other accelerated-aging conditions.

Jerry had gone to work, but as he texted Petra that afternoon, he wasn't getting much done and wasn't much help to his lab associates, who looked to him to validate or question their work.

"I should have stayed home, like you, let it sink in."

. . .

"Okay," he says, once they've sat down with their drinks and a bowl full of nuts. "You've had more time to think about this than me. What have we got?"

Petra swirls her glass of Primitivo and looks at the legs, the droplets of wine that form on the inside of the glass. "I don't have any idea what I'm looking for when I do this, but I like how sophisticated it makes me look." She smiles, takes a sip, and puts the glass down. "Before we get too excited, can we agree that there's a chance this might be an error on our part, or something that's already discovered, and you and I just don't know about it?"

Jerry laughs and slaps the table. He leans back, his ponytail dangling for a moment on the shoulder of the startled man at the table behind them. The front legs of his chair rise off the floor for a moment before he rights the ship. "I thought to myself this morning: Petra's going to come in and first thing, she'll knock this down a notch or two."

Petra's stone face holds for a moment, then gives way to a broad smile. "Fair enough. Honestly? I think it's a big deal. Maybe bigger than 'big.' But I spent a lot of last night and this morning remembering how many times I've gotten my hopes up about some discovery or another, just to wind up disappointed later." Her smile wavers for a moment. "I just realized how much my scientific life mirrors my dating life."

Jerry smiles. "I'm thinking of Ed's analysis of the three of us. He says that I'm the eternal optimist, my glass always some-where between half-full and overflowing. That's why everyone brings their ideas and projects to me first. Ed's got a lab to run, and schedules and budgets to meet, so he's more the half-empty guy. As for you, my dear, your glass is always bone-dry."

Petra chuckles. "Normally, Ed's right. But I've had all day to talk myself and our discovery down, and I haven't come up with anything." She takes another sip of wine. "If this is what I think it is—unique and age-related—then we're on to something bigger than either of us has ever dealt with. The more I thought about it, going back to my MIT research, the more I realized that, if we can manipulate this protein's characteristics, it could have implications for not only aging, but also some of the diseases I've been studying."

"Including your mother's?"

"Too soon to tell. But maybe."

"I spent my day somewhat differently," Jerry says. "Jotting down some notes for your Nobel Prize acceptance speech. My only ask for using them is a photo of the two of us holding the statue. Or am I getting this mixed up with the Oscars?"

"I don't know. I've never won either one."

"Speaking of the Oscars, when they make a movie about this, I want Harrison Ford to play me."

"Harrison's eighty, Jer. He'll probably be dead by the time Hollywood discovers us."

"Okay, then Brad Pitt. With hair extensions." He sees Petra's smile widen, a look that has been missing for too long. "So, where do we go from here?" he asks.

Petra thinks hard before answering. "We've got a protein we've never seen before. Right?" Jerry nods. "So, first thing, we need to double check everything we did to get to this point. Research any proteins of similar nature. Confirm that our mystery protein is truly novel and that no one else has discovered it. If they haven't, we determine if its universality has to do with aging, as we suspect, or if there's another commonality that we're not thinking of. And then, finally, if it has to do with aging, are we able to discover the aging mechanism, and edit it out or reverse it?'"

"Agreed on all counts," Jerry says. "And if all of that checks out, we need to figure out how to get this out for peer review, without raising suspicions about what we're up to. Agreed?"

"Agreed. We'll need outside validation of our discovery at some point. But that's a ways off."

"Have you decided what to tell Cheryl Aynesworth? And when? You know she's going to want to claim ownership for Salvana, at least in part."

"I've been wrestling with that one all day, too. I've been so careful, up until now, to keep my Werner work separate from my Salvana work. And in my mind, those are still separate. But I am worried that using the Salvana lab equipment, and your involvement, to run the blood tests might muddy the waters around the discovery of the mystery protein."

"Look," Jerry says. "Much as I'm excited to be a part of it all, you need to be really careful about giving me, or more to the point, Salvana's lab equipment, any credit here."

"But Jer, you've been ..."

"We're not the Wright brothers, Petra. We're more like Don Quixote and Sancho Panza. You've been working on this most of your professional life. I'm coming into this movie way past the halfway mark. So no more 'we', legally or otherwise. Okay?"

"I don't agree. We're partners in this discovery. I couldn't have done it without you."

"I appreciate your saying that, Kid, and I'm enjoying this partnership. But you start crediting me, then you're crediting Salvana, at least in their minds. I've been in the corporate world longer than you. We don't need to give them any more information than necessary. Just remember to mention me in your Nobel acceptance speech. Deal?"

Petra hesitates, then: "Deal."

"Good. Now, since it's just the two of us, can you at least acknowledge this might be a big fucking deal?

Petra smiles into her wine. "It could be."

"Could be what? I need to hear you say it."

"It could be a big fucking deal."

* * *

The others arrive at The Speak Easy within minutes of each other. Alice gives Petra a kiss and waves at her husband, taking a seat across from him. Zoe and Izaak have shared a ride, so they come in together. Ed has already sent word that he'll have to skip tonight's get-together. His in-laws are in town, and they're going out to dinner.

Zoe springs her newest drink on The Speak Easy bartenders, but this is the rare one they're familiar with. The two bartenders, it turns out, have different ways of preparing Double Vision, so they send two large glasses of their concoctions to the table. Zoe is the only one who opts for one. The rest have their usuals.

"Okay, you two," Alice says, as their server departs. "What have you been up to? You've been like a couple of middle-school girls, huddling together and gossiping about the boys. What gives?"

Petra looks at Jerry, who shrugs. "Go on," he says. "They've been through all the shitty times with us. Time for some encouraging news."

Petra hesitates, then plunges in with an animated history of their discovery. When she's done, the table sits in a stunned silence.

"You bastard," Alice says to Jerry. "That's why you were so frisky when you got home. I just thought you'd been on Pornhub again." This to cries of 'ewwww' and laughter.

Zoe looks at Petra. "Seriously? You cracked it? And for once, don't go all humble pie on us. Did you crack the code on aging?"

Petra takes her time formulating her answer. It's a question she's been asking herself ever since the discovery of the protein. "There are a lot of *if*'s involved," Petra begins.

She sees Zoe and Izaak roll their eyes. "Come on," she continues. "You can't think that there's a one-word answer to that question. But *if* the protein's presence means what we think it does, and *if* we can unravel its mechanisms of action and find something that we can modify or turn off, then the answer is most likely *yes*."

The table is silent for a long moment. Then Zoe speaks up. "That's the most boasting I've heard from our Petra in all the time I've known her. What's next?"

"We've got to analyze and validate every step—every theory, every test—that brought us to this point," Petra says. "Then we need to pick the right outside resource—someone who will test our findings and not either alert the scientific community or try to claim the discovery for themselves. If we can get validation for the existence and properties of this mystery protein, then we'll know we have something significant."

"I'm going to ask a question you're going to get over and over," Izaak says. "Who actually owns this discovery?" Everyone turns to him. "I know you've been careful about keeping your work separate, but ..." He nods at Jerry. "... I can feel Salvana creeping into the picture, especially with you using their equipment. Does anyone else at Salvana know about this discovery?"

Jerry answers. "No. All conversations have been just the two of us, and the tests all took place after hours."

"What about Ed?"

"He knows something's up, the way Petra and I have been huddling. But no, no one at Salvana knows."

"What about the lab equipment? Would it have records of what you did?"

"I would assume so," says Jerry. "But maybe I could explain them away somehow."

"What if Jerry just deleted records of the tests?" Zoe asks. "Because it sounds like those tests are what Salvana would use to claim ownership, partial or full."

Jerry doesn't respond initially. He plays with the tip of his ponytail, a habit he has when he's working through a problem. "A few standard tests don't give Salvana anywhere close to equal footing with something Petra's been working on for years. It would be like saying the medical lab that runs tests on your blood work should get credit for diagnosing and treating your illness. But maybe I should go back to the lab and figure out the best way to delete evidence of our work."

"Don't do that," Izaak counsels. "Pharma companies are rightfully concerned about IP and theft. They've all got someone like me on staff or retainer to monitor their different data silos, and the first thing we look for is activity out of the normal."

"What do you suggest we do, then?" Petra asks.

"First off, consult an IP attorney, tell them all the facts, and see if Salvana has any right to your findings. If the answer is *no*, then don't do anything. If it's even a cautious *yes*, let me know. I'll come over during a regular workday, we'll bring in lunch from the café, and I'll find a back door into the system. Jerry can show me where the tests are, I'll check out the security, and unless I see any traps out there, I'll delete the tests."

* * *

The next day, Jerry and Petra meet with a Stanford law faculty member who specializes in intellectual property. They walk him through the discovery at a high level, not mentioning Salvana or the nature of the protein in question. They stop after each step to see if he has a question or problem, but the professor just waves at them to continue. After they finish, he sits with his notes for a few minutes.

"There's no question about primary ownership," he says, finally. "But a major company, which I'm assuming yours is, will have an interest in at least co-owning the protein in question. And they have the deep pockets to force the two of to spend your time protecting your discovery rather than taking it to the next scientific level. So be ready for that."

He nods at his notes. "There are a few other issues to consider here, too."

"Like what?" Jerry asks.

"The company's equipment," the professor says. "Even if it was limited to performing standard blood tests and providing the raw data that was analyzed elsewhere, the company still might have policies decreeing that any use of their equipment, for any reason, gives them the right to claim a partial stake in the discovery. And they might claim another inroad to ownership because an employee was involved in running that equipment for the tests."

Jerry and Petra thank the professor and walk across campus to Izaak's office in the IT facility. They summarize their meeting for Izaak, who nods, as if this were what he expected. "I'll meet you tomorrow for lunch at Salvana," he says. "And I'll bring my laptop."

11

Seeing the Flop

CHERYL LEANS FORWARD, forearms on the table, sleeves on her tunic rolled up to the elbow. She's got two plastic bottles of water in the middle of the small conference table in her office. Now she's waiting for Petra.

She's not sure what to expect of this meeting. Normally, she and Petra meet on an as-needed basis, with the need always on Cheryl's part, like an update for a 1:1 with her boss, or in preparation for a board meeting. But Petra is the one who called this meeting, which has Cheryl curious and cautious in equal measure.

In her first three months at Salvana, Cheryl has given Petra a wide berth in terms of management. Unlike Cheryl's other direct reports, Petra isn't required to do a weekly summary of her activities or attend Cheryl's weekly management meetings. At times Cheryl will drop by the café, pick up two lattes, and stroll down to Petra's office for an unscheduled update on Petra's progress against the grid on her wall.

The adjustment to her senior responsibilities at Salvana has taken some time, as she's had to take crash courses in the science behind the company and the products it yields, as well as come up to speed on the basics of what Petra is up to. But it's nothing like the adjustments she and her family have had to make over the past two years.

It's been toughest on the girls. Her two daughters enjoyed a comfortable Silicon Valley life, with their father a heart surgeon at Stanford, and their mom a prominent fundraiser and advisor to a number of nonprofits. The challenge for Cheryl and her husband, Kurt, was keeping the girls grounded in a culture where high school parking lots are filled with BMWs and Teslas, with the price and model of each line known to most kids, resulting in an informal caste system. And what college you get into defines both you and your parents. It's not uncommon for a kid to get into a school like Colgate or Syracuse, topnotch by any standard except the Valley's, and receive commiserations from their peers' parents, accompanied by the reminder that they can always transfer to a better school if they maintain a 4.0.

Kurt and Cheryl had responded by keeping their lifestyle low-key and their expectations for their girls more on the personal growth side than the academic. Both drove practical cars—he a Jeep Cherokee, she a Camry—and both expected their girls to accompany them and take an active hand in their volunteer work.

But that lifestyle underwent a major change two years ago, when Kurt, mountain-biking with a group of friends on a single track up in the Santa Cruz mountains, went over the handlebars and broke his neck. Despite all the efforts of his colleagues at Stanford, he wound up paralyzed from the chest down, with his hands able to negotiate the controls of his wheelchair and bed, but little else.

Knowing that Stanford's generosity and benefits were finite, Cheryl and Kurt had discussed their options. Kurt was determined to contribute to the family income once his recovery was complete and he knew what his limits were. He would have to shift from making his living with his hands to relying on his brain instead. But the process would be long and arduous. So while the benefits were still in place, they'd had a day nurse in four days a week, leaving Friday and the weekend for Cheryl and the girls to take over, learning the ropes of what looked to be lifelong care.

For her part, Cheryl had realized that her nonprofit work wouldn't cut it for a single-income family, not for where they lived and where the girls went to school. Finding a job in the private sector was not a problem, not with the reputation she had gained among the Valley's moneyed class for integrity and accomplishment. The question was what kind of job and which company.

Acting on her own impulses, as well as the advice of VC friends, she had concentrated on finding a senior-level job in Business Development. She'd joined a chip manufacturer and managed both Biz Dev and vendor relations. Both the job and the travel were enjoyable, and she could have stayed there a while. But then Salvana called, with a salary and a challenge she couldn't resist.

. . .

She reads over her notes one more time, which she's divided into two stacks. The first has her observations from initial meetings with the different departments at Salvana, including their financial goals and contributions to the company's product line. The second is her notes on Petra and her longevity project, starting from the Detective Perkins briefing. It's a thin file.

There's a knock at the door and Petra enters without waiting for a response. After a quick exchange of pleasantries, they take seats at the conference table. Petra opens her laptop and jumps into a recitation of the events of the past few weeks, starting with her mother's symptoms and ending with the battery of tests run the past week. She leaves any mention of Jerry and his tests out of the report. Cheryl listens without interruption for the 20 minutes it takes Petra to go through the steps leading to the discovery and the science used with each step. When Petra concludes her presentation, the two women sit in silence for over a minute.

"This protein," Cheryl begins. "You're the first to discover it?"

"It looks that way, though I won't be sure until it goes out for peer review."

"Then let's start with the obvious. Congratulations. I may not be a scientist, but I know a breakthrough when I see one. It *is* significant, isn't it?"

"Potentially."

"Jesus, don't wet yourself with excitement, Petra. How did you celebrate the discovery? Crack a smile?"

Petra beams a genuine smile. "I've had a bottle of Veuve Clicquot in my pantry for the past seven years. To celebrate with if I came up with a cure for Werner Syndrome. I opened it last night, after I checked and re-checked the tests and data for this meeting."

Cheryl sits back and looks admiringly across the table. "I wasn't sure what you wanted to meet about today, given that we met just two weeks ago. I sure as hell didn't think it would be something like this."

"I was as surprised as you," Petra says. "My mother's new symptoms sent me in a new direction, which ultimately led to the protein in question."

"So let me get this straight," Cheryl says. "In language the board can understand. Are you saying you've discovered a cure for aging? And forgive me if I'm drooling." With that question, and the sharpness in Cheryl's voice, the atmosphere of the room goes from passive listening to a charged electricity.

"To call it a cure would be overstating it. But if this protein is what I think it is, if we can characterize and manipulate it, we can dramatically change the way we age—and the way we treat aging. It all depends on what we—and other researchers—find when we crack it open."

Cheryl's face loses some of its enthusiasm. "What do you mean, 'other researchers?' Salvana is a for-profit company. We're not in the business of sharing with our competitors."

Petra takes a breath and relaxes into her chair. She knows this next sentence won't be well-received, and she doesn't want to make Cheryl an adversary. "Actually, the discovery was a product of my research into Werner Syndrome, not as part of my longevity evaluation work for Salvana."

"But done on Salvana time and equipment."

"No. If you check with Ed and Jerry, they'll tell you I have a fairly sophisticated AI-powered system at home that's able to do advanced analytics and modeling. And I've always kept my Werner research separate from my Salvana work, both time and equipment."

She sees the frustration growing on Cheryl's side of the table, which she had anticipated. "That said, I'm a Salvana employee and I appreciate what the company has done for me. I also appreciate the talent and resources within the company that could be put to use against this discovery. All of that earns Salvana first rights."

"First rights or sole rights?"

"First," Petra says firmly. She sees Cheryl's face start to harden, a dash of color coming into her cheeks. "Put yourself in my shoes, Cheryl. I got into this field initially to try to come up with a cure for Werner and to design new ways to diagnose and treat diseases that are currently incurable. While I certainly feel an obligation and gratitude to Salvana, my primary allegiance as a scientist is to the people suffering from those diseases. And now that I have this discovery, the more brains, labs, and tests applied against it, the quicker we'll have a solution."

"Brains, labs, and tests," Cheryl repeats. "We have all of that here."

"Agreed, though they're all being dedicated to end-of-life palliatives. I'm not sure how much help they'll be on this new initiative, or whether you'll need to hire new personnel. It's early days, but I think it's the latter."

Cheryl looks across the table, her facial expression now back to the one Petra has trouble reading. She gives Petra a tight smile. "Let's back up for a moment, maybe back to where we were cracking open the Veuve Clicquot. You've made a tremendous discovery, and Salvana would be foolish not to take full advantage of it." She pauses. "Let's do this. Give me a week to put together an initial plan from the company side— what we can do and how we propose to do it. You do the same, from a scientific standpoint, and what you need to validate your findings and take them to the next step. Let's get together next Friday and compare notes. I think—or hope, at least—that we'll both be pleasantly surprised at where we come out."

Cheryl stands, as does Petra. Cheryl walks her to the door, congratulating her one last time before ushering her out. Then she returns to her desk and calls Legal.

12

A New Dealer

"I HEAR OUR MS. ALEXANDER has had a major breakthrough," Mike Perkins says.

Cheryl frowns. It's only been three days since Petra's announcement, and besides Legal, Cheryl has told only two people, both of whom she'll need for the next meeting with Petra, both of whom she trusts. Perkins isn't one of them. But she's found in her few encounters with Perkins that he's more wired into Salvana than she is, and she's always prided herself on her inside knowledge.

"Is this the point where I'm supposed to say I can neither confirm nor deny?" she says in a light tone, watching his face for a reaction.

She gets one. The skin at his temple tightens and there's a flash of anger in his eyes before he eases into a practiced smile. "It would be except ..." He holds up two fingers and folds them down, one at a time, as he continues: "A: I've already confirmed it, and B: We're on the same team. What can you tell me?"

She recounts the basics of the meeting with Petra, closing with: "I've spent enough time with her to know she's underplaying her discovery. It's a trait common to scientists, this cautious stance, and Petra seems even more cautious than her peers. So we may be looking at a real breakthrough on the longevity front, the kind Salvana has been looking for."

The skin around Perkins' eyes tightens. "That's incredible. One person—someone we know, no less—coming up with something that significant. I guess it's not unheard of. I'm thinking of all the single contributors from my history classes: Madame Curie, the guy for penicillin, Edison." He shakes his head. "Still, impressive." Then he comes back to the moment. "But I'm hearing there's some question about ownership?"

"It's more than a question, from what I'm gathering from Legal. It's a real problem. Legal says if Petra can prove that her discovery happened away from Salvana, and didn't rely on either our equipment or human resources, she has full ownership."

"But based on her personal history—especially that thing with her father—I'd assume she wants to develop it here at Salvana, rather than start over somewhere else. Or go out on her own."

"I hope you're right, but this is personal for her. We need to keep that in mind."

"What do you mean?"

"The foundation of her discovery was the work she's been doing to find a cure for the disease that killed her sister. And now her mother's showing signs she's got it, or something like it, too. So Petra's going to be hell-bent to develop this discovery, even if it means sharing it with other scientists to get to a solution faster."

"That could be a problem on two fronts." At her raised eyebrow, he continues. "The first is obvious. If longevity is the future of Salvana, we need to own this product and the technology it's based on."

"And the second?"

"It can't happen on her timeline. It has to happen on Salvana's."

"I know where you're going with this. It came up in my interviews and it was the first thing I asked when they put the longevity project under me. How it fits into Salvana's product strategy and bottom line."

"And what did management tell you?"

"That longevity may be the future of Salvana, but the present is in making the last phase of life as comfortable and pain-free as possible. How to get from the present to the future— that's a big part of my job."

He nods. "That's more or less what they told me as well, but they got more specific, saying that the transition you're talking about— getting from here to there—will take at least ten years. Maybe more."

"How could they know that without seeing the science? I don't know that. You don't know that. And we're closer to this situation than they are."

"It's not a question of science, but of business. Once there's a breakthrough of this nature—and for the purpose of this meeting, let's assume Petra has cracked the code—the company needs time to integrate this science into their portfolio, and this new development into its product line and into the way Salvana is viewed by the buying public. All of that will take time, and in the meantime the company has to maintain profitability."

"Specific to Petra's project, what are you saying?"

"Let's see what her numbers are first. They may be in line with ours. But if they're not, if we find ourselves at cross-purposes with her goals, my job is to ensure that Salvana's objectives prevail."

"And that directive comes from the CEO?"

"Above him. Quite a bit above." He cocks his head and shrugs boyishly, but it doesn't play.

Cheryl's smile has a touch of acid to it. "You're not an HR consultant, are you?"

His lips thin as he draws in a breath. Then his mouth relaxes. "I'm on HR's payroll. And I do vet major new hires, such as yourself. But I have a second boss, the one who told Salvana to hire me. And that's all I can say about that."

"Or you'd have to kill me?" She's teasing—and isn't.

"Let's hope it doesn't come to that." She looks hard at him and realizes he's teasing—and isn't.

13

On the Clock

PETRA AND JERRY ARE IN PETRA'S SALVANA OFFICE. They're running through the numbers one more time in advance of Petra's meeting with Cheryl. On one of the whiteboard walls are the steps they established as milestones for their projections:

- CONFIRM EXISTENCE (done)
- CHARACTERIZE PROTEIN AND DNA SEQUENCE
- CREATE ANTIBODY
- IN VITRO TESTS: (REMOVE, DOUBLE-DOWN)
- IN VIVO TESTS (NEMATODE WORMS, FRUIT FLIES, MICE)
- MANIPULATE DNA TO DECREASE ACCUMULATION
- CREATE ACTUAL INTERVENTION (DRUG)

• • •

Petra finishes her notes and gives them one more read and tabulation. She places the piece of paper face-down on the table and nods at Jerry, who's been going through the same exercise.

"Okay. What've you got?" she says.

"Forty-eight months, assuming that your AI tool can do most of the heavy lifting. You?"

Petra shows her sheet. There are two sets of numbers. The first totals 38 months, the second, 60. "I went best-case, worst-case." She nods at his sheet. "I'm glad we're in the same ballpark."

"What do you think Cheryl will do with these numbers?" Jerry asks.

"She's out of her depth on the science front, so I hope she just defers to us. Ed tells me that she's asked for his help, so she may have her own set of numbers."

"Have you shared your numbers with Ed? Because I haven't."

"No," Petra says. "I don't want to put him in a tough spot. You can tell he's already uncomfortable with Cheryl's request, though I've told him not to be. It's not like we're on two different teams. If he validates us, great. If he doesn't, we'll bring him around."

· · ·

Petra walks into Cheryl's office the next morning and sees Ed talking to Cheryl. A woman she's never seen before is seated next to him. The unknown woman is in her late twenties, dressed like someone on their way up, a contrast to Cheryl's casual outfit and Petra's workout/work gear. Her hair is up, her makeup just right. She's sitting a bit straighter than the others around the table.

Cheryl motions Petra to the empty seat on the far side. As Petra settles in and opens her laptop, Cheryl takes a yellow pad, manila folder, and Mont Blanc pen from her desk and joins the table. Then she turns to Petra. "I thought it would be helpful for this meeting to bring in some resources who can help us create the most complete plan possible. Ed, you obviously know—I'm counting on his knowledge of equipment and tests to help us with our schedule. And this," she inclines her forehead towards the mystery woman, "is Ashley Eastman. Ash is a Research Director in our Marketing department."

Ashley Eastman half-stands and reaches across the table. Petra shakes hands, then turns an inquiring eye to Cheryl. "Marketing? At this stage?"

"You'll see in a minute." Cheryl looks around the table, holding each person's eyes for a moment before continuing. "Let me kick things off, then turn it over to Petra. In my experience, success in any major initiative like this one comes down to three components: product readiness, market readiness, and company readiness. We've got the owners of all of them here at this table. Product is Petra, obviously, with Ed to determine what we'll need to support her plan, people, budget, and space. Marketing and how prepared the market is for our discovery is Ashley. I'm responsible for company readiness. We combine these three elements, we should have a solid plan we can present to the board and start implementing. You're up, Petra."

Petra is impressed by the way Cheryl has taken command of the meeting. She also likes the categories that Cheryl put forward. She has come into the meeting thinking the burden was all on her. Instead, she finds herself a partner on a team. She walks the group through a quick history of the discovery and the steps that she and Jerry have articulated. She concludes with "If everything goes right—and it rarely does—three years. On the more conservative side, five."

Cheryl nods. "Okay. Let's come back to those numbers once we've discussed the other components." She turns to Ashley. "Market readiness?"

Ashley nods to Cheryl, but then speaks directly to Petra. "My job, whenever Salvana is developing a new product, is to determine, first, how large the potential market is. Then I measure where that market is currently. Do they foresee a need for this new product, what have they been doing in its place, and how much are they willing to pay for this new solution. Those are the external metrics. The internal metric is: How much market education will it take to move the market from neutral or negative, to positive, then from positive to buyer." She nods at Petra's laptop. "In this case, the potential market seems at first massive. I mean, living a long, healthy life, who wouldn't want that?'"

Petra gives her a tight grin. "Why do I feel a 'but' coming on?'"

"Because you'd be right. Every new product is up against the status quo. And in this case, the status quo is life expectancy. To be clear, your potential customers don't *want* to die. Not anytime soon, anyway. But they *expect* to die. And while life expectancy has inched up to over 80, our audience's goal is to live those years as healthily as possible, a longing that has made Salvana into a billion-dollar company."

She points her finger at Petra, but it's a friendly gesture. "You're talking about adding 50 to 60 years to that equation. There will be a small core group, call them 'the early adopters,' who'll be excited and eager to be guinea pigs. But the vast majority of our target audience is going to take a helluva lot of convincing."

Cheryl motions at Petra and Ed. "Give them the numbers you gave me."

Ashley looks at her screen. "There are personal and societal components to this. When it comes to themselves, 38 percent of Americans want what is currently called 'radical life extension,' or RLE, for themselves. Another 56 percent don't. Societally, 41 percent believe that RLE would be good for society, while 51 percent think it would be bad."

Ed speaks up for the first time. "Wouldn't that depend on your definition of living?"

"Exactly. Looking at the data, it's clear that few, if any, of the people surveyed had given this much thought. If pollsters introduced positive elements to their questions, such as more time with grandchildren, the numbers spiked up. Same spike with negatives, such as questions about retirement, social security, elder care, and impact on the environment. So the lesson is that the market can be moved, but, given how major a shift in attitude this would be—to opt in to living to 120, say—this market education campaign will take years."

"In other words," Cheryl says, "it's not too soon to start."

"Exactly. But it can't have Salvana's fingerprints anywhere near the campaign. This has to look like an academic discussion, not a company promotion." She turns to Cheryl. "I've done a little digging since you invited me here, and I know of at least three market analysts who, with the right sponsorship, can start the discussion. And on our terms."

Cheryl looks at Petra. "You see why I invited her today?"

Petra gives a wistful smile. "Any more fun facts like that and I'll go home and delete all my findings."

"Now to my part of the formula, company readiness," says Cheryl. "The big question, if your solution proves out, is how— both internally and externally—we can integrate this science and resulting products into Salvana without cannibalizing our current product line. We can and should start today, but without Salvana anywhere near the discussion. But once we've started to accomplish enough of the items on Petra's list, when it's clear both that the product works and that we have a significant edge on our competitors, then we can start sponsoring workshops, public halls even, as part of the market education campaign. And while we're doing that, as Ed and I have been discussing, we can start extending the Salvana product line to include what I call 'bridge products,' versions of our current product line of palliatives that include some of Petra's breakthrough, adding to our bottom line and beginning to change the way the market views Salvana."

She opens a manila folder and takes out three pieces of paper. "I've met with Finance and a few members of the board to get their reaction to how quickly we can move into the longevity business without losing our core constituencies. Then I met with Ed to determine the equipment and personnel a major initiative like this would require." She distributes the papers. "Don't respond now. Take it with you and give it a solid read. See how it fits with your agenda. Then let's reconvene in a week."

14

Being Slowplayed

"EIGHT TO TEN YEARS?" Petra says, waving Cheryl's one-pager at Jerry. "That sounds more like a prison sentence than a product schedule."

It's the evening of Petra's meeting with Cheryl and they're sitting in Petra's office, beers from Petra's small refrigerator in front of them. As Cheryl requested, Petra gave the document time to settle. Once the meeting was over, she retired to a nearby Peet's, where she read the document twice, making notes in the margin. Then she routed herself by The Ascent for a grueling workout, hoping that would alleviate some of her frustration. Now it's 7 pm and she's sharing the document with Jerry for the first time.

She has to hand it to Cheryl. If this were a poker game, Petra would say that Cheryl was playing with a stacked deck. As she recounted to Jerry, Cheryl had let Petra lead out, giving her as much time and encouragement as she needed to get her schedule across. But Cheryl had some hole cards that Petra wasn't prepared for, starting with Ashley Eastman's figures on market readiness and acceptance. "She sounded like Alice on Wednesday nights at The Speak Easy, except with numbers to back it up."

"Did it seem like she was presenting them to educate or to dissuade?" Jerry asks.

"Educate. Like I said, even though Cheryl realized her schedule was twice as long as ours, she didn't push anything on me. Remember, she didn't know what our numbers were going to be, so when she saw our schedule, she tailored the rest of the meeting to explain the thinking and the logic that went into her schedule."

"And did they change your thinking? Or your schedule?"

"No, but I understand Cheryl's perspective a little better. Her priority is Salvana, and her measurement tool is the company's bottom line. You and I have a different bottom line. It's how fast can we get this into the market and start impacting people's lives for the better. And we have the AI capability on our side, which I haven't begun to share with Cheryl yet."

"Do you see this being a conflict or something you two can work out?"

"Hopefully the latter. Because as the news of what we're doing gets out, and the market starts to raise some of the issues that Ashley Eastman raised this morning, Cheryl is going to be the public face of longevity. There can't be any space between us."

"Why Cheryl as the public face? Why not you?"

"Can you imagine me on CNN? Or better yet, Fox?"

"Yes, I can," Jerry says. "But it doesn't sound like you can."

"She's the better spokesperson. It'll be a lot easier to teach her the science she'll need for these shows than to teach me all the media skills I lack."

Jerry takes a sip of his beer and looks at the figures again. "Before we get our chains wrapped around the axle here, are any of her figures and calculations flat out wrong?"

"Not wrong. Just overly cautious. At every turn." Petra stands up, beer in hand, and goes over to the far wall, which is covered with a new set of calculations. "I went back to our original calculations, and I can see where someone could argue that we're too optimistic by a year or so. But off by five to seven? No way."

Jerry looks back again at the paper. "I'm wondering where she got her numbers. She certainly didn't run them by me. You said Ed was in the meeting?"

"Yeah, but he hardly said a word. And he didn't look very comfortable, either."

Jerry looks out the office window. "He's still here. Let's buy him a beer and see what he thinks."

A minute later Jerry is back, Ed in tow. "I hope you like IPA, 'cause it's all Petra is pouring tonight."

"What happened to the Stella?" Ed asks. Jerry pats his stomach in answer.

Petra opens the last Blind Pig and hands it to him. "I want to ask you about the numbers on Cheryl's schedule," she says. "If that puts you in an awkward spot, let's just enjoy our IPAs— sorry about the Stella— and talk about your beloved Niners."

"Ask away. I was surprised to be invited, to be honest. She told me yesterday afternoon about your discovery." He fixes a scolding eye on Petra, then on Jerry. "Tell you the truth, I was a little pissed to be hearing about it from her and not from you guys."

"That's on me, not Jerry," Petra says. "Until I've got a better feel for Cheryl and her role in all this, I didn't want to put either of you at risk. I did need Jerry's help on a couple of tests, but only the three of us know that."

She looks at Ed, who wears the same look of discomfort as he had in the morning meeting. "This schedule doesn't smell right to me," she says. "What do you think?"

Ed doesn't refer to the paper with the numbers on it. "Those numbers didn't come from me. Not sure where they came from." He shifts in his chair. "She called me in as she was prepping for the meeting and asked if I thought her numbers were reasonable. I told her I was out of my depth when it came to longevity, but she kept at it, saying I know more about bringing a product to market than anyone on her team. So I looked hard at the numbers, then told her they looked high to me."

"And how did she respond to that?" Jerry asks.

"She never raised her voice, but she never came off her eight- to ten-year schedule. She kept saying she had to factor in 'the greater good,' like we were in Sweden or something. I got the impression that the greater good had to do with Salvana's market standing. It's clear she needs to build a bridge from Salvana today to Salvana, the longevity company. So every time I gave her a number, she padded it, citing 'the greater good.'"

"Here's my big issue," Petra says. "The more I think about this new protein, the more I believe it has ramifications, not just in aging, but in the arena of incurable diseases. We won't have the bandwidth to pursue all the possibilities, which is why I want to publish our findings as soon as possible. Cheryl's measurement tool is Salvana's profit line, but mine is the thousands of people who might die unnecessarily in the five years between her schedule and ours. If Cheryl won't budge off her schedule ..." She looks over at Jerry. "It might be a bigger problem than we think."

15

Moving Tables

"EIGHT TO TEN YEARS?" This time it's Izaak questioning the schedule. "I know guys who've launched and sold two companies in less time than that." He and Petra are strolling down University Avenue, Palo Alto's major artery. It's 10:30 and the city is in different stages of closing down for the night. Izaak had called Petra earlier that day and suggested a night out would do them both good. She didn't disagree, though she asked if they could meet at 8:30, since she still had a number of things left to do in the lab.

Petra takes Izaak's arm as they stroll. She's glad Izaak called. She can feel herself slipping away, socially, as the scope of the challenge ahead takes charge of her calendar and moods. She makes a promise to herself that she'll make priorities of Wednesday evenings at The Speak Easy, and of her friendships.

One of those friendships is with Izaak. While she respects his decision to curtail their romance when he learned of her bisexuality, she doesn't understand it, emotionally or otherwise. Both men and women have their unique sexualities and forms of expressing them, she reasons, and she doesn't appreciate or understand why someone would limit themselves to only half of what the world has to offer. Izaak, to his credit, tried to roll with the punches, though his broader perspective didn't extend to other men, either for himself or Petra. Women were okay as

Petra's sexual partners—he told her he even found it arousing—but men were off limits, a restriction that Petra wasn't comfortable with.

She drapes her arm loosely through his as they walk the length of University, turning around at the Alma overpass. Over dinner she had brought him up to speed on what she and Jerry had discovered as well as the development stages ahead. It was nice to be able to have this conversation with someone other than Jerry. Ed, by mutual agreement, was keeping his distance from Petra and Jerry until the issues around ownership and schedule were resolved.

Even though Izaak is at Stanford and Zoe at Oracle, he is more the Silicon Valley insider. First off, as Zoe noted, HR is technology-ambivalent. She doesn't need to know how databases work to do her job. Izaak, on the other hand, is in charge of the IT research center at Stanford, which has spawned more startups than any other educational institution. When a project or person graduates from the center and heads out into the make-or-break world of startups, they often offer Izaak a job. But, as he told Petra on their first date after she relocated to Silicon Valley, he loves the variety of technologies that he's exposed to in his work, as well as the perks that come with his position, especially the ability to audit any course, undergrad or graduate.

"What's Jerry say?"

"Same as me. And we came up with our schedules independently."

"Does Ed agree? He was quieter than usual at The Speak Easy this week."

"He's in an awkward position. Cheryl is using him to validate our numbers and to help her come up with her own. Officially, he has to be on Team Cheryl. But off the record he says she's padding every number he gives her by three years."

As they enter the parking garage that holds both their cars, Izaak stops, causing Petra to slip her arm out of his. He takes hold of both her forearms and waits for her eyes to find his. "Listen to yourself, Petra. 'Team Cheryl. Deleted tests. Padded schedules.' Can you honestly see yourself living the next ten years in that kind of environment? Because I can't."

"That's big talk from the gallery, Izaak. I don't see you in the arena." She sees the hurt in Izaak's eyes, but plunges on. "You're always telling me about the startups coming out of Stanford that recruit you to join. And yet there you stay, running the computer lab and taking all those classes tuition-free. So don't tell me to get in the game."

Izaak drops Petra's arms and takes a step backward. "That isn't fair, Petra. I'm not the one who ..."

"That's right. You're not the one who cleaned her father's brains off his desk and the wall behind him. You're not the one who watched her sister age a year every week as her life circled the drain. When you're *that* person, you can advise *this* person what to do with her life."

Izaak starts to respond, then he steps back in and regains his grip. "Before you say another word—before you do any more damage to our friendship—let me say my piece. I know your aversion to startups, but there's someone I'd like you to meet. Do that and I'll never mention startups again. What do you say?"

"Who are we talking about?"

"Keeley James. Ever heard of her?" When Petra shakes her head, he continues. "She used to be a VC, took a number of startups public, made her millions, and retired. Now she splits her time between philanthropy and advising startups, with an emphasis on women-run companies. I'm sure she'd agree to meet with you if I asked her, since I've helped her with some of her companies. What do you say?"

Izaak's gentle tone and touch have a calming effect. Petra looks around the parking garage and sighs. She sits down on the small wall dividing the garage from the street and motions for Izaak to do the same.

"I'm not going to apologize, Izaak. It's not in my DNA, as you know. But I'll try to explain." This time she takes his hand. "You know the phrase 'Failure is not an option'? Well, that's been my mantra since I can't remember when. Maybe before my father's death, but certainly after. And ever since. This isn't some kind of NASA slogan—it's how I live. How I stay sane. Because if there's one thing I know, it's that failure is contagious. Usually between people, but in my case, between me and myself. I saw where a single failure took my dad—first to laying off staff, then to closing his beloved company, then to lying to family so that they'd think they were investing in a growing company when it was just to pay off his creditors. And when that didn't work, he took out his pistol and left a note for me on how to make it look like he was cleaning his pistol rather than ending it all."

She drops Izaak's hand and stands up. "So keep your friend's card. I'm staying where I'm safe, where my failures and consequences are my own, nobody else's."

16

Face Up

THE TWO WOMEN stroll the Stanford campus, arm in arm. It's February, so evening comes early, and they're dressed for the chill. Eleni called Petra earlier that day and proposed the walk, saying she had some shopping to do at the Stanford mall but afterwards there was something she wanted to discuss with Petra. They meet in front of the Apple store and stroll seemingly aimlessly, though Petra knows where they'll wind up. The Rodin sculpture garden is her mother's favorite place on the peninsula.

One of the least publicized but most enjoyable parts of the Stanford campus, the garden is a collection of 20 of Rodin's most famous sculptures. Eleni takes a seat on a bench near the heads of the Burghers of Calais and pats the seat next to her.

Petra joins her. "So how do I merit a mid-week sleepover? You said you wanted to talk to me about something."

"I said I wanted to *show* you something. I'll show you when we get back to the apartment. But since we're talking, I want to run two things by you. They've always been on my mind, but this change in my condition makes me feel like the clock is now no longer ticking but speeding up." She holds up a hand to stop Petra from chiming in. "And unless you're going to tell me you've found a cure to what I have, please don't give me a pep talk."

Petra nods. "Fair enough. So, the two things."

"The first is, I'd like to go back to Greece, see the village I came from. And I'd like to do it with you. I know you can't do it now, but it's a bucket list for me, so I just want to put it out there."

"Okay. What's the other thing?"

"Grandchildren." Her hand goes back up, even though Petra hasn't opened her mouth. "I know we've never talked about it. I just want to know if it's even remotely in the picture. I don't want an argument here, just a discussion. You know Greeks and family." She looks tightly at her daughter. "Well?"

Petra looks at her mother, at the earnest expression, at how she's leaning forward unconsciously. "I think you're expecting me to be a hard no. Right?" Eleni just shrugs. "But the real answer is, I haven't given it any thought. And I'm serious, Mamá. In my mind, given my schedule now and for the foreseeable future, I can't imagine meeting that ..." fingers in the air, "'special some-one.' Male or female. Someone I'd like to spend the rest of my life with. That's kind of a prerequisite to having a child, at least for me."

Eleni nods, as if this were the answer she was expecting. "What about adoption? What if we—you and I—adopted? With whatever time I have left, I'd be the stay-at-home and do the heavy lifting. After I'm gone, you could bring in a nanny." She pauses and looks in earnestly. "What do you think?"

"What do I think? I thought the trip to Greece was a reach, until you opened Door Number Two." She sees the water gather in the corners of Eleni's eyes. "I hope you didn't expect an answer tonight, or am I wrong?"

"Actually, I expected a 'let's see' on Greece and a hard *no* on grandchildren. But I needed to raise both topics."

"Well, you're half right. The Greece trip is a possibility, depending on work. The adoption...? When you called and said you wanted to talk to me about something, I thought you were going to tell me that you and Jeff were getting married. But you and me adopting ... can I sleep on that? For a year or so?"

．．．

When they get back to Petra's apartment, with dinner on its way from one of the local restaurants, Eleni tells Petra she'd like to take a shower before she gets into her pajamas. Petra nods and says she'll set the table. Eleni disappears into the bathroom, along with the plush white robe that she keeps at Petra's apartment for sleepovers.

Ten minutes later, Eleni comes out, scrubbed clean. With no makeup, the lines on her face are canyonesque, clear and deep. Her remaining hair is stiff and grey, with parts of her scalp showing through. Eleni registers the shock on Petra's face. "One of the few times I've seen you without your poker face."

"My God, Mamá. What happened?" Petra catches herself. "I mean, I know what happened, but why have you been hiding it from me?"

"From everyone, honey, not just you. And the reason should be obvious. You should have seen the look on your face when I came out. I can do without that, from people I know and people I don't. Luckily, one of my neighbors is in the make-up department at the ACT. She helped me with the wig as well."

"Well, she did a helluva job," Petra says. "And so have you. I'm sure no one at work has noticed a thing. I just figured you'd been getting better at your makeover skills. But why haven't you at told me, at least? I'm your daughter, for God's sake."

"A daughter who is under more stress than anyone should be. And what could you do about it?"

Petra sits there quietly, eyes fixed on her mother, taking inventory of the disease's advances. "I feel awful. With everything that's going on—and that's no excuse—I've ignored my research on Werner. Mamá, I'm so sorry."

"See? This is why I didn't want to tell you. Because you're going to do what you just did, blame yourself. Which is the last thing I need right now. And the last thing either of us can afford."

Petra starts to speak, but Eleni holds up her hand. "I've told you now. And I've shown you. That's enough. This is our secret. I'll be the one to decide who to tell and when. Understand?" Petra nods. "Good. Let's eat."

• • •

Dinner was a forced affair. Petra had tried initially to learn more about her mother's symptoms, but it was clear from Eleni's re-direction that she'd said all she was going to on the topic of her health. So Petra had made light conversation while looking across the table at the ravages that the disease had exacted in the recent few months. The lines were deep and pronounced, rivers running down her mother's cheeks and neck. And her hair, a source of pride for Eleni, had gone grey and straw-like. Her mother was dying in front of her.

An hour later, dinner is done and Eleni is cleaning up the kitchen. Petra retreats to the bathroom, where she sits on the toilet, sobbing quietly. Mindful that Eleni might be listening, she tries to suppress the sound, holding a small towel in front of her mouth. When one large sob involuntarily escapes, she turns on the shower for more cover.

As soon as the crying subsides, she picks up her phone, turns off the shower, and makes a call. "Izaak. It's me. Can you set up that meeting with your startup friend?"

She listens for a moment. "Yes, I'm sure. The sooner, the better."

17

Backing the Play

"ZELDA, REMEMBER TO SHARE, HONEY. You've got two. Let your friend Murphy have one." The woman turns to Petra. "God, the names these days. I was in Whole Foods yesterday and I heard a woman calling out for her precious kid. Tallulah. Can you imagine?"

"Petra isn't the most common name. I caught some grief for that growing up. I imagine the same for Keeley."

"Yeah, but at least there's some heritage there. But Tallulah—my god. I hope that kid's got a good middle name."

The two women are seated on a green metal bench in the playground reserved for children of Stanford faculty. Petra's host is Keeley James. She agreed to the meeting as a favor to Izaak, who phoned her as soon as Petra called him from her bathroom. Zelda is her granddaughter, the daughter of Keeley's son Jeremy, an associate professor in linguistics. In her early 50s, Keeley has shoulder-length hair gone almost completely grey. She has a round face and slightly upturned nose and wears just a touch of makeup. Round rimless glasses and a dash of freckles complete the picture. There's nothing in either her looks or posture that indicate she's one of the most powerful and successful women in the Valley.

"Thanks again for meeting with me. I know from Izaak how busy you are."

"Thank *you* for not starting this meeting by telling me I look too young to be a grandmother. I get that buttering up crap all the time. Yeah, Izaak. That boy's a keeper. I've tried to recruit him for a number of my startups, but he likes it where he is. And I've heard about you for as long as I've known him. He's very fond of you, by the way."

Keeley looks to Petra for a response, but Petra just nods. "I assume you know I'm semi-retired these days," Keeley continues. "My main job now is keeping up with that one." She nods at Zelda. "Four years old and thinks she's fourteen." She looks back to Petra. "I've done my own due diligence on you as well, plus what Izaak tells me. So how can I help?"

* * *

When Izaak told her he was available if she wanted to rehearse her pitch, Petra was initially surprised. "I thought this was a conversation and I'd just bring her up to speed on my situation, see what suggestions she had."

"Ignore the playground location. She's expecting to be pitched. Even though she's mostly retired, there's still a bit of the shark in her. Figure you've got five minutes, ten tops, to grab her attention. The nice part of her will give you advice, perhaps even agree to be your startup coach. The shark side of her will be looking for an investment opportunity, something she can get involved in from the ground up. So treat this as a business meeting, but in casual clothes. And be compelling, because you're competing with her only grandchild for attention."

With Izaak's coaching, Petra had honed her narrative. "You've got two things you need to get across, then a possible third, if she's interested. The first is the problem you're looking to solve, which translates into 'opportunity' for investors. The second is your personal narrative—how you got involved in it and why you're uniquely positioned to solve the problem. This is where you bring up Thea, how you changed majors and concentrated on aging and disease, and your accomplishments at both Chicago and MIT. And Petra, this is no time for modesty. VCs like arrogance. If you can't be arrogant, at least be proud of your work to date. Let her know about your work with artificial intelligence and how that changes the game in terms of discovery and testing, and how it shortens time-to-market. She'll be interested in that."

"The third thing you mentioned—her level of interest." Her voice rises at the last word, indicating a question.

"You're the poker player, so you'll have a feel for that, I'm assuming. But to use Jerry's baseball analogies, if she gives you the names of some folks who might be interested in funding you, that's a single. If she gives you her phone number and says she's available to be your startup coach, that's a double. And the home run is if she wants to invest in you. Especially since it's her own money."

. . .

Keeley tilts her head back and lets the sun play on her face as she listens to Petra. She doesn't pretend to know enough about longevity and the science behind it to challenge Petra's theories and tests, but since Izaak vouches for her, Keeley focuses on the underlying psychology at work—namely, how prepared and emotionally ready Petra is for the startup life.

Keeley gives Petra an A- for dedication and intensity, but a C for presentation. Based on what Izaak told her, there's no question on the IP and ownership fronts. It's Petra's discovery. As she listens to Petra discuss the implications of her discovery, not just for longevity but for certain currently incurable diseases, she's impressed. But she hears a scientist, not a CEO. In her world of technology startups, Petra would be a Chief Technology Officer.

"Out of respect for both you and Izaak, I'm going to be direct with you," Keeley says. "You come across as a scientist who is deigning to step into the distasteful world of commerce." She waits for an objection, but there is none. "Let me tell you what I look for in every founder we meet. It's not arrogance exactly, more a hunger to succeed, to make a mark. And the attitude to do whatever it takes to get there. Are you following me?"

"I am," Petra says, "and if we're being honest here, I'd have to agree with your assessment. I don't know too many scientists who would fit that description."

Keeley throws up her arms. "See? That's what I'm talking about. That was your opportunity to tell me nicely that I'm full of shit and show me why. Not agree with me."

Petra smiles weakly. "This meeting isn't going that well, is it?"

Keeley smiles back. She likes this woman and is impressed by her discovery and its implications. Plus, there's Izaak's recommendation, which counts for a lot. "Let's do this," she says. "There's a Starbucks two blocks from here. You go there and rework your pitch. Take some hubris pills, if you've got any. Get rid of the modesty and the scientific disclaimers. I'll take Zelda home and then join you. I want to hear a different pitch from a different woman, someone who thinks she's discovered something huge and wants to bring it to market. That sound fair?"

This time Petra does show her surprise. "More than fair. I thought you never get a second chance with VCs."

"You can thank our mutual friend for that. Plus, I think you're onto something big here. But before I leave, let me tell you what I say in every lecture I give to gatherings of would-be founders. We VCs suffer from two diseases. The first is ADHD, which means you've got five minutes to grab our attention, and another five minutes for us to be interested. At that ten-minute mark, if you haven't grabbed us, we either call it a day and show you the door—or we go into fake-listen mode, nodding our head as we scribble notes that have nothing to do with you."

"Got it. What's the second disease? Maybe I can cure that while I'm at it?"

Keeley laughs loudly. "Good for you, girl. Keep that attitude when you're presenting. The other disease is greed. And your discovery rings that bell—loudly. Make sure you keep ringing it." She reaches into her purse and comes out with her car keys. "See you in an hour."

* * *

"You're trainable," Keeley says. "I'll give you that."

"Better?" Petra asks.

"Much. I'm impressed, both by you and your discovery. Now my only question is why I shouldn't make you Chief Science Officer and bring in one of my EIRs to run things. You know what an EIR is?"

A nod. "From Izaak. Entrepreneur in Residence. A would-be CEO warming up in the bullpen."

"*Would* you be comfortable in that role?"

"I've given that some thought, and the answer is no. Not for egotistic reasons—at least I don't think it is. But all the startups I know about focus only on tech, and so will most VCs I meet with, I imagine. But with a science startup, a tech-based CEO—or one with a general business background—won't have much to do for the first two or three years, at least. It's better to have a scientist or a science-oriented person in that role initially, one who can not only understand what the scientists are up to, but who can contribute to the process. And who can definitely challenge their thinking, if not their findings. I'm not being proprietary about my discovery, but I know it best. The corners I cut that we need to fix, the different thinking that led to the protein and its use. If it's not me, then someone like me."

"Okay, last question: What will Salvana do if you go out on your own?"

"Izaak put me in touch with one of the Stanford Law professors. Legally, Salvana can't stop me, since my notes and computer files will show the history of the solution and that it has nothing to do with Salvana. But I can see my new boss—do you know Cheryl Aynesworth?"

"Only by reputation. And that was from the non-profit world."

"She's someone my pal Zoe would call 'a bulldog with pearls.' Charming, but tough. I can see her trying to tie me up with litigation. Or she gets her IT guys to dig deeper into the lab's database, which might prove embarrassing—or worse." Petra paused. "But I've got something in mind that should forestall that and protect the people there who helped me validate my findings."

"Care to divulge what that is?"

"I'm willing to give Cheryl a copy of all my research to date in return for Salvana agreeing to let me go out on my own—a clean break on both sides. In return they get a one-year head start on the competition before I release that data to the world."

"I haven't had a client suggest anything like this before," Keeley says. "Are you that worried about this Cheryl or are you that sure of yourself?

"A bit of each."

Keeley purses her mouth as she thinks through the offer. "If you go that route, then two things. First, Salvana has to agree to forego any legal action—get an attorney to word it just right—and allow you to hire up to three Salvana employees without penalty." Petra nods her agreement. "And second, you never tell a soul—

especially the VCs—about this agreement. VCs, like Salvana, are not in the sharing game."

Keeley nods at Petra's empty coffee cup and raises her own. "I'm getting another. You?" Petra nods.

"Here's my take," Keeley says, when she returns with the coffees. "First, I think your discovery is a big fucking deal. I like big fucking deals. So do VCs. Second, you've *really* got to want to be a CEO. And show it. Not occasionally, and not just in your initial meeting with funders. You breathe it and exhibit it in your everyday demeanor and behavior. Investors can smell ambivalence a mile away. So can employees, for that matter."

"What about my lack of business and operational experience?"

"That's par for the course with most first-time CEOs. As long as we're convinced that you're the best person for the job—and in your case, you can make a compelling case that you're the *only* person for the job—we'll provide the training, resources, contacts, advice. That's our job, to turn you into a CEO."

The two women continue sipping their coffees and spend the next hour getting acquainted. Petra pries VC and startup stories out of Keeley, and Keeley extracts info about Petra's awards and patents, as well as her climbing experiences. Finally, with the coffee long gone, Petra says, "Thanks for all the time today. You've given me a lot to think about." She starts to stand. "I'll ..."

"Sit down," Keeley says. "Don't you want to know if I'll invest in you?"

"I thought you'd want time to..."

"The day you resign from Salvana, I'll write you a check for 50K in return for 2 percent of the company. Your first job—and there won't be a second one if you fail at the first—is to turn that 50K into 250K. That will buy you and one key employee a year at a science incubator, including lab facilities. You don't get the 250K, I write the 50K—and you—off, and we part company. Got it?"

"Got it. I'll get back to you next week to let you know if I'll take you up on your kind offer."

"Trust me, there's nothing kind about it. Either that 50K is going to make me millions or it'll be a write-off. And I hate write-offs."

18

Seeing the Flop

"SO WHERE DO WE STAND?"

Petra is sitting at the table in Cheryl's office. She has spent the couple of hours before the meeting rehearsing and re-rehearsing in her mind what to say and anticipating how Cheryl might respond. She's now in full poker mode.

Her senses are on high alert. She notices that Cheryl is wearing what Petra thinks of as 'serious business' clothes—a simple but impeccably tailored grey skirt, silk blouse in a lighter grey, single strand of pearls hitting just below her collarbone, and simple pearl earrings. This is not the Cheryl she first met, either in attire or mood.

The office looks as it always does, tidy and with scant evidence of what Cheryl is working on. But a tasteful vase of fresh orchids decorates the windowsill, and a pitcher of water and two glasses sit off to the side of the table. Cheryl has a leather-bound notebook and her Mont Blanc pen already out and on the table in front of her chair.

During the week since their previous meeting, Petra has gone through the numbers repeatedly—first on her own, then with Jerry, and finally with Ed. Ultimately, though, it's not a matter of math but of trust. She doesn't trust Cheryl, and, by inference, Salvana. Or she doesn't trust Salvana, and, by inference, Cheryl.

"I could give you all the reasoning and calculations that went into my decision," Petra says, "but I think you're only interested in yes or no. And the bottom line is no. I can't sign on. Our priorities and schedules are too different."

Cheryl nods, as if this were the answer she was expecting. "I'm assuming it's a waste of my breath—and both of our time—for me to try to change your mind." She raises her tone on the last word, making it both a statement and a question.

Petra shrugs slightly, as if the decision were obvious. "I tried to make it work, but I'm betraying too many people in need with your—Salvana's—schedule. Speaking of which, I'm assuming that while I've been crunching numbers this past week, you've spent some of that time with Legal." It's half a statement, half a question.

"I met with them twice," Cheryl says. "The first, to walk them through the history and basis of your discovery including the Werner angle, the six areas of longevity you were investigating while drawing a Salvana paycheck, your mother's symptoms, and finally, the discovery of the phantom protein."

"And the second meeting? What did Legal say?" When Cheryl doesn't answer at first, Petra continues. "If I were them, I'd propose playing it—and me—two ways. The first is to dig into my work here at Salvana and go back as far as my work at MIT, looking for ways to challenge my ownership." Cheryl doesn't respond, so Petra keeps going. "When that comes up empty, you propose I work with you to modify the Salvana schedule to five to seven years, knowing that once I'm on board there can be any number of ways—product delays, more tests, legal issues—that could stretch it out to the ten years the company needs." Petra smiles sweetly. "Or do I owe both you and Salvana an apology?"

Cheryl's face slides from neutral into an admiring smile. "God, I wish you were on my team." The smile dims a bit. "So that's that, huh?"

"Almost." Petra takes a manila envelope from her briefcase and slides it across the table. Cheryl stops it with her palm but doesn't open it. "That's a summary of all of my research and the results of the most recent tests," Petra says. "Legally, we both know Salvana has no rights to this information. But the company has been generous to me, and you've been more forthcoming than you need to be. So I'm giving this to you, as well as my word that I won't share this with any of your competitors for at least a year. That gives you a head start with them, and an equal start with me."

Cheryl looks down at the envelope but still doesn't open it. "This is a generous offer, one that both of us know you don't have to make. What do you want in return?"

"Call off Legal. I'm not worried about my rights to the discovery, but I can imagine Legal tying me up with lawsuits, the result being that Salvana gets the ten-year schedule it wanted in the first place."

Cheryl looks down at the manila folder. "Done. Anything else?"

"I want to be able to hire three Salvana employees without any repercussions. On them or on me."

"Would one of those hires be Jerry?"

Petra shakes her head. "Jerry's a lab rat, and Salvana has a better lab than anything I could offer."

"Ed?"

"Ed's a manager. He needs a big operation to be at his very best. I don't know if I'll be doing any hiring from Salvana—I just want the option. So do we have a deal?"

Cheryl is about to say something more, then stops herself and extends her hand. "You have my word." She puts the envelope in her briefcase. "Personally, I wish you the best, Petra. Professionally, I hope you fail, because there will always be a spot for you on this team."

Petra isn't gone more than a minute before Cheryl jabs a number on her phone. Her assistant comes on the line. "Jenna, can you call HR and get me the number for Mike Perkins?"

19

Who's Not In?

"SO I'M A ... what do you call athletes who no longer have a team?"

"If they were cut, I call them unemployed. But I think you're talking about free agents, players who can sign with any team. Right?"

"Yeah," Petra says. She looks around The Speak Easy, which is relatively quiet at 4:45. She returned from her two o'clock meeting with Cheryl with the news for Jerry and Ed that she had resigned. The two had insisted on taking her out to celebrate then and there, but she said she had some things to do. She suggested 4:30, which worked for Jerry, Ed saying he'd be along after his four o'clock team meeting let out.

"Do you want to order or wait for Ed?" she asks.

"Let's order. Those lab team meetings can go anywhere from ten minutes—nothing to report—to two hours. What are you having? My treat, remember. We're celebrating, appearances to the contrary," Jerry says.

"Sorry. I'm just a little overwhelmed. I've never been unemployed before. What red wine goes best with Imodium?"

Jerry closes one eye and cocks his head. "Seriously? This is the mood we're going with on this momentous occasion?"

"Again, sorry. I know that going the startup route is the goal of seemingly everyone in this Valley. Everyone except this girl."

"Then why did you resign? You can stay put, retract your resignation, and we'll keep the band together. You're like Eric Clapton leaving Cream. Or Blind Faith or Derek and the Dominos, for that matter. Always leaving just when things were starting to get going."

"I thought about staying. Long and hard. I love the sense of safety and all the resources at Salvana. And I'm not kidding about the Imodium. My stomach has been doing flip-flops ever since I walked out of Cheryl's office."

"How'd she take it, by the way?"

"She took it graciously, had nice things to say, wished me luck. At the same time, I could see the wheels turning. Was I already around the bend with my decision or could she persuade me to stay? And if so, with what? Was I bluffing—and if so, what did I want, other than an accelerated schedule, which she couldn't grant. But in the end, it was an amicable parting."

At that moment, the door to the bar opens and the Wednesday crowd—Zoe, Izaak, Ed, and Alice—comes noisily in. "We met in the parking lot," Ed explains as everyone takes turns hugging and congratulating Petra, who accepts it all with a frozen smile.

"We'll get to our normal drinks in a bit," Zoe tells their server as he approaches the table. "But for now, bring us a bottle of champagne. Something in between Dom Perignon and Cold Duck."

"You excited?" Izaak asks Petra.

"Wrong question," Jerry says. "She's petrified, no pun intended." He turns to Petra. "Tell us how we can transition you from Imodium to Petra's Fabulous Adventure."

"I'm a simple girl at heart," Petra answers. "All I need is financing, breakthrough science, a place to work, a great team ..." She raises her eyebrows at him. "And a wonderful partner I can trust."

Before Jerry can answer, Alice jumps in. "I can help on that last one. Your work husband—my *actual* husband—has two sons about to enter college. I love you, Petra, but it's too risky."

Petra tries not to look directly at Jerry, but out of the corner of her eye she sees him redden. Whether it's because he's sorry to be saying *no*, or is embarrassed that Alice spoke for him, she can't tell. She's happy when the champagne arrives, ending the awkward moment.

Zoe nods to the server to leave it, then does the pouring herself. She raises her glass. "To a long and happy life, not just for us, but for the rest of the world as well."

Once the glasses are back on the table, Petra speaks up. "The next toast is mine. If this whole episode turns out to be a spectacular failure, I owe it all to the people around this table." She waits a beat for the smiles. "Now, to be what Zoe calls 'faux serious.' I know I'm not the easiest friend—or partner—at times. But I appreciate all of you more than I can express. Everyone here at this table has made me a better scientist and hopefully a better person, both of which I'm going to need in spades for this next chapter of my life. So thank you. For everything."

She starts to raise her glass, then stops. "At the risk of pissing Alice off, I need to single out my partner in crime—my work husband—for special thanks. Without him, there's no mystery protein, no breakthrough, no startup. When I put in for a patent on our discovery, Jerry's name will be on the application."

"Totally unnecessary," Jerry says. "You did all the work—I just tested it."

"With tests that were absolutely crucial to the discovery. I talked to Keeley James, who I'm hoping will be my initial funder, and she says that while it's a little unorthodox, you'll qualify for founder's stock—assuming I can secure the funding to get this whole venture off the ground. For the rest of you losers, Izaak

says there's something called 'Friends and Family' stock alloca-
tions. So I'd suggest you be nice to me for the next couple of
years."

After that the table breaks into side conversations. Ed has
some lab news for Jerry, with Alice pretending to care. Izaak and
Zoe have taken positions on either side of Petra.

"You scared, honey?" Zoe asks.

"Terrified," she says. "I don't have an entrepreneurial bone in
my body. I loved the security and independence Salvana gave me."

"Why'd you leave, then?" Zoe asks. "Was it just the ten years
or something more?"

"I'm not a spiritual person, you know that. But ..." She thinks
for a minute. "You know how people will tell you that from an early
age they knew exactly what they wanted to be? Like all those musi-
cians who saw The Beatles and decided right then and there, even
though they were ten years old, that this is what they wanted to be?
That isn't me. I was going to be a mathematician until Thea died.
But something sparked in me when we discovered the protein. I felt
like I'd found my life's calling. This protein could change everything, not just aging. I'm revisiting my MIT research into incurable
diseases and finding some interesting things. Hell, this protein may
even hold the key to what's going on with my mom."

She looks into her empty champagne glass. "I thought I
could do it at Salvana, with Jerry. But ten years ..." She shakes
her head. "I couldn't deal with that, having a country-club
schedule while people might be needlessly dying."

Two large tears roll down her cheeks. Izaak puts a hand over
hers. "Everyone at this table will be there for you, you know that.
And that was before you mentioned the Friends and Family stock."

"Izaak's right," Zoe says. "Although nothing says 'thank you'
more than stock. And remember, I should get more than anyone
else because I helped you crack the code."

20

Bottom Dealing

"I CAN GET USED TO THIS. My own private eye on call. Before you get going, can I offer you something to drink?" Cheryl nods at the dorm-size refrigerator built into one of her wall units.

"Diet Coke, please."

She fetches two and places one in front of him. "Okay. What have you got for me?"

"You want to start with Ms. Alexander or with our internal candidate?"

"With Petra, please."

It had been a month since Petra and Salvana parted company. Without incident, due to Cheryl's admonitions to Security and HR. By mutual agreement, Petra cleaned out her office over the weekend and met with HR after hours the following Monday, to finalize her separation from the company. Security had wanted to walk her out, but Cheryl had put the kibosh on that. She also vetoed Security's demand that they delete or remove all Salvana-sensitive data from Petra's workstation, which Cheryl had gifted her in recognition of the data Petra was leaving behind. "This is to be a civil parting of ways," she told the head of Security. "I want her to know that there will always be a home for her at Salvana, should things not work out." Also, she had pointed out, if Petra wanted to steal anything, she'd have done it long before announcing she was leaving the company.

"Our gal isn't encountering much success, so far, at least," Perkins starts out. "To save a lot of money on surveillance, I just put a tracker on her Subaru. Here's a list of the angels and VCs she's visited so far."

He hands Cheryl a sheet of paper that she skims. "The report is informal and incomplete. I've got connections in most of the big firms, but the meetings she's had so far have been with small fry. Maybe that's all she can get in to or maybe Keeley James is holding back on the big boys until Petra fleshes out her team and has her pitch down pat. Anyway, the feedback, little as I've been able to get, is that she's not off to a good start. She doesn't have a partner, which for most firms is now a critical factor, since Uber and WeWork have exposed the dangers of a CEO without strong lieutenants. Also, she comes across as a Chief Scientist, not a CEO. And these smaller firms don't have an EIR ..." He sees Cheryl's confusion. "Entrepreneur in Residence. They don't have anyone they could put over Petra, letting her stay in the lab. So it's either a hard *no* or 'come back when you've got more to show us.'"

"I did some digging into Keeley James, since you mentioned her in our last meeting," Cheryl says. "If she's coaching Petra, I'd expect better initial results than this." She nods at the piece of paper. "I tend to agree with you, that she's putting Petra through boot camp, letting her learn from her failures. Which is smart, since I don't think Petra's acquainted with failing."

. . .

It had been a busy month. Once Petra was out the door, Cheryl turned her attention to Project L, Salvana's clever term for its own longevity project. First step was finding and hiring the project leader, who needed to be a major player in the field to attract the necessary talent and represent the initiative, if successful, to the public.

After a month of considering internal candidates to head up Project L, her assessment of the top scientists at Salvana was that none of them was up to the task, an opinion that Ed seconded. It wasn't a reflection of their talents as much as their areas of expertise. None of them was even remotely connected with longevity.

So Cheryl engaged a headhunting firm to lead the search, a process that was just getting under way. While the search went on, she and Ed put together a preliminary budget, including staffing, facilities, and equipment, as well as a rough schedule. Impressed with Ed's work, Cheryl asked him if he wanted to join the project, building out and running the lab, the right hand to the major player they still needed to find. But Ed passed, saying he was happy where he was. She wondered if that were true, or if he were passing out of loyalty to Petra.

• • •

"Shall we turn to the internal candidate?" Perkins asks. Cheryl nods. She's been looking forward to seeing the possibilities for filling this very special, and very confidential, role. Perkins spins his laptop so she can see the screen. A clean-cut, smiling face greets her. The smile is a little forced, as is the case with most security ID cards. His hair is stylishly messy, causing Cheryl to wonder how much time and effort he spends to get that careless look. His cheek bones are pronounced, even sharp. She looks at the detective. "Marathoner?"

"Triathlete."

"Type A or A+?"

It's his turn to smile. "A. Just local races so far. If he competes in the Hawaii one, I'll change him to an A+." He nods at the screen. "I was going to bring you four or five to look at, but the more I qualified this guy, the more he seemed to be what you're looking for."

"Let's hear about him, then."

"Jake Montgomery. Twenty-nine. Local boy. BS in biology and an MBA from Santa Clara University. He's what we need: a semi-nerd who can hold his own with other science nerds but who also has the social skills to work with Sales and Marketing."

"You're right, he sounds good. What's his history, here and before joining Salvana?"

"I can tell you that Sales here at Salvana thinks the sun shines out this guy's ass. They fight over who gets him for sales calls."

"What's so special about him?"

"He knows science and he's good with people. They created a new position for him, one that requires two business cards. The first is Medical Science Liaison, meaning he goes out on sales calls to handle scientific questions and objections. The other is Product Marketing, meaning he gives his field feedback to product management and helps them design and launch products."

"He sounds great. But it sounds like he's doing great where he is. Why would he be interested in this position?"

"Because our boy wants to be a CEO someday. Since he's already established his technical and scientific chops, he wants to build out his business side."

"What was he doing before he joined Salvana?" Cheryl asks. "Any skeletons I need to be aware of?"

Perkins touches his keyboard and a logo appears. "Once he graduated from Santa Clara with his BS, he was recruited by a number of companies. He joined a biotech startup that looked promising but that went tits up." Perkins looks at Cheryl to see if that last turn of phrase crossed a line, but she shrugs and motions for him to continue. "He's got startup experience as well. I think he's our guy."

"Sounds like it. I'll have my EA schedule something. Thanks, Mike."

He stays seated. "Assuming we go with Jake, do you want to manage him or do you want me to?"

She frowns slightly. "I was planning to. Why do you ask?"

"It's just that I've got a bit more experience than you in this field, where the legal lines are and how to get around them. Or smudge them."

21

Stepping Up

"YOU KNOW I HAVEN'T PLAYED competitively in over a decade, right?" the auburn-haired woman says, looking down as the foam from the incoming wave laps against her bare foot.

"I know, Annie," says Petra. "But you've forgotten more poker than I'll ever know. And I've got no idea how to get into a cash game. Not the kind I'm looking for."

"I might be able to help you there. I can coach you a little, but only if I know the players. I looked you up online. Your winning percentage is impressive. And you've done well in the few tourneys you've entered."

"Tournaments won't get me there. The money's good, but they take too long and are too risky. My only path to getting the funding I need is with a cash game. A high-end one."

"What kind of game are you looking for?"

"Ideally? A game full of fish—guys with more money than sense, who bet as much with their little heads as their big ones."

Annie laughs. "You're not asking for much, are you? Hell, if I knew of a game like that, I'd be in it, not getting you an invite."

Petra is walking on the beach in Manhattan Beach, a boutique town near the Los Angeles International Airport, with Annie Duke, the unofficial Queen of Poker and an acquaintance from Petra's MIT card-counting days. During the hour-and-a-half flight to LAX from the San Jose airport, away from both work and home routines, Petra had time to really think about who she was going to meet, and why. And she had a startling realization. She was scared, really scared, that she was staring at failure for the first time.

The feeling was so foreign, she wasn't sure what to do with it. In every other challenge she'd faced in her life—and she'd had plenty—she could follow some familiar thread that would lead to a solution. Now, she felt like she was treading water in a huge, unfamiliar, and potentially hostile ocean, with nothing and no one to grab hold of.

Her meetings with Keeley's list of VCs had been disasters. Even though Petra's ask was minor and attractive—two hundred thousand in return for 6 percent of the company—the response had been consistent and negative. In feedback sessions, each of the VCs had asked Keeley, where was her team? Where was the market research? How ready was she to run her company? And for that matter, how eager was she to be a CEO?

With the VC route showing little promise, Petra decided her best—or last—option to secure the needed $250K to move forward with Keeley was poker. So she'd contacted Annie.

No stranger to achieving in a male-dominated profession, Annie invited Petra to visit her in Manhattan Beach so they could talk in person. Though she retired professionally in 2012, Annie's career winnings of four-plus million dollars still rank her fourth on the all-time women's list. She is also one of the few women to win a bracelet at the World Series of Poker.

Annie never fit the profile of a professional poker player. A National Science Fellow and a PhD candidate in cognitive psychology and decision science, she grew up playing cards with her brother, a top poker pro. On his advice, and with some coaching, she entered the world of professional poker. Applying her psychology skills to both read her opponents and calculate her likelihood of success, she moved up the ladder quickly, from local games, to smaller tournaments, to Vegas cash games. And ultimately to the World Series of Poker. Her breakout year was 2004, when she won a World Series bracelet, took home six hundred and fifty thousand in tournament winnings, and made the final table in 13 events, a remarkable run.

She walked away from poker in 2012 and became a bestselling author and lecturer. Combining her cognitive psychology and poker background, she wrote books about decision-making in life and business that gained her a large and appreciative audience. She was about to embark on a promotional tour for her new book when Petra contacted her.

Now in her mid-fifties and still very attractive, Annie looks ten years younger. Lively and healthy, she's a contrast to both her former self and the current poker crowd, most of whom spend the bulk of their lives indoors under a constant bath of fluorescent light.

As they stroll in the damp sand toward the Redondo Beach pier, Annie listens as Petra recounts her lack of success with a variety of audiences: individual investors, called angels; seed money firms; and a few VC firms. Since her retirement from poker, Annie has turned her decision-making and poker skills into a lucrative career as a consultant, with some of her clients coming from the VC community.

"I know you won't raise the issue, so I will. Do you think sexism has anything to do with the response you're getting? I know the Valley a bit, and it's about as welcoming to women as poker has been."

"Thanks for the excuse," Petra says, "but I think I've earned the lack of enthusiasm all on my own." She looks out at the horizon. "I can change my pitch a bit—and Keeley is helping me with that—but the lack of a partner, and the fact that the Valley is more tech-oriented than scientific in nature, means I'm running out of time. And options. Hence my call to you."

They reach the pier and turn around for the two-mile return trip. The wind has picked up slightly, causing the waves to stipple and lose their shape, but there's still a crowd of surfers around the pier.

"I think I know a game I can get you into," Annie says. "If there's still a seat left, it's what you're looking for. High buy-in, probably 50K. No pros in the mix. These guys are a combination of the Hollywood crowd and some money guys from up north. I love playing with actors because they think they can act their way into winning. VCs, on the other hand, are great to play with because they're used to being the smartest guys in the room, even when they're not." She shields her eyes against the afternoon sun. "Yeah, this could be your game."

"If I get in, who am I? And how should I play things?" Petra asks.

"You're yourself. They can research you the same way I did, though I can see some of them being too lazy—or too egotistic—to do so. They'll see your tournament results and think you're one of those players who thinks they're ready to move up to the big leagues—the high-end cash games. They'll think they can bully you. You should let them, at least for the first two hours. Look like you're in over your head. Maybe run a bluff, but make it slightly obvious so that you're called. When it fails, they'll look to see if you go on tilt. You don't, but you're now once-burnt, twice-shy, and start playing conservatively after that. Until you don't. And you're the only one who can determine when that is."

"Got it. What else?"

"The next part is true, so it won't require much acting on your part. You're the only one in the game who can't afford to lose. Make sure they can smell your desperation. They'll try to take advantage of it, which will leave them exposed."

"This is great stuff, Annie. Anything else before we hit the parking lot?"

"Only the obvious thing. You're the only woman at the table, and an attractive one at that. These guys aren't used to playing with women. So, as we discussed, you start out slow and cautious, you get caught on your bluff, and you're a little emotional, though you're trying to keep it in. You grow more conservative, almost timid. Keep an eye on the different ways these guys respond to you and use it in the last hour."

"How do you do in cash games, if you don't mind my asking?"

"I've won more than I ever did in tournaments, and you know that number. It's easier in cash games to use my academic training. I've used part of that training to develop a series of stereotypes for the male players I encounter. Not everyone fits them, but enough do to make me—and hopefully you—a lot of money."

"What kind of stereotypes are we talking about? Risk-takers like Sammy Farah, grinders like Mizrachi?"

"Those are more poker stereotypes. I read the man first, then see what parts of his personality transfer to his game, and which he keeps in check. I know that, between my looks and fame, I'm still an attractive commodity. So the first stereotype is the guy who wants to sleep with you. With this guy, you don't flirt with him—at least not obviously—but be just a little more impressed with his play than it merits. Let him think you're out of your league."

"And how do I play that? Specifically."

"If you're up against him and it's a big hand, talk it through out loud." Annie adopts a girlish tone, with just the right amount of cute. "'You're representing trips, but if you had them, why did you ...'"

She sees Petra smile. "This guy is dying to show you his cards, especially when he's bluffed you. Give him a little of your money early, then go after him at the end. He'll have that early memory of you, where you seemed to be out of your league, and will think any time you beat him is an aberration."

"Okay. I'll work on my girlie voice."

Annie nods. "The second guy is the misogynist. He's not crazy about having a woman in the game but can't say anything in this day and age. He won't give you credit for any poker intellect. If you bluff him, don't show the bluff at the end. Don't humiliate him—you want him around at the end, along with Mr. Sleep-With-Me.

"The third guy will resent you, not because you're a woman but because you're new to the game, which he thinks of as *his* game. Take this guy on only when you've got the nuts."

"Any other types to watch for?"

"Yeah, the quiet guy who plays fewer hands than the others. Stay the hell away from him. He's probably there for the same reason you are, to take their money."

Back at the parking lot at the Manhattan Beach pier, Annie retrieves her phone from her car and makes a call. She says a few words, then listens. She raises her eyebrows at Petra and nods. After hanging up, she says, "You're in. Two weeks from tomorrow night. Someone will text you the details."

22

A Wild Card

HE HAS NO IDEA what's about to hit him. Cheryl is a big football fan. Her image of him for this meeting is of a wide receiver coming across the middle, eyes fixed on the oncoming pass, fingertips twitching and reaching, unaware that the oncoming safety—her, in this scenario— is about to separate him from both the ball and his senses.

It's the first meeting of the day, and the air in the room is dry, stiff, and stale. The conference room itself is a study in bland, each wall a slightly different hue of beige, as if this were the room the painters used to finish off their leftover paint from other, more important offices. This lack of attention is further evidence that no department, including her own, owns the room. An orphan, it's there for the taking. She uses it for all her initial meetings, with subsequent meetings taking place back in her office.

She sees him arrive through the half-open blinds. In deference to Salvana's corporate culture, which is more conservative than its high-tech neighbors, he's wearing a navy blazer and white shirt. She imagines him agonizing that morning over whether to wear a tie or not. He's opted not to.

Cheryl knows she's an object of speculation around the company. It's not just the precipitous and rather public firing of her predecessor that has sparked the interest, it's that she seems an odd fit for a senior management position at Salvana. Although the company is based in Silicon Valley, it has East

Coast roots, which means that the executives still wear suits and have a strict, hierarchical process for making decisions. But Cheryl's style—both in dress and management—is either at odds with, or is a welcome change from, 'the Salvana Way.'

She weighed early on whether to maintain the mystery around her, even adopt a Dragon Lady persona that keeps people on edge. Instead, she's made it clear that she's open to suggestions from anyone, regardless of status or department. In terms of style, she opts for outfits that her two daughters lay out for her the night before. If she's honest, they often do a better job than if she did it herself, joining colors in unexpected, playful ways she wouldn't have thought would work, but do.

Today, though, she dressed herself. Because today's meeting calls for "the shark suit." A belted blazer over a silk blouse and pencil skirt, it takes its name from its varying hues of grey, and because she always gets really serious when she puts it on. Those are the days the girls know to stay quiet on the ride to school.

As he raises his hand to knock on the door, she catches his eye through the office's internal window and waves him in with a hand her daughters manicured and tended the night before. Normally the nail color, like Cheryl's outfits, tends toward playful. Today's nails are blood red.

She watches him go through his last-minute mental checklist. A quick run of his hand through his short, slightly spiked hair—no gel, thank God—while he assembles just the right kind of smile. In the extra beat before he opens the door, she envisions him checking his fly with his free hand.

She does her own last-minute audit, starting with her eyes. She's been told many times that her eyes, in their neutral state, are serious, almost fierce. And if she concentrates and doesn't remember to relax her facial muscles, the resulting intensity can be intimidating, which is not how she wants to start this meeting.

His entry freshens the room's air slightly, though it also brings a hint of cologne. Nothing overpowering, but she's not a fan of men who wear cologne. She stands and extends her hand. It's a grip and shake she's worked on over the years, guided by her father's statement that he places a lot of value on a man's handshake. Hers is firm but not overpowering, nothing that would cause a man to shake his hand and offer some lame joke. But she'll be damned if she's going to be one of those women who offers a limp three fingers, as if she's some delicate thing.

"Jake Montgomery," he says, as she motions for him to sit down. She doesn't offer her name—that would come across as false modesty. Everyone knows who she is by now. She watches to see if he crosses his legs, displaying an ease he hasn't yet earned. But he keeps both feet firmly planted on the floor and looks directly, expectantly, at her. He's got a confident face— tanned, high-boned, the cheeks slightly hollow, bordering on anorexic. She would have guessed he was a marathoner or triathlete even if the HR file hadn't mentioned it.

She taps her finger on the file. "You've got an impressive background, Jake. Tough to tell if I'm talking to a scientist or a business associate." She speaks in a clipped, almost terse style, with little waste.

"I'm a scientist first and foremost, Ms. Aynesworth, but ..."

"Cheryl."

"I'm a scientist first, Cheryl, but I think it's helpful to learn the business side of my field as well."

"Because ...?"

"Because I don't want to spend my life creating products that never go beyond the lab. I want any product I develop to be something the market needs, or at least wants. Which is why I got my MBA and why I'm interested in working in Biz Dev."

She nods briskly, letting him know he's off to a good start. "Don't get too excited, Jake," she says, giving him a slight, but disarming, smile. "Biz Dev is one of those jobs—like being a restaurant critic or archaeologist—that's attractive from the outside, but insiders know better. And it's risky as hell, as my predecessor found out."

She leans forward and lowers her voice, as if she's bringing him into her confidence. "Biz Dev is like taking money from the mob. You're placing million-dollar—sometimes billion-dollar—bets with someone else's money. Bet wrong and you get kneecapped. Or you wind up working the drive-through window at McDonald's, asking if they want fries with that order." She sits back, the confidentiality at an end. "Still interested?"

"I am, but thanks for the caution."

She waits to see if he wants to take this opportunity to toot his own horn about his qualifications. But he sits there in a comfortable silence—it's her meeting, after all. The silence is a point in his favor. But as he sits back, he now crosses his legs. Cheryl looks down to hide her smile.

"I imagine you're wondering what this meeting is all about," she says.

"Your assistant just said you wanted to discuss a possible opening in your department."

"Correct. It's nothing that we're going to post, either in-house or in a search. Our HR consultant has examined a number of candidates, and you're his first choice."

"Can you tell me more about the position?"

"I can, but you're probably going to have questions that I can't answer. So I'm going to bring in the HR guy I just mentioned."

She gets up and goes to the door. Mike Perkins, who has been sitting in a chair in her EA's cube, stands and follows her back into the room. After introductions, he brings out a file.

"If I'm in this meeting," he begins, "it means that Cheryl agrees with my assessment of you and that you've expressed interest in the position. Correct?"

Both Cheryl and Jake nod. "Then at this point I have to inform you that Salvana is terminating your employment. Effective immediately."

Cheryl's momentarily as stunned by Perkins' bluntness as Jake, whose mouth opens and stays that way as he turns to Cheryl. She watches his reaction progress through the HR version of Kubler-Ross's stages of grief: Shock. Confusion. Outrage. She jumps in before he gets to Anger.

"Listen to the entire thing before you respond," she advises.

"And now that you're unemployed," Perkins continues, "I'd like to offer you a job. At twice your current salary and with a two-year commit. And a possible future in Biz Dev."

Cheryl sees Jake cycle back from Outrage, stalling at Confusion.

"I don't understand," he says. "But I guess that's obvious." An edge enters his tone. "And perhaps intended."

She's glad to see a bit of spine, but Perkins doesn't seem impressed. "Or there's Option B. You're still employed and this meeting is over. You can go back to your office, go about your day, and this conversation never took place."

Perkins motions obliquely towards the door, but Jake stays put. Cheryl notices that he's uncrossed his legs. "Can I hear more about this offer before I decide?" he says, though his voice is a little thinner than before.

"Certainly. But first, how would you describe Salvana's product line?"

Jake is long in answering, to the point that she's wondering if he's pouting or considering the best way to end the meeting without endangering his career. She waits.

"I'd say our strength is in palliatives, with curatives a distant second," Jake finally says.

Perkins turns to Cheryl. "Same question."

"I agree with Jake. We exist to make the last years of a person's life as pain-free and productive as possible. And when they do die, we use the knowledge gained to improve the life—and death—of the next person."

Perkins motions for Jake to close the blinds. He fumbles at first with the dangling plastic pendant, raising the slats. Then he grabs the other pendant and twists, bringing the slats flat. The room seems to shrink as it darkens, bringing both an intimacy and sense of confinement.

"Here's the problem, Jake," Perkins says, his voice suddenly warm. "Can I call you Jake?" He doesn't wait for an answer. "The future of our industry, according to the board, is in longevity. Ms. Aynesworth's job," he nods towards Cheryl, "is to make Salvana a major player in the longevity market. And for that she's going to need help."

Perkins pauses, leaving room for a response. Or question. But Jake seems to have decided that silence will serve him better than a potentially wrong response.

"How do you think Salvana is positioned for this coming market?" Perkins asks.

"Not very well. I've never even heard the word 'longevity' mentioned in my time here," Jake says.

"On a scale of one to ten, I'd put us at a two," Cheryl says. "Over 80 percent of our revenue comes from palliatives, from end-of-life treatments, medications, and accessories."

She slides her sleeves up slightly and rests her bare arms on the table. "The company hired me to get it off its ass and into the game. To evaluate all the longevity solutions out there and pick the one we should either acquire or partner with. And then work with product management to create a plan, complete with schedule and budget, to transition the company to a leadership position in this new market. It's a big job and I'm in the process of building my team. My biggest need, at this point, is to get eyes and ears into that market and start tracking our future competition."

"By eyes and ears, you mean ..."

"A spy," Perkins interjects, his voice again devoid of any warmth.

There. The meeting is at its critical point. By mutual agreement, it's Perkins' meeting from here on. Cheryl keeps her eye on Jake and likes what she sees. After the initial shock of his 'firing,' he now seems to be thinking through his situation, trying to sort out the questions and angles.

"I'm interested, but aren't we talking about competitive analysis, which is standard practice at most companies? I don't see why I can't do that as a Salvana employee."

"Because this job has to be ...," Perkins seems to be genuinely looking for the word, not pausing for drama, "fluid. There are things this job entails that can't be associated with Salvana. That's Legal's call and it's non-negotiable."

"How would it work?"

"If you accept the position, you'll stay at Salvana for the next month, but on special assignment. During that month you'll focus on two things. The first is to start complaining, initially just in conversation, then in written form, about the company's testing procedures, both on animals and humans. The second is to become familiar with Salvana's work in longevity—and there has been some—to date, as well as the personnel involved in it."

"Competitive analysis on people in my own company?"

"You'll see why in a minute," Perkins continues. "After a month, we've had enough of your complaints about us putting 'profits before people.' Remember those three words. Make them your mantra. You repeat them whenever anyone asks why we fired you. They should make you a hero and martyr in the communities we're trying to reach."

"And what communities are we talking about?"

"Anyone involved in extending human life significantly. Start with the startups in this area and extend out from there. Lie low for a week or two, licking your wounds. I'll leave it to you how you insinuate yourself into these groups, whether it's meetups, or online, or over drinks. Learn what you can, interview where appropriate, then report back to Ms. Aynesworth and myself regularly. My guess is that you'll be kissing a lot of frogs. But eventually you'll get a handle on who we should be keeping an eye on, whether it's to compete with or acquire."

"At which point my assignment is over?"

Perkins inclines his head in Cheryl's direction. She picks up her end of the conversation.

"At which point you'd have a variety of options. Speaking for Salvana, you would have your choice of a senior-level job in either the Longevity division or in Biz Dev. I'd also imagine you could join any of the startups you're researching."

"And what part of what you just said can I have in writing?"

Perkins puts on a wry smile and turns to Cheryl, making one of those 'these kids' gestures. He turns back to Jake. "You wouldn't be here if you weren't bright, Jake, so I'll assume you know the answer to your rhetorical question. The answer is none. No chance. This is a verbal agreement and you'll be paid by a shell company, nothing that can be traced back to Salvana. Still interested?"

"I am," Jake says, then turns to Cheryl. "What happens if you get fired?"

Perkins jumps back in. "Then you're screwed. Because the only three people who know about this offer are here. Right here."

Jake is quiet for over a minute. Then he again gives Perkins the shoulder. "This wasn't the meeting I was expecting, Cheryl. I'd like to think it over, if that's okay. But my first impression is that I'm interested. Very."

She also doesn't acknowledge Perkins. "Take your time. You know where to find me."

23

Call or Fold

"I LOVE THIS PLACE," Alice says. "Especially when someone else is buying." She swings her hand between Jerry and Petra. "I'll let you two fight it out for the check."

The three are sitting at a corner table at The Left Bank, a French brasserie in Menlo Park, a few miles from Petra's apartment. Jerry had called Petra that morning and proposed that the three of them have dinner, that he and Alice had something they wanted to discuss with her.

"This is the only place where I order Pernod," Alice says. "It's like someone melted down my black licorice from when I was a kid and turned it into a grown-up drink." She looks at Jerry, who has opted for a diet Coke with lemon, and Petra, with her glass of Grenache. "Peasants," she says.

After a few minutes of catch-up, Alice takes control of the conversation. "The reason we wanted to get together with you is that Jerry's been bugging me about joining your startup. He says it's the challenge of a lifetime for a science nerd like him and could possibly put us on Easy Street. I've gently reminded him of our financial situation, not just now, but what's ahead, college-wise, but he's determined. I told him I need to hear more, that this is one of the biggest decisions we're going to make as a couple."

Petra frowns as she looks at Jerry, then back to Alice. She would love to have Jerry as a partner, but this is exactly the reason why she doesn't want to run a company, to have someone—in this case a number of someones, since she knows Jerry's sons—she feels responsible for. But she's determined, with Keeley's help, to present an honest picture of the market and her company, then let them decide. It's all she can do.

"Here's the deal, Petra. Jerry trusts you. And I trust Jerry. But one of us has to have one or both feet in reality. Before I sign up for the startup life, I want to know what's ahead. I've asked Jerry to net out the scientific challenges ahead in a language that I can understand, with you chiming in, where appropriate. And I'd like you to acquaint me with the financial challenges and timing, and how you're addressing them. Are we good?"

Petra nods.

Alice then turns to Jerry: "Anything to add, honey bunch?"

Jerry looks over at Petra. It's a different Jerry than she's used to being around. A little less sure of himself and definitely deferring to Alice. "I've told Alice a bit more about the mystery protein. Do you have a name for it yet?"

Petra smiles. "BFD150. Keeley named it. I thought it was too casual and full of itself, but Keeley said it shows confidence and is memorable. The BFD speaks for itself and 150 is the longevity goal. And we'll keep that name for whatever product we eventually develop based on the mystery protein. Unless Marketing, when we hire someone, comes up with something better."

He chuckles. "Okay, BFD150 it is." He turns to Alice. "You know how we discovered it, so I'll go from there. We see it unfolding in five steps. Step 1," Jerry says, "is to fully characterize the protein, including its DNA sequence and 3D structure. We need to know exactly what we're dealing with here. This first step will take a few weeks to a couple of months at most," Jerry continues, with Petra nodding.

"Got it," Alice says. "Keep the rest of the steps at that level."

"Step 2 is to create a way to detect the protein in future tests.

The best way to do that is to develop an antibody." He cocks an eye. "You know what an antibody is?"

"You'd think after 30 years with you I would, but it's just one of those words you hear and think you know what it is, but you really don't."

"Think of an antibody as a security guard. It's a protein the immune system develops to recognize and neutralize harmful substances. Each antibody has specific regions that bind only to a particular protein, kind of like how a key fits only a particular lock. We create an antibody to BFD150, then tag that antibody with something like a fluorescent substance. Any time that fluorescence shows up in future tests, we know that BFD150 is present."

"Schedule?"

"A few weeks," Petra says.

Jerry continues. "Step 3 is testing to confirm that the protein has an effect on aging at the cellular level." He looks at Petra. "Are you settled on using fibroblast cell senescence assays to do that?" When she nods, he returns to Alice. "Do you want one of us to explain what that is and how it works, or is that too detailed?"

"Too detailed. I just need enough to get a sense of what you're doing and how long it'll take."

Jerry nods. "At this stage, we'll be finding out what happens when you remove the protein entirely. What happens when you add a bunch more? What does the protein interact with when aging symptoms increase or decrease?"

"There are basically two types of testing," Petra says. "'In vitro' is all about controlled lab experiments. Think petri dishes and cell cultures. Once we have proof of concept that our protein affects aging symptoms at the cellular level, we can move to step 4." She motions to Jerry to continue.

"After validating all the workings of BFD150 at the cellular level, we'll continue our in vitro tests, using genetic techniques to manipulate—or alter—DNA so that the cells make less of the mystery protein, or make a version that doesn't accumulate in the cells. At that point, we take some solutions that work at the cellular level and move from in vitro to in vivo testing, which is on living organisms."

"Not to sound like a broken record," Alice says, "but how long do you project that taking?"

"To do in vivo experiments related to aging," Jerry says, "you want to start with organisms that have very short lifespans, so you can get results relatively quickly and do additional tests. We'll start with nematode worms, with a lifespan of two to three weeks. Then we'll move on to fruit flies, with a lifespan of five to seven weeks. So we're talking a year or so at least, up to this point."

"Once you've completed those tests, you'll have a longevity product? Something you can sell?"

"No," Petra says, "but we'll have everything we need to go to Step 5, which is designing one or more formulations and testing them higher and higher up the animal kingdom, starting with mice, and eventually doing human clinical trials."

"Are you talking about things like dog and monkey experiments? And don't those animal tests and clinical trials take a long time?" Alice says.

"That's where the other half of Petra's background comes in," says Jerry. "Her math skills. Once artificial intelligence—AI—came on the scene, Petra was one of its early practitioners, applying it to her research. The initial AI models she built were around discovery, which led to us finding our protein. Her latest uses of AI focus on creating simulations that will replace a number of the tests, speeding the process considerably and letting us skip ahead faster. Good news for the animals, better news for us."

Alice nods. "Okay, I almost followed most of that." She turns to Petra. "Now to something I can understand. Money."

"Right now, I'm wearing two hats," Petra says. "Chief Scientist—moving through the steps Jerry just outlined—and CEO, raising money. It's all about money at this stage. I need to raise $250,000 just to get in the game. That will get me lab space in an incubator—a shared workspace for startups—and allow me to hire a Chief Scientist."

Alice and Jerry glance at each other.

"I'm guessing that's where you see Jerry fitting into all this?" asks Alice.

"That would be my ideal," Petra answers. "To be honest, I can't imagine doing all this without Jerry." She pauses. "But I also realize this is a huge decision for you and your family."

Petra stops talking and holds her breath. Her poker senses tell her that Alice and Jerry are moving toward a decision. After a long pause, Alice speaks.

"Obviously, Jerry and I have discussed this possibility. He really, really wants to join you, Petra. I'm the one who's been pushing back, for all the reasons I mentioned earlier." She pauses again, looking at Jerry, who flashes a grin. "Hearing you lay all this out, I think I'm as comfortable as I'm ever going to be about life with a startup Chief Scientist."

Petra practically beams. "Well, this calls for a celebration. Or at least a toast."

"To BFD150 and bringing it to the world," says Jerry, as they clink their glasses.

"And to becoming solvent as soon as humanly possible," adds Alice. "Which makes me wonder, long-term, is your goal to go public or be acquired?"

"Keeley, my initial investor and advisor, says you always posture that you want to go public, but you plan for acquisition. It's quicker, cleaner, and usually more lucrative."

"Let's talk finances, then. What kind of package are we talking about if Jerry joins?"

"In terms of salary, nothing until we get the real funding. The 250K is for workspace and our initial hires. If I get funding, and Keeley's coaching me to shoot for ten million, both Jerry and I would take 200K in salary."

"Equity?"

"The standard distribution is 40 percent to the founders, 40 to the investors, and 20 for employees. I'd like to see it a little fairer—a third to the founders, a third to the investors, a third to the employees. On the founder stock, Jerry and I would split that equally."

"That's too generous," Jerry says, looking at Alice to see if she's going to jump in. But she just nods. "You discovered the protein ..."

"*We* discovered it. Together. And you'll be doing the heavy lifting going forward, if you join. So fifty-fifty. No discussion."

Jerry starts to speak, but Alice puts a hand over his mouth. "Quiet, honey." She turns back to Petra. "Actually, I agree with Jerry, but it's your company, your call."

Petra nods to Jerry as Alice removes her hand. "If you join the company—or if you can't and you're advising me in return for stock—who would you recommend the first hires be?"

Jerry thinks for a long moment. The two women, used to his long pauses, wait patiently. Finally, he says, "I'd hire Bao and Josef, no question. They're not just whip smart, they're young and can afford to take the risk. Yeah, Bao and Josef."

"And the third slot?"

"I'd leave it open, at least for now. You're going to need someone with rockstar CRISPR skills. Not immediately, but hopefully sooner than later. Bao and Josef can be up and running from Day One, and I'll put out feelers for a CRISPR person."

24

A Fresh Deck

JAKE OPENS THE DOOR to The Ascent and eases in. He looks around awkwardly—part natural, part an act—to get his bearings. It's nine in the morning and the gym has just opened. His is only the third car in the parking lot.

He sees Spyder, who took his membership fee and walked him around the gym earlier that week, hunched over his desk, not looking up at the opening door. The rest of the gym looks empty, though he knows, from Cheryl's detective, that Petra—whose car he recognizes from Perkins' description—is somewhere inside.

Clad in loose-fitting drawstring shorts and a T-shirt, he sits on the bench and puts on his climbing shoes—which he will bill Cheryl for—and walks over to the bouldering cave. Petra is there, clinging to the ceiling with both feet and one hand. With her other hand, she's reaching into a bag dangling from a carabiner fixed to her climbing belt. She pulls her hand out, fingertips white with chalk, and gathers herself, coiling her body for a long moment, the muscles on her legs becoming more defined, then she pushes off with her legs.

Reaching with her chalky hand, she targets a hold that seems beyond reach. But with a final lunge she grasps it, her fingertips pinking with pressure. As she wedges her hand in for a firmer grip, her fingertips slip. She holds her position for a suspended moment, then her hand releases, and she falls. She turns her body slightly in mid-air so that she lands not on her back but on her side, slapping the mat in a move that Spyder showed Jake in his intro session, one intended to absorb the shock.

Lying on the mat, Petra sees Jake and nods a greeting, then turns her gaze back to the ceiling. After a brief rest she chalks up her other hand, walks over to the side wall, and scampers up the eight feet in seconds. It seems to Jake as if the rocks fastened to the wall have springs in them, each one launching Petra to the next until she's back on the ceiling attempting the same move as when Jake walked in.

Jake moves to the wall Petra just accelerated up and tries to repeat her route, though more slowly and cautiously. Suddenly he's on the mat, looking up in surprise and frustration. He repeats the moves, with the same result. But each attempt sees slight progress, until he can touch the ceiling. He knows better than to try to mimic Petra's current activities, and so drops back to the mat and ponders his next move.

Moving around the room, he tries different routes, increasing the distances between holds or the difficulty of a certain move. After 20 minutes, in a full sweat and with quivering arm and thigh muscles, he calls it a session. He stays within the room, sitting on the mat, back to the wall, sipping water, and watches Petra. Ten minutes later, soaking wet, she drops to the mat and sits there for a moment, gathering herself.

"Sorry to interrupt," Jake says. "It's Petra, isn't it?" She looks at him suspiciously but nods slightly. "I'm new to climbing, and when I told Spyder I wanted to come in first thing in the mornings, the goal being to make a fool of myself with the least number of witnesses, he told me you're usually here in case I had questions and he's not around." Petra doesn't respond but also doesn't make to leave, so he plunges on. "Is bouldering the best way to learn?" Jake says. He inclines his head toward the entry to the cave. "Or should I be out there on the wall?"

"I'd start in here. You can do it on your own, without needing a partner. Like you said, you can make your mistakes in here." She pats the mat. "You don't fall far, and these mats are forgiving. You'll develop more strength and confidence in your holds in here, on your own." She repeats his nod toward the rest of the gym. "The wall's great for technique, but in here you can build your strength and learn holds a lot quicker."

She catches herself. "I should have asked you first: What are your climbing goals? Do you want to be primarily an inside or outside climber?"

"I'm not quite sure what you mean," Jake says. He motions with his hand, taking in the entire club. "I thought all of this was a practice area to get ready for outside."

"That used to be the case. But now that climbing's an Olympic sport, you can be a world-class climber and never leave the gym. Come here in the afternoon or evening, you'll see climbers whose only goal is getting to the top in the fastest time."

"Spyder says you hold the record for time to the top."

"That was one time, and just to settle a bet. I prefer the outdoors." She nods around at the gym. "Outside or inside, though, this is the place to start. And to keep coming back to, so your current skills stay sharp, and you learn new ones."

"Thanks. This is helpful. I'm Jake Montgomery, by the way." He doesn't stand or reach across to shake hands.

"Petra Alexander."

"I know."

"Then you should also know that Spyder exaggerates my climbing ability."

"It's not that," Jake says. "I used to work at Salvana, where you're a bit of a mystery woman."

"Used to?" She says. "Where are you now?"

"It's a long story. Maybe another time." He rises. "Thanks for the information."

Petra watches as he heads for the front door.

25

A Three Bet

"WHO'S READY TO BE HUMILIATED TONIGHT?" Gordon—
"call me Gordy"—Anders asks the table. He nods at Petra. "For
the new player tonight, let me make my standard offer. If you
give me half your stack right now, I'll let you keep the other
half." He smiles, his small teeth at odds with his large drinker's
nose.

Petra politely smiles, then looks away and surveys her surroundings. The suite is in a tasteful Westwood hotel near the
UCLA campus. It's sparsely but elegantly furnished, some of
the furniture moved to accommodate the poker table. A wet bar
sits in a far corner, a Scandinavian-looking couch next to it.
Floor lamps rather than overhead lighting illuminate the space.
There's a friendly, welcoming vibe in the room, one that Petra,
based on what she's observing and what Annie has told her,
knows won't last more than a half hour.

Petra goes through Annie's last-minute counsel one more
time. Earlier that afternoon, Annie called her with a rundown of
the participants. She started with Gordy. "Don't let the pinkie
ring and chains fool you. That's him being a cartoon of a
Hollywood mogul. If he didn't already have chest hair, he'd have
some surgically implanted so he could nest his gold chains in it.
But he's a walking abacus, can carry the line items of a film's
budget in his head. So be careful.

"Then there's Billy Crenshaw, the actor. He's the one who'll want to sleep with you. Or be mystified that you don't want to sleep with him. But, like Gordy, he's no mark. He'll play the vacant pretty-boy routine while he's trying to get a read on you. He drinks, so wait until the liquor kicks in to challenge him.

"The third guy, Eric Tippett, is an entertainment lawyer. He plays tight to begin and loosens up as things go along. The last two players are money boys from up north. I've never played either one. I've heard a little about the young one, Zac. Loose player, which figures. He's a Bettencourt, which means he was born on third base and thinks he's hit a triple."

"How about this Jason Fredericks?" Petra asks.

"I've got nothing but what you've already found from Wikipedia and Google. I've played with a number of VCs in the past. Most of them need to be the smartest guy in the room, which, when it comes to poker, they usually aren't. But you're going to have to do your own read on Mr. Fredericks."

Petra watches as everyone refreshes their drinks. Gordy and Billy make a show of their scotch and sodas, though she notices they go soft on the former and heavy on the latter. Freddy goes with a diet Coke, as does Petra. Eric stays with a plastic bottle of water, while Zac has a Red Bull and vodka.

Everyone returns to the table, where they draw cards for position. This is a critical but overlooked part of the game, as Petra explained to Jerry as he drove her to the airport. "Position's huge. If the player to your right is aggressive, you're always reacting, defending. A cautious player to your right lets you dictate the action." They take their seats and turn their attention to Betty, the professional dealer who, Gordy explains to Petra, has been with the game since its inception, four years ago. A bottle-blond in her sixties with a Lauren Bacall smoker's voice, she's pleasant but all business.

She gives Petra a tight smile and indicates her seat, in between Gordy and Zac.

"Betty is judge and jury," Gordy explains. "She handles all dispute, and there's no appeal. Though it never comes to that." He pauses dramatically. "There is one rule unique to this game. Since it's called the Zac rule, I'll let him explain it to you."

Zac adopts a look of half-embarrassment, half-pride. "Anyone who says 'Read 'em and weep,' has to pay each of the other players 10K and leave the game."

"Guess who wore that phrase out in his debut?" Freddy says. And with that Betty starts to deal.

As planned, Petra plays tight the first 45 minutes or so. Not that she has much choice—the cards aren't coming her way. She attempts two early bluffs, one of which succeeds, the other called by Gordy. She decides to play tight until the first break and spend most of that time studying her opponents for tells.

Tells in poker range from the flagrantly obvious to the incredibly subtle. Over her years of playing, Petra has found that, with the number of players at a table and time clocks now a part of the game, she has to read her competition quickly and accurately. She focuses first on the eyes: Are they calm or darting? Do they look at their opponent's stack before betting? But eyes can be controlled. Mouths and the swallowing mechanism are tougher to control. A dry mouth, tight lips, an involuntary swallow—all can tell a lot. Hands: Do they change their association with the chips—shuffling, stacking, hovering—depending on the strength of the hand? Some players focus their eyes on the temple or the neck, to see if there's any involuntary flinch.

All of these activities can tell her a lot—or nothing, if in fact they're deliberate and intended to confuse. The only solution is time. It's hard for an opponent to stay in total control of all emotions and expressions over four hours (cash game) or four days (tournament).

Playing tight, Petra is down $5K at the first break. But she now has a read on the table. Gordy is, as Annie cautioned, bombastic on the surface but surprisingly solid. Billy's acting skills extend to the table. He's either getting the cards early on or is a real player. Eric is tight, though he seems to relax a notch every 15 minutes or so. He parts with his money more grudgingly than any other player at the table.

The two Silicon Valley guys couldn't be more different. Zac, not Billy, turns out to be the one, in Annie's hierarchy, who wants to impress her, if not sleep with her. He plays loose, almost sloppy, and it doesn't appear to be an act. Freddy, on the other hand, is a tough read. He varies his game from tight to semi-loose and chases at times, but only in small hands. More importantly, when the cards are dealt or turned up, his eyes are not on the cards but on the other players, looking for even the slightest reaction. He's the one to avoid in a showdown.

When they resume play after the first break, drinks refreshed and legs stretched, Petra wins the first hand, a substantial pot that puts her $20K in the black for the first time. She then deliberately gives it all back, looking flustered at one point, broadcasting that she's loose when ahead, tight when behind. At one point, Zac is clearly running a bluff, one she can beat. She pretends to agonize over it, talking herself through her options *sotto voce*, before saying to Zac, "If I fold, will you show me?" When he shrugs, she pushes her cards towards the dealer. To her delight, he shows his bluff and crows to the rest of the table. Freddy seems pained by the boorish behavior.

After three hours Petra is up $75K and change. She's also narrowed her field of prospective targets to Zac, Billy, and Gordy. Eric is too tight, and Freddy still mystifies her. She remembers Annie's caution as she prepares for the final hour of play. "Don't pretend to get sloppy. They won't buy it. If you do win a big pot mid-game, go a little girlish for the winning moment. That'll piss off the misogynists."

Which is what Petra does. This time she doesn't fold against Zac's bluff. When she turns over her queens and starts gathering her winnings, she lets out what seems to be an involuntary laugh. She doesn't pay attention to Zac—she knows his reaction already—but glances up as she stacks the chips and is surprised to find Eric frowning slightly.

Her winnings bring her to $140K. She thinks about playing tight the rest of the way, preserving her gains, and going back to the Valley with only another $110K to hit Keeley's goal. She'll see how the rest of the game goes. After a few nothing hands, Betty announces there are 15 more minutes in the game, time for three more hands. Unless the cards break her way, Petra will take the $140K and call it a night.

The next hand brings Petra two diamonds, the 10 and Queen. With the night winding down, she expects the players to be a bit looser, to stay in hands longer. Which proves to be the case. She leads out with $10K, which everyone matches. Except Zac, who raises another $10K. Again, everyone matches. The odds are that no one has a made hand, that everyone is waiting for the flop, where the dealer reveals three cards at once.

The flop comes: two kings, neither one a diamond, and the eight of clubs. She checks her bet, which is almost the same as folding, given that everyone is still in. Eric bets another $10K, which drives Gordy and Freddy to the sidelines. Zac raises to $20K and the bet's back to Petra.

She knows she should concede the hand to Zac and live to fight another day. But her years of playing are telling her that he's bluffing, though she's not sure. She is still considering folding, her eyes seemingly on the flop. But out of the corner of her eye she notices Zac's throat tighten, a dry swallow.

"All in," she says, pushing all of her chips into the middle. Betty is still counting Petra's raise when Eric folds. The attention is now on Zac. He looks at Petra with hard eyes.

This is where she needs to sell her own bluff. He's seen the seemingly nervous Petra, the anxious Petra, the girlish Petra. Now she needs him to realize that all three of those weren't real, that the real Petra is the one staring back at him. This Petra's eyes are hooded, her gaze flat. Her face, her hands, her posture—all of them are new to him. Now the only question is whether Zac will bet with his heart and call her or fold. If this were the final game of the night, Petra is pretty sure he'd call—but then, again, she wouldn't have bluffed had it been the final hand. But there are still two hands for him to get his money back—or more.

She sees him glance over at Freddy, who has a bemused smile on his face. After staring at Petra for the full minute allotted to him, he tosses in a time chip, which buys him another 30 seconds. Betty starts the clock. With ten seconds to go, he reaches for his chips—all he needs to do is throw one into the pot to let Betty know he calls—and Petra's heart stops. She has no idea how she'll tell Jerry she's lost all of Keeley's money.

But then Zac's hand slides off his chip stack and over to his cards, which he pushes into the middle, smiling sickly, as if he swallowed something gone bad. "Let's see 'em," he says.

Petra is dying to show the bluff, but she doesn't want to humiliate Zac. She pushes her cards towards Betty, face down. An angry Zac reaches to turn them over—an egregious breach of poker etiquette—but Betty's hand covers them, and she brings them into the muck.

Zac gathers himself and, to his credit, nods at Petra. "Nicely played," he says, and seems to mean it.

With $280K in front of her, Petra takes no chances, folding the last two hands. Zac, on tilt now, loses two more hands, one to Billy, the other to Eric. Petra notices that Freddy tends to stay away from taking on Zac directly, and wonders what that's all about.

As the game concludes and everyone cashes in, Freddy walks over to Petra, her coat over his arm. Helping her put it on, he says, "We're flying back tomorrow in the Headwaters jet, if you'd like to catch a ride." At her surprise, he says, "You think you're the only one who researches their opponents? You're a strong player; it would be great to have you in the game. But I get the feeling this was a one-time shot." When Petra doesn't answer, he says, "Let me know about that ride. And tell Keeley I say hi."

26

A Garage Game

"COZY, HUH?" KEELEY SAYS, motioning around the small conference room. "Get used to it. Every incubator I've ever been in is a bit claustrophobic. They all maximize their real estate, getting as many people or companies into the space as possible. Then they market it as 'collegial,' as if you're going to learn secrets about longevity by overhearing the conversations from the agtech startup next to you. So invest in a good set of headphones."

Keeley is sitting with Petra and Jerry in Bioscape, an incubator for biotech startups in Menlo Park, a largely serene town that blends pleasant residential neighborhoods with a mix of tech and biotech companies. In addition to its proximity to Stanford University, the town has the advantage of having a rail station in its downtown, which allows companies to base themselves there and attract commuters from San Francisco and up and down the peninsula, a distinct advantage over locating in the office complexes that dominated the early Silicon Valley landscape.

"When you guys outgrow this place—and I hope that's soon— you're going to have a decision to make about where to base yourselves. Not just which city, but what kind of facilities you want. When I first came to Silicon Valley, all the tech companies wanted to be in the office complexes next to the freeways. No personality but functional. Location wasn't important, since most nerds just nuked their Ramen noodles for lunch and went back to work, and they didn't need anything much in the way of equipment besides computers.

"But these days, quality of life is factoring into the equation. Remember, companies like Oracle and Apple and Google, with their mega-campuses and all the perks, have set new expectations for work environments. The big biotech companies, like Genentech and Amgen, have added similarly impressive perks, and you'll be competing for talent with them. Startups can't match the perks, but they have advantages large companies can't offer. Like locating in a city with a nice downtown, both for strolling and for lunch and after hours. And walking distance to a railroad station is a huge plus. Palo Alto is a good example, but it's beyond most startup budgets. But you should keep Mt. View and Burlingame in mind as you grow."

"I know the traffic on the peninsula sucks," Jerry says, "but are the trains that popular? Seems like more of a New York thing."

"The appeal is varied, depending on your audience. The workaholics like the extra time to work, rather than sitting in traffic. Young singles like the San Francisco scene more than the peninsula. And young marrieds can't afford to live on the peninsula, so they go someplace south, like Morgan Hill or Gilroy, and then take the train."

Keeley drains her Diet Coke. "Okay, let's get started. Since this is our first official business meeting, let me begin by welcoming Jerry to ... does the company have a name yet?"

"Elethea," Petra says, then spells it out. "It's a combination of my mom and sister's names. Plus, *alatheia* is Greek for truth." Keeley looks at Jerry to see if the name's okay. He nods.

"What do you think of the lab facilities here?"

"For our early work, it's more than adequate," says Jerry. "I'll start sourcing some of our own specialized equipment, but that's six months out at least."

"Is there a minimum lease?" Petra asks.

"No," Keeley says. "That's part of the beauty of these incubators. They want you up and out, so they can point to you as one of their success stories. In addition to the wet lab, shared equipment, office and meeting space, and cafeteria, they bring in experts on growing a company and VCs to coach you on pitching and funding. It's a model that's been honed in the tech space and works well for everyone. In your case, 10K a month buys you two workspaces and full lab access." She focuses on Petra. "So you need to start fundraising. Today. I'll make the intros. The rest is up to you. Speaking of which, I got an interesting call from your poker pal, Freddy. He wants to meet."

"With me? Jerry and me?"

"Me, to start, then the two of you." Keeley says. "I don't know which Freddy you'll be meeting with, the managing partner at Headwaters or Freddy the Big Swinging Dick. Either way, you're off to an interesting start. So get your pitch together and start rehearsing."

. . .

It's after eight in the evening and the incubator is still humming. The café serves dinner, so Petra has stayed there to eat and to catch up on her email. Jerry has gone at his usual time, 6:30, to have dinner with Alice and the boys. He's intent on keeping the same schedule as at Salvana, though he'll come back after dinner, if needed.

Her inbox empty, Petra is packing her briefcase when her computer pings with an incoming email. The title reads: "Welcome, Neighbor!" Smiling, she clicks on the message and grabs her coat. With one arm in the coat, she looks back at her screen just as the Welcome message dissolves and is replaced by a photo of her father. Frowning, Petra takes off her coat and sits back down. A pistol appears next to her father's temple. As she watches, the gun fires and her father's head explodes.

A second photo, this of Thea, replaces that of her father. On the screen, Thea ages quickly and dramatically, until the old face dissolves into a pile of ash.

The next photo is of Eleni. The aging process begins again, but then stops midway through and a series of question marks. The screen goes dark for a moment, then a photo of Petra comes up. The photo is of Petra from her MIT days, receiving an award. Then the screen goes blank.

27

All In

"THANKS FOR HOSTING, FREDDY," Trina says. "I'm so sick of that fucking yacht. There's only so much great food, sunbathing, and being catered to hand and foot that a girl can take."

The Dicks are meeting in Freddy's house in Atherton, Silicon Valley's version of Beverly Hills, with lots starting at five mil and ramping up sharply from there. Freddy's house is a stunning ultramodern home—all glass and steel, with cedar highlights. It's also a showcase of Freddy's investment in modular construction, where the house is built off-site in the controlled environment of a factory, then brought to the site and assembled in the space of a week. Though normally publicity-shy, Freddy and his wife, Annika, have allowed the house—and themselves—to be profiled in a number of magazines, both because they believe in the environmental benefits of modular construction and because it promotes Freddy's investment.

"I remember when this place was under construction," Max reminisces. "I was sitting on the patio at The Flea when I saw your living room go by on a flatbed."

"Yeah, I got lots of calls all that week," Freddy says. "We had the entire family plus our neighbors over to watch the cranes drop the rooms into place. It was like a huge Lego exercise. One of my kids filmed it and then did one of those fast-forward treatments. I'll send it to you, if you want."

Annika comes in with everyone's drinks and then takes a seat. "I want to hear this conversation," she says. "Think of me as a silent Dick."

Freddy holds up the presentation that Kerry prepared and sent around in anticipation of tonight's meeting. "What do you think?"

"It's a helluva ask," Vinod says. "We've never invested that much in a single venture before."

"She must be a helluva poker player," Max says.

"Ask Zac," Freddy says. "Most of her winnings are his."

The group turns their attention to Zac, who looks like he's about to pout, but then loses the attitude and nods. "She played me like a fiddle. If she's as good at longevity as she is in poker, then I think Freddy's on to something."

Freddy looks at Zac with fresh eyes. He saw the defensive attitude starting to rear its head and was surprised when Zac reined it in. He nods slightly at Zac, who acknowledges it with a slight nod back.

"But sole funding," Max says. "We've never done anything like that. Even close. We always spread our bets around."

"And how's that working out for us so far? Like I said last meeting, we need to find the next big idea. And the next Steve Jobs. It's not the poker game that led me to make this suggestion, though she did impress me there. It was talking to Keeley James." He notices the group perk up. "We all know that Keeley doesn't exaggerate. And Keeley thinks Petra is the real deal and on to something big."

"She's never run a company before," Vinod says. "And I know what you're going to say, that most of our founders haven't. But most of our founders aren't asking for eight million of our dollars."

"To be clear," Freddy says, "Keeley and Petra aren't asking for anything. This is my idea. I know this is a big ask. Just meet with her, that's all I'm asking. If after that you don't agree with my proposal, we drop it. No harm, no foul. But if she and her idea impress you, this might be one they'll be talking about for years." He smiles. "But don't let public admiration and phenomenal wealth be determining factors in your decision."

28

Breaking the Seal

KEELEY AND FREDDY are in the living room of her house, a Craftsman within walking distance of downtown Palo Alto. The house has a casual elegance and a warm feel. The two are sitting on a large couch, glasses of red wine on the low table in front of them. Freddy's in his standard uniform—khakis and a starched Oxford shirt; Keeley's in jeans and a Stanford sweatshirt. She's barefoot.

"She's good with the terms?" Freddy asks. At Keeley's nod, he adds, "And you?"

"They're fine. Generous, even. Eight mil for 33 percent. I'm surprised you're not spreading the risk, bringing in other groups."

"This is something I've always wanted to try. And this one, especially with you involved, seems like the time to try it out."

"Well, you'll get no argument from Petra and Jerry. From their standpoint, every day spent fundraising is a day away from building the company—and the product. So yes, they're good with the terms."

A doorbell rings. Keeley stands up. "There she is."

A moment later Keeley returns with Petra. Freddy walks over to greet her. Petra and Freddy stand there awkwardly, and then Freddy goes in for a brief hug at the same moment Petra extends her hand. They settle on a bro-hug, shaking with one hand, patting on the back with the other.

"We're off to an awkward start," Freddy says.

Petra smiles. "I'm not much of a hugger."

"I'll remember that." While Keeley pours a glass of wine for Petra, the three settle down, Petra in a wingback chair across from the couch. "Since it seems like we're all good with the numbers," Freddy begins, "let's talk board. We'd like three seats: me, Zac—who you've already met—and Trina, who you'll meet next week. I'm assuming the same for Elethea?"

Keeley speaks up. "Just two. Petra and Jerry." As Freddy raises his eyebrows, she continues. "You're making a helluva investment with these guys, so we think you should have the controlling votes."

"What about you? What's your role?"

"I think I'm more valuable to Elethea as a consigliere than a board member. Someone needs to keep a little distance here."

Freddy smiles. "To paraphrase LBJ, you want to be outside the tent pissing in, rather than inside the tent." When Keeley raises her eyebrows in agreement, he turns to Petra. "What questions does our new CEO have for us? Our job, starting this moment, is to get you off to the best possible start."

"Since you both know my family history and my fixation on failure," Petra says, "let's start there. Your first-time CEOs who failed. What did they do wrong?"

"It's a long list," Freddy says, "for both of us. Both in terms of number of CEOs and the reasons for their departure." He looks at Keeley. "You want to go first?"

"Most of my founders possess this dangerous cocktail of pride and ignorance," Keeley says. From the corner of her eye, Petra sees Freddy nod. "These people, like you, have had an abundance of success in their lives. Their failures, if any, have been few and short-lived. As a result, when they don't know something, they won't admit it. And when things start to track wrong, they're too proud to ask for help, thinking the board will see it as a sign of weakness. That's when they start to spiral."

"Also," Freddy says, "you need to take criticism seriously but not personally. Like Keeley says, people like you, people who have excelled most of their lives, aren't used to criticism. Even though you swear to us that you're good with it, that you welcome it, most of you sulk like children when you hear it."

He thinks for a minute. Then a smile slinks across his mouth.

"You ever work with Israelis?" Petra shakes her head. She looks from Freddy to Keeley, who is smiling as well. "They're an acquired taste. Personally, I like working with them, though that puts me in the minority." He looks at Keeley.

"I'm not sure where you're going with this," Keeley says, "but I'd agree on both fronts. You always know where you stand with Israelis. I find that refreshing."

"What's that got to do with criticism?" Petra asks.

"I've worked with over a dozen Israeli companies," Freddy continues. "One of them paid me the ultimate compliment the other day. He said, 'You don't speak a single word of Hebrew, Freddy, but you're fluent in Israeli.'"

"Meaning what?"

"He said that when he's dealing with Americans, let's say he's got a problem with the website, he says he can't just jump in with his question or complaint, the way he would with another Israeli. He has to ask his American counterparts first how they're doing, how's the weather out here, maybe even a brief conversation about their kids and how they're doing in soccer. Only then will he broach the subject of the website. And if he's critical of it, he has to couch his language—remember what I said about criticism. With me, he can just jump in and say: 'What the fuck's going on with my website?' He says he's at least 30 percent more productive working with me and other Israelis than with Americans."

"In other words, you want me to be more Israeli in our relationship?"

"The more time I spend being sure I'm not hurting your feelings, the less productive we both are. Just remember that Zac, Trina, and I are as invested in Elethea as you and Jerry, just in a different way."

"What about hiring? What's your advice on that front?"

"My advice is to hire deliberately but fire quickly," Freddy says. "I know Jerry has two research scientists he likes, both of which he can vouch for because they've worked together at Salvana. Your job is to vet them. Dig into their past. Ask the hard questions. If you hear any alarm bells, pay attention. If you're still unsettled, either pass on the hire or bring one of us in for another set of eyes. That's part of our job.

"Once they're on board," he continues, "you'll know soon enough whether they're Elethea material or not. If not, admit it—to Jerry at least, if not to us—and fix it. Fast. Most first-time founders have very little experience managing people. They've never fired anyone in their life. If you do need to fire someone, do it early and fast. You're running a business—you don't have time for reclamation projects."

"As for Jerry's two hires," Petra says, "how should we be compensating them?"

Freddy extends his hands, palms up, forming a scale. He then lowers his right hand and raises his left, exaggerating the imbalance. "This hand," he nods at his left, "is cash. The other is equity. Stock. Right now, you've got more stock than cash, so use it on your strategic hires. Because they're the ones with the greatest value and the ones taking the biggest risks."

"What's an example of a package for Jerry's hires?"

"Some of that depends on how you're allocating your equity. I understand you're not going with the standard 40/40/20 rule?"

"Correct. The fairest distribution, at least in my mind, is one third for you, one third for the employees, and Jerry and I will split the remaining third."

"I told her that's more generous a distribution than any of my companies had—or have," Keeley says to Freddy. "You?"

"Same."

Petra shrugs. "Back to the employees. Say Jerry's got a candidate who's making 250K, which is the case with one of the Salvana guys. What do I offer him?"

"Offer him one-forty and a half percent of the company," Keeley says. Freddy nods.

"And those terms are acceptable?"

"If they've got any experience in the startup world, yeah, they are. If not, have them meet with Freddy or me. And if we can't convince them, then you should probably pass on them, because they'll be a managerial headache from Day One."

Petra takes a small pad of paper from her front pocket, produces a pen from the other, and jots down some notes, the scratching filling the silence. "This is good stuff. Now what about hiring beyond the lab? What are my priorities?"

"The key word here," Freddy says, "is 'virtual.' When Keeley and I started in this business, headcount was the heaviest part of our startup budgets. Why? Because everything had to be done in-house. That's all changed over the past ten years. Now all your support functions—Legal, HR, Finance, even Marketing in the early days—are done virtually and part-time, by experienced professionals who do the same function for multiple startups. I know a ton of them, so does Keeley. They're experienced professionals who have decided there's more upside and freedom in applying their expertise across a number of startups, like they're their own mutual fund. And five to ten hours a week—not forty—is all you're going to need from each of them.

"Bottom line," Freddy continues, "is that the board will want you to justify any full-time hire beyond your key scientists. And we'll mean it."

"That's fine," Petra says. "For the immediate future it'll just be Jerry, his two guys, and me."

"Not quite," Keeley says. "There's one other hire you need to make. Freddy agrees with me on this one. You need an office manager, though that's not an appropriate title. This person is far more than that. In addition to managing all the daily operations, such as ordering in lunches and dinners and equipping the office, they'll manage all those virtual functions Freddy just mentioned—Legal, HR, Finance. More importantly, the right office manager will be at the heart of your company. She—and it's usually a 'she'—will keep an eye on the employees and be able to voice their concerns if they're too shy to bring them up. She'll monitor corporate culture and let you know when it—or you, for that matter—are drifting off-course."

"Do you have anyone in mind?"

"I do," Keeley says. "She's done it twice for me in the past, which has made her rich. But I think she's bored in retirement. I'll give her a call if you'd like."

"Please."

"Last piece of business," Freddy says. "For legal purposes we need an official start date for Elethea. Any objection to making it tomorrow?" When no one objects, he hoists his glass. "Then that's that," he says. "You're in business, Petra. Good luck."

. . .

Petra opens the door to her apartment, pours herself a glass of wine, sits on her couch, and phones Izaak.

"Hey there, I just wanted you to be the first to know. I did it. Elethea is officially in business. I guess I'm the CEO of a startup."

"Elethea?" asks Izaak.

"It's a combination of Eleni and Thea and a variation on *alatheia*, the Greek word for truth."

"I like it. So, how does it feel, to be the head of your very own startup?"

"Terrifying. Confusing. Strange. But also kind of exciting. Thanks again for encouraging me to meet with Keeley. This would never have happened if you hadn't pushed me in her direction."

"What are friends for?" Izaak says with a laugh. "Seriously, though, thanks for letting me know. And for the record, I think you're going to make a great CEO."

"God, that just sounds so weird, you know? All these years of feeling like a scientist, through and through. Never once imagined I'd be on the business side. Never."

"Give it time. Who knows, maybe it'll grow on you."

"Thanks for the confidence boost. Anyway, enjoy the rest of your evening, and I guess I'll see you at our next Speak Easy get-together," she says.

"Sounds good. See you then, Ms. CEO."

Petra smiles, sips her wine, and pulls up her laptop to check messages. After reading and responding to a few, she sees one from an unfamiliar address. She opens it, and it starts scrolling the names of Valley startups. All failed, out of business. The names roll by for what seems like a full minute, then stop. A question appears on the screen: "Are you next?"

Petra closes the laptop, shaken. She wonders who is sending her these messages. And what do they know that she doesn't?

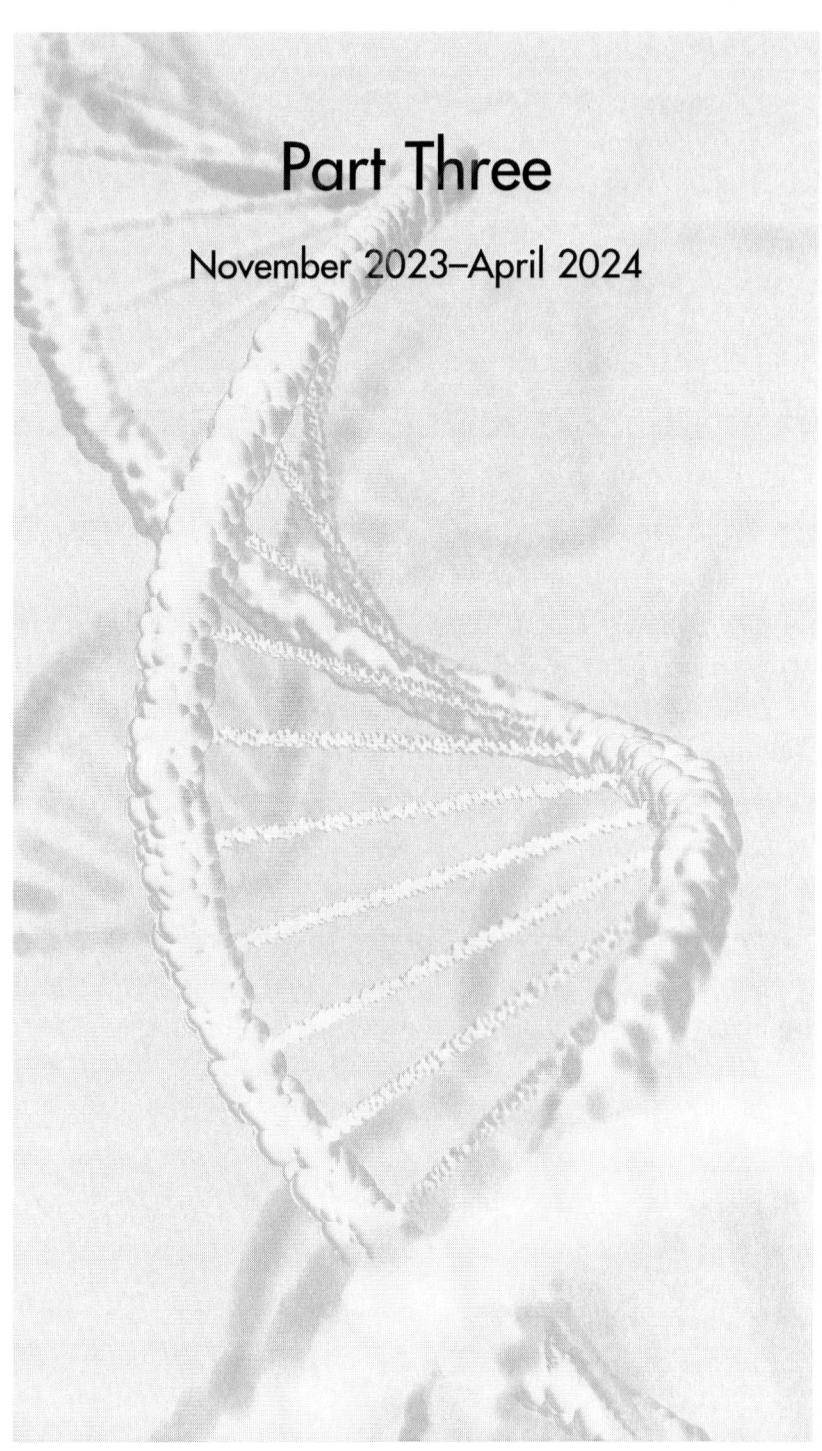

Part Three

November 2023–April 2024

29

ONE YEAR LATER

Upping the Ante

CHERYL POURS HERSELF a second cup of coffee and returns to the living room, where a small whiteboard is perched on the armrests of a chair. On it are five categories, with notes scribbled beneath each. She sits on the couch and stares at the board. She's done all she can. The rest will have to wait for Jake's arrival.

It's an October Sunday morning, crisp enough to merit a small fire and the heat on. Cheryl's house, a Craftsman bungalow, is tucked into one of the winding streets of Portola Valley, a semi-rural/horsey town nestled at the base of the Santa Cruz mountains that mark the western edge of Silicon Valley.

Cheryl's husband, Kurt, knowing the importance of this annual board presentation, has sacrificed his Sunday football routine to take the girls up to San Francisco for the day. They're visiting the Exploratorium, the hands-on science museum on the wharf, a favorite destination for the girls. For trips like this, Kurt asks their live-in nanny/caregiver to drive. Even though Kurt's a guinea pig for Elon Musk's self-driving cars—anything for more autonomy—he's not willing to risk his girls until a reputable someone other than Elon certifies the safety of the vehicles.

Cheryl appreciates Kurt's gesture and the quiet that comes with it. This is her second presentation to the board since Petra left and work began on Project L, the in-house longevity project, and she wants to nail it. She's divided the presentation into two parts: Biz Dev in general and Project L. Biz Dev is her bailiwick, and she's got nothing but good news on that front: new partners, new revenue streams, and new prospects on the horizon. She'll run through it one last time with Jake, but she doesn't expect much, if anything, to change.

Project L is another matter. The first six months were rocky, as Cheryl refused to hire the scientific team until she'd found and hired the right leader, arguing that the head of the program must be able to pick their own team. The long list of candidates her headhunter had put forward was exclusively male. No surprise there. She'd been warned by Ed that some of the best candidates to fill out his org chart were old school and might have a problem reporting to a woman. She felt both cowardly and practical with her decision and hoped that there would be other opportunities to advance her feminist goals.

Part of the problem had been finding a leader whose ego was okay with working from Petra's research, rather than demanding that all work originate from the point of his arrival. It took over two months to identify and hire Drew Loper, a scientist from one of the longevity institutes that had sprung up in the past few years. An academic by background, he looks the part: semi-longish hair perpetually mussed; no tie; a narrow, earnest face culminating in an even narrower chin. All that's missing is the pipe and tweed jacket with leather elbows. Hiring him away from the longevity institute took quite a bit of convincing, but the intellectual challenge and almost unlimited budget, plus the chance to hire and work with scientists whose work he admires, finally brought him on board.

Loper knows nothing about Jake, either his off-the-books assignment or his longevity tutorials with Cheryl. The scientist is impressed by her grasp of Project L's technology and the emerging competition, especially in the startup market. He also appreciates that, other than requiring that half of his research stem from Petra's findings, she gives him wide latitude on hiring and managing his group of scientists.

She does, however, encourage him to eschew big-company schedules and thinking in his research and culture. "Think of Project L as a startup with deep pockets," she told him in their final interview. "For example, management wanted to put the project on-site in one of their vacant buildings, but I insisted it be off-site, with no signage and no link to Salvana. Think of yourself as the head of that startup. Dress like it, act like it. Most importantly, think like it."

"Speaking of 'startup thinking,' ever since your recruiter contacted me, I've been reading everything I could get my hands on about how startups work. And a couple of their favorite phrases—Move fast and break things' and 'Throw things against the wall and see what sticks'—don't apply to the scientific world, especially biotech."

"Agreed. But what we can learn from startups is that many of them began by assuming nothing and challenging everything, especially status quo thinking. When it comes to death and longevity, I want you to encourage your team to look at their past research with fresh eyes. Share it with the team but be prepared to start over. No sacred cows, no egos. Fresh thinking at every step."

It took Dr. Loper a few months to get his sea legs, to finish hiring his team, and get his hands around Petra's research, but once he did all three, he proved to be the leader Cheryl had hoped for. That included pushing back on the technology front and standing his ground.

Cheryl wanted him and his team to pursue Petra's research full-speed and with all resources. He disagreed. Vehemently.

"While I appreciate Dr. Alexander's genius as well as her generosity," he said, in a closed-door meeting, "there are two reasons not to go full-bore on her solution. The first is that you can't bring in a team of all-stars like we've just hired and tell them to ignore their own work and ideas to date. If you want their full buy-in, you need to at least give their own research a hearing."

"Got it. What's the next thing?"

"The fact that Dr. Alexander might be wrong. Simple as that. She has a theory. A fascinating theory, to be sure. And she has a unique approach, of attacking aging from infancy. Both are intriguing, but if either is wrong, the whole thing collapses."

"How do you recommend we proceed, then?"

"The budget allows for twin tracks. The first track, call it 'the Blue Team,' will work from Dr. Alexander's research and mirror Elethea's efforts—ten scientists working full-time and full-speed. That's more manpower than Elethea currently has, based on what you've told me."

"And the second track?"

"The Red Team is made up of seven scientists who want to pursue their own theories. Here's the deal I've struck with them. Mornings, they pursue their own solutions and at key points present their progress and results to the rest of the team. Afternoons, they review and critique the work of the Blue Team. This arrangement, to my mind, has two benefits. It accelerates work on the Alexander solution by having an ongoing review process to catch early mistakes. And it gives us other approaches in case her solution turns out to be flawed or mistaken, but still salvageable, which is often the case in research like this."

. . .

At noon, Jake knocks on the door and then, seeing Cheryl through the window, lets himself in. He's brought lunch—burritos from a taqueria near his house in Mt. View—and nods to Cheryl, who is on her knees writing on the small white board.

"Help yourself," she says, pointing with her chin to the refrigerator.

"Beer or diet Coke?" he asks.

"What's Mr. Triathlon having? Water?"

"You can't watch football without a beer in your hand."

"Make it two, then."

He puts their burritos on a plate and nukes them in the microwave for 30 seconds. Then he unwraps them, pops the tops off two Stellas, and grabs napkins and salsa from the bag. It takes him two trips to bring lunch into the living room.

With the struggles she's had getting Project L up and running, Cheryl is impressed by how smooth and productive her relationship with Jake has been. Over the course of the year, they've evolved from employer/employee—or 'spy and handler,' as Jake refers to it jokingly—to allies, even friends. Like Ed, Jake has the science chops to listen to her issues with Project L and make suggestions. But unlike Ed, his MBA training and perspective allow him to offer advice on the business ramifications of the scientific decisions under consideration.

Still, it's the undercover work that is his primary assignment, and he's exceeded her expectations on that front as well. He has become a fixture at the meetups and informal gatherings of individuals and startups that populate the six major categories on Petra's grid, getting job offers from some, doing product marketing consulting for others.

Most impressive, though, has been his ability to insinuate himself into Petra's world, seemingly without raising any alarms. By trading business advice for climbing lessons, he's developed a friendship of sorts, with Petra occasionally using what's going on at Elethea as examples. As he has reminded

Cheryl, extracting any information from Petra is going to be a slow, at times frustrating, process. She's not a forthcoming person by nature and he's sure she's been cautioned by her investors about loose lips and corporate security.

Jakes takes a seat on the floor and looks up at the television. "Any surprises in the morning games?" NFL Red Zone is on but with the sound down. Both of them are huge football fans—not just of the Niners, like so many in the Bay Area, but of pro football in general—to the point that they have a number of bets on the point spread and over/under for a handful of games each weekend.

"You know, I've been so busy, I haven't had a chance to follow any of the games.". As she says that, the screen splits into quadrants, enabling them to catch the scores of at least four of that weekend's slate of games. "I love The Red Zone," she says at one point. "It's football for those of us with ADHD."

With her pen, she gestures at the whiteboard, where she's written:

- Staffing
- Facilities
- Technology
- Schedule
- Integration/Transition

"These are the categories I'm using to present Project L updates to the board, going forward," she says. "I sent them to you a minute ago in PowerPoint. If you could use that template for your Elethea update, they'll have an apples to apples comparison, which is how they think."

"Not a problem. I'll do it during the first half. Do you want me to do one for any of the other startups I've been following?"

"Nah. Elethea's the only one they care about at this point. Both because of its Salvana roots and because they're the ones furthest along. Okay, let's watch the game and we'll review at halftime."

They turn the set to the Niners-Seahawks game, though each one keeps the RedZone up on their laptops. At the end of the game, and after RedZone has signed off, they compare notes on today's bets. Cheryl is up almost $200, Jake up $80.

Cheryl has added Jake's slides to her own. After spending a few moments reviewing the complete presentation, she puts the laptop on the table and does a final rehearsal, with Jake taking notes. When she's done, she raises her chin at him to take over.

"Headcount: Elethea's at eight scientists and holding. Facilities-wise, they've moved out of the incubator and into their own space in Mt. View, just down the street from my place. That's always a positive sign, when a startup moves. The board wouldn't allow it without some form of major progress. And from what I can glean from Petra, they're at or near the proof-of-concept stage. They've got a CRISPR expert on board, which would normally mean they're past POC, but she's been there a while now, so I'm not sure what's up. I've shown about as much curiosity on that subject as I'm comfortable with, so I'll hold off on any more Elethea questions to her. At least for now."

Half an hour later, Cheryl walks Jake to his car. The air has a snap to it, perfect football weather. Kurt has texted that they're on their way home, there in 45 minutes. Just enough time for her to do a Zoom call to preview tomorrow's agenda and presentation with Detective Perkins.

"I can't believe you have to brief that guy *before* the presentation," Jake says. "That's a pretty ballsy request."

She nods. "I ghosted his initial request, just ignored his calls and emails. Then my boss called me in and asked me—nicely but with no room to say no—to bring him into the tent. To remind me that, after all, we're on the same team. But it was the way he said it, not rah-rah encouragement but more like he was as confused—and intimidated—by our detective as we are."

Jake nods. "It's like that scene from Butch Cassidy: Who *is* that guy?"

30

In the Pit

"OUR FIRST DISAGREEMENT of any sort. She says to me, 'I've already got a mom.'"

"And what did you say?" Eleni asks.

"'Well, now you've got two.'"

The two women laugh and return to laying out the new office and lab space, which Mona Rodriguez, the office manager and Petra's right hand, has secured on the second floor of a renovated warehouse two blocks off Castro Street, the main drag in downtown Mt. View. A touch over five feet and solidly built, Mona has unlined skin and bright almond eyes that seem to never leave your face. Squat without being fat, she moves through every place with purpose. Using real-estate contacts from her previous startups, she was able to find the space before it went on the market, getting in while it was being gutted and working with the owners to customize it to Elethea's needs. She solicited and welcomed input from every employee on what was needed and how the layout could be optimally deployed. Then she huddled with Petra.

"I've got a preliminary layout," she said, "one I think gives everyone what they asked for ..." She smiled sweetly at Petra. "Except you."

Before Petra could respond, Mona plowed ahead. "Jerry tells me how much you liked your privacy at Salvana, especially the office. More specifically, the door." She paused. "I think you're better off in a cube in the new space, but you're the boss."

"I'm not so sure about that sometimes," Petra said with a slight smile.

"A cube sends the right message about equality and privilege. Plus, it keeps you in touch with not only what's going on in the lab but what's going on in the lives of your people, which is just as important."

"What about privacy for phone calls?"

Mona unrolled a blueprint and tapped a mid-size rectangle. "You've got the conference room. Plus, you can also use the sleep room. It's got a futon. The scientists say they want it for power naps. But trust me, more than one of these guys'll be using the room overnight on occasion."

. . .

Mona was Keeley's contribution to the team. "I met her eight years ago," she told Petra and Freddy, when the topic of an office manager first came up. "She was running the garage where I took my car. The place was immaculate, the schedules were sacred, the bills were never a surprise. And everyone, including her husband, whose garage it was, deferred to her on anything that didn't have a motor. It took me a month to explain to her and Ramon what her job at the startup would entail and to convince her it would be more challenging, and potentially much more lucrative, than the garage."

"How'd she do with the first startup?" Freddy asked.

"She took to it like a duck to water. Had the place shipshape within a month. Was supportive where she should be, and hardline where she should be. When the company shipped its first product, the CEO brought in a tattoo artist for anyone who wanted one. The product team dared her to get one that they had already designed, a tasteful 'Tough Mother' on her right bicep. She agreed, showing it off to me, saying she took each word equally seriously."

Her work was so impressive that the founders, with the board's backing, upped her stock shares twice in the company's first three years of operation. When Cisco acquired them, Mona cashed out and used the money to establish an educational fund that paid for college for her two sons, plus eight others in her extended family. As well as for two new bays in Ramon's garage.

"Did she quit then?" Petra asked. "Or go back to the garage?"

"She thought about both options, but she wound up going with one of the founders from her original company on his next startup." She saw Petra's surprise. "That happens a lot in the Valley. Large companies like Cisco are buying the technology and the development team. They don't need more executives. So they pack up the founders up and say 'good luck—just don't compete with us in your next venture.'"

"How'd the second company do?" Petra asked.

"That one put her on Easy Street. She was done with the pace and demands—or so she thought—and went back to the garage. That was a year ago. I'm surprised she lasted that long. You should have heard the relief in her voice when I called her about Elethea."

"She wasn't put off by us being a biotech company?"

"Not at all. She didn't need to be a car mechanic or a software expert to whip the garage or the two startups into shape, and she doesn't need to be a scientist to do the same for Elethea."

"I'm glad I listened to you, about hiring her right after we got the funding. It seemed premature at the time, but now I can't imagine this place without her."

"I tell my founders that 'Office Manager' doesn't begin to define someone like Mona—and most successful startups have a Mona. 'Director of Operations' comes closer to capturing her value—finding the space, selecting your vendors, managing all your virtual services. But her job also includes what I call 'Chief Culture Officer.'" She saw the skepticism on Petra's face. "Let's say you'd won the argument with Mona about having an office by promising to have an open-door policy. Mona would keep an eye on just how well you lived up to that promise. And if you retreated to your Salvana ways ..." She saw Petra's eyebrows rise. "Yeah, I know about your hibernation tendencies. If you started to backslide, Mona would either call you on it, or she'd have one of her sons come in one evening and take the door off. And good luck getting it back."

She saw Petra's smile grow rigid. "Think of her in two ways," Keeley continued. "First, as the company's conscience. If you've got a set of values, either informal or up on the wall, she'll hold you to them and let you know when you're slipping. She's also your eyes and ears into your employee base, especially as it grows. She's the one who knows which employees need a break, maybe a day at a spa to rejuvenate. Which ones are having trouble at home. In her first company, one of her most important functions was making sure the two founders' zippers were up before they left the building."

"How long do you think we'll be in this space?" Eleni asks Mona.

"I signed a two-year lease, based on the numbers Petra and Jerry gave me. But, as I cautioned them at the time, I've seen boards who, when they hear good news on the product or technology front, pressure the CEO to increase hiring. Based on the calculations I made about space in the bullpen, I think we could get to 23 employees before we're on top of each other."

Eleni and Mona are talking over lunch, sampling some of the catered fare from local restaurants. When they were looking at potential office space, the two women knew that, with almost every restaurant in the South Bay signed up to bring in lunch to startups, food wouldn't be a consideration in their choice of locale. But Mona counseled Petra and Jerry that they should encourage their employees to leave the building at least twice a day, either for lunch or a walk. And that studies showed improvements in both productivity and mental health with breaks in routine and locations.

● ● ●

Even though Mona is technically Eleni's boss, it hasn't stopped the two women from becoming friends. The relationship had its genesis in a staff meeting, when Mona was complaining about her problems finding a virtual CFO/accountant to round out her virtual team. Either ignoring or not seeing Petra's warning look, Jerry told Mona that Eleni was an accountant. He then shifted his legs to the side of his chair, sitting side-saddle and out of reach of Petra's kicks. Eleni came in the next day and started that afternoon. Now the two women are a team on a number of fronts.

Knowing that Petra was concerned about her mother's presence within the company, Eleni had taken the initiative and called her. "If you've got a problem with me being there, I just won't do it. It looks like Mona could use the help, but not if it makes you uncomfortable."

"It's just that I'm only starting to get my hands around running my own company, and now my mom is going to work for me."

"Here's what I propose. First, I'll come once a week, twice at the most. When I do, you call me 'Eleni,' not 'Mom.' You don't manage me, Mona does. And we do it on a three-month trial, with the promise on this end that there will be no hard feelings if it doesn't work out."

"You sure you want to do this?"

"I wasn't, at first, when Mona called me. Then I looked around at everyone so hard at work, at how the team was coming together, and I wanted to be a part of it. Also, I've walked every neighborhood and street in San Francisco, and I'm bored."

There turned out to be no need for the three-month review. Eleni fulfilled all of her promises, and she dazzled Mona—normally a tough sell—with her financial acumen. It was Mona who suggested a small stock grant for her at the six-month anniversary, and the board approved it unanimously.

· · ·

Today, as they sample from the new Indian restaurant, they're discussing Petra's dating life, or lack thereof. While Freddy and Keeley see Petra's lack of marital and dating status as a positive, allowing her to focus exclusively on Elethea, Mona is all-in with Eleni that marriage—and especially grandchildren—is a central component of a complete life. A Nobel prize would be nice, Eleni says, but it's no match for a grandchild. Or four.

"It took me years to come to accept Petra's bisexuality," Eleni says, dabbing at the corner of her mouth with a napkin. The skin on her face has sagged slightly in the last year and her test numbers are on a slow rise, but she has forbidden Petra to bring the topic up, given the stress she's under running the company. "But now, whether it's just that I realize that's who she is, or living in San Francisco, I'm used to both the word and the fact that it applies to my daughter." She laughs slightly. "I even suggested she ask Zoe out."

Mona looks up in amazement. "Aren't we the modern one. I can't see me doing that with either of my boys, and I consider myself a fairly worldly woman. What did Petra say?"

"She almost choked on her salad. Then she said, 'Mom, Zoe's straight. And even if she weren't, I'm not going to risk losing my

best friend and climbing partner because you want grandkids.'"
She looked at Mona. "Not trying to get you to betray any confidences, but do you know if she's seeing anyone? Of either sex."
She blushed slightly and lowered her head.

Mona shook her head. "Not that I know of. There's this one guy, Jake, that I've heard her talk about, but I think they're just friends. If I learn otherwise, I'll let you know."

Eleni looks out at the open lab area, where a small group has assembled around one of the large microscopes. A blonde woman is talking as they take turns looking through the ocular, then back over at her.

"I never got the story on that one," Eleni says, gesturing at the blonde, "just her name. I go back to Chicago for a week, and when I come back, she's not only hired, but she's been at work for the past three days. I'd ask Petra, but she and I have agreed not to talk work."

"Well, you know her name, since I introduced you the first day. That's Layla Clements, our CRISPR expert, but it turns out she's great with the other stuff as well. And that's from Bao and Josef, who're tough to impress."

"You sure they weren't just smitten? I mean, just look at her."

* * *

Layla had walked into what qualified as Elethea's waiting area—the space between Mona's desk and the front door—unannounced. Not noticing the manila file in her hand, Mona had just nodded to the conference room. "You can just set up over there. You got something for me to sign?"

In telling the story to Eleni, Mona puts a hand over her heart. "Swear to God, I thought she was delivering the lunch. I mean, she looks eighteen, for God's sake."

"Excuse me," Layla had said. "I'm here about the CRISPR position."

That got Mona's attention. She looked at her visitor with fresh eyes. Long blonde hair—no highlights or additions, best Mona could tell—pulled back in a loose ponytail that made it halfway down her back. No makeup, though none was needed. She wore men's Levi's, running shoes with no laces, and a hoodie from a Santa Cruz surf shop. On closer examination, she was in her twenties, the skin around her eyes beginning to show lines, as if she spent too much time squinting. Maybe she was a lab rat, after all.

Mona was right about the squinting, but it was into the sun, not a microscope. Aside from those people who actually live on their boats, Layla had probably spent more of her life in and on the water than anyone her age. The child of itinerant surfers who were also coders-for-hire, she had spent her youth up until the age of 14 being home-schooled, with no fixed address except a customized VW van with a pop-up camper top.

Since infancy, Layla had accompanied her parents as they roamed as far north as Oregon and as far south as Peru in search of surf and adventure. Mornings were spent on dawn patrol, early morning when the waves were the cleanest, the winds the calmest, and the crowds the smallest. When the winds or tides caused the waves to lose shape, the three would paddle in and Layla's school day would begin. Dividing the work, her father took the morning session, concentrating on a rotation of math, English, history, and social studies. Her mother took over after lunch, working on science and coding, as well as Spanish grammar. All three of the Clements were fluent in spoken Spanish, accumulated from summers spent in South America. It was an annual foray, avoiding the dreaded summer wave slump on the North American west coast, where their favorite spots could go weeks at a time with waves only small enough to be called 'whale farts.' Late afternoon, if the winds eased off and the tide dropped, they were usually back in the water for the evening glass-off.

At 14, Layla had a heart-to-heart with her parents. While she still loved the lifestyle, she wanted to be a scientist, and wanted to study at the kind of schools that would require transcripts and recommendations from someone other than her parents. So they'd parked the van in a long-stay Santa Barbara RV park and enrolled her in a local high school. They bought an old Karmann Ghia, which Layla used to commute to school.

But surfing took priority over academics and acculturation. If the waves were good, her parents would unhitch the van and head down to Rincon. Or the three would ride their bikes, with surfboard carriers attached, to Leadbetter's. Since Layla's grades were excellent and her teachers knew of her background, the school let the absences slide.

Between her grades, test scores, and unique life experience, she had no trouble getting accepted at her first choice, UC Berkeley. She took an eclectic approach to her first two years, exploring majors in physics, chemistry, psychology, and philosophy before deciding on molecular and cell biology, which incorporated elements of physics and chemistry, while touching on both psychological and philosophical issues as well. Berkeley also had the advantage of being within driving distance of San Francisco's Ocean Beach and its thick, cold waves.

She chose to stay at Berkeley for her doctorate, drawn to the opportunity to work in proximity to Jennifer Doudna, a Nobel laureate and pioneer in the CRISPR technique. Inspired by her parents to think freely and to be open to other views—academic and otherwise—she was more ambitious with this new technology, willing to try and fail as she stretched it to its limits. Her doctoral thesis employed CRISPR in its investigation into how targeted cancer mutations affected various molecular pathways.

. . .

"There's no CRISPR position," Mona had told her.

"Not yet, there isn't. But my professors suggested that Dr. Martin might be interested in my work to date." She handed the folder to Mona.

Mona opened the folder and scanned the resume. The topics and terminology were over her head, but not the schools, the degrees, and the recommendations. She told Layla to wait for a moment and headed across the lab floor to consult with Bao and Josef, who took one look at the resume, glanced over at the waiting Layla, and put their conversation on hold.

Mona set them up in the conference room. When lunch arrived, she set it out on chairs outside the room, allowing the interview to proceed without interruption. At one point, the three emerged, grabbed and filled plates, and returned to the conference room. The next time Mona looked over, Layla was up at the whiteboard, Bao and Josef taking notes.

Finally, Bao came out and crossed the floor to Mona's desk. "She needs to see Jerry. Now."

"He's at Stanford with Petra. Izaak's reviewing our security system. Both Jerry and Petra should be back by two."

"Call him," Bao said, with an urgency she hadn't heard before. "Tell him not to let her leave this building without a job offer."

Summoned by Mona, Jerry hurried back and took Bao and Josef's place. Unschooled in HR dos and don'ts, he started at the top. "Layla. Based on your coloring, I'm thinking you're not Arabic or Israeli, but rather that your parents were big Eric Clapton fans."

She nodded. "It was between that and Aja. They're both huge Steely Dan fans, too."

"Two great albums. You couldn't go wrong either way. Good thing they weren't Iron Butterfly fans." He ignored her confusion and pointed at the whiteboard. "Let's get down to what we're up to and why you're here. On my way back here, I checked with your thesis advisor, Dr. Stein. She's an old friend. She says you're the best CRISPR jockey she's ever had. And Sarah is stingy with her praise. But before we talk further, I do have one question. Why's there nothing in your CV since you finished your PhD?"

Jerry was referring to the year that had elapsed since Layla earned her doctorate degree, an unusual gap in a scientific career. Most scientists, especially those interested in a research path, maintain their career momentum by moving as quickly as possible from PhD thesis to either a post-doctoral position or a job.

For the first time in her impromptu interview, Layla looked slightly ill at ease. "I know I was supposed to go straight to a post-doc or something, but after finishing a decade of structured schooling, I needed a break. So I spent a year chasing waves all over the world. Now, sanity restored, I'm ready to get to work." She smiled. "Though I'm not giving up surfing, not for any job."

"No problem on this end," Jerry said. "Ok, so now let me talk to you about what we're up to and where CRISPR fits in."

Layla walked out that day as employee number thirteen. As Jerry told Petra, who okayed the hire by phone, Layla fit the CRISPR requirements and then some. Even more importantly, Bao and Josef both swore she was capable of jumping in and contributing to their efforts until her CRISPR skills were needed.

She rented a studio cottage in Pacifica, a 45-minute drive from Elethea in good traffic. She went back to her dawn surfing habits, stopping home for a quick breakfast and shower, then heading over the hill to Silicon Valley once the morning traffic stopped. If the surf was particularly good, she'd arrive at work at about 10:30, stay and take her dinner there, and head home in the evening. She also kept a change of clothes in her cube, and when she worked late, as Mona predicted, the sleep room came in handy.

31

Dealer's Choice

"TALK ABOUT PERFORMANCE ANXIETY," Jerry says, surveying the assembled group.

"Just imagine us naked," Zoe says, helpfully.

"That's usually how his performance anxiety begins," Alice says.

Jerry waits a beat for the laughter to die down. "Thanks, hon. Okay, let's get started."

The training session has its roots with Mona. With her previous two startups—one a cybersecurity company, the other developing algorithms to track population trends—she'd made no effort to learn what they produced. As she explained to Eleni, you don't need a PhD to order office supplies. But longevity, especially if it had to do with her own life and that of her children, was another issue. In their monthly operational review meetings, when she started asking Petra to explain the technology and her thinking behind some of her decisions, Petra suggested that if she wanted answers she could really understand, Jerry was her guy.

"When we were being courted by the Hydras," Petra told Mona, "I kept losing them, trying to explain our underlying technology. Finally, Jerry gently suggested that he give it a try, that he'd had to explain science to Alice and his two sons for the past twenty years. And voila. The funding was approved the next day. So yeah, Jerry's your guy."

Once Eleni heard about the informal tutoring session, she was eager to join, saying she wanted to be able to talk to her daughter semi-intelligently about her work. When Petra mentioned the training at the Wednesday night gathering, the class size grew to five, with Izaak, Zoe, and Alice inviting themselves along for the ride. "I know you and Petra try to keep company business out of these sessions," Zoe had said at their most recent Wednesday get-together, "but when it does arise, you lose us. If you're going to be soaking in this science for the next couple of years, it would be nice to have an idea of what the hell you're up to."

· · ·

The group is using a conference table and chairs that Mona found on one of the repo furniture websites she follows. With startup failure rates in the 90 percent range, bargains are a must. The chairs are plastic of varying colors. One splurge came at Petra's request, with Mona having the conference room walls sprayed with the whiteboard treatment Petra enjoyed in her Salvana office.

Jerry starts from scratch, explaining how Petra combined her MIT and Werner work with the technologies on her grid. Having gotten the okay from Eleni to talk about her medical condition, he explains how their attempt at diagnosis was the final piece in the discovery of what one of the Hydras termed "the Methuselah protein."

Wrapping up the introduction, he turns to Eleni. "I hope you're impressed at what a genius you raised."

"She says you're an equal partner in the discovery."

"Hardly. She's Michelangelo. I'm the guy handing up the paint brushes. I'll take credit for performing the tests that led to the discovery, but the ideas and the research, that's all Petra."

He takes a sip of his cappuccino, the yield from the other luxury item that Mona purchased, arguing that coffee was a necessity, not a luxury. Licking the foam from his mustache, he walks over to one of the whiteboard walls. "The discovery of this protein is a big deal, potentially a huge one, depending on where it leads. We're not going to be the only ones developing solutions based on it, but if things go as we hope, we'll be the first. Unlike major biotech companies, however, we've got the time and resources for only one shot, so we'd better get it right.

"Alright, now let me tell you what we intend to do with Petra's discovery." He writes "5 Steps, 3 Bets, 1 Secret Weapon" along the left side of the board. "Everything I've discussed with you so far, that's all theory. Our job now is to prove that theory."

Jerry briefly outlines the same five steps he described to Alice when the two of them met with Petra at The Left Bank restaurant: characterizing the protein, including its DNA sequence and 3D structure; creating an antibody to detect the protein in subsequent tests; confirming the protein has an effect on aging at the cellular level (proof of concept); manipulating DNA to prevent the protein from accumulating in the cells and then testing those manipulations in short-lived animal species (nematode worms and fruit flies, in Elethea's case); then designing one or more formulations and testing them in mice and higher up the animal kingdom, with the ultimate goals being human clinical testing and FDA approval.

"So far, we've established proof of concept, which means we've established that the protein we've discovered has some effect on the aging process."

He turns back to the table. "You like to gamble, Eleni?"

"On occasion. Not like Petra, but a girlfriend and I go to Vegas twice a year."

"Ever play roulette?"

"Rarely. It feels like a loser's game. I like blackjack. I feel like I have a little control there."

"You're a smart woman. Back to roulette. The more squares you put your money on, the better your chances of winning, right? Large companies like Salvana have the luxury of putting their money on as many squares as possible in their search for a longevity solution."

"While startups like Elethea don't have those resources and have to be extremely careful where they place their bets," Izaak chimes in.

"Exactly. We've put all our resources—money, time, and people—behind three bets related to our mystery protein." He points to that line on the board. "Bet number 1 is that this protein's activity can be influenced by something called 'epigenetics.'" He pauses and smiles as the group looks around, as if seeing who's following him and who's lost already. "Before your eyes glaze over, I've had to explain epigenetics to friends for years. For a complicated technology, the explanation is pretty simple."

He writes *DNA* on the wall. "Think of your life as a movie, hopefully a long one. The cells that make up your body are the actors and other elements you need to make that movie. DNA, or genetics, is the script, telling both the actors and the crew what to do and say. So if genetics is screenwriting, epigenetics is the director, turning that script into a movie. You with me so far?" To a person, the heads at the table nod.

"The director doesn't have to change the lines in the script to determine how those lines are delivered, and which parts get more or less emphasis. In the same way, epigenetic changes don't necessarily change the DNA itself but can influence how the DNA is read and used."

Zoe raises her hand. "Can you give some examples of what kinds of things could be considered epigenetics?"

"Sure. All kinds of things, including diet, exercise, stress, and exposure to pollutants, can trigger epigenetic changes, meaning how the DNA 'story' is experienced in the body. You've probably heard that exposure to UV radiation from the sun can trigger premature aging of the skin and skin cancer, right?" Everyone nods. "Well, UV radiation is an example of epigenetics in action. UV rays don't do anything to change the sequence of DNA in your body, but they can cause changes in how the genes you *do* have act. In one person's body the UV rays might suppress just enough of certain protective processes to allow skin damage or cancer to take hold."

"Thanks, that helps," Zoe says.

"Okay. Let's stay with the script metaphor to discuss bet number 2. This one comes from Petra and, in addition to the protein itself, is a major distinguisher between us and the competition. Most, if not all, of the companies in the longevity space start with the ending of the movie—death. And they think, now that they know the ending, they can work backwards from there and develop a great script for a long life. Petra believes in starting from the beginning, with our core DNA. And since we know what ending we want—a long, healthy life—we make corrections the moment we see the script going off track."

He cocks his head and looks at Mona. "You're the one who calls herself techno-phobic. You still with me?"

"Yeah. The movie analogy helps."

"OK, on to bet number 3. Staying with our movie analogy, we just need to determine the best editing tool for our script. And for that we're going to use something called CRISPR. Think of it as a DNA editor. Just like a movie editor reviews multiple shots and arranges them in a certain sequence, CRISPR does the same with your DNA. It's like a molecular pair of scissors that can delete, change, or repair your DNA, like deleting, moving, or adding scenes to the movie. Using Petra's approach of identifying aging in its earliest stages, CRISPR can edit out the harmful or malfunctioning part of specific genes in their earliest stages, ideally making it possible for that person to live a long, full life."

Jerry looks at the faces in the room. "Any questions so far?"

Izaak shifts in his seat and says, "The three points make sense on their own, but I'm confused about how the CRISPR part, which makes changes to the DNA, jives with the epigenetics part, which doesn't change the DNA. And how would they work together to increase longevity?"

"Great question," Jerry says. "It turns out that, in addition to using CRISPR to edit DNA sequences, we can also use it as an epigenetic agent, meaning it can control how genes are expressed. We project that we can use CRISPR to turn specific genes on or off without changing their sequence, or to change how cells respond to other epigenetic changes."

He looks at the mix of frowns and nods. "Think of it this way. Imagine your genes as light bulbs in a house. Epigenetics is like the light switches and dimmers that control those bulbs. Epigenetic factors can flip some switches on or off or adjust how brightly particular genes 'shine.' While the light bulbs—genes—themselves don't change, how they're used and controlled can vary greatly."

Izaak points at the white board. "What's the secret weapon?"

"That's our magic accelerant for every phase of our solution. And it's something no one else has. It's Petra and her AI system. As most of you know, she's been creating and refining sophisticated AI systems since her grad school days, when AI was still considered some futuristic mumbo-jumbo. As AI has matured, she's been able to further supercharge her system, giving her—and

Elethea—the ability to do simulations and projections with far less data than was previously possible." He looks around the table. "Petra's AI system will shave years off our research trajectory."

"OK, now play all of that out in terms of longevity," says Izaak.

"And don't forget your audience," Alice cautions. "Not all of us have the training or background that Izaak has."

"Okay," Jerry says, smiling. "As we age, some of the genes that repair components in our cells become less active. We need a warning sign, like a flickering light, that tells us that one of the bulbs in our house is about to go out. The problem may be fixable, like a loose wire, or it may be permanent, like a failing bulb. We believe in fixing it either at first flicker or before, if we can anticipate it.

"To Izaak's question about how this fits into extended longevity. We believe the protein we discovered—you all know it as BFD150—is involved in the aging process, perhaps even critical to it. We believe we can use CRISPR technology to turn certain genes associated with this protein back on—rebooting them, so to speak—or turn off other genes, to affect how much of this protein accumulates in the body's cells. Those are just suppositions for right now, but we're not only confident in its impact on the aging process, we think this discovery could have major implications for diseases that, until now, have been regarded as incurable."

"Which is what Petra has spent her life before Salvana studying," Eleni says, the pride seeping into the words.

"How far along are you in this process?" Izaak asks.

"Just getting started. Remember, the Hydras funded a theory. We're in the process of proving that theory correct. Once that's done, we'll determine what processes—in both aging and disease—our protein affects and how. Then we'll put CRISPR to work, changing or deleting the things that cause us to age. Or die. And throughout the process, Petra's AI system will keep us moving along well ahead of what we believe any other groups will be able to achieve. And that's Elethea 101. Or, as Zoe puts it, Elethea for Dummies."

32

Under The Gun

IT'S THE MORNING OF the board presentation. Petra decides to go for a run rather than head to The Ascent. She dresses in layers and is lacing her running shoes when her email alert pings. Thinking it has to be Jerry at this early hour, she opens it. She recognizes the photo on the screen immediately. It's the Eiger, one of the most dangerous and difficult climbs in Europe. That photo then fades and is replaced by a series of photos, all of them climbers who have died pursuing their sport. The message closes with the warning: *Be careful out there*.

Unnerved, Petra sits down in her home office chair and stares at the screen. This is the third anonymous email she's received since she left Salvana. There was the one about her family, a second one that scrolled the names of startups that failed, with a query at the end: *Who's next?* And now this one. After the second message she called Izaak and brought her laptop to Stanford. Izaak tried all morning to crack the identity, or at least the point of origin, of the messages, but came up empty.

"Whoever this is, they obviously know a lot about you as well as how to avoid detection," he said. "That makes them doubly dangerous."

. . .

She starts to initiate her own security search, but then stops. This is exactly what this attack is intended to do. Make her lose her focus and spend her time pursuing the source. She shuts down her computer and heads for the door.

She drives in the early morning light to a park in the hills to the west of Stanford. Open sunrise to sunset, the Dish is a unique Bay Area destination. A combination of hiking/running trail and eco preserve, it takes its name from the 150-foot diameter radio antenna dish that dates back to the Sixties. In an area where technology recreates itself every five to ten years, the still-active Dish is a revered dinosaur, its jaw gaping open to the heavens.

As she stretches before starting her run, she assesses the weather and decides to keep her lightweight jacket on. Then she starts off.

The park has three paths, each with its own level of difficulty. She goes with the hilliest of the group, wanting to drain the anxiety she's feeling about both the email and the upcoming presentation to the board. But because of its hills, it's also the least-traveled route, so she puts her Mace and whistle in the jacket pocket before starting out.

She runs easily, but at a crisp pace, taking the hills as they come. She normally runs with her earbuds in, listening to music or a podcast. But today she keeps the buds out so that she can monitor her surroundings.

Halfway through the run she becomes aware of a runner behind her. She picks up her pace, but so does the trailing runner. Petra reaches into her pocket and takes out her Mace. Then she slows her pace, allowing—or forcing—the runner to pass her by. Which he does.

She picks up the pace again and puts the Mace back in her pocket. Up ahead, she knows, the path forks, the main route continuing flat until the parking lot, the less-traveled route hillier and arduous. As she nears the decision point, she sees a runner stopped up ahead. She tries to remember what the earlier runner was wearing, but nothing stands out as distinctive. She takes the hillier route and attacks the inclines, her knees pistoning.

She feels, more than sees or hears, the runner behind her. Whether it's the same runner as before or not, she can't be sure. Taking no chances, she takes a hard left turn and leaves the path, running and climbing up the steep wooded face. She hears a voice from below but can't make out what it's saying. She gains the top of the hill, gets her bearings, then heads back to the parking lot.

• • •

"What's your take?" Jerry asks her. They're in the bar down the street from to the Headwaters office where the board meeting took place, waiting for Freddy and Keeley to join them. "Was it a stalker? Or worse?"

"I don't know," Petra answers. "But between the email and then the runner on a trail I usually have to myself, I was pretty shaken."

"This is scary stuff, Petra. Is it something we want to tell the board about? Or the police?"

"Not the police, for sure. And tell them what? As for the board, I may tell Freddy, and we can give his security firm another shot at the emails. But if Izaak and his team can't crack it, I'm not optimistic."

She shakes her head, as if to clear her thoughts and move on to another topic. "Speaking of the board, how do you think we did? I think we nailed it."

"I do, too," Jerry says. "But I'm still confused about why we were meeting in the first place, and why we were presenting so soon after our last meeting. Not that much has changed with the product or the company."

"That's all Freddy. He calls it a dry run for future investors, that we're presenting to them not as our board, but as if they were new investors."

"Why do we need more money? We've been careful with our spend so far and we've got plenty in the bank."

"Freddy and Keeley both agree that the best time to raise money is when you already have money. You're working from strength rather than desperation. Also, do it when you've got good news, which we do. Now that we can show proof of concept, it's an indicator to new investors that we're for real, that this is the time to get on board."

· · ·

As Elethea marks its first anniversary, there's plenty to celebrate. Hiring has gone well, with Jerry and Petra assembling a world-class team. Over the past 12 months they've added six scientists: cell and molecular biologists with expertise in genetic engineering, gene expression, protein structure, and preclinical testing.

As with the office equipment and facilities, Mona has worked her magic in outfitting the lab. Though she still doesn't know what each piece of equipment does or how it fits into the longevity solution, she takes Jerry's wish list and uses her own network to find biotech companies in distress or those that have recently closed their doors. Then she swoops in, checkbook at the ready, and secures the needed equipment for a fraction of its list price.

Legally, as Freddy and Petra have reported to the board in previous meetings, Elethea is ahead of the competition in two key areas. Sandy Beukema, their part-time general counsel, has done a good job on the regulatory front, working with the FDA to determine which division they'll need to work with, what tests need to be conducted and under what conditions, and how to present their findings.

Just as important, Sandy has worked with an intellectual property firm to begin the patent process. "Being first to file is important," she explained to Petra. "But explaining and validating the technology you used to verify its existence is critical."

Naming is also a part of the IP/patent process. Initially the Dicks referred to the discovery as "the Methuselah protein." Then Keeley came up with BFD150 as a stopgap. Though the name was never intended as an official moniker, the board surprised Petra and Jerry by suggesting they use it for their filing— not just for the protein, but also for future compounds they'll develop based on the protein's properties. Legal blessed the name as it tracked the common convention of letters and numbers.

"It *is* a Big Fucking Deal," Zac opined. "And the 150 reminds people of how long they could live. I say go with it." And so they did.

• • •

"I don't know how much scientific detail investors want—or need—to know," Jerry had said as they prepared for the presentation. "I mean, do they want to know why we used fibroblast cell senescence for our early proof of concept tests? Or how CRISPR works? Should I prepare at that level?"

"I wouldn't, unless they ask," Petra says. "But who knows? Maybe they'll want to nerd out on everything. Since science is our major differentiator from the competition, I'd go deep until they tell us to stop."

"OK, so how about this for my closing slide?" Jerry turned his laptop around to show a multi-colored, spiraling image, equal parts science and psychedelia, reminiscent of a light show from one of Jerry's revered early Dead shows. In reality, it's an AlphaFold 3D image of the protein, replete with spirals and interlocking components.

"Absolutely. Let's keep it up there for the Q and A."

Jerry closes his computer and the visual goes away.

"You want to grab a quick bite before we head over?" Petra asks.

"Won't they have food there?"

"Probably. But I don't want to present with food in my mouth. And I don't want to present on an empty stomach. Come on. My treat."

• • •

Elethea's first year of operation has been a learning curve for all parties. For the BSDs it's been ongoing training in the world of science, biotech especially. Schedules, government regulations, the importance of peer reviews—all this is new to Freddy, Zac, and Trina. As is directing a team as reserved and new to the business world as Petra and Jerry.

The standard Valley startup model doesn't pertain to Elethea. The Dicks are used to what Freddy calls "the Penn and Teller" model, named for the magic act in which one of the performers never says a word. In the tech-based Valley startup world the role of Penn—confident, business-savvy, a strong communicator—is played by the aspiring CEO. While he (and it's almost always a man) may be as technically versed as the Chief Technology Officer, the would-be CEO has absorbed every book, blog, and podcast on leadership they can find and lapped up advice from other CEOs and VCs like a thirsty dog. He tends to do all the talking in meetings, putting the CTO (Teller) in the role of color commentator. It's almost always the case that the board has to restructure the company's early pitches to give the CTO a stronger role.

Elethea has been different from the start, not just because of its scientific focus. Not only is biotech new to most of the board, it's proven to be a different species of startup. Not just because of its science-based caution, but because the hubris that is inherent in tech startups is missing. Of the two, Jerry is the better storyteller, so he tends to play a larger role in presentations than a CTO would on the tech side. His casual style, plus his open admiration of what Elethea has developed so far, evokes contagious enthusiasm. Which is a nice balance to Petra, whose presentations are still a bit stiff. It's clear that she'd rather be giving Jerry's part of the presentation than focusing on the business components. And unlike many of their tech counterparts, both are scrupulously conservative when it comes to schedules and product capabilities.

The challenge for the board is to get Petra ready to be the public face of Elethea and longevity. Media training will help, but that's still a ways off. A quick study when it comes to learning the operational side of the business, she has a command of all the components of the company. But there's little joy in her delivery, little excitement. Her answers are exact, but don't encourage the second and third questions that lead to lively discussions and a favorable ranking of the team. And "she's too damned honest," as Zac puts it. Meaning she hasn't learned the corporate art of diverting hard questions in ways that are truthful but shade that truth in a positive light.

On-site at Elethea, Petra is guilty of spending too much time in the lab, either working through some of her own ideas or interfacing with the team. Keeley, speaking on behalf of the board, has told her more than once to stay the hell out of the lab and to concentrate on leading the company. Petra counters that, even with her AI models speeding up the review process, delivery of a finished product is still years off, giving her plenty of time to build out her business skills. While the product is in its nascent stage, she argues that she's needed in the lab, at least part-time.

. . .

Today's board meeting was in response to the good news coming out of the Elethea lab. With the company on the right track science-wise, the BSDs will soon face a new funding decision. After making the extraordinary decision to be the sole funder of Elethea, the board will have to decide whether to double-down on its investment or open it up to other firms or individuals. Which is why they scheduled today's presentation, a dry run to see whether Petra and Jerry are ready to meet with a less forgiving crowd.

"If we're treating them as investors, are you worried that our presentation was a bit too technical?" Jerry asked.

"I don't think so. They need to know what they're buying. And our science—the theory, the protein, epigenetics, and all the rest—that's our core and what makes us such a good investment."

33

A Bad Beat

AS IT TURNED OUT, the board had no questions about DNA or CRISPR or any other part of their presentation. Petra and Jerry, sitting in the bar waiting for Freddy—and Keeley, who also attended the presentation—to join them, regard this as a good sign. More than that, they take it as a sign that they nailed it. Naturally humble by nature, they're damned proud of themselves. Now they're just waiting for confirmation. And kudos.

Nursing an IPA and a glass of Primitivo respectively, they keep an eye on the door. After a few minutes it opens, and Freddy and Keeley enter. Petra tries to read their faces as they approach. She gets nothing from Freddy, which is par for the course. He was hard to read in the poker game in LA and is even harder to read in board meetings. The closest hint she gets is that his walk is more purposeful than casual. Keeley, on the other hand, should never play poker: Her face is drawn and she's not looking over at their table as they approach.

They order drinks before getting down to business. Freddy orders a scotch neat, Keeley does the same but on the rocks. Petra breaks the ice.

"I'm gathering from your expressions that the meeting didn't go as well as Jerry and I think it did."

"I'm surprised, as good as you are at poker, that you didn't pick up on that during the meeting," Freddy says. "And make the appropriate changes."

"I was too nervous, too focused on the presentation. What did I miss?"

"A lot," Freddy says. He turns to Keeley. "I saw you taking notes throughout the presentation. Why don't you start?"

Keeley settles herself on the stool, then looks at Petra. "Way too technical, to begin. Especially you, Petra. The whole thing felt like we were meeting with two chief scientists and waiting for the CEO. Who never showed up."

"That's a bit harsh," Jerry says. "Petra..."

"I'll defend myself, Jer," Petra says, then turns back to Keeley. "Go on."

"Science-wise, you guys were fine," Keeley continues. "Especially you, Jerry. You explained things, including new developments, without making your listener feel stupid. But Petra, you came across like someone trying to impress us with her science degrees. If I were an investor—and remember, that was our role today—I'd say we're all buttoned up on the science side—maybe too much—now let's find us a CEO."

"Let me chime in here," Freddy says. He faces Petra, his face still a mask. "What do you think your major responsibility is as CEO?"

Petra's eyes leave Freddy and pick a spot on the wall just past the top of his head. This feels like one of those moments of Rubicon-like importance and she's not clear what her own answer is, much less what Freddy's looking for.

"To marshal all of Elethea's resources and direct them to bringing our product to market," she says finally, trying to sound authoritative, though she feels anything but.

"Even after I told you the purpose of the meeting?"

"Can we stop with the Socratic questions, Freddy? What am I missing here?"

He holds her gaze. "Speaking for your current investors, and for the future audiences we told you to prepare for, we have one question: How are you going to make us money? You didn't answer that. You didn't even come close."

Petra doesn't show any emotion. She just turns her head toward Keeley and raises her eyebrows. Keeley shrugs, her face somewhere between sad and disappointed. "Freddy showed me the PowerPoint presentations for companies at the same stage as Elethea that he gave you to help prepare for this afternoon. All of them began with the problem at hand, the market opportunities, and the different paths to a solution—meaning your competition. You did a solid job of differentiating yourself from the competition, but your focus was all on their scientific approaches. Jerry could have—correction, *should* have—done that. You should have focused on your funding, go-to-market plans, and projected early market traction."

Petra feels her footing beginning to give way, then corrects herself. It's past that point. She's slipped, she just doesn't know how much. "I thought those presentations were for structure— on how best to communicate where the different companies and their technologies stand."

"Even if that were the case," Freddy says, his voice as tight as his face, "I don't know how many times we have to say this: The underlying science, the theories and tests—those are Jerry's responsibility, not yours. Your job is to manage the business, find the right market for your solution, and make us a ton of money. I got no confidence today that you were the best person to do that."

Petra feels the heat flow into her face and hopes it's not a visible tell. There's no money on the table, but she feels like far more than chips or money are in immediate play. And there's no room to bluff.

"I advised you that today could be your opportunity to take a big step forward as CEO," Keeley joins in. "When I saw your presentation open with the science behind Elethea, I moaned to myself. But then I thought that slide—two slides, tops—would be the bridge from science to business, which would then direct the meeting from that point on. But ..." She shakes her head, a sad gesture, not a contentious one.

Petra is flustered, then gathers herself. Her initial reaction is to push back, but as she looks for traction in what Freddy and Keeley are saying, she finds none. As she replays the separate conversations with the two, she realizes they were dropping hints she hadn't picked up on.

Her second reaction is to take an aggressively defensive stance, to remind both Keeley and Freddy that she didn't want to be CEO in the first place, that both had pressured her to take the job. But she plays that conversation out on both sides quickly in her head, realizing it comes off as whining and petulant.

Petra is aware of a warning tickle in the back of her mind. In poker she's proud of never having gone on tilt, which is when a player, after suffering a bad beat, acts angrily and irrationally, playing recklessly, almost out of control. It's embarrassing to watch, and she feels herself slipping into that territory. She starts to take a stalling sip of wine before remembering that the glass is empty. She puts the glass down and looks first at Keeley, then Freddy.

"Is this the moment when the board shows the floundering CEO the door?" Petra asks.

Freddy looks surprised at the directness of the question. "Before I answer that, let me share an analogy—or metaphor, I never know the difference—that might help this conversation. Do either of you follow baseball?"

Petra nods at Jerry. "He's a fanatic. I've picked up a bit from him over the years."

"In baseball," Freddy launches in, "there's a constant struggle between the pitcher and batter, each one constantly adjusting to the other." He looks at Jerry. "Right?"

"'The game within the game,' they call it," Jerry says.

"And in that game, there are two kinds of hitters. There are the ones who know what pitch they hit best—let's say it's a belt-high fastball away—and they wait for the pitcher to make a mistake, and they hammer it. It's a successful strategy initially, but only short-term."

Again, he looks at Jerry, who nods and picks up the narrative. "Every year there are five or ten guys like that. They look like they're headed for Cooperstown, and then they're out of baseball three years later."

Freddy smiles at Jerry's knowledge. "The other type of hitter—the one who *does* make it to Cooperstown ..."

Keeley looks at the confusion on Petra's face. "Cooperstown is where the Baseball Hall of Fame is located."

"Sorry," Freddy says to Petra. "That hitter sits down with the catcher on his own team and says, 'how would you pitch to me?' Or he asks, 'what are the holes in my zone?' And then he spends the off-season learning to hit the pitches that have been getting him out."

Freddy quits talking. Petra is grateful that he doesn't bore in on her with his famously flat eyes, putting all the pressure on her to respond. He looks instead at Jerry to see if Jerry has another baseball anecdote. But Jerry, sensing the gravity of the moment, just nods, a single dip.

"And you're saying I'm the one waiting on the fastball," Petra says.

"You are," Freddy says. "You're spending way too much time in the lab, where you're comfortable. And you're not pushing yourself in the areas where you're not. Or at least we're not seeing any evidence of it."

The last few words hang over the table, deadening the atmosphere. Petra appreciates Freddy's frankness and that there's no meanness behind the words. But she's not sure where he's leaving things.

"So who's got a decision to make at this point, you or me?"

Again, the direct nature and tone seems to catch them off guard. But Freddy's response is equally direct. "You've got a decision to make. We've already made ours."

"And that is ..." She's not sure she wants to hear the answer, but she needs to ask.

As if tired of dominating the conversation, Freddy turns to Keeley and hands her the reins with a lift of his chin. "The board is agreed that they want you to succeed as CEO, but you have to convince us ...." She motions with a wag of her hand at Freddy, then herself, "that you want the job. Really want it. And if you do, show us that you're open to some changes, such as Freddy taking on the role of COO and being on-site one day a week."

"And if I don't convince you? Or if I don't want to remain as CEO?"

"Then we—and you—have a problem. Because we already have a Chief Scientist, one who's got twenty years' experience managing other scientists. And I don't think it would work, the founder joining the team as just another scientist."

"So you're saying what, that there's no role for me in my own company?"

"It quit being your company the moment you accepted the Hydras' money," Keeley explains, her tone patient but with a cautioning tinge. "There would be a role for you, but I don't know how attractive you'd find it. Let's call it Chief Evangelist. Under this scenario, the board hires an operational CEO. You become the face of longevity, both in recruiting partners and early customers, and later, with the press."

"I would have no scientific role?"

Freddy answers this one. "Off-line you can be as involved with the product as Jerry is comfortable with. You can feed him ideas and he can keep you up-to-date on how everything is progressing. But you do it from home. The lab is off limits."

Petra feels hollow. The conversation doesn't feel scripted and yet she doesn't see how they could have wound up anywhere except where they are at this moment. She may not be in danger of tilting, but she needs to regroup.

"Do you need an answer tonight?"

"No, but soon."

"I'd like to take a day then, to think things through on my end and to talk to Jer. Can we do a Zoom tomorrow at this time?"

"A decision this important. Let's do it in person," Keeley says. "How about right back here tomorrow at five?"

34

Doubling Down

PETRA DOES HER MORNING WORKOUT at home but forgoes The Ascent, opting instead for a long walk on the Shoreline bike/hike trail. The trail hugs the shore of a finger of the San Francisco Bay, extending down to northern San Jose. Dressed in layers against the early morning mist, she walks for over an hour, her hands warming in her pockets, her face rosy from the cold.

As she walks, she rewinds the past year in her mind and all the crossroad decisions she came to, what she might have done differently, and then plays those scenarios out as if she'd made those alternative decisions. She envisions herself staying at Salvana, joining another startup as Chief Scientist, starting Elethea but with an Enterprise-In-Residence in her position. Each decision would have lessened the pressures and still advanced the protein, but as she runs through each in her mind, she comes to the conclusion that she'd made the right decision, leaving Salvana and going out on her own.

But Keeley was right: It wasn't her company anymore. Still, she and her AI system—along with past simulations and those to come—were critical to the company's long-term success. The question was, in what role?

Petra walks briskly initially, establishing a rhythm that lets her concentrate on the decision ahead. Her mouth tastes of copper, like it's filled with melting pennies. It's a foreign experience.

She wonders if there's a new type of pollen in the air, then realizes it's the taste of failure.

As a scientist, failure is a familiar experience. But that kind of failure is academic, clinical; it's to be expected, even welcomed, as part of the scientific process. This is different; it's an indictment of her and her abilities.

She ups the pace into a half run. The taste dissipates but doesn't go away completely. She plays back the meeting with the board, then the prep meetings with Keeley and Freddy. The poker player in her is embarrassed at misreading the room so badly. She remembers the sideways glances among the Hydras and Keeley. What she interpreted as nods of affirmation at her updates she now accurately and embarrassingly reinterprets as notes of shared concern. Alarm, even.

The rational side of her recognizes the rabbit hole of self-recrimination she's heading down. She allots herself another few minutes of flagellation and then it's time to get to the business at hand.

The walk doesn't bring the clarity she was hoping for. Not ready to face the office and the questions from the team about how the presentation went, she routes herself to The Ascent.

She parks and lets herself in. Instead of getting into her climbing gear, she walks over to the main climbing wall and looks at her route. This time, instead of lowering herself into her normal viewing position, she walks back and forth in front of the wall, stopping now and again to get a different perspective. She spies a singleton off to the west side of her regular route. It's black, signaling that it can be used by any color route. She knows that Spyder likes to use singletons as feints, so she's dismissed it in the past. This time she incorporates it into her mental image of the wall.

She moves 20 feet to the left, keeping her eye on her route. She lowers herself and settles in, back against the wall, her knees drawn up. She closes her eyes and envisions the route, this time with the singleton as part of her mental picture. Not meditating, exactly, but calming her mind and letting the ideas come.

She sits there, eyes closed, for ten minutes. When she opens her eyes, her gaze goes directly to the singleton. And there it is.

• • •

She is in her climbing gear when Spyder walks in. He nods at her and starts towards his office, then he turns back and looks at her closely.

"You solved it, didn't you?"

"Maybe. Let's find out. You up for a little belaying?"

Once the two are in their harnesses, Petra takes off. This time, instead of heading straight up, she moves off to the left side, where there are two green holds that Petra has always dismissed as more of Spyder's distractions. But from this perspective the singleton makes sense. She moves her left hand to grab it and swings her body up, using the momentum and leverage to bypass the ledge that has defeated her for the past two months. A minute later, she's at the top. In all her time at The Ascent, she's never rung the bell at the top of the wall. Too much look-at-me for her taste, too amateurish. Not this time. This time she's Quasimodo.

• • •

She arrives at the office mid-morning to find Mona waiting for her. The look on Mona's face dampens the enthusiasm of her victory at The Ascent.

"What's up?"

"Got a minute? I need to discuss something with you."

The two walk to the conference room. The moment the door clicks shut, Mona turns to Petra. "It's your mom."

"What happened?"

"I went to the bathroom and found her on the floor, trying to get up. She said the floor was wet. Then she saw herself in the mirror, the wig off to the side, and just broke down. We sat on the floor and I just held her, let her cry. Then she told me about her disease."

Petra stares out the heavy glass and across the lab at her mother, who is at her desk, a little unsteady. Petra starts to head over, but Mona puts an arm out, blocking her path.

"You can't go over there. She swore me to secrecy. But if this is a symptom of her disease, it'll happen again."

Petra returns to her cube, occasionally sneaking glances at her mom. Finally, she gets up and walks over to Jerry's cube. "I'm working on something new. But I need fresh blood. Can you draw some of mine and do one of our standard scans?"

"No problem." He looks at her closely. "What are you going to tell the board tonight about your decision?"

"I'm still working it through, trying to figure out what's best for everyone."

"Well, you know my vote. And I'm speaking for everyone in this building."

"Thanks." She looks around the work area, then back at Jerry. "I can't think straight here. I'm heading home. Please send the blood results there."

• • •

It's 4:15 and Petra is getting dressed to meet with the board when the blood results arrive from Jerry. She loads them into her system, the screen showing her BFD150 levels from the earlier bloodwork, a 1.2. As the data gets processed, a new line forms. It moves past 1.2, ramping up quickly and settling in at 2.7."

"Well, damn," she says. She erases the data and repeats the analysis. The number settles again at 2.7.

"Damn," she says, and heads for the door.

. . .

At a quarter to five, Petra and Jerry are sitting in the bar awaiting the board members. Keeley walks in and makes a beeline to
their table. "Anything you want to discuss before they show up?"
she asks, taking a seat without being invited.

At Petra's confused look, she says, "This is where I earn my
2 percent, and why I didn't take a seat on the board. So I could
represent them to you, and you to them."

"In that role, you might have given us a heads-up that we
were walking into a meeting where the trap was already set."

Keeley lets the anger hover over the table before answering.
"I could have, but that would have been unfair to the board.
Also, I happen to agree with them."

"Good to know which side you're on," Petra says.

Keeley again takes her time. "You know, the time we have
right now is going to be a lot more productive if you lose the attitude. You're not a victim here. You're a CEO who's in over her
head. Which, by the way, is the majority of startup CEOs at
some time or another in their first year. Yesterday was your
wakeup call. How you respond is entirely up to you."

Petra lets her eyes roam the bar, taking her time before
answering. She's embarrassed at the tone she just took, not just
because it was rude but because she showed her hand.

"Jerry and I talked earlier this afternoon. As you'd guess, he
was supportive of whatever I decided." She smiles at him.
"Which was no help. He said we could make Option Two work,
but I don't think that option would be fair to him or his team."

"I know you didn't ask my opinion," Keeley says, "but I
think that's a wise decision. So what about Option One?"

"Let's wait for the others. I don't want to say this twice."

Keeley and Jerry spend the next few minutes talking baseball and the two trades the Giants made that week. At five o'clock, the door opens, Freddy holding it so Trina and Zac can pass through. He motions to the waitress and points toward the table where Petra, Jerry, and Keeley are waiting.

"However this plays out," he says, pulling out a stool, "it'll go better with a drink." The waitress takes their orders and leaves. All eyes turn to Petra.

"I don't quit things I start," she says. "You can fire me—and I'd understand why—but I won't quit."

"No one's asking you to quit," Trina says, "but tell us your thinking." Petra nods at the waitress as she puts the glass of wine in front of her. She waits until everyone has a sip and the waitress has departed.

"Yesterday caught me by surprise. And I don't deal well with surprises. So I went home, felt sorry for myself for an hour or so, cursed you guys for another hour or so, then poured myself a nice Zin and did an honest assessment."

She takes a sip of wine and looks around the table. "I want to be the CEO. And with the right training, which I gather will come from Freddy, and the right coaching," she nods at Keeley, "I can be a solid CEO. Maybe better than solid."

Surprisingly, it's Zac who speaks up. He raises his glass. "We hoped this would be your answer. And we agree with your assessment."

After they all clink glasses, Freddy says, "I'll be on-site Wednesdays, until we determine—you and I together—whether you need a full-time COO. Until then ..." He reaches down next to his chair and comes up with a large manila folder. "These are the three best business plans I've seen in my years at Headwaters. This time, yes, use them as templates. But learn from them as well. You'll present your business plan to the board a month from now. It will include your product plan, your sales strategy and initial sales plan, your hiring projections, and your go-to-market strategy, which will be heavy on influencing the market. Any questions?"

Petra has none. Neither does Jerry. "Great," Freddy says. "Then no more talk about work. Let's hear from Zac, who just got back from Burning Man."

35

The Inside Game

"WORMS AND FLIES? Really? When Jerry said the animal testing was going really well, I've gotta be honest, I wasn't thinking insects."

"Well, technically, the nematode worms are roundworms, which aren't insects. But I get what you mean."

"It's just that worms and insects sound so ... pedestrian, so unimpressive, given what we're up to here. Are they even in the animal kingdom?"

Bao and Josef both laugh. "They're definitely in the animal kingdom," says Josef.

Freddy has dropped by the Elethea lab and is talking with the two researchers. In an earlier meeting, Jerry encouraged Freddy to talk occasionally to the scientists, to give him first-hand access and insights into what's going on.

Josef and Bao explained the importance of moving from in vitro ("in the glass," the glass being test tubes) to in vivo ("within the living") experiments. It's common practice for labs to spend months or even years doing in vitro testing before moving to the in vivo phase. But Petra has collapsed that schedule at Elethea by putting AI to work. Combining her AI-powered models with her knowledge of the protein and desired solution, she's been able to quickly determine the appropriate tests for their proposed solution, as well as predict the outcome of different approaches.

"Got it," Freddy says. "But why begin with worms and flies?"

"For starters," says Bao, "specific species of nematode worms, as well as the *Drosophila melanogaster* species of fruit flies, are acknowledged as model systems for studying biology, meaning there's tons of data from years of research on them that we can employ as baselines. More importantly, both species have relatively short lifespans. That means we can do an experiment, track its progression over the full life of the worms or flies, get the results, adjust things, and do new experiments and refine things quickly, almost immediately. Obviously, you can't do the same with animals that live for years, rather than days or weeks."

Adds Josef, "And with the data from the short-lived species in hand, Petra's AI system will enable accurate, and very rapid, predictions in the longer-lived species, such as mice."

. . .

"How was the visit from Freddy?" Jerry asks Bao and Josef later that day.

"He gets what we're up to," says Bao. "But I don't see him bragging to his golf buddies about how this hot young company he's funding is doing amazing things with worms and flies."

Bao and Josef have been colleagues since their days at Salvana, where they were working on different projects. Now, at Elethea, they've become good friends, with the rest of the team referring to them either as "the boys" or "the odd couple." Born in China, Bao moved to California as a 3-year-old, when his engineer father took a job at Sun Microsystems. Growing up, Bao found most things easy: school, friendships, sports. His short but athletic stature and quick wit led to plenty of Jackie Chan references, which he chose to enjoy rather than find offensive.

Bao decided to study biology—undergrad at Stanford, graduate school at the University of Chicago—because it combined aspects of many of the other sciences, including chemistry and physics. His interest in the practical applications of biological research drew him to Salvana, where his research skills led Jerry to recruit him to Elethea.

Josef is also an immigrant kid, coming from Munich to Ann Arbor at 18. He followed a similar academic trajectory to Bao, studying biology first at the University of Michigan before getting his PhD at Yale. He's nearly a decade older than Bao, with a wife and a couple of kids whom he dotes on.

Standing a couple of inches over six feet tall, with elegant facial features topped by a plume of blond hair, Josef looks more like a Germanic warrior of old than a modern-day scientific researcher. His reserved manner, at least with people he's just met, gives no hint of his sharp intellect or technical prowess in the lab.

"They're like a married couple who complete each other's sentences," Jerry once noted of the two scientists. "But they come at the problems from such different perspectives that it's like one plus one equals three."

Jerry follows up with Freddy to make sure the new COO appreciates how far the team has come in so short a time. He explains the significance of the worm and fly tests exhibiting the same results as the in vitro proof of concept tests in the cell cultures, with higher concentrations of BFD150 causing the animals to age and die earlier than the control animals. Also, animals with higher concentrations of the protein have shorter-than-expected telomeres, the protective caps at the end of chromosomes—a classic sign of aging. What the team needs to do now, he explains, is figure out how to reverse whatever it is that BFD150 is doing to accelerate the aging process.

"So if I'm talking to prospective investors," Freddy says, "the takeaway is that, while we're still a long way from a longevity cure, we're definitely on the right track and ahead of the rest of the pack."

"Also, that thanks to Petra's AI simulations," Jerry pointedly adds, "we'll be far quicker to market than the competition."

36

Out of Position

AS GLASSES OF RED WINE are set down in front of the two women, Cheryl hands the server her credit card. "Keep it open." She raises her glass and tilts it at her companion. "I like a woman who drinks red wine. Primitivo, huh? I'll have to try it. I'm a Pinot girl, myself, but I'm always open to a new blend."

Petra raises her glass in answer. "Try it now, then. Seriously. Before my lips sully the rim." She extends the glass until it's next to Cheryl's. Cheryl puts down her Pinot, swirls Petra's wine a few times, then takes a sip. She nods approvingly. "A little stronger than I like usually, but it's smooth. I may have a new wine."

"Primitivo's just a new name for Zinfandel, I believe," Petra says. "But as I'm learning quickly, marketing and terminology matter."

"Tell me about it," Cheryl says. "I grew up in the South, and whenever I go back home, I marvel at how my side of grits at Waffle House is basically free, whereas the same food, now rebranded 'polenta,' is ten bucks at my favorite Italian restaurant."

"My favorite version of that is a wilted spinach salad. Regular spinach salad: seven bucks. Wilted spinach, add an extra two bucks. When the hell did 'wilted' become a positive attribute?"

It's five o'clock on a Sunday afternoon. The football games are over for the most part, with the exception of the Sunday Night game. Cheryl told her husband she'd be home in time to watch the second half with him. She and Petra are meeting in a bistro in Burlingame, a town just south of the San Francisco Airport, one safely out of the list of Silicon Valley watering holes where they might be spotted.

There's a pause in the conversation, one that's beginning to get awkward when Cheryl says, "Thanks for agreeing to meet. I have to think this wasn't how you envisioned spending your Sunday afternoon."

"Put it down to curiosity, if nothing else. Once you assured me this wasn't about Salvana versus Elethea, I was both curious and looking forward to it. Do you mind my asking what prompted the call?"

"Not at all," Cheryl says. "In a word: estrogen. I don't have a female counterpart in either Biz Dev or Project L." Petra looks confused: "The clever name we came up with for our longevity project. Also, I'm one of only two women on the management team: the other one is the recording secretary."

"I've never been a 'female counterpart' before," Petra says, though with a smile.

"Actually, this meeting was my husband's idea. I was moaning yet again about the lack of support and infrastructure I'm feeling at Salvana, as well as the unintentional sexism, and he said, what about you, that I'd always spoken highly of you and was disappointed when you left Salvana. I thought about it, and he was right. If we stay away from the proprietary stuff, there's no reason we can't be resources for each other. Hell, even friends. That is, if you're interested."

"I am. Once you called me, I remembered our first couple of meetings, how impressed I was with you and what I could learn from working with you. I'm not a big fan of the word 'mentor,' but you get the idea."

Cheryl nodded. Triggered by the suggestion from her husband, this meeting was the result of the frustration and management challenges that came with her dual role. While the Biz Dev part was running smoothly, managing Project L was proving to be more a managerial challenge than a scientific one. Thanks to Jake and the team, from Dr. Loper on down, explaining their approach and accomplishments in terms she could understand, she found herself capable of representing the project at all but the most technical levels. To the point that Loper wanted to give her an office in the Project L space, but Cheryl told him to keep it for the team, that she planned to be there one to two days a week at most, and a cube would do just fine.

The problem came with Salvana management. Her direct boss, Salvana's CEO, Scott Bonsall, told her at the start of Project L: "Welcome to matrix management. You may still report to me on paper, but everyone from the board on down is going to want to know how it's going, even though most of them have no idea what *it* is."

Which had proven to be the case. By phone or in person, people she barely knew but who were above her on the org chart would call at random times, asking for updates, pretending to be more familiar with the project and its underlying science than they actually were. And while everyone was aware of, and committed to, the ten-year schedule, the interest in Project L, at least initially, had to do with how the project was doing in comparison to Elethea, which they all knew to be on a three- to-five-year track.

Cheryl paused and smiled crookedly. "Those are the moments where I miss you the most. To handle all those goddamn updates."

Petra listened to Cheryl with a combination of interest and sympathy. She hadn't given Salvana much thought since leaving the company, but when she had, it was always with a nostalgia for her life there—being free to run her operation entirely as she saw fit, without having to deal with anything but the science. She realized now, listening to Cheryl, that this wouldn't have been the case had she stayed at Salvana. She would have been caught up in big-company politics and would have been even further away from her discovery than she was at Elethea.

She had been surprised at Cheryl's call but impressed at the honest emotions behind it. She remembered Cheryl's directness in their one-on-ones and in how she managed Biz Dev. She could have benefited from her counsel during her rocky initial tenure as CEO. "I'll tell you where I missed a mentor like you the most. It was when the board of my own company almost fired me."

An hour later they were still going strong. Cheryl never spoke of her private life at work and had told no one at Salvana—with the exception of HR—about her husband's accident. But she found herself sharing that information with Petra, along with the additional pressures it put on her, both on the salary front and the need to take health care insurance into any decision she might make. Petra, for her part, talked about the self-doubt that plagued every non-scientific decision she had made over the past year.

"The dreaded imposter's syndrome," Cheryl says with a chuckle. "You probably never suffered from it, growing up with math and science, a couple of very measurable fields. Management's a different world completely. Everyone's got some background in it, which makes them experts in their eyes. In my case, after fifteen years in the nonprofit sector, I finally shook the imposter feeling. But Kurt's accident forced me to join the world of big business—of stock prices, executive compensation, and multi-million-dollar budgets. And I was back to Imposter Syndrome 101 all over again."

Driving home from the meeting, Petra was encouraged by the restart of the relationship. Cheryl, outside of work, proved more relaxed, more caustic in her appraisals of everything from herself to Salvana. But what Petra had liked most about the past hour and a half was how constructive the conversation had been. Neither one had felt the need to trot out the 'woman in a man's world' complaints. In fact, both had commented on how egalitarian they found the world of scientists. The ability to do the work, making a breakthrough, that was what defined you. The conversation focused more on the challenges of being a stranger to new environments—science and big-company politics for Cheryl, CEO responsibilities in Petra's case.

When they parted that afternoon, Cheryl had surprised Petra—and possibly herself—by drawing Petra into a hug. And Petra, who had made it a practice over the years to get her hand outstretched early in any parting, eliminating the awkward hug-or-shake moment, had deliberately held her hand back. While it wasn't in her DNA to initiate a hug, she was glad that Cheryl had, and she was happy to reciprocate. And to agree to meet again.

37

Rules of the Game

"HERE'S THE GOOD NEWS about this phase of our relation-ship. I can teach you what I do. There's no way in the world you can teach me what you do."

"Do you mean what you do as a VC, or as my interim COO?"

"The latter. VCs all believe what we do can't be taught, like you can give us an ultrasound and we can predict what the full-grown individual will look like. No, I'm talking about the COO job. There's nothing magical about it. It's all common sense and basic business. Once you learn that, you could be a COO or CEO in any number of industries, not that you'd want to be. It's just a matter of breaking down the complexity of a corporation or business into measurable components, then managing your MBOs."

"MBOs?" Petra asks.

"Management By Objectives. Create measurable objectives for each component, track your progress, take corrective action as needed. Have a plan and make sure everyone's aware of it and their role in it. Then manage them—and yourself—by how well you achieve them. I can't imagine it's that different from what you scientists do in conceiving an idea or theory and then proving it out in different stages."

"Maybe not. Let's find out."

Two weeks have passed since Freddy and Keeley had their come-to-Jesus meeting with Petra, leading to her doubling down on her role as CEO and Freddy's installation as COO on a once-a-week basis. Today is his first day on-site in his new role. He's spent the morning with Jerry and the team and now has commandeered the conference room for a working lunch with Petra.

"Let's start with the most basic question," he says. "Why does Elethea exist?"

"After all the talk about measurable goals, you're starting with philosophy?" Petra says.

"I'm starting with the most practical issue: your reason for existence. What problem do you solve? What need do you meet? And who, specifically, needs it? If you can't answer those questions, you'll be out of business within a year. On the other hand, if you had an answer for all those questions, you'd be ahead of most startups. And you wouldn't need me."

"Doesn't death qualify as a problem?"

"No. Death is an inevitability, even with your breakthrough. The issue is when, and under what conditions, we die. Find a compelling way to state the problem and then begin every presentation, no matter who your audience is, with that slide."

Freddy stands up and walks over to the white board. Marker in hand, he turns to her. "There's someone I'll want to bring in when we're getting closer to going to market. She's the sharpest marketing mind I've ever encountered. Her name is Lisa Carroll. You'll like her. She challenges you, makes you think."

He uncaps the marker. "First time we met, she told me something so basic but so compelling that I use it with every startup I work with. She said the essence of marketing comes down to two questions: 'So what?' and 'Who cares?'" He writes both questions on the board, then taps the top one.

"Most companies, including mine, are great at the 'so what,' because it's their opportunity to explain what they've developed, usually in painfully excruciating detail."

He taps the other question. "But almost every company I've ever funded fell short when it came to the 'who cares' part of things. And the reason is that the 'who' is a lot more complicated than most companies know."

He draws a long line the width of the whiteboard, with arrow tips on either end, then a large "V" at the left arrow tip, an "F" on the right.

V  F

He caps the pen but stays standing. "The V stands for Vision, the F for Function. A successful company, by the time it goes to market, has to be equally strong on both ends of the spectrum. But here's the deal. Everyone thinks there are one or two audiences, or customers, for their product, when in fact there are six. And by the time you go to market you'll need a plan for each one."

He taps the V. "Vision is your long-term plan for the company. It shows the full range of your science, how that grows into a family of products, and projected initial revenue. Think of it as a blueprint of a house. When the Elethea house is well under construction and your target market can walk around in it, then you're ready to either go public or be acquired."

Under the V he draws three boxes. "Here's half of your six audiences—or 'who cares.'" In the boxes he writes: Investors. Analysts. Influencers. "Investors you already know about. They're your lifeblood. The Hydras are your investors for now, but at some point you're going to need to dazzle future investors who don't know you the way we do. So consider investors customer number one. Number two are the analysts, the ones who follow your market, assess your viability, and make recommendations to their own customers, who pay them a ton for their expertise and opinions. You need to pay these guys to follow you, regularly update them, keep on their good side. But they're worth it. People listen to them."

He takes a bite of his sandwich and dabs at the corner of his mouth with a napkin. "This too basic?"

"When it comes to the world of business, you can't be too basic. For me, at least. Jerry might be a different story, though I doubt it."

"Okay, then. The third group is harder to identify and reach, but it's probably the most important one for Elethea. Influencers are the critical component for your early customers. If Elethea were a computer company, you'd be focusing on that guy or gal who everyone in the family—or in the bar—turns to for advice on what computer to buy."

He goes back to the table and sits down. "This is a group you and I, and Lisa, when she comes on board, will spend a lot of time identifying and then targeting with early information. Because think about it. Elethea doesn't make a computer you can give an influencer for a trial weekend and then hope for a rave review and early sales on Monday." He takes a sip of water and looks at Petra over the rim. "How long will it be before your first human influencers will be able to report measurable benefits of your product?"

"Years. We'll need to give the science time to do its work before we can create actual products, then there'll have to be clinical trials."

"So your influencers are going to have to come from the scientific side. Fellow researchers, scientific journals, professional societies, and pertinent publications and bloggers. You'll need to cultivate them, same way you do analysts."

Freddy's up and back at the board. He draws a box under the three targets but leaves it empty. Under the box he writes one word: "Disruption."

"Vision is all about disrupting the status quo. If successful, Elethea will disrupt the way people think about death, both scientifically and practically."

Now he goes to the empty box and writes "CEO." He turns to Petra. "You own this half of the board, the Vision half. It's your company, your vision. And it's your job to represent that vision to the market. Got it?"

Petra nods, more not to disappoint Freddy than to show complete understanding. "It's a different way of thinking, but yeah. I think."

"Which makes this a great time to take a break. Take a walk, clear your head, check your email. I'll see you back here in thirty."

. . .

While Petra is gone, Freddy fills in the rest of the white board. Upon returning, she notices and tilts her chin at the board.

"No dramatic reveals this time?"

"No drama. Because you don't own this half of the board. I'll explain in a minute."

He turns back to the white board. On the F side of the board he has written in the three boxes: Press. Partners. Prospects. "We call these guys the three Ps. The thing to remember about them is that they hate disruption." He steps over and draws a dramatic circle around the word on the V side of the board.

He turns back. "What this side of the board cares about is ..." Another dramatic circle around "Relevance," on the F side. "It's all about meeting your audience's needs. These prospective customers say, 'Yeah, yeah, your vision's fine. But what can you do for me today?' The press is on deadline. What story can you provide them today? And your partners want to know why they should join forces with you and not the other guys. These three audiences are all selfish, with immediate goals. Vision won't cut it."

Petra seems overwhelmed. Then she frowns. "If I don't own that half of the board, who does?" She gestures at the empty box, the only missing component on what is now a crowded white board.

Freddy writes "CMO" into the empty box. "Your CMO, when you hire him or her, will own this part of the board. But only at first. Once you have a product to sell, your CMO will hand this half of the board off to the VP of sales and will move up to ..." He draws another dramatic swooping arrow to the top of the board, "...and develop plans for each of the six targets. Your six *Who's.*"

"It'll be years before we come close to having a product to sell. How do we fill that CMO box in the meantime?"

"If Elethea were a tech company, you'd be hiring product marketing specialists. But as a biotech company on the road to becoming a pharmaceutical company, you'll want a market development specialist. Someone who can provide strategic insights into market dynamics, educate and engage your various audiences, and build relationships and create awareness early on. The goal is to position Elethea as the leader in the longevity space starting now, to lay the groundwork for when you transition to clinical trials and eventual commercialization."

Petra's dull eyes and slightly drooping shoulders betray the tiredness she feels. Freddy notices. He's seen that look with almost every founder he's worked with. "And with that, let's call it a day," he says, gently.

Petra waves a hand at the board. "What should I do first?"

"If I were you, I'd keep two docs—Word or Google—open on your laptop. For the first one, work on *Who cares?* Make a list of individuals, institutions, and publications regarded as experts when it comes to evaluating and reporting scientific advancements and new pharmaceutical products. Start with anyone involved in longevity or aging research, of course, but that list may be small at this point. So broaden your thinking to include adjacent areas of research. Because those influencers are the difference between Make and Break."

He holds up a cautioning hand. "You don't need to do it tonight. Or next week, even. As you've pointed out, we're talking years here. But start the list, then bring Jerry into the picture, then anyone else from your university or Salvana days, whose opinion you trust."

"What's the second document for?"

"BFD150 and whatever products it generates are going to trigger a variety of ethical, cultural, and economic concerns that you're going to need to address. From what Jerry says, Alice is a great starting point. Meet with her, start the doc with her concerns, then build from there. Then we hand it off to Lisa Carroll, the marketing consultant I told you about. She's been building her own list for us—the Hydras, I mean—ever since we got into the longevity game. I'll bring her in for a brainstorming session as well."

"Do we need to begin addressing those concerns now?"

"No. Just collect them and start developing your positions for each. Hold them for your launch. The list will grow organically, as people learn about your discovery and react. Eventually, as we get closer to market, Lisa and I, and your market development or strategic marketing person, will build a council of experts in those areas and bring them inside the tent well before we announce. They'll be the go-to resources for the networks and business press when we launch."

Freddy stands and puts a hand on Petra's shoulder. "It's a lot to think about, I know, especially for a first session. But as you've pointed out, we've got time." As he leaves the conference room, he sees her studying the whiteboard, as if willing the words and images to implant themselves in her brain.

38

Showing Your Hand

"YOU'RE KIDDING. He's got an interview at Elethea?" Perkins' voice is somewhere between excitement and disbelief. "Hell, I'm taking the rest of the day off. You should, too, Cheryl."

"It's tomorrow," she says unenthusiastically.

"This is the kind of thing I wish I could replicate and bring to my bosses. Think of having someone like Jake in every longevity startup out there. Though, to be honest, Elethea is the only one I'm worried about. Maybe it's only because Jake is finding out so much more from his coffee and climbing arrangement with Petra, but my intel on the other longevity initiatives is that they're far behind Elethea."

He sips his water. "What's the news on Project L? Still on schedule?"

"We're still in the discovery stage," Cheryl answers, "which means we're on our schedule and behind Elethea, which, from what I can gather from Jake, has their protein in proof of concept." She doesn't like using 'our' when it comes to Perkins—he has grown on her in the past few months, and not in a good way—but it's accurate. They meet once a month, usually by Zoom, to check on Project L and what she's learning about Elethea. On the Salvana front, there's no basis for concern. While the ten-year schedule is nothing Dr. Loper is aware of, he and his team come from environments where that kind of projection is par for the course. On the Elethea front, though, the news about Jake is a game-changer.

"What's our boy think about the new gig?" he asks, almost giddy.

"He's excited at the possibility, as you might guess. But you should know, he thinks this either changes the nature of his assignment or brings it to an end."

Perkins' face loses its excitement. "Hardly. It just means he'll be entering a new—and potentially more lucrative—phase, depending on what he brings us." There's a long pause, then he continues. "Actually, if Jake becomes an Elethea employee, that changes the nature of our relationship as well."

Cheryl looks into the screen. Her eyes narrow. "How so?"

"It makes sense for me to take over handling Jake. I've had more experience managing personnel in this area. And besides, at some point I may—and I stress 'may'—have to ask him to do something that you're better off not knowing about."

"Mike," Cheryl begins, a timber to her voice that she hates, because it has a pleading tone to it. "I'm fine being kept in the dark, especially when you start hinting at illegal activities. But as far as I'm concerned, Jake has fulfilled his contract to us. He should be allowed to ..."

"Which is why it's better that I take over things from here on with our boy. Thanks for your help, Cheryl. Bet you're glad to be out of the spy game." He hangs up before she can reply.

39

Splashing Around

JAKE SPENDS THE MORNING balancing two items competing for both his time and attention. There's the upcoming interview at Elethea and the looming specter of a meeting with Mike Perkins. The former he feels prepared for. Not the latter.

When it comes to subterfuge, Jake knows he's up against a grandmaster. While he's determined to tell Perkins that he's more than fulfilled his obligations under the initial agreement, he knows that Perkins will anticipate this and have either a sweetened offer or threat to keep him on the job. The offer he's comfortable rejecting—this assignment, at double his Salvana salary, has given him the financial comfort to tell Perkins to stuff it. The threat, though… He has no idea how to prepare for that.

There's also the professional opportunity to consider. The more time he spends with Petra, and the more he learns about Elethea, the more he realizes this could be the opportunity of a lifetime. He knows, even as he continues to weigh his options, that he's going to say *yes* to the offer and try to navigate things as they develop.

• • •

For her part, Petra is meeting with Zoe, as both her BFF and HR advisor, to discuss the idea of hiring Jake as Elethea's market development manager. She reviews Jake's qualifications with her and how they match with Elethea's immediate and long-term needs.

"There's just one thing that worries me," she says.

"You've got a crush on him," Zoe says confidently.

"Not a crush. Come on, I'm not sixteen. But I like him. Maybe a lot."

"Whoa. TMI. Don't go all mushy on me." Zoe wags her head back and forth, as if sorting options. "At Oracle, that wouldn't be a problem. I think half the population is fishing off the company pier, following the example of upper management. In fact, in HR we regard it as part of our employee retention program. But I can see how it might be a problem at a company the size of Elethea."

Zoe eyes Petra over the edge of her glass. Since it isn't Wednesday, she hasn't played stump-the-bartender, instead ordering her go-to drink, a Texas Mule. "I guess it comes down to which you need more, a boyfriend or a marketing guy."

Petra smiles slightly. "Or which one is harder to find."

"Since you're the bisexual—which means you've got twice the marketplace that the rest of us do—and since even Oracle has trouble finding good marketing people, I think you better hire the boy, girlfriend. And rein in your libido."

. . .

Jake interviews with Jerry first, the idea being that if he doesn't pass that one, there's no need for him to see Freddy or Keeley. But Jerry comes away impressed with Jake's technology chops. "I mean, I expected him to know the core stuff, given his time at Salvana. But he surprised me with how much he knows about our space and the other folks in it. Plus, he's a closet Deadhead, so what's not to like?"

Freddy is next and has the same reaction but on the business side. "I can work with him," he says. "He's already done some research into our TAM ..." He rolls his wrist at Petra playfully and raises his eyebrows.

"Total Addressable Market," she answers.

"... as well as some thoughts on our go-to-market strategy. Since he's proven he can hang with Jerry and the other scientists, I vote *yes*."

Keeley is impressed as well but suggests a final test. "Since he's going to be educating analysts and the press about Elethea, I'd like to see him present something formally. It wouldn't be fair to do something with our technology, but something from his MBA program would be good."

Freddy thinks for a moment, then turns to Petra. "Have you ever heard of the Chasm Exercise?"

· · ·

At lunchtime the next day, Petra, Jerry, Keeley, and Freddy, by unspoken agreement, are standing at the back wall, ceding the seats to the rest of the team: the lab's dozen scientists plus Mona and Eleni. The remains of lunch have been cleared and the healthy waters, diet Cokes, and espressos have come out.

Jake opens his laptop and presses a button. The Chasm—a visual familiar to almost every Silicon Valley company and every marketing professional—shows up on the Elethea conference room white wall.

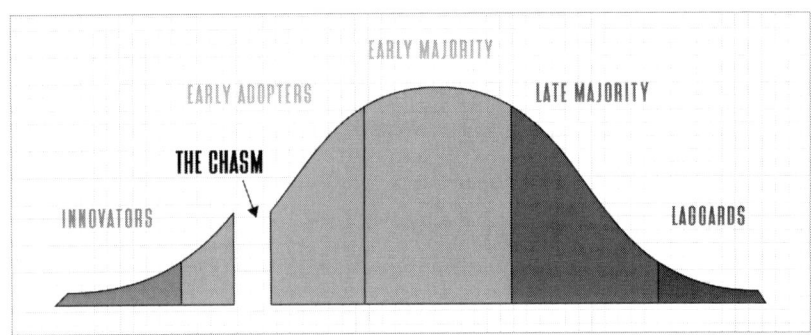

"I know today's presentation was supposed to be a generic look at The Chasm Exercise, but as I refreshed my knowledge of it, I realized that, with what I've learned about this market in general and the little bit Petra has told me about Elethea, I could make this presentation a bit more longevity- and Elethea-specific."

Jake stands up and moves to the wall. Gesturing at the visual, he says, "The bottom line of the Chasm Exercise is that any technology or scientific endeavor will face two markets: an early one and a mainstream one. A chasm exists between the two, and most companies fail because they can't get across that chasm."

He taps on the left side of the visual. "The early market has two audiences: innovators, who play with your product while it's under development, and early adopters, who use it in its earliest form. Think of a car that's being developed in Detroit. Innovators might visit the lab, maybe even take a prototype out on the track, then come back with recommendations. Their goal is to be able to show a friend the finished car and say: 'See the curve on that fender? That was my idea.' The early adopter will be the one who takes the first cars off the assembly line out for a spin and then hopefully buys one and raves about it to their friends."

"I can't imagine we'll have any innovators," Jerry says. "Given the complexity and risks involved with our solution, not to mention the FDA approval process, they'll have to wait to see what we develop and then critique it. On the early adopter front, I can see the line going from here all the way to Castro Street of those who want to be guinea pigs. But we're a long way from that. And those early players will be testers, not adopters."

"Whatever we call them—influencers, testers, adopters— they're critical to your success. Change, even if the benefits are obvious, won't come easy. Don't be surprised if Elethea is on the left side of the chasm for years."

He sees the group react to that last statement, processing it, then scanning the table to see how it landed with the others. "On the left side, you're going to need a focused and fact-based early education program, where influencers and experts can share their thoughts—including their concerns—with you and each other. Then you'll need a strong program to get information out to the people on the other side of the chasm. And that's just the beginning. This program, done right, will unfold slowly, over years."

The rest of the meeting is interactive, with those at the table having questions for Jake first, followed by those standing at the back of the room. It's a healthy exchange, with Jake being both moderator and recorder, putting the ideas up on the whiteboard walls as quickly as they're put forth.

As the meeting hits the 90-minute mark, Mona catches Petra's eye and taps her watch. Petra nods and walks over to Jake, thanks him, brings the meeting to a close and walks him out.

"How do you think it went?" he asks, as they stand on the sidewalk facing each other.

"Better than I'd hoped, given that crowd," Petra says. "They're all very protective of our discovery. Your tough words about the chasm took them outside their comfort zones, which is good." She extends her hand. "I'll call you tomorrow with our decision. But if I were you, I'd expect an offer."

"If there is one," he says with a slight smile, "how much room will I have to negotiate? I recognize I'm dealing with a poker pro."

She returns the smile, but then gets serious. "When we were still in discussions with Freddy and his team, I told them how I wanted to run Elethea when it comes to offers. We're trying to attract an extremely high caliber of people. So our offers, both in salary and equity, should be at the top of their ranges. I'll tell you what I counsel every person we're looking to hire: This is our best offer. Put another way, our only offer. Take it or leave it, but don't counter."

40

Pot Committed

JAKE WALKS THE SIX BLOCKS from his house to Stein's, a brewery just off Castro Street, where he's meeting with Perkins. He always enjoys walking Castro, Mt. View's Main Street. His first day as a Mt. View resident, he walked the length of commercial Castro, from the train station to El Camino Real, a distance of only four large city blocks. But in those four blocks he counted more than 40 places to have a bite, formal or casual, or a drink, from coffee to exotic mixed drinks. Three new breweries had popped up in his three years in the town, but Stein's is still his favorite.

Perkins is already there, commanding a small table out in the "Biergarten" part of the restaurant. He half stands and waves Jake over. Two pints of beer sit on the table. "There was a crowd that came in right after me, so I just took a chance and ordered for us both." He points to the lighter of the beers. "A German pilsner." His finger slides over a notch. "And an IPA. You pick. Or if you want something else ..."

"No. IPA's fine. Thanks, Detective."

"Call me Mike."

"Okay. Thanks, Mike."

"Happy to do it. Just wanted to celebrate your new position and tell you ..."

"It was just an interview. I haven't received an offer. And I'm not sure what I'll do if they do make an offer."

"Do?" Perkins smiles, but it's just his teeth—it doesn't reach his eyes. "You take the job. You draw two salaries. You keep me in the loop. By the way, Cheryl's swamped with Project L, so I'll take over working with you."

"I'm not sure I'm comfortable with joining Elethea if my contract with Salvana ..."

"As I told you when we first met, Salvana isn't paying your salary. I am."

"You, Salvana. Whatever. Either way, you're working at cross purposes to Elethea. And that's fine. I know how corporate espionage works. And I'm happy to keep digging into those other longevity companies, since it would be part of my job, and report to you my findings. But I won't be an inside man. Sorry."

"Well, as you've pointed out, you haven't got the job. If—or when—you do, we can talk more about this. But for now, let's just enjoy these beers. How's the rock climbing coming?"

"Fine. Look, Detec ... Mike. We need to resolve this here and now. Otherwise, I'll decline the offer, if it comes, and we'll just keep things as they are."

The smile grows a few more teeth, but the eyes remain flat. "Oh, you'll take the job when it's offered. Are we clear?"

Jake looks at Mike with disbelief. "Do you hear yourself, Mike? You sound like a mobster."

"I sound like someone with a job to do, Kid. Someone who answers to people you don't want to know about."

Jake stares across the table. Then he stands. "Tell you what. Keep my last check. Let's part company right now. No hard ..."

Perkins reaches down and picks a manila folder off the floor. He slides it across the table. "Before you make your dramatic exit, take a quick look at what's inside. Then let's talk about your new role at Elethea."

Jake sits back down.

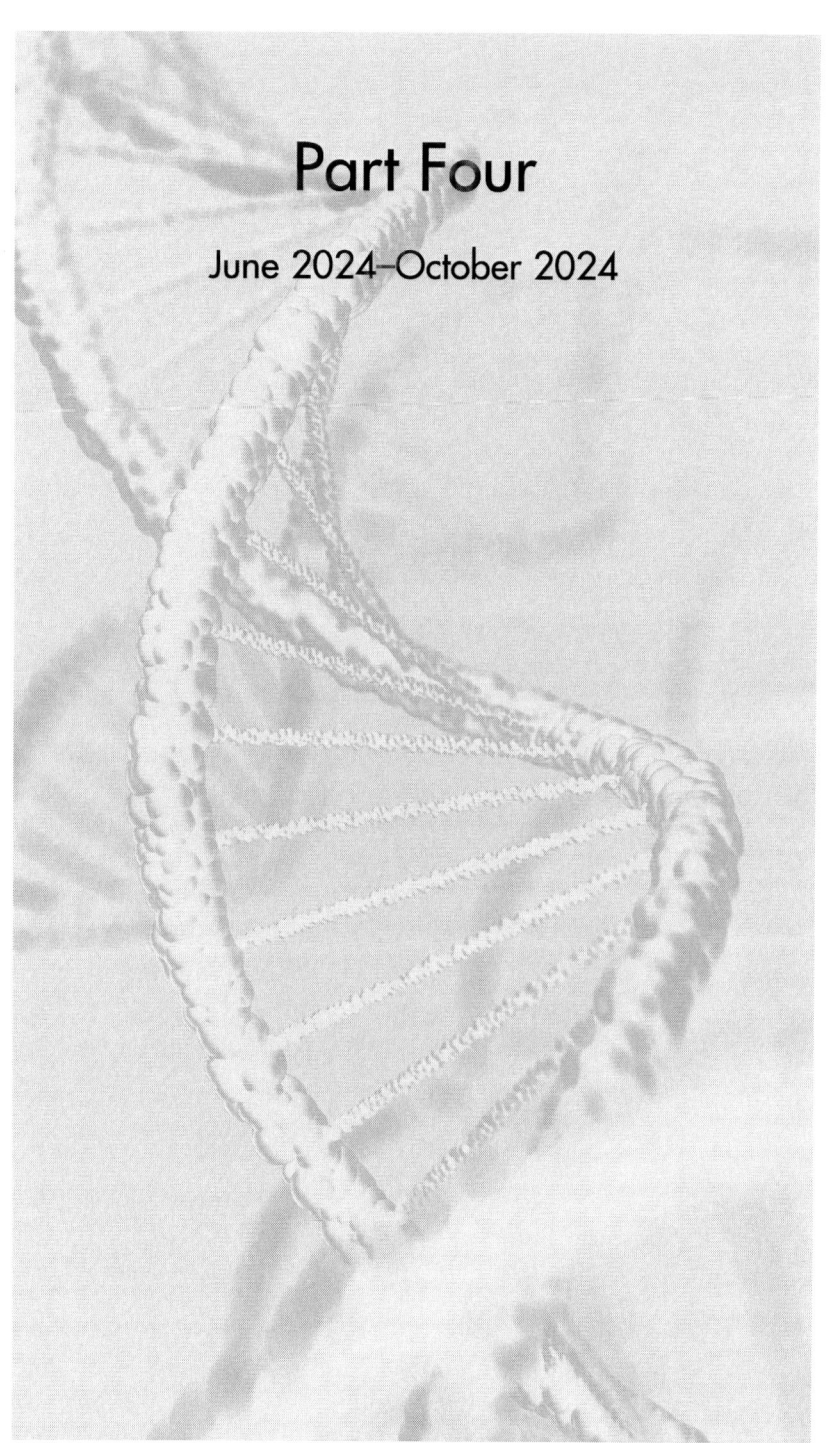

Part Four

June 2024–October 2024

41

Filling the Table

"I WANTED TO HAVE THIS MEETING ever since Freddy told me about you," Petra says. "But he said it was premature. Then he sets this up. What changed?"

Lisa Carroll tips her head in Jake's direction. "Him. Freddy knows I won't take on any job where the CEO is my client. It's just a matter of productivity. And focus. I need an active partner to do my work, and the CEO, despite all best intentions, doesn't have the bandwidth to be that partner. Freddy urged me a couple of times to change that rule, but when I did and he saw the results, he told me to reinstitute it, that he'd honor it going forward. This time he lived up to his word. The day you made Jake an offer, Freddy called me on his way home, told me to give Jake a week to get his feet wet, then come in. So here I am."

The three are in the Elethea conference room. It's the Monday of Jake's second week at Elethea. He spent the first week in a crash course with the scientists, getting detailed explanations of their tests and results and asking questions that impressed the team with his depth of knowledge. He also tried out analogies and metaphors with them, in his attempt to turn their intricate science into terms the general public could understand.

"So, Jake's your client, not me?" Petra asks.

"Jake's my partner. You're my client."

"What's the difference?"

"A client can fire me. But the person I'm going to meet with regularly, who'll team with me to build out your website and PowerPoint presentations, that person is my partner."

• • •

In her forties, with a strong-boned face, tight chin, and piercing eyes, Lisa Carroll comes across as formidable at first. But her self-confidence and easy laugh create an environment that sets her clients at ease while allowing her to maintain control of the room.

She earned her spurs as CMO at two tech companies, one that proved to be a Silicon Valley titan, the other a hot startup. When the startup went public, she took a severance package, though the founders begged her to stay, took a year off, and traveled the world on her own. When she came back to the Valley, the offers were waiting. But she'd done a bit of self-analysis on the trip and had reached a decision.

"I'm too young to retire," she told Freddy upon her return, "but I'm too old for the startup grind again."

"So a big company?"

"Naw. No interest. When I was thinking about returning to this life, I started thinking about what invigorates me. I found that the answer had changed over the years. Early on, I liked being part of something organic and growing, a community working toward the same goal. I liked digging down into the technology and then determining the best way to package it and educate the market. I became what I call a 'Silo Person,' staying in a prescribed area and then digging down. You know what I mean?"

"I hadn't thought of it that way," Freddy said, "but that's the essence of the Valley. Almost everyone is a Silo Person."

"I realized I wasn't a Silo Person anymore. During my year of traveling, what I loved most was experiencing one culture after another, none of them the same. I realized that's what I wanted to do back here. Instead of a Silo Person, I wanted to be like a hummingbird, flitting from flower to flower. Except my flowers would be startups. I'd become their initial CMO, applying everything I learned about putting a company on the map. I'd join the team for its first year, launch the company, then hire my successor and move on to the next flower."

· · ·

"When Freddy first told me that he wanted to bring you in as initial or temporary CMO," Petra says, "I asked him why Jake couldn't do it, now that he's on board." She inclined her head at Jake, who nods his agreement.

"Let me guess what he said," Lisa says. "First, he asked how many launches Jake's done, right?" Petra nods. "Second, he told you that launching a company is like what your grandmother used to tell you: You only get one chance at a first impression."

Petra laughs out loud. "Almost in exactly those words."

"Well, I've trained him well over the years," Lisa says. "My model has worked for over fifty startups, so I'm comfortable it will work here as well. At this stage, as Elethea prepares to introduce itself to the market, your CMO should be strongest in corporate marketing, or what some companies call corporate communications. That's what I do. What Jake does is market development and product marketing—meaning he's versed in your science to the point that board members at first—and your sales team later—will take him on client and partner calls. That's because ideally he'll be able to answer questions about what Elethea does and how it works—in English for the executives and in scientific language if they've brought their scientists to the meeting."

"Whereas you, as CMO..."

"I start off every engagement with a twelve-hour workshop that gets us all on the same page, about the company and the product. No more than five attendees. In this case, you, Jerry, Freddy, and Jake. Add Keeley, if you like. The input from all of you will serve as the basis for Jake and me to develop all the tools you'll need to tell the world about Elethea: a preliminary website that will grow as you come out of stealth; presentations for partners and analysts; and the beginnings of PR outreach and market education. Your launch is going to be the most critical part of your go-to-market strategy. It's a complicated event with a number of critical and moving parts." She pauses to see if Petra is following. "Think of me as a wedding or party planner. You could do it yourself, but you've got other things on your plate. And you don't have the time, experience, or resources of someone who does it for a living."

Petra looks at Jake. "You good with all this?"

"More than good."

To Lisa: "Let's get started, then."

Lisa looks around the conference room, which holds a variety of notes, test results, and to-do reminders. Lisa notices the V<—>F spectrum and smiles. "Goddamn Freddy. Always takes my best stuff. Did he do *So what* and *Who cares* as well?"

"Yes, but he attributed them to you."

"Well, that's better than nothing. Okay, let's get started. Since Freddy has already stolen most of my opening, I'm going to go with the other opening exercise I use for most of my clients." She goes to the whiteboard and writes the numbers 1, 2, 3, and 4 in stacked format, with 1 at the bottom.

"For the sake of the exercise, let's assume you're a toothpaste company." She writes next to the "1" the word "dexahydrochlorophine." She turns back to the table. "That's Level One, your critical ingredient, the thing that makes your toothpaste so special." She moves up to the next number. "Level Two is whiter teeth. Level Three is more dates. And Level Four is 'get lucky.'"

She nods at their smiles, then back at the whiteboard. "Most technology companies start at Level One and stay there. They're so enamored with their technology that they think they just need to explain how dexahydrochlorophine works and their work is done. I'm assuming biotech companies suffer from the same syndrome, falling in love with their key discovery?"

She waits for Petra and Jake to nod, then circles the '1.' "Starting at Level One is the number one sin in tech marketing, and I'm assuming science marketing as well." Her hand slides up to the '4.' "You need to start up here, at 'get lucky.' Promise your audience they'll get laid more with your toothpaste than any other on the market. Once you've got their attention, you'll need to prove it. At which point you can trot out dexahydrochlorophine and explain, in terms they'll understand, how it works." She stands back. "But always—with your pitches, with your website—start at Level Four, not Level One. With that in mind, tell me what Elethea does—not what it makes—and why I should care."

For the next hour, Jake tells her about the discovery of BFD150 and the subsequent theories, tests, and results that have brought them to this point, with Petra joining in whenever he gets stuck with the science or details. Lisa pushes back occasionally with Socratic questioning that forces Jake and Petra to look at the discovery and initial results not in terms of the self-congratulatory "aren't we smart" tone that works in a VC pitch, but that shifts the focus to the needs and desires of their target audiences. After this hour of back and forth, Petra and Jake have modified four key slides in their core deck, all of which Lisa blesses, telling them she likes their thinking.

"That's enough for today," she says. "Except for one thing. And it's a biggie. I'm just going to raise it for now; we'll develop it later. But I want you to give it some serious thought, because it's critical to how we introduce Elethea and your solution to the market." She stops and looks from Petra to Jake. "How old are you guys?"

"Thirty-three," Petra says.

"Thirty-one," Jake says.

"Then you may be too young to have experienced this analogy. But indulge me for a couple of minutes. Not too many years ago, going out on the road meant heading out with an eight- to twelve-pound laptop on one shoulder. We called them 'luggables.' And over the other shoulder you had a garment bag packed with everything we still carry with us on any business trip. You were weighted down on both sides, with straps digging into your shoulders."

She takes a sip of bottled water and shifts her shoulders unconsciously. "At night, when you checked into your hotel room, you ordered room service and took a long, steaming shower, with the spray focused on your shoulders. Then while you watched TV in your pajamas, you kneaded your shoulders."

She stops. "Does that person know they have a problem?"

"Well, sore shoulders, obviously," says Petra.

"Except they don't see it as a problem. It's just the price of being on the road. If you asked them about what they hate about being on the road, sore shoulders might not even register. It was just the way things were.

"And then one day, a flight attendant or pilot got the bright idea of putting wheels on a suitcase. And all of a sudden people remembered their shoulder pain and realized they had a problem after all."

She dangles two fingers on her left hand in front of her. "That's what we call a 'two-step sale.' The first step is educating or convincing your prospect that they have a problem. The second step is convincing them that you have the best—or only—solution."

She pauses. "Are you following me? I may need to update my sore shoulders analogy, since my clients keep getting younger."

"No, I get it," Petra says. "I remember my father with that tan garment bag, heading out on the road." Jake nods as well.

"Great. Now imagine that I've got terminal cancer. I know I have a problem. A big one. I just want a solution. That's an extreme example of a one-step sale."

She stands up and pulls some papers out of her briefcase, which is soft and as much a backpack as a briefcase. "Your assignment for our next meeting is to tell me whether Elethea is a one-step or two-step sale. This is one decision we don't want to get wrong."

She motions at the door to the conference room. "And now, Petra, I have to ask you to leave." She smiles. "My partner Jake and I have work to do."

42

Showing Your Hand

"WHO'S GOT TODAY'S PLAYLIST?" Jerry says, as he steps into the lab.

"You know how it works. We wait until we see which T-shirt you're wearing, then one of us'll build a compatible list, but from this century." This from Nigel, a proud Brit who likes to feud with his American colleagues about everything from what they call "football" to beer temperature. Who exits conversations by saying he needs to "crack on" with his work. And who can be counted on to bring a six-pack of Bass Ale—but never Guinness—to every potluck he's invited to.

Jerry pirouettes, giving all the scientists a view of his outfit, which he narrates as he turns. "Today's scientist is smartly attired in jeans by Levi's, footwear from Nike, and a stunning mustard-colored shirt from the Creedence Clearwater Revival Green River collection."

"I'm up today," announces Leslie, a West Coast native who, after a couple of years as a post doc at the University of Chicago, is delighted to be back in northern California. "God's Country," she tells Nigel. "Okay, Jerry, you're going to like my list. Creedence today would be classified as 'Americana.' So I'll mix them in with Nathaniel Rateliff, The Black Keys, and Jason Isbell. And we'll top it off with something for both your generation and ours: John Prine." She turns to her phone. "Give me ten minutes."

It's a great crew Jerry has assembled. He's happy, and frankly a bit surprised, that they've gelled so well and so quickly. "You never know," he explained to Petra during one of their catch-up sessions, "when you bring together a group like this— smart, motivated, ambitious, all from different backgrounds— whether they'll play nice together or get protective about their individual responsibilities and discoveries."

Though Petra won't admit it, these meetings with Jerry are the highlight of her day. Knowing how much she wants to be part of the lab and its work, he makes a point of dropping by once or twice a day and bringing her up to speed. These drive-bys accomplish the twin goals of keeping the CEO informed and out of the lab.

As she has promised the board—and herself—Petra has committed herself to the role and responsibilities of a CEO, as reflected by the whiteboard walls that ring her cubicle. Walls that used to be filled with experimental categories, central research questions, sketches of molecular pathways, and preliminary data plots now are crowded with funding strategies, patents to file, and the ever-growing list of business books that Freddy has assigned her to read.

Jerry puts his head over her cubicle wall. "Got a minute? The kids have something they want to show us."

As they walk through the lab, Petra's eyes travel from one station to the next. They pass incubators and lab benches filled with cell culture trays and pipettes, all arranged neatly and orderly, with microscopes and computer screens mixed in.

At one lab bench, Bao and Josef are in animated conversation with Layla, who's showing them something in a microscope. Bao looks up at their arrival. "Your timing is perfect. There's something here you should see."

The Bao/Josef/Layla triumvirate has emerged as the power-house within the Elethea scientific team. Bao and Josef bonded right away, having already worked together at Salvana. Different from the traditional scientist in so many ways—looks, background, her path into the company, the hours she keeps—Layla took a bit longer to work herself into the group. But her impressive CRISPR skills, coupled with her willingness to consider and pursue even the most extreme suggestions, eventually won the pair over.

With summer bringing the usual extended periods of flat surf in northern California, Layla is in early and stays late. Out of either hope or habit, she still wakes at dawn's light and checks the surf reports. Even with the forecast calling for only knee-high swells, she jumps on her balloon-tired bike and rides the five minutes to her local spot, just to be sure. Once she confirms the surf report, she heads home, grabs a quick shower, and heads into work, often arriving before anyone else.

These early-morning arrivals don't change her evening pattern. Unlike many of the other scientists, who are a decade older and have families, she'll often stay late into the night finishing up an experiment or wrestling with the challenge of the day. Or week.

Today, as Jerry and Petra approach, they clock the excited look on Layla's face. "We've been pursuing your idea, Petra, that it's some kind of deterioration over time in the lysosomes that causes the BFD150 build-up."

Petra nods. Once the team established that BFD150's effects on aging was associated with too much of the protein accumulating in cells, Petra theorized that the key was in the lysosomes, which act as the "digestive system" of cells—that the lysosomes somehow lost their ability to clear out the BFD150 protein. For the past month, Layla had been experimenting with using CRISPR to change the function of the lysosomes that are responsible for breaking down the BFD150 protein. The hope was that manipulating the lysosomes would prevent the accumulation of BFD150.

"I've been trying various edits to the lysosomes in both the nematode worms and the fruit flies," Layla says, "seeing if the CRISPR'ed lysosomes can retain their ability to keep BFD150 quantities in check over more cell divisions."

She motions to her microscope. "Take a look. These first two samples are from the control group, with no CRISPR alterations, with the BFD150 protein tagged with fluorescence. The sample on the left is from newly hatched fruit flies. The one on the right is from six-week-old flies, meaning they're nearing the end of their lives and have gone through multiple cell divisions."

Petra peers into the microscope. "The one on the right has a lot more of the fluorescence-tagged BFD150 protein in it."

"Which is just what we'd expect, right?" Layla displays a new set of samples. "Now look at these samples. Same thing: on the left from newly hatched flies, on the right from elderly flies. Except these ones had their lysosomes CRISPR'ed with my latest edit."

Petra looks into the microscope. "There's practically no difference between the amount of BFD150 in these two samples." She looks up at Layla, who's grinning broadly.

Jerry takes his turn at the microscope, then looks at first Layla, then Bao and Josef. "This is fantastic. If we can replicate this, we've just cleared a major hurdle." He looks over at Petra. "The board's going to be happy."

Petra takes one more look, then nods to the team. "Great work, guys. Really great work."

She turns to Jerry as the two of them start to walk away. "We need to name what's happened here, both for the patent process, and for Jake and Lisa to use in their marketing plan."

"Those CEO lessons must be sinking in," Jerry says. "You're starting to sound like a real businessperson."

Petra looks at him sharply. "I hope you're not implying I've turned to the dark side."

He laughs. "Not at all. It's a good thing, trust me. Just that the Petra of a few months ago would never have been able to think that way." He pauses. "I'm proud of you, Kid. I mean it."

• • •

It's a week later. Further tests have confirmed both Petra's lysosome theory and Layla's CRISPR technique. Jerry has gathered Bao, Josef, and Layla, along with Petra and Jake, in the conference room.

"Rule number one for brainstorming meetings," Jerry begins. "There are no stupid ideas. Just stupid people with ideas. Let's just get words up on the board that are associated with our breakthrough." He writes feverishly on the wall as the group tosses out candidates. When they've finished, he caps his marker and joins them to stare at the wall.

"What is it you're doing with CRISPR exactly?" Jake asks Layla.

"We're using CRISPR as an epigenetic agent to selectively repress specific lysosomal genes," she says. "To reverse their inability to clear the BFD150 out of cells."

"There's a lot we can work with there," says Jerry. "Can we shorten it?"

"How about 'lysosomal gene repression'?" Josef suggests.

"Not bad," Jerry says. "But I'm guessing that phrase could apply to too many different things."

"'CRISPR-induced gene repression'?" This from Bao.

"Same problem."

Jake closes one eye and surveys the whiteboard. "How about 'epigenetic selective repression'?"

A collection of nods and murmurs greets the suggestion. Jerry writes it on the board, then stands back. "I like it," he says.

"Epigenetic selective repression. We can abbreviate it as ESR. And we can also break down and explain each term in more detail. The board or the patent attorney might have a different idea, but for now, let's go with ESR."

He caps the marker. "This calls for a celebration. Grab the others and let's meet at The Oasis. Petra, bring the corporate credit card."

43

Reading the Room

"OKAY, THAT'S IT FOR BUDGET, facilities, and headcount. The board might have questions about our burn rate. If so, the details are behind bullet number three."

Mona and Petra are sitting outdoors at a wine garden within walking distance of Elethea. They're wrapping up the first part of Mona's quarterly state-of-the-company meeting, where she gives Petra everything she needs from an operations perspective for the upcoming board meeting.

Mona has two requirements for this part of her job. The first is that they do this formal meeting every quarter, more frequently if needed. The second is that they meet outside the office, preferably with something alcoholic in hand.

Now that Petra is all-in on the CEO position, she relies heavily on Mona. Not just for the virtual departments that Mona manages—Finance, Legal, HR, Facilities—but also for checking in on company morale and kicking around ideas on how to keep the company's culture fresh and inviting. Petra knows scientists and what they do and don't like; Mona knows startups and the toll they can take. Between them, they've created and maintained a relaxed but productive work environment.

"One thing I can't get a handle on," Mona says, changing topics. "Gaming. Do scientists like the same games as tech nerds? Or do they like board games at all?"

"I'm not sure. I'm a scientist, but outside of poker, which serious players will tell you isn't a game, I've never been a gamer. Why do you ask?"

"Because, in my previous startups, gaming was part of the culture. A big part. What games your employees played—usually a couple days a week, on-site, and on company time—was part of attracting your software and security folks. I've asked Jerry, but he's like you—not a gamer. I've asked a few of the other scientists, and they seemed interested if we got something up and going, but I didn't feel like they were chomping at the bit to play."

"I'll ask around, but I don't think they'll be that honest with me, afraid to look like they're not serious about their job. You know?"

"Then I'll bring it up at the next all-hands. I'll have a list of the five most popular board games and..." She looks at Petra, cocking her head slightly. "You *do* know what I'm talking about when I say board games, don't you?"

"Like Risk? Stratego?"

Mona barks a laugh. "Why don't you throw Chutes and Ladders in there, while you're at it? I'd tell you that you need to get out more, girl, but these games are all played inside. I'm talking about adult games. Some are fantasy, some are warfare. They've got happy titles like Doom, Pandemic, and Settlers of Catan. They can go on for weeks. The gamers I supported in past companies took their games very seriously. Some of them asked during their interviews which games the employees played."

Petra shakes her head. "You better be the one who brings it up, then. I'd just embarrass myself. Okay, what's next?"

"Human resources. Which brings me to a delicate topic. Office romances, or the threats thereof."

"Who are we talking about?"

"Well, you, for starters."

"I didn't know I was dating anyone."

"That's not what it looks like. Give it a moment and it'll come to you."

Petra takes a sip of wine and then sits back. Her face, especially her eyes, stay blank, as if she's at the poker table. Then her eyes widen. "Jake?"

"Bingo. Everyone knows how you guys met and how you coached each other. That's the kind of thing that in the movie business they call 'meet-cute.' I just need to know if that's the extent of the relationship or if it's gone deeper. I wouldn't blame you if it did—he's easy on the eyes and a great listener, something I value in a man." She holds up her hand. "Before you get pissed, it's part of my job to raise the question. In both of my previous startups it was a problem. Fishing off the company pier, peeing where you drink, whatever you call it, it can screw up a corporate culture faster than you would believe."

"No, I'd believe it. And no offense taken. We're just friends, but I'll curtail the climbing, tell Spyder to find another partner."

Petra drains the last of her wine and is about to call for the check when Mona puts a hand on her arm. "There's one more thing I need to go over with you." She motions to the waiter and points to Petra's glass. "Can we have one more of those, please, and split it between the two of us." He nods and departs.

"This last thing is a bit awkward. It's part me doing my job, part none of my business. But I don't think Eleni should be living alone."

"Why? Has she fallen again?"

"No, but since that first fall, I've kept an eye on her," Mona says. "She's moving tentatively, has her hand slightly out, like she's getting ready to grab something for support. So I asked her if she'd fallen again."

"Did she tell you to mind your own fucking business? Because that's the answer, any time I ask."

"I'm not her daughter, so it's easier for her to talk to me. She said she'd fallen a couple of times, but they'd been in her apartment, not in public. As if that mattered."

Petra sighs. "I know how she loves San Francisco, and I know how much she prizes her independence. I've never raised the subject of her moving in with me. But it may be time."

"You know you're going to have to be the one to bring it up. She'll never ask."

They sit there together, the silence comfortable. Then Mona raises her glass. "Here's to Eleni, one tough broad."

44

In the Hole

"YOU REMEMBER THAT BEACH BOYS LYRIC, 'Two girls for every boy?'" Zac asks.

"It was actually Jan and Dean," Freddy corrects him. "And what the hell do you know about that? That wasn't just before *your* time, it was before mine."

"I also know about Beethoven and Gershwin, and they were before my time as well."

"Point taken. Why did you bring up *Surf City?*"

"I'm thinking of revising it and having a friend record it. But instead of Surf City we're talking about New Zealand. 'Five sheep for every guy.' See what the government and Chamber of Commerce think of that."

"The government still playing hardball with you about the visa and bunker?" Trina asks.

"Yeah. All the publicity from Peter Thiel and folks like you embarrassed them. Since they can't broadcast the package anymore, they're upping the price." He belches slightly and looks apologetically at Trina. "Fuck 'em. I'm looking into Greenland."

"By the way, how's your hacker pal doing?" Max asks. "The one with the implants and fecal doping?"

"Fecal *transplants*, Max. Transplants. He's okay on that front, but his implants have placed him on the government's 'no-fly' list. They set off the security scanners and no one believes him when he tries to tell them what they are and what they're for."

. . .

The conversation stops as the door opens and Kerry, this time in her role as Freddy's Headwaters assistant, escorts Lisa Carroll and her three guests into the conference room. Petra joins a few minutes later. They all shake hands and exchange names, then give their drink orders to Kerry, who departs.

After a few sidebar conversations and the delivery of the drinks, Lisa calls the meeting to order. "Before I do formal introductions, let's review the purpose of this meeting, specific to Elethea, and how it came to be."

The Headwaters conference room is actually the second choice for today's meeting. The Dicks initially wanted to meet on the yacht, but Lisa vetoed it as too distracting for their guests, who are already out of their element in the elegant setting and hospitality common to most VC firms.

Lisa is seated at the head of the table, with the Dicks and Keeley, joining at Freddy's request, on one side, and their three guests on the other. Petra is there as well, but she tells Lisa that she'll be in 'listen-only' mode.

The guests are Dr. Mitchell Bruckner, a social economist who specializes in projecting the impact of various technology and scientific discoveries; Dr. Maggie Jaspers, professor of Environmental Impact at UC Berkeley; and Sister Mary Vincent, Ethicist-in-Residence at The Futures Institute, a program at Santa Clara University's business school.

"Today's guests have been working with me for the past year," Lisa begins. "Our work had its start before Elethea, when you guys decided to get into the longevity game. Freddy and I met to discuss what getting into this new market—science, not technology—years before the benefits would become obvious, would require. We agreed that we were out of our depth, so I invited these three experts ..." She sweeps her hand at the three on the other side of the table, "to forecast the impact of longevity from a variety of perspectives. With that, let me introduce them."

Once introductions are concluded, Lisa continues, "Our method during this first year has been to consider the implications of advanced longevity with as wide a lens as possible. The goal of this meeting is to share our findings and opinions with you and get your reactions and insights. Once that's done, I'll work with Petra to formalize their role as Elethea's Advisory Board, including NDAs and equity grants, which will be their sole form of compensation."

She surveys the BSD side of the table. "Questions?" There are none. "Okay. The meeting will consist of two parts. The first is our experts giving their findings. The second will be a brainstorming session on what to do with these findings, how we prepare the market for our solution, and begin to respond to concerns and objections. And with that, let me turn the meeting over to Dr. Bruckner, from the Economics Department at Stanford. Mitch, the floor is yours."

Still in his thirties, Dr. Bruckner is a hot property. He has an informal, engaging way of breaking down social and economic issues and making them relatable to a general audience. He is almost a stereotype of the cool professor—hair stylishly long, clothing by Zegna, rather than Brooks Brothers—but he doesn't try to ingratiate himself with his audiences, either in class or over the air. As one admiring producer noted, he wears well.

"The bottom line is not going to surprise anyone at this table. Incorporating longevity into an already fraught world is going to be a challenge, economically and socially. Some questions are obvious. How do we care for a larger and longer-living population? How long do we continue to work, if we're now doubling our life span? What's retirement and when does Social Security kick in? What role does government play in all this, or are we on our own?"

He takes a sip of the natural soda provided by the helpful Headwaters staff. "Before we all feel overwhelmed, bear in mind that every major development brings with it a sense of chaos and concern. But we eventually accommodate it and integrate it into our lives. The three of us, working with Lisa, have created a list of what we call 'macro concerns,' which we'll be articulating and validating. We'll then have specific—or 'micro'—concerns within our own fields. But for this meeting, let's stay at the macro level."

He pauses and looks around the table. When there are no questions, he continues. "The impact on health care systems will be huge. The labor force will mean people in their seventies and beyond will embark on second and third careers. Or choose to stay longer in their current job."

He stops for a moment. It's tough to tell if he's doing it for effect or if he's lost his place. "But all of this is only possible if our mental capacities keep up with our new physical longevity." He looks around the table, his gaze settling on Freddy. "If I were a VC or had a group like the Hydras ..." He smiles. "I prefer 'BSDs,' by the way. But if I were in this group, knowing what you do about the Elethea solution, if I had the bandwidth and money, I'd be looking for a counterpart to what Elethea is doing with the body, except focusing on the mind. One without the other is an incomplete solution."

Dr. Bruckner goes on like this for another ten minutes, then looks down at his notes. "Making room for my two partners, I'll sum up. An aging population doesn't just mean more health care costs. The fear of an extended future will mean more saving and a new approach to consumption and investing. Politically, since elderly people are more conservative, more averse to change, look for the political parties to tilt right. I could foresee a schism within the Democratic party, while the Republican party will continue its shift toward autocracy, which will play well in this newly uncertain populace." He smiles. "And with those cheery predictions, let me turn it over to Maggie."

Unlike Dr. Bruckner, who gave his presentation seated at the table, Dr. Jaspers stands up. A petite woman in her late forties, she's in jeans and a loose-fitting silk top. Her hair is long, shot with grey, and gathered in a braid that looks like it's about to come undone.

"Thanks, Mitch." She looks around the table. "If Mitch hasn't depressed you enough, let me pile on. The impact of Elethea's discovery will be as significant environmentally as economically. Maybe more so. Part of it is simple math. More people—dramatically more people—on an increasingly fragile planet is not anything our models have planned for. Unless we change our relationship to the planet in a number of fundamental ways, by the time your first clients start living longer, the added burden that this new population will place on the planet will constitute a tipping point from which the planet can't recover. Unless we recognize the burden and plan accordingly."

Dr. Jaspers pauses for questions or objections, but again there are none. It's clear that the Dicks are completely engaged, but equally clear that the ramifications are only now starting to sink in. "Consider all the major areas of environmental impact that will accompany longevity—resource consumption, waste generation, energy consumption, biodiversity conservation. The Elethea solution will, once we get over the personal shock of adjusting our lifespan, bring us to a crossroad about the climate. Perhaps your discovery and its implications will be the trigger for the world to realize it needs a dramatic reset, on many fronts, to preserve its viability in the long term. Or it will validate the school that believes we've already passed the point of no return with our existing population and that the planet is just going to become unlivable that much faster, so, to steal a phrase from Prince, let's party like it's 2049, leaving the hard work associated with a dying planet to the next generation."

"Do you honestly think your second option is a valid one? That we'll do nothing?" Zac asks.

"How long has global warming and climate change been staring us in the face?" Maggie says. "Our politicians have politicized science in a way we haven't seen since the Inquisition. And not letting the general public off the hook, how many of us have adopted the changes to our lifestyle required to slow, if not eliminate, the damage we're doing to our environment?"

She goes to the whiteboard and quickly sketches a circle with a horizontal line bisecting it. "Even if global warming stabilizes in the next few years—which is unlikely, given our lack of appetite for hard decisions—we're going to be seeing major migrations." She taps the middle of her drawing. "This area, the middle band, is fast becoming unlivable. And just like animals during the Ice Age, we're going to see major shifts, this time from the equator to the poles. Think of the political and cultural implications. Right now, America's got a political crisis because Latin Americans are coming here to escape the gangs and political repression of their home countries. And that's just a small minority of those populations. I'm talking about a majority of those populations—gangs included—moving north and south, toward livable climates."

"How do you think the destination countries will accommodate this influx?" Vinod asks. "If my home country of India is any example, there's no room at the inn. We'll just keep piling one on top of another."

Dr. Jaspers nods. "The first option is just that—accommodate them and integrate them into our current cities and cultures. But the more efficient model, if we start acting now, is to build new cities in currently uninhabited or lightly inhabited areas. Since we're building from scratch, we can use all the best practices we've learned, from renewable energy to new construction techniques to ways to promote and facilitate multigenerational living."

She sees that this last point isn't hitting home. "Take Cancun as an example. Back in 1970, it had three residents. Now it's close to a million, most of the growth planned for. The Chinese are also exceptional at building major cities where none used to exist. We need to learn this form of urban development as well, starting now. If we start planning and building new cities from scratch, not only will we be able to accommodate an aging but growing population, but we'll be establishing models and tools for existing cities to emulate." She looks across at the BSDs. "Since Mitch had the temerity to offer you investing advice, let me do so as well. On a personal level, I'd start investing in land, the farther north the better. Think Montana and Wyoming as possible sites for these new cities. And at an institutional level, I'd be investing in those companies and technologies focused on designing and building these new types of cities."

With that, she sits down.

"Sister, you're up," Lisa says.

Sister Mary Vincent stays seated. In her early sixties, she's spent much of her career writing and teaching about the ethical ramifications of modern developments—from computers to social media to income gaps to global warming. "Ethical ramifications aren't as predictable or measurable as the environmental or economic, but I see the impact of your discovery occurring in two stages. The first is when you announce your discovery and the world reacts. That's our focus in today's meeting as well as subsequent meetings prior to your launch. And people such as those in this room will need to have answers that will reassure a population already jittery about global warming. The second is harder to pin down, at least its date. It's when the impact of your discovery begins to take effect in a way that the world has to recognize and respond to it. And that I place at about twenty years from now." She looks at Freddy, who nods.

"The launch will be about projections and reassurances. We're strong on the former and have a few years to come up with the reassurances. The twenty years out scenario will be out of your hands, because it won't be about science, it will be about policies. Governmental to be sure, but social contracts as well. Who does what? Who gets what? If we don't retool our health care systems, the rich will dominate this generation of elderly in terms of services and their own general health. Societies like ours will need to look at other cultures, where familial obligations come into play, in terms of multigenerational families living together and providing care for this new advanced citizenry. End of life issues will crop up. Suicide will become a viable medical procedure. And death panels—or the same thing under a better name—may finally become a reality."

Sister Mary smiles slightly. "We're a happy group, aren't we? One last point, then I'll shut up. Since we're talking end of life, we need to talk beginning of life as well." Her smile broadens and her eyebrows lift. "… an area that my church has fumbled more than once. I can foresee the increasing numbers from this solution forcing governments to adopt some form of China's one-child policy to counteract the numbers and impact of the aging population."

Sister Mary looks around the table. "Without being overly dramatic, I believe your discovery will have more impact than any other invention on the horizon. If we're still as polarized as we are today, longevity and its impact will either bring us together in common cause or cause a tribal hardening, with each group protecting or extending its interests at the expense of other tribes."

With that, all eyes swing back to Lisa. "With Kerry's help, I've stacked the refreshment table with razor blades and hemlock," she smiles. "The Sister here has agreed to give you last rites." After a bit of nervous laughter around the table, she adds, "Now, let's open up the floor to questions."

The question period extends to the hour mark, at which point they take a 10-minute break. When they return, Lisa says, "Since no one fled during the break, let's turn our attention to how to counter or re-frame the objections and concerns our panel listed."

She stands next to the whiteboard wall, marker in one hand, a sheet of paper in the other. "I asked all of you last week to send me your thoughts on the positive aspects of enhanced longevity. I've grouped your responses into a number of categories, so let's consider them in turn.

She writes "Productivity" on the wall. "This one came up the most, so let's start here. Who wants to go first?"

"I'll go," Vinod says. "If we think of productivity as 'idea meets expertise,' we'll be seeing significant advances. Think about the advances we would already have if our greatest inventors had another 30 years of ideas and inventions. You couple more innovation with greater expertise—as people practice their trades longer—and you have a powerful formula."

Others chime in on the productivity front until Lisa writes "Health" on the wall. "I received a wide range of suggestions on this topic. Freddy, you had a good one."

Freddy shifts his eyes upper right for a second, recalling what he submitted. "From what Petra has told me about BFD150, it has potential beyond longevity. If CRISPR can do what Jerry and Petra think it can, there will be ramifications across a wide range of diseases, many of which were incurable."

"If we're trying to educate the general populace," Trina chimes in, "I'd design an image where Elethea and the breakthrough are the trunk of a tree. We then show the branches that will extend off this trunk—all the fields of science and medicine that will benefit from this discovery, all the startups that will use Elethea's solution and Petra's AI formulas as the foundation for their work. That should address—or at least mitigate—the number one concern that I can imagine will arise, and that's *what happens if my mind doesn't keep up with my body?*"

"That's going to be your biggest hurdle," Sister Mary adds. "Is one hundred going to be the new sixty? Otherwise, the general populace is going to envision themselves living the last third of their lives, if not more, in a nursing home, rather than living an extended, vibrant life."

The conversation goes on in this vein for the remainder of the meeting. Topics range from intergenerational family living to multi-careers being the new life path to economic models. The wall is full of ideas under the major categories. Lisa, who has taken a seat for most of the conversation, stands up. Before she can speak, Dr. Bruckner interjects. "Before you wrap things up, Lisa, I've got some good news on the economic front. Good for the average citizen, that is, not so much for the government. Let's say a 25-year-old invests $15,000 at an annually compounding interest rate of 5.5 percent, which is today's going rate. At 65, that 15k will be worth around 125K. Good return, huh? But if you let it build until you need it at 125 years of age, that 15K will be worth $3.2 million. Individuals, banks, and governments are going to have to adjust to this new math."

"I wonder, though," muses Trina, "about people already being left behind economically, who live paycheck to paycheck and have nothing left over to invest. The good-news scenario you raise, Dr. Bruckner, would benefit only people who are financially comfortable and able to plan ahead, rather than live day to day. I can see this solution widening the income or wealth gap, rather than reducing it."

Lisa Carroll wraps things up. "This is more than I hoped for from this initial session. Jake and I will integrate they key points in our rollout or launch plan. Speaking of which, we'll be contacting you to be references for the analysts, potential clinical trial partners, and the press."

She claps her hands once. "And with that, we're done. Thank you, Freddy, for hosting. And speaking of the wealth gap, everyone, make sure you raid the Headwaters kitchen on your way out."

• • •

After seeing the guests out, Lisa goes back to the conference room and takes photos of the whiteboard. The Dicks are gone as well, Freddy to his office, the others to their homes. She is surprised to find Petra still in her chair, her notes in front of her.

"You got a few minutes to talk?" Petra asks.

"Sure. What's up?"

"That was sobering."

"It was intended to be. Think of me as a lawyer preparing their client for trial, especially if, like you, they're going to be testifying. My job is to anticipate all the questions—or damaging evidence—you're going to encounter."

"If that's your job, you do it well."

"Thanks. But remember: This world is new to you—not longevity, but the public arena. And I've been working with our panel for the past year, ever since the BSDs got serious about the longevity market. The reason they didn't have that many questions today is because I've kept them up to speed on Elethea for at least the past year. Today was Scare the Client Day. Don't worry. The panel also has a separate presentation on all the good news associated with your discovery."

Petra lets out a long breath, followed by a grimace. "I'm looking forward to it, because maybe it's the Greek in me, but these days I feel like Pandora about to open her box. Or Oppenheimer with his goggles on for the first test of the bomb."

"A little dramatic, but I get your point."

"You remember what Oppenheimer said after viewing the first test of the atomic bomb?

"It was something from the Bhagavad Gita, right?

"I am become Death, the Destroyer of Worlds."

"Damn, girl. You need new role models. And a slightly more upbeat message." Lisa eyes Petra carefully, wondering how seriously to take this moment.

"Most of my clients think they've invented something 'world-changing' or 'life-changing.' You're one of the few that actually lives up to those terms, so I'm glad to see that you're taking the implications of your discovery seriously."

"How could I not? Listening to your panel made me look at what we're doing in a new light. If what your panel—*our* panel—says is right, my idea could result in famine, and it could be the last nail in the coffin for this planet." She smiled bitterly. "How's that for grandiose thinking?"

"There's a quote from a French philosopher that I tell my founders if they're concerned about the consequences of their technology—or in your case, science."

"Is it going to make me feel worse or better?"

"You tell me, but here it is: *When you invent the ship, you also invent the shipwreck. When you invent the plane, you also invent the plane crash. And when you invent electricity, you invent electrocution.*"

It's Petra's turn to nod. "Sounds like I'm not the only one who can bring a party down."

Lisa has been nodding as Petra talked. Now she stops and her eyes bore in. "It's too soon for media training, but if I were advising you today on how to handle the question about consequences, it would go something like this: All inventions displace part or all of the status quo. But ask your audience this: If the Wright brothers could have foreseen Hiroshima or Dresden, should they have quit work on the airplane? If Tim Berners-Lee foresaw the spike in misinformation and teen suicides due to social media, should he have stopped work on the Internet? It's the job of society and governments—parents, in the case of social media— to *determine how best to use your creation*."

45

Burn and Turn

"ANY GOOD NEWS?"

"Afraid not, boss. None of the treated worms or flies are living any longer. In fact, they're going backwards, dying slightly earlier than the controls."

"But the CRISPR'ed lysosomes are still clearing the BFD150 out of the cells, right?"

"Kind of. We're not sure why, but the CRISPR'ed lysosomes become less efficient the longer the animals live. Plus, they're creating toxic aggregates in the test animals' cells that are obvious in the microscopy."

Bao and Josef's report to Jerry, though presented in measured tones, portends a possible disaster. If the treated flies and worms aren't living any longer and are in fact suffering from toxins caused by the treatment, it calls into question their entire theory that reducing the accumulation of BFD150 in the cells, which is what the CRISPR'ed lysosomes are doing, is the secret to their longevity solution.

"OK, let's not throw up the white flag quite yet," Jerry says. "Layla, can you tweak the ESR process any more to see if that helps?"

"I can definitely try."

"Let's do a few more rounds of tests. Keep me posted."

Despite Jerry's upbeat tone, he feels the full weight of their disappointing news. They've put all their research eggs into the ESR and lysosomes basket. If it's the wrong bet, then they may not be back to square one, but they'll be close.

The news is especially surprising because things have been going so well. The experiments were working, and the lab environment has been humming, with the scientists working tightly together, examining and critiquing each other's work without a concern about ownership or praise. Many mornings, Jerry overhears people talking and joking about a movie, concert, or dinner they shared the night before.

Then there's Petra to consider. The pressure she's under is showing, big time. He knows he needs to bring her up to speed, but he's dreading the conversation.

"Got a minute?" Jerry says as he peers over the wall of Petra's cube.

"Of course." She looks up. "Uh-oh. You've got your bad-news face on. Or are my face-reading skills rusty?"

"No, they're accurate. We've hit some snags. Nothing major yet, but just want to keep you in the loop."

"What kind of snags?"

Jerry leans forward, resting his arms on the cube's wall. He looks down at Petra and sees strain etched into her face. Dark smudges underline her eyes, and her skin somehow looks both waxy and brittle. Even her hair looks tired, clinging limply to her scalp.

Jerry looks past her to the whiteboard wall, avoiding eye contact. "As you know, we've succeeded in demonstrating how doing ESR on the lysosomes is clearing out the BFD150 in the worm and fly cells."

"Why do I get the feeling there's a 'but' coming up?"

"But it's not having the effect we expected. The treated worms and flies aren't living any longer, and as they near the end of their normal lifespans, they're actually showing signs of toxicity in their cells." Jerry lets the sentence hang there. Petra's expression registers surprise, then shock, then settles into a worried state.

"Are you sure?" she asks.

"Layla's going to try some more tweaks, so we'll see how it goes. But so far, yes, I'm sure."

Petra slumps in her chair. "This could be devastating. Obviously, we can't move forward with the mice until we solve it. And what if we can't? Or we solve it at this level but then it crops up again when it comes to the mice? With their lifespans we won't be able to ..."

Jerry walks around the chest-high wall and into her cubicle. Since there's only one chair, he takes a knee and rests a hand on Petra's arm. "It's not good news, but it's hardly fatal. You know how it works. It's like a locked house and our key no longer works. So now we try the back door, windows, even the chimney. Or we make a new key. We'll get back on track."

Petra doesn't return the encouraging smile.

"This is the last thing we need. The last thing *I* need. The board's going to ..."

"Don't jump that far ahead, Kid. I'm focusing everyone on this. All hands on deck, and all that. We'll get there. And if we don't, *I'll* be the one to tell the board. It's *my* lab. *My* fuck-up."

"Thanks, Jer, but as far as the board's concerned, it's *my* company, *my* responsibility. They'll expect to hear it from me." She looks over at the lab area. "Can I help? I feel responsible, handing you guys a faulty theory."

Jerry shakes his head. "I know the team would love to have you, but it would set a bad precedent. If we can't solve things ourselves in the next few days, you and I can come in over the weekend, just like the old days."

As he turns and walks back to the lab area, the upbeat look disappears. "This is not good," he mutters.

46

Table Talk

"IS THERE ANYTHING YOU WANT to say to me before we get started? Anything you want to get off your chest?"

"Let's just get to work. If I say what's on my mind, it'll just lengthen the meeting and piss you off. Or maybe not. Maybe you're used to being called an asshole. Or worse. I'm assuming I'm not the first person you've blackmailed."

Perkins leans back in his chair, one of those ergonomic office affairs with umpteen settings. He usually gives his spies this moment, to clear the air or vent, before getting down to business. He surveys Jake with more admiration than affront. He's been called worse.

"Do you want to know how I sleep at night?" he asks. "Or how I got into the spy-running business in the first place?" When there's no answer, he continues. "I sleep well, thanks for asking, though my wife says my snoring is getting worse. As for what you call blackmail—what I call 'encouragement'—I was in Internal Affairs when I was on the force. So I've heard it all and then some. No one can swear like a crooked cop that's just been outed. But go ahead. I'll give you five minutes to vent. No consequences, no anger on my part."

"I'll pass on the kind offer," Jake says. "Only because I think it's more for you than for me. You let me rant and you think that evens the score somewhat."

Perkins shrugs, but there's something to what Jake says. He finds his spies are more manageable after venting, but he doesn't like it when they're on to his tactics, as Jake seems to be. "I didn't like having to bring your father into the picture," Perkins says. "It's a tribute to you that you don't have anything I can compromise you with. But your father, between the embezzlement and the mistress, he's a gift that keeps on giving."

Jake uncrosses his legs and plants both feet on the floor. He leans forward, his chin out. "Given that we're talking about blackmail—the term I prefer since I'm a stickler for accuracy—how do I know you're going to honor your promise to never use that information about my dad, especially with my mom?"

"You don't. All you have is my assurance that I will show that file to both the government and your mom if you don't continue your assignment at Elethea. So let's hear what you've been up to."

Jake glares at him, making no attempt to hide his disgust. "You want to know what I've been doing in the three weeks I've been at Elethea? I've poured maple syrup in all the computers and killed all the lab mice with a hammer. What the hell do you think I've been doing? I'm learning the business. And as I'm doing it, I'm looking for ways that I can give you what you want without drawing attention to me. That's what I've been up to."

"What's your impression of the operation? And the people involved."

"I'm sure you've got a file on each of them, so I'll assess them as a team. It's almost all scientists and they work together extremely well. They've got specialists in a number of fields—molecular biology, immunology, bioinformatics, CRISPR, and so on—and they hold a daily 15-minute meeting right before lunch, where they update each other on recent progress, in case the new work could have implications for what others are working on."

"Management? Especially your pal, Petra."

Jake scowls, as if those words, coming from Perkins mouth, are distasteful. "What you'd expect. She's over her head in some places, competent in others. But she's got a good COO and ...."

"That's Jason Fredericks, right?"

"...and good coaching from Keeley James."

"And now she's got you."

"And now she's got me." His face still has that sour look. "Look, Detective ..."

"Mike."

"Detective. As you can guess, I hate being in this position. And I'm still not sure that I won't just call your bluff and let my father deal with what you have on him. A lot of it will depend on what you ask me to do. Information is one thing. Sabotage is a big step beyond that. And even if you could threaten me into sabotage, what do you think I'd be able to do that wouldn't be immediately discovered and traced back to me? These people are all geniuses in their field. I go in and alter an algorithm or poison a test—even if I knew how to do it—they'd be at my cube 10 minutes later. With the cops."

Perkins keeps the languid pose, resisting the impulse to lean forward and go chin-to-chin with the outraged Jake. But the kid's right. Perkins doesn't even know what to ask, much less how to evaluate success. He needs a number of these updates before he'll have any inkling of the weak spots in the process. Which means he can't afford for Jake to be any more of an adversary than he already is.

"Alright, let's do this. Let's see how far information alone will take us. You update me by phone—no emails, no written reports— once a month. More if there's a breakthrough I should know of immediately. And we'll meet face to face once a quarter for a plan-ning session. If I can satisfy my bosses with the information you provide, that'll be it. If I can't, then we'll have that awkward conversation about your father again."

Perkins watches as Jake's face goes through that familiar dance that is part of turning innocents into spies. Past the surprise and outrage stages, now Jake is trying to figure out two things. What's the minimum he can do and still satisfy Perkins. And, just as he'd asked Perkins, how he'll be able to live with himself afterward.

"I don't know if this is going to help you adjust to your new role," Perkins begins, "but this is how I justify my job and what it entails. You and Petra are in the creation business. I'm in the consequence business. Someone has to be, and it's usually not the inventors. It's someone like me. Or my client."

47

Tilting

"YOU THINK THIS IS A GOOD IDEA? I've never been a part of one of these before. Just seen them on TV."

"It was Izaak's idea. Then he recruited Zoe. They know her a lot better than we do. It's worth a try, at any rate."

Keeley and Freddy are in his car, on their way to The Speak Easy. It's a Wednesday night, and with Petra having missed the last four gatherings, Jerry has shamed her into attending tonight, saying that he and Alice will be bowing out of the group if she's no longer attending, that they're only there at her invitation. Mona's job is to make sure that Petra leaves the office on time, then race to the bar ahead of her to join the gathering.

"Let's compare notes," Keeley says. "You're there once a week. I'm more of an on-call resource. And she seldom calls. What's your take?"

Freddy smiles slightly. "When it comes to women, I'm only smart enough to know what I don't know. So I went to the source."

"Mona?"

"Who else? She says Petra's hanging on by a thread. There's the day-to-day CEO stuff, which she's getting better at, but which is still foreign to her. There are the snafus in the lab. There's the growing list of responsibilities that Lisa is laying out for her, especially after the meeting with the ethicists. Plus, the answers she'll need to have down pat about the impact of longevity in a variety of areas—social, economic, environmental, and financial. And Mona tells me that her mom is now living with her, that the disease is advancing more rapidly. I've never had a CEO under this kind of stress, especially so early in their company's history."

"I've been talking to Izaak," Keeley says. "He says she's running on fumes. She's quit climbing, quit socializing with her friends. As he says, she's got no outlets these days." They ride together in silence for a few minutes, then Keeley says, "Should we be looking for a new CEO, do you think?"

"I hope not. I don't know if there's a company without Petra. So I hope tonight works."

Petra is five minutes behind Freddy and Keeley, though she doesn't know they'll be at The Speak Easy. She's looking forward to seeing the group, but without Jerry's reminder she'd still be at work. It's been a tough stretch for Elethea in general, but Petra in particular, culminating this week in the firing of Reuben, one of their top molecular biologists.

Silicon Valley is proud of the maxim "Move fast and break things," but that doesn't apply to the scientific community. The science that Elethea is developing is so new, so dramatic, that any mistake can be serious—or fatal—if unchecked. Each Elethea scientist is responsible for validating their work, either double- and triple-checking it on their own, or enlisting a peer to confirm results. Reuben, anxious to get to the critical next phase in his work, had done neither. He made an error that had worked its way into others' work, setting everything back two weeks.

Petra had made Reuben topic number one for her weekly one-on-one with Freddy on Monday. "How serious was the error?" he asked.

"Serious enough on its own. But errors happen. To everyone. It was his not validating the work—either on his own or having someone like Bao look at it—that was the real mistake."

"Isn't this a Jerry problem? You've done a great job of staying out of the lab. Why get involved now?"

Petra hesitated. This was the question she was hoping she wouldn't have to answer. But it was the right question. "Because Jerry isn't 100 percent sure it was an innocent mistake." As she saw a frown creep over Freddy's face, she nodded. "It's a long shot, but there's a possibility that this could be ...'sabotage' isn't the right word, but deliberate. It's possible Reuben wanted to create a problem, then ride to the rescue. He's the new guy on the team and I think he's envious of Bao and Josef. Solving a problem like this would put him on the same level as them."

"What's your take? Sabotage or just sloppy work?"

"I was up much of last night wrestling with that question," she said. "And then it dawned on me that it doesn't matter. We can't afford either one at this point."

"Meaning?"

"Meaning Reuben has to go."

Freddy nodded, pleased with Petra's conclusion and the logic behind it. "I know it's hard, but it's the right decision." He reached over and patted her arm. "You're growing into the job."

Jerry had come to the same conclusion but hadn't shared it with Petra until she told him where she stood. "I'll do it," she said.

"Like hell," Jerry said. "I hired him, I'll fire him."

The firing had been emotional and personal. Reuben copped to the mistake but again blamed it on eagerness and nothing more. He reminded Jerry of what he'd given up in salary to join Elethea and how devastating his firing would be for his family. Jerry told him to write his own version of events that led to his departure—something like the startup lifecycle being too tough on his family—and that Jerry and Petra would both corroborate his story if called for references.

The exit interview with Reuben, which Petra had insisted on doing herself, had been tough. She knew Reuben's wife, and knew they had two children under the age of five. A part of herself was self-pitying, thinking of this episode as one more log on the pile that was her life these days. But a larger part was pleased with how she'd handled it—and of Freddy's validation.

• • •

She opens the door to the bar and steps in. Looking around the room for her regular cluster of friends, her eyes skim over the large group at a table across from their regular one. Then her eyes swing back and take in the table and its occupants. Freddy and Keeley, seated next to Mona and Ed. Then Jerry, Alice, Zoe, and Izaak.

She strides across the room and stops in front of the group. An empty chair sits between Izaak and Zoe, but she doesn't take it. "I know it's not my birthday, so someone better explain what the hell is going on here."

Izaak starts to speak, but Mona puts a hand on his arm. She turns to Petra. "We're worried about you, honey. All of us, from different angles. Go around the table and you'll hear what's got each of us concerned. We want to help."

Petra, still standing, crosses her arms and glares at the group. "So this is what, an intervention?" She spits out the word. "Seriously?" She looks around the table, her eyes defiant. Then she holds out her arms. "Anyone want to look for track marks? Or maybe I'm shooting up between my toes. Who wants to check?"

"You're running on empty," Zoe says. "And you're not yourself, at least the self I know and love. You won't talk about work, though it's clear that a part of you is still back there, no matter where we are. You won't talk about your mom. You seem worried all the time. And you look like hell."

Petra looks from Zoe to Izaak, who shrugs and nods. "She's right. You're not an entirely different person, but you're not yourself."

"You're running flat out, Petra," Jerry chimes in. "No breaks, no downtime. You can't keep pushing yourself like this. It isn't healthy. For you or the company."

"Is that a nice way of saying I'm not doing my job? Is it, Jerry?" There's an edge to her voice that she's never used with Jerry—or anyone, come to think of it—before.

Freddy speaks up. "I'll speak to that, both as your chairman and as your COO. You're making better progress on the CEO front than I would have guessed. But it's come at a cost. Because it comes on top of everything else you've got going on. Plus, you're a perfectionist. You're trying to do too many things yourself and do them perfectly. In the VC world we call it 'Founder Syndrome.'"

"Your mom's worried about you as well," Mona says. "She wanted to be here tonight, but we thought it would be too much. For you and for her. She's worried that her condition, on top of everything else ..." Mona stops as she sees the tears pooling in Petra's eyes. "My girl," she says quietly, and puts a hand on Petra's arm.

Petra is determined not to cry, not in front of this group, not in front of Keeley and Freddy. And if she does cry, she realizes with alarm, she has no clue if they're tears of anger, frustration, or self-pity. No one at this table, including Izaak and Zoe, has ever seen her cry. And it dawns on her that this stoicism, which she thinks of as a source of pride, is anything but. As she feels her anger crumble, she lowers herself into the empty chair, holding onto the sides of the seat.

"Everyone at this table wants to help you," says Mona. "And everyone knows they're risking their relationship with you by coming here, myself included. But it's a risk we're willing to take. Because you're worth it."

Petra dabs at her eyes with the pads of her hands. "If this is a true intervention," she says, "then either someone from rehab is waiting outside, or you're bringing in a bulldozer to clear out 40 years of hoarding. What's the plan?"

This time it's Keeley. "You need time off, Petra. That part's non-negotiable. What *is* negotiable is how much and in what form."

"What are my options?"

"There are two," Freddy says. "The first is you take a full month off from work. All contact with Elethea will go through me. I'll give you regular updates, daily if you want. But you don't come in, you don't call, you don't email. You concentrate on righting your own ship, taking care of your mom, and then coming back to your company ready to bring your solution to market."

"And option two?"

"You go to Yosemite, leaving tonight. Zoe's got you packed, with your mom's help, along with all your climbing gear. You spend the next four days hiking and climbing. No computer, no phone. When you get home, you take another week off to just let things settle. Then come back to your company and take it to the next level."

"What about my mom? I can't be away from her for that long."

"I'm staying with her," Mona says. "We've got some girl things already planned, starting with a day at a spa."

Petra looks around the table, emotions pinballing. Outrage. Embarrassment. Self-pity. Gratitude. But it is exhaustion that carries the day. She lets out a long sigh. Most of the table leans forward slightly. She looks around and sees the concern written on each face. Her eyes settle on Zoe. "Drink up," she says. "I'll drive the first leg."

48

On the River

"IF THIS IS YOUR IDEA OF ROUGHING IT, we can stay more than four days, as far as I'm concerned," Petra says.

"It was too late to check into Camp 4," Zoe responds. "Can you imagine us driving in there, arriving after 11? Keeping the headlights on as we make camp? We'd catch no end of shit, spoiling their beauty sleep. God help us if one of them fell tomorrow. They'd blame it on us." She rolls over in the king-size bed so that she's facing Petra. "The plan is to sleep in tomorrow, have a nice late breakfast—room service would be my vote—and make camp, then do some bouldering just to get the rust off. That leaves us all day Friday and Saturday, and part of Sunday, if we want to, for climbing. Or since we're both a little out of shape, we can hike a little or a lot. Sound okay?"

"Everything except room service. If we're staying at the Ahwahnee, we need to eat in the dining room. Trust me."

With almost a hundred rooms, most of which bear Native American themes or artwork, the Ahwahnee is a gorgeous example of what is termed either 'rustic' or 'parkitecture,' since the same architect also carried the rustic themes over to other western parks, from the Grand Canyon to Bryce and Zion. The lodge sits in a large meadow with an expansive view that takes in Half Dome, Glacier Point, and Yosemite Falls. With his copious connections, Freddy was able to secure a reservation for one night in the always-booked lodge.

The two sleep long and hard, waking at 10, a luxury for both. They take their time getting ready, then head down to the dining room for lunch. The Ahwahnee dining room is a cathedral-like hall with 30-foot ceilings, enormous pine trestles, and granite pillars. Zoe, who has been climbing steadily, at The Ascent as well as outside with casual climbing friends, orders both an impressive omelet and a side of French toast. Petra sticks to the fruit and yogurt plate.

After checking out, they drive to Camp 4, where the serious climbing crowd recognizes and welcomes them back. Zoe had called in a favor and secured a camping spot at the last moment, so they pitch camp and then head off for a quick bouldering session. They join some of their fellow campers for dinner. Most of the Camp 4 crew are poor, living for the climb, with no job during climbing season. They can stay at Camp 4 for up to 30 days at a time. After that they settle into a game of hide-and-seek with the rangers.

Knowing the diet of these climbers is based on budget more than health, Zoe has brought the makings for a large pot of minestrone the first night, enough to share with the group, who for their part contribute beer—which they buy in bulk and never seem to run out of. After dinner she surprises everyone, including Petra, with two pies from Marie Callender's, a move that makes her the unofficial mayor of Camp 4 for the rest of the weekend.

Tired from the day's climbing, the two women are in their tent and sleeping bags by 9. They spend the next hour, before sleep takes hold, planning their next three climbing trips, which they agree will have to wait until Elethea releases its hold on Petra.

"When do you think that's going to be?" Zoe asks. "Honestly. I'll wait for you. I just want to know how long."

"Hard to say. Especially given the recent setback in the lab. When I closed the deal with Freddy and Keeley, I told them I'd give them four years. I figured that's enough time on the science side to demonstrate the function of the protein and develop our solution for longevity. Once that's done, we all agree it's time to reassess my role. But if the product is viable, there are two options. The first is to go public, which would mean replacing me with a CEO with a history of success with IPOs. Under that scenario I morph into a spokesperson and evangelist for longevity in general, and our solution specifically. In which case, I'd be free to get back to serious climbing in three years."

"What's the second option?"

"We get acquired. Which Freddy says is the likelier scenario. VCs are okay with IPOs—going public—but on a tech time-frame, which is a lot shorter than a scientific schedule, with all the initial testing, long product dev cycles, clinical trials, and government involvement. The Hydras aren't interested in that scenario, and neither am I. We both want the biggest return in the shortest period of time. So, yeah, someone buys Elethea for a gazillion dollars. Under that scenario, you and I take a year off—my treat—and we hit as many climbing destinations as we want."

"How soon could that happen?"

"Sooner than I thought. AI changes everything, not just in helping me develop theories and models, but in demonstrating the product's efficacy. If I can use AI to take our work with insects, worms, and mice, and extrapolate those results into higher species, Freddy can take those results to interested parties and start the bidding. But we need to nail all our tests and prove the validity of the AI tests, neither of which is a given."

"But to be crass, either way you're going to make a gazillion dollars."

"Or they don't work and we're all out on our asses and I'm working the drive-thru window at McDonald's. But yeah, if the tests get back on track, and Jerry thinks they will, then Freddy's talking about an acquisition number north of a billion." Petra shakes her head. "That's Monopoly money. It doesn't seem real. At least not now." She looks over at Zoe. "But if we hit it big, I won't be the only one in this tent who benefits."

"Meaning what?" Her BFF says hopefully."

"Weren't you the one who helped me discover the protein?"

Zoe nods in the dark.

"There you go, then."

• • •

The next day is a full one. The two hike an hour to a wall that few climbers know about. Tackling a route they've done before, they rope up and climb for much of the morning. After lunch they park themselves at the base of the wall. Zoe takes out a folded piece of paper, smoothes it, and shows it to Petra. It's a printout of the rock face they're looking at, with some words off to the side.

"That's Spyder's handwriting," Petra says.

"I told him we might be coming up here and he sketched out this route for us to try. He says only do it if we're up to it and do it when we're fresh. Your call. We can either spend this afternoon plotting a route for tomorrow or go back to camp and do some more bouldering."

Petra squints at the massive granite wall, so much of it smooth, even to the practiced climber's eye. Then she looks over at Spyder's route. "Let's try this."

Zoe takes a pair of binoculars out of her backpack and passes them to Petra.

They take turns with the binoculars, pointing out possible barriers, first gesturing up at the wall, then marking it lightly in pencil on the sketch. As the paper fills with marks, the excitement in the women's voices grows.

"I know we're a little rusty," Zoe says, "but I think it's doable. How about you?"

"You're being kind, saying *we're* rusty. You're moving great. I'm the one who's holding us back. But it's coming back to me." Petra shrugs, but her voice betrays her enthusiasm. "Let's try it."

Zoe spends the next 15 minutes with the binoculars, studying the route and calling suggestions to Petra, who acts as recording secretary. They then change roles, with Petra tracking from the mid-mark. Suddenly she sits straight up and hands the binoculars back to Zoe.

"Let's head back," she says, in an excited voice that causes Zoe to look at her oddly.

"We're not done mapping," Zoe says.

"I've seen enough. We'll make it. But I need to get back to camp. I just thought of something. It's important."

"If it's work-related, I'm vetoing it. That's my job this weekend."

"I just need 30 seconds with a phone. I won't talk to him, just leave a message on his work phone."

"On whose phone?"

"Jerry's. I think I just came up with a solution to the lab problem that has brought us to a stop." She looks at Zoe's frustration. "I wouldn't have come up with it if you hadn't brought me up here. I've been wrestling with this problem ever since Jerry told me about it. But the more I tried, the more frustrated I got." She gestures at the granite. "But staring at that smooth face is like a Zen exercise. It forces your mind to relax. And once my mind quieted down, the solution was there." She looks over at Zoe. "Thirty seconds."

Zoe looks at her for a long moment. "Does giving you a phone mean more stock for me?" Without waiting for an answer, she reaches into her backpack, brings out a phone, and hands it to Petra. "Go for it."

Petra takes the phone, then looks at Zoe. "I thought you surrendered your phone to Freddy. Just like I did."

"I figured Freddy would pull something like the 'no phones' trick, so I brought him one of my old ones." She looks over at Petra. "Come on. What if you'd fallen? Or worse, what if I'd fallen?"

Petra smiles and punches in a number. She speaks in excited tones, with words that Zoe can't understand. Then she clicks off and hands the phone back. "See? Thirty seconds. And no more calls, I promise. Let's climb."

· · ·

It takes them two hours to summit, but it goes faster and smoother than either expected. They hike back to camp, full of themselves. When they get there, Zoe announces that, to celebrate their summitting and Petra's breakthrough, as well as to thank their neighbors for securing the campsite, she's taking the group to dinner in El Portal. "That's a generous gesture," Petra says, as their six pals head off to change. "I'll split it with you."

"No need. I got Freddy's credit card. One of those heavy ones that say: I'm rich. Who do you think paid for the Ahwahnee?"

On Sunday, done with climbing, the two go for a hike. Veterans of Yosemite, there's little of the park that's new to them. But the rangers have just opened a new trail, so the two women explore this part of the park, one rich with fast-running streams, mini-waterfalls, and bushes exploding with small flowers. Back at Camp 4, they break down the tent, take a climber's shower, and say their goodbyes.

As they exit the park, Zoe hands Petra her phone. "Go crazy, girl."

Petra dials her mother's phone and is slightly surprised when Mona answers. "Let me guess," Petra says, "she's in the shower."

There's a long pause at the other end, long enough to cause Petra to hold the phone away from her to see if the call has dropped. Finally, she hears Mona: "Honey, your mom's in the hospital. She either slipped or passed out in the shower. I don't know if she hit her head when she fell or if..."

"How is she?"

"She's in a coma. They've stabilized her, but that's all the news so far. I tried to explain her condition to them, in case that matters, but they're going to want to hear it from you. How soon can you get here?"

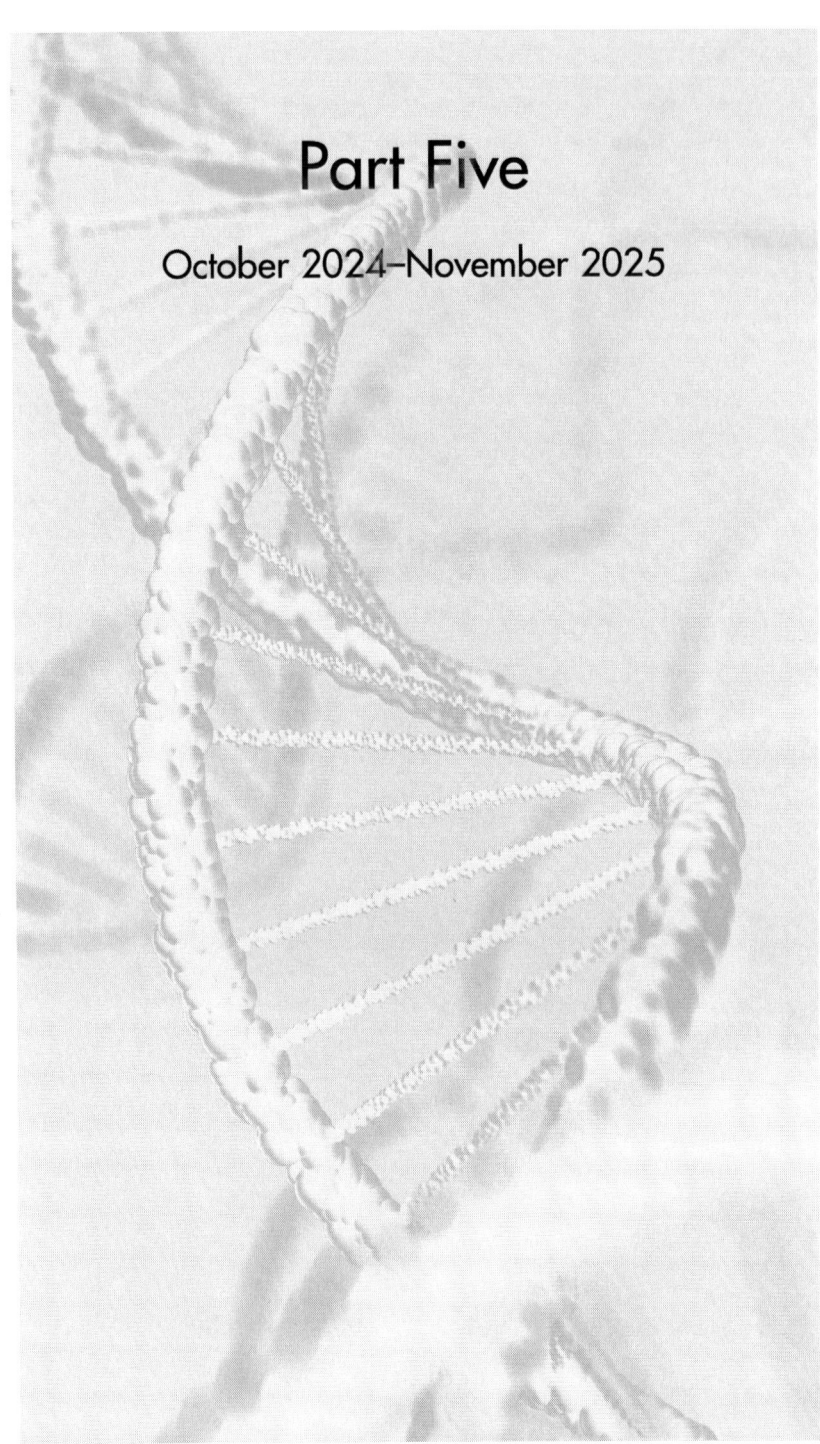

Part Five

October 2024–November 2025

49

Full Tilt

"THEY DON'T WANT to go into details with me on the phone," Petra says. "What's her status?"

"No change. She's in a coma. They're still trying to figure out the cause. I don't know enough about her disease to answer any of their questions. They're waiting for you to give them more details before they decide on the next test."

"Thanks, Mona. For everything. Tell them I'll be there in three hours. Who's with her now?"

"Izaak. He's been here the whole time. I had to call him to help get her out of the shower, which is where I found her." There is a gulping sound. "I'm sorry, Petra. I tried to be around her as much as possible without making it seem like she was under house arrest, but I couldn't follow her into the bathroom."

"Don't even go there, Mona. You did everything you could. If there's anyone who should be apologizing, it's me."

"Then don't you go there, either, honey. We all did the right thing this weekend—you getting away, me getting to spend more time with Eleni, my daughter joining us for dinner Saturday night. It all went perfectly. Until it didn't."

"You said she has a bruise on her cheek?"

"The doctors said it's from the fall. But they don't know if the fall caused the coma or vice-versa. Which is what they want to test for once you brief them on her condition."

With Zoe burying the needle on the speedometer, they make it to Sequoia Hospital in three hours. Petra hustles past the nurses, intent on room 308. Inside the room, no doctors or nurses are in evidence—only Mona, holding Eleni's hand and speaking to her in a low, soothing voice, and Izaak, sitting in a chair at the foot of the bed, silent, his eyes rimmed red.

Eleni looks peaceful, the bruise just starting to show. The wig is gone, as is most of the makeup. The lines on her face have deepened, her skin slackened. If she were a man, they would call her "weathered."

Mona yields Eleni's hand to Petra and, taking Izaak by the arm, leaves the room without a word. Petra sits for an hour, her hand clenching Eleni's, her eyes never leaving Eleni's face, fearful of missing even the slightest encouraging sign. Mona eases back into the room and stands next to Petra, not touching her. "The doctors are hoping to talk to you now." She extracts Petra's hand and nods to the doorway, where a nurse is waiting. "Shelley will show you the way."

Her feet shuffling, as if picking them up is too much work, Petra follows Shelley down the hall. They stop in front of a closed door. Shelley knocks twice and eases the door open. Two doctors are waiting for her and they stand as she enters the room. The one who steps forward is a man in his forties, lean, with a widow's peak of rust color with a few shoots of grey. His handshake is gentle but not weak.

"Ms. Alexander, I'm Dr. Cummings, your mother's admitting doctor." He gestures to the other doctor. "This is Dr. Lawrence, our resident neurologist. We're sorry to be meeting under these circumstances. We've treated your mother as best we could, given how unique her condition is. Anything beyond making her comfortable and watching for any swelling, especially in the brain, we were waiting on, until we talked with you.

Our understanding is that you know more about your mom's condition—a Werner-like variant, if that's what we're looking at—than anyone here. If so, we want you involved in any decisions we make."

For the next hour Petra walks them through her family's history, her early work with Werner, and the mutation that she believes to be the cause of her mother's symptoms. Dr. Lawrence, who tells Petra to call her Sheila, is the one with the most questions. A small woman in her sixties, she has an angular face, a helmet of grey hair, and a no-nonsense way of asking questions and answering Petra's queries, even though she qualifies most of them with, "But I've never seen anything like this."

As they wrap up what the doctors assure her is just the first of many diagnostic meetings, Dr. Cummings says, "I know you've got a company to run, but I hope we can reach you with any..."

"I'm not going anywhere," Petra says. "I'll be here until she wakes up."

A small smile. "Your friend Mona predicted that would be your answer. She also secured your mom a single room and a rollaway cot, which will be in your mother's room when you return." He stands. "Now, if you'll excuse me, I've scheduled a Zoom with a number of my colleagues to get their input."

"Do you want me to participate?" Petra asks. "As a researcher, not as the patient's daughter."

"Absolutely, if you're up to it. I didn't want to interfere with your time with your mother, but I know the group is going to have questions that only you can answer. So yes. Absolutely."

• • •

When Petra returns from the Zoom call, she finds Mona back at Eleni's bedside, their hands joined. A rollaway cot, looking like a mattress clamshell, stands in the corner, next to the door to the bathroom.

"They have any new insights?" Mona asks.

"They're asking the right questions, which is encouraging. But they're also looking to me for answers I don't have, things I've spent a lot of my life asking and trying to answer myself."

"What do they say about the coma?"

"That she could wake up tomorrow. Or never." Petra hears the sharp tone of her answer and shrugs an apology at Mona, who waves it off. "When I was doing my graduate work at MIT, I worked on incurable diseases. One of the doctors I was working with told me that Harvard did a study of over a hundred hospitals. And the conclusion at the macro level was that 35 percent of cases that come through a hospital door will wind up in a file they call GOK. For 'God Only Knows.' So it's not just the coma that's wait-and-see. I think the diagnosis will either be GOK, or some word-salad diagnosis that includes the word 'idiopathic.'"

"Which means?"

"That same doctor told me to never settle for a diagnosis that includes that word, because it's just another way of saying GOK."

Mona nods at a small duffel bag next to the rollaway. "Zoe and I didn't think you'd be going anywhere for the next few days, so she went to your place and packed a bag. She figured your hiking gear probably wasn't appropriate for this place, not for an extended stay, at least."

* * *

By Eleni's fourth day in the coma, with her condition showing no signs of improving or worsening, and with Petra having no intention of leaving her mother's side, Mona takes over. She integrates Petra's hospital and Elethea responsibilities into a single schedule, then tells everyone, employees and board alike, to go through her for any requests of Petra's time. The two sit together and consider the options, either delegating to a combination of Freddy and Jerry, or designating a few uninterrupted hours a day to Elethea business. If neither option proves sufficient for handling the responsibilities of a startup on the verge of major developments, they'll need to talk to Freddy about bringing in one of his Entrepreneurs in Residence.

Jerry is the first one to conduct Elethea business at the hospital. He and Alice have been visitors since the day after Petra returned from Yosemite, but today is all about business. Mona has commandeered a table in a quiet part of the cafeteria, which she adorns with a Reserved sign, to which no one, hospital staff included, takes any exception.

The lack of any progress on the Eleni front is clearly plaguing Petra, who sits passively as Jerry brings her up to speed about BFD150. He's clearly excited but holds back out of respect for Petra and their surroundings.

"I don't want to disturb you, but I thought you'd like to know what we've done with your idea." Petra looks at him blankly, her eyes somewhere else. "The one you called in from Yosemite. About using ESR to work directly on BFD150 to change how the protein folds, in addition to using it on the lysosomes."

"God, that feels like years ago. With everything that's happened, I completely blanked on the idea, much less calling you."

"When I got your message, I called Layla right away. With the 3D model we have of BFD150, she was able to use her CRISPR skills to alter the protein's folding. At least one of those prospects is causing the nematode worms and fruit flies to stop showing signs of any toxic aggregates. Whether they live longer, we don't know yet, but it's start. Better than a start, actually."

"Did you notice any changes in the telomeres in the treated animals?"

"It's too soon to know for sure, but their telomeres don't seem to be shortening. Again, we need to let all the tests run for a bit longer, but my gut feel is that this is the answer. So thanks for the breakthrough. And the call."

"No, thank you both for taking the idea and running with it. This is great news, Jer. Now we just need the same in Mom's case."

Two days later, Keeley visits. As instructed, she calls Mona first to get the lay of the land. She's told not to ask about Eleni, that repeat accounting of the lack of progress to each visitor seems only to deepen Petra's mood. As she settles at the cafeteria table, she sees the toll the past week has taken on Petra. Her cheekbones are sharper, even as the skin below them is sagging, and her eyes seem to be sinking into her skull. Petra asks after Keeley's granddaughter, but it's a hollow question.

"Petra, I'm here as a friend first. Anything you need, work or otherwise, you get the word to me through Mona, and it's yours. As for these visits, I'll try to keep them few and short, unless you want Valley gossip to distract you, in which case I've got hours' worth of material."

Petra almost smiles. "But you're here representing the board as well," she says. When Keeley just raises her chin once in assent, she continues. "And they're wondering if they've still got a functioning CEO, aren't they?"

Keeley doesn't object to the question or the tone. "They're all concerned about you," she says. A smile tickles the corners of her mouth. "Even Zac." When Petra doesn't respond, she continues. "But yes, they're worried about the company as well."

"Have you talked to Jerry? I understand there's been progress on the product front."

"Due to you, I understand."

"Hardly. He had to remind me I'd even called him. It's my idea, true, but Jerry and Layla are the ones who are making it work."

"However we got there, it's major progress. Jerry's hopeful that it's the last major barrier to cross before testing the discovery's viability in mice."

"Yeah, well, we'll see ..." Petra's voice drags down and then drifts off.

Keeley shifts in her chair, then leans forward. "Listen, Petra. You know I've got this hybrid role—representing the board to you and vice-versa. This is one of those times where I want to tell you where things are—or where I think they're going. But I want to make sure you're following what I'm saying, and I don't think that's the case right now."

Petra raises her head. Her eyes become a little clearer. "If it's something I should hear, go ahead. I'll listen. Just don't ask me to think. Or decide anything."

"Fair enough. Yesterday the board asked Jerry to update us on the breakthrough. The news he gave us was the best they've heard in a while. It's sped up their thinking about an end game. Which is part of why I'm here."

"Acquisition?"

Keeley nods. "Which I'm assuming would sit well with both you and Jerry. Neither one of you strikes me as being interested in shepherding a major company through the next seven to ten years. Not when you could be out coming up with new breakthroughs."

"I can't speak for Jerry," Petra begins, then catches herself. "Actually, I can in this case. You're right—neither of us is interested in an executive position with a major company, even if it's one we created."

"The board thought as much. And they're all in on the acquisition front as well. But if we go that route, with the shortened timeframe, it increases the demands on everyone in the company, starting with you. Which is part of why I'm here—to see if you're up to it."

"Update me and we'll both see whether I'm capable of what's needed or whether I need to step away."

"According to Jerry, the most recent breakthrough, if it proves out in mice experiments, should be enough to provide us with what we need to start engaging with potential suitors."

"I'd agree, based on what Jerry told me."

"But if we go that route, we need to know your availability, both time-wise and psychologically. Jerry was clear that the last two breakthroughs were wholly due to you. He was adamant on this point. I quote: 'Elethea *is* Petra, and vice-versa.' He said there's genius and there's diligence. According to him, you're the former and he's the latter."

Keeley waits for a protestation, but none is forthcoming. "And that's just the science part. As far as the board goes—and I agree on this front—you're at least as important to the acquisition process. Any prospective buyer will do their homework and come to the same conclusion that Jerry has. You're at the core of Elethea."

"And if I'm damaged goods or not available, that will..."

"Impact the price. Considerably."

Keeley looks around the cafeteria, which is emptying, now that it's almost two in the afternoon. "Before we go any further, the board has asked me to raise a delicate issue. This condition your mother has. Is there any chance that you have it as well?"

Petra falls silent. This is the question she's waited for the doctors to ask, but they haven't. She's thought about telling them about her own test results, but she doesn't want to distract from her mom's situation. But now it's the board that's asking.

"Tell the board I've tested myself periodically ever since I became aware of Mom's condition. So far, so good."

"Then here's what I'd propose. Short-term, things are moving ahead. Jerry's running the lab and taking your discovery to the next level. Freddy's running the company in your absence. And Zac is just starting to nose around about possible buyers. You stay here and concentrate on Eleni. I'll update you on Elethea and you let me know what role you want to play in the company going forward. I'll support whatever that decision may be. The board will, too."

. . .

The next visitor catches Petra by surprise. Mona had received an email from a Cheryl Aynesworth, saying that she was a friend, that she'd heard the news about Eleni and wanted to visit. Mona waved her off, but she persisted. Given that the request came from a Salvana address, she asked Jake if he knew her. Which is how Petra finds herself sitting across from Cheryl, this time in the quiet of the chapel, since there is an event in the cafeteria.

"I'm sorry to hear about your mom. I met her once in the café. She couldn't get over that her cappuccino was free, and lunch only cost three dollars."

Petra smiles, but it's a sad smile. "I think she wanted me to stay at Salvana just for the food. We had to buy one of those espresso machines for Elethea just to keep her happy." Off Cheryl's confusion: "She's a CPA, does all our accounting."

"Keeping things at a conversational level," Cheryl says, "how are things at Elethea? Ed explained the derivation of the name. Nice touch."

"I don't have any basis for comparison, but the pace feels fast but controlled. It's great to see a bunch of very talented people turning my idea into a reality. How about you? How much of what you do is longevity and how much standard Biz Dev?"

"The longevity project is coming along well. The guy who's running it is a gem. He's a big fan of yours, by the way. For the first year, he gave half his team full rein to pursue other approaches. The other half worked on developing the research you gave me when you left. At the end of the year, it was no contest."

"Call me when you guys discover the three sabotage points I hid in the research. You should be hitting them in the next six months."

Cheryl laughs gently, respecting the surroundings. "I miss you and Jerry. Happy for you guys, to be sure, but I wish we could have gone on this ride together."

"You ever think about doing a startup? You'd be a great CEO. Seriously. Freddy's always looking for Entrepreneurs in Residence for Headwaters and their client companies."

"Maybe when the girls are a bit older. And if Kurt's condition improves." She sees Petra's confusion. "That's right. We didn't know each other long enough for me to tell you about him. Only HR knows. Their benefits were a big part of why I joined Salvana. And why I stay."

· · ·

An hour later, the two women are still talking. The reference to Kurt took the conversation in a fresh direction, with Cheryl finding herself sharing with Petra the demands that Kurt's accident have put on the family. There's hope among his team of neurologists that he may regain some of his mobility, that a breakthrough is still possible. Still, she says, no one has given her a schedule.

"I'm sorry to unload like this," Cheryl says at one point. "I only talk about Kurt to my therapist. I'm not sure why I'm comfortable telling you." She gestures around her. "Maybe it's the surroundings, like I'm in a large confessional."

Petra looks at the relief on Cheryl's face as she shares the pressures she's under, of the tragedy that has scarred her family at every level. She takes a deep breath, then says, "The disease my mother has? The moment Jerry and I confirmed its link to whatever my sister had, we assumed it's hereditary, so I started testing myself."

Cheryl leans forward and takes Petra's hand. "And?"

"And the news was good. Until recently."

Five minutes later, Mona opens the door to the chapel to summon Petra to yet another doctor conference call. She finds the two women sitting closely together, their foreheads touching as they talk in low, almost sacramental tones. Petra sees Mona, nods, and stands up. Cheryl follows suit, and the two embrace— a long, genuine hug that catches Mona by surprise.

As Petra moves down the hall towards the conference rooms, Cheryl starts to ease past Mona, who's still standing in the doorway. Mona stops her with a gentle touch on her shoulder.

"I don't know who the hell you are, but you're welcome back here any time."

50

Misdeal

ELENI EMERGES FROM HER COMA on Day 9. At first, it's just a slight change in pressure on her little finger as it rests in Petra's grasp. Then the fingers all close around Petra's hand, gripping it loosely. A nurse sees Petra suddenly sit up, then sees the hand, and hurries out to alert the doctors.

Dr. Cummings hustles in just as Eleni opens her eyes. The peaceful mask that her face has settled into over the past eight days stays in place, as if Eleni is aware of, and comfortable with, her setting. But her eyes tell a different story, wide and shifting side to side. It looks like she wants to talk, but the lower part of her face hasn't come back to life yet.

The doctor leans over her bed, so that his face takes up most of her vision. "Eleni, can you hear me? Blink twice if you can." The shifting eyes steady, then two quick blinks. "Good, good. I'm Dr. Cummings, and you're here in Sequoia Hospital." He holds out a cupped hand to Eleni and closes and opens his fingers, motioning for Eleni to do the same. He eases back so that his face is still in Eleni's sight, but Petra's face can take primacy.

Petra leans forward and whispers in her mother's ear, first in English, then in Greek. Whether it's Petra's voice or her private message, Eleni's eyes lose their wild, trapped look. At the same time, the rest of her body starts to catch up with her eyes. Within an hour, she's able to move arms and legs. The nurse pushes the button on the bed, allowing her to sit up.

"Welcome back, Mamá. We've missed you." Petra looks gratefully at the doctor, who shakes his head.

"This is all her, not us."

Petra smiles at him. "GOK?" He nods.

With Eleni's awakening, Mona adds her visitation schedule to Petra's work calendar. She monitors her patient, who is delighted at the attention and the visitors but tires easily. The hospital wants to keep Eleni for at least three days for additional testing, and to gather more data for Dr. Cummings and the team. Despite the urging from Eleni, Mona, and the doctors, Petra refuses to go home, as if the change in routine might send her mother back into the coma.

Freddy visits Eleni on the second day after her awakening. The two have become friends during his weekly time at Elethea. He brings in lunch from Eleni's favorite gyro shop and visits with her for over an hour. He then heads down to the cafeteria, where Petra is waiting at a table.

"She's looking and sounding like her old self," he says.

"She's mortified that people are seeing her without makeup and her wig," Petra says. "I've told her that enough people have seen her now that she should just go with short hair when she comes back to work. She won't give up the heavy makeup, though, and I can't blame her."

"How about you? This thing has to have taken a toll on you as well."

"Yeah, well..." Petra gazes out the window, then comes back to Freddy. "Listen, Freddy. I know the intervention was your idea..."

"Mine and Mona's."

"I just wanted to thank you. You've been a friend, as well as my COO and my boss. Can't always be that easy for you, wearing all those hats."

"It's been...unique. Going all in on the funding with you guys, being on-site once a week—that's all new territory for me. We're both making it up as we go. But it looks like it's paying off. Not bad for two amateurs."

Petra nods. "Keeley told me about the meeting with Jerry. And about the plans for acquisition. Sounds like things are moving ahead."

"They are, but before we go any further, I need to take your temperature. Officially. I know Keeley told you that, whatever you decide, we'll support you, but hers was an unofficial visit. I'm here as head of the board to reiterate what she said." He waits until Petra nods. "If, after I lay things out for you, you tell me you need to be at home full-time with Eleni, we'll move ahead without you. Zac will find a buyer, he'll get a good price, we'll all make a ton of money, and Elethea will be regarded as a major success."

"With that setup, I'm dying to hear what the *but* is."

He chuckles and tucks his head slightly, like a kid caught in a lie. "What if there is no *but?*"

"There's always a *but* with you, Freddy. That's part of your charm. Your *but* in this case is that the acquisition you just described will feel incomplete, both from a science standpoint and a financial one."

This time Freddy laughs out loud. "I can't wait to hear what I'm going to say next in this conversation. You're right, on both counts. On the science front, Jerry is employing yet another of his baseball analogies. He says we're in the seventh inning, and if the game is called on account of rain—or acquisition in this case—it will go down in the books as a win. But it won't be as satisfying as a complete game. He says there's one more major step to achieve before your solution is truly validated and you two can feel like you've achieved what you set out to accomplish. Do you agree?"

She nods. "Yes. We need to show that our tweaks to BFD150 work to extend the lives of mice, at least. And on the financial front?"

"Put your modesty aside and look at this acquisition from the other side of the table. They've got this young, attractive, articulate woman who broke the code to aging and who can assure the public—and investors in the acquiring company— that longevity is attainable, with the unspoken message that the acquiring company got a helluva deal."

"And if I can't be that person?"

"Then I'd cut my purchase price by a third. Or more."

"So no pressure, is what I'm hearing."

"None." He smiles and starts to stand. "But that conversation can wait. For now, take Eleni home, get her settled, and stay away from the shop. I'll let you know if and when we have something further to discuss."

Eleni is released after three more days of observation. The doctors, in recognition of Petra's involvement in the diagnostic process, don't pretend that they had any role in her recovery. They admit they don't know what caused the fall or coma—or which occurred first. They suspect, but can't say with certainty, that her Werner-like condition played a role. And they have no prognosis on whether it will recur. "In short," Dr. Cummings says with a smile, as he wheels Eleni down to the hospital's driveway to where Mona is waiting in her car, "there's no need to tip."

. . .

Cheryl waits a few more days before visiting again, this time at Petra's apartment. She and Eleni sit at the kitchen table and talk while Petra tidies up after the lunch Cheryl brought. Then Eleni retires to Petra's bedroom—now hers—for a nap.

"How's she doing?" Cheryl asks. "And how are you? In that order."

"She's doing great. It's like the coma never happened. She's declining, no doubt about it, but it's her disease, not the aftereffects from the fall. Or coma."

"And you?"

"Hanging in there. I put everything on hold—work, my emotions, my friendships—until we were released." She stops. "Listen to me. 'We' were released. I sound like Eliot talking about E.T. 'We're fine.' But yeah, we're both coming to grips with our situations and wondering what's ahead." She looks cautiously at Cheryl. "How about you? You hanging in there?"

"Barely. I told my headhunter to start looking around. Benefits are the critical factor, but I need to be doing something I'm proud of. And that's not at Salvana. Not anymore."

"Well, whatever you decide, I'm happy to be a reference. I mentioned the EIR path to you before, but a startup might not be the right place for you, given the other demands on you. Trust me, I speak from experience on that front."

"Speaking of which, do you think you'll be able to resume the CEO role, with everything that's going on in your life?"

"Honestly, I don't know. Without trying to make this a pity party, I'm hanging on by a thread. Or I'm the camel, waiting for that one more straw. Take your pick."

Cheryl's eyes move around the room, then out the window. Anywhere except on Petra's face. Finally she says, "I need to tell you what our friend Mike Perkins has been up to. It's about Jake."

51

An Open Seat

"HOW'S YOUR MOM DOING? I wanted to visit her in the hospital, but Mona said that if she let me visit, especially since I'm the most recent hire, she'd have to let everyone visit."

"I'll tell Mom you were asking after her. She'll appreciate it," Petra says in a cold, almost informal voice.

Jake looks at her oddly. "Is everything alright?" He catches himself. "That's a stupid question. I just hope..."

"Speaking of hope, I was hoping, as I was driving in this morning, to come up with some witty or cryptic remark that would let you know that I know what you've been up to."

"It's not a secret. Lisa and I have been working with the professors to..."

"You've been spying on us, Jake. The only open question is if you've been sabotaging us as well."

Jake's shoulders slide back, touching the back of his seat. His eyes leave Petra and look down at his lap. "It's not what you think, Petra. I was hired to research the entire market, not just Elethea."

"Did the other CEOs teach you how to climb as well? Or should I be flattered?"

"I was going to tell you. I promise I was. I just didn't know how. I told the guy who was in charge of the program...

"I believe he's called a 'handler' in the spy world."

"Stop it!" His voice rips through the air, startling them both. Jerry and Bao, the only others in the lab this early, both look up, then return to their work when Petra waves them off. "You don't know what it's been like this past year. I signed up for a research position, and then, when I tried to quit to join Elethea, this guy..."

"I believe his name is Mike Perkins. I've met him, remember?"

"When I tried to quit, he showed me two files. One was proof that my father has been embezzling from his company. The other was photographic proof that my father has been having an affair. Perkins was going to release the first file to the government and the second to my mom if I didn't cooperate."

"By sabotaging Elethea? Was that the trade-off?"

"I'd never do that. But I pretended to go along and report back to him—he wouldn't know I was lying to him—until I could find a way out of this situation."

"Well, let me give you that way out. You're fired. Effective immediately."

Jake sits there, a vacancy taking over his face as he goes back to staring in his lap. Finally he says, "I'll go ..." He catches himself. "As if I have a choice." Petra doesn't return his weak smile. "But I have one request. Tell Eleni about your decision. She'll..."

"That's the last thing I'm doing," Petra says. "First, because of her condition, and second, because she really liked you. We all did." She stands up. "I'm going home now. I want you gone by lunch."

She stays in her cube, ensuring that Jake leaves, hopefully without speaking to anyone. Whether it's out of shame, or that he hadn't yet filled his cubicle with personal items, he doesn't pack a box. He simply leaves, staying at the door for a moment, looking back one more time before departing.

Petra beats herself up on the drive home, her mood vacillating between sadness and anger. She has no idea how she's going to tell the board—and the rest of the company, for that matter. How to explain hiring a spy/saboteur, though what the hell, he got past everyone, not just her. She's determined to keep the news from Eleni for as long as she can, until her recovery is complete. Her mom really liked Jake, and Petra's sure her mother also harbored some hope of a relationship there. And, if she's being honest with herself, she did, too.

52

Fourth Street

"GREAT TO SEE YOU BACK IN THE LAB," Josef says a couple of days later as he passes Petra, Jerry, and Layla deep in conversation at one of the lab benches.

"Trust me. No one's happier about it than me."

With Eleni now home and acquisition increasingly likely, Petra has, at Jerry's invitation and with Freddy's approval, returned to the science side of things. She still works from home for part of most days, but Jerry updates her by Zoom at day's end, a Stella in hand from the dorm refrigerator in the conference room. At Petra's urging, he treats her like just another scientist, giving her regular assignments. She also works with Freddy, again remotely, on a new company pitch, this one intended for possible acquiring companies. This latter project focuses on two items: translating her AI models and predictions into terms an acquiring company would understand—what Freddy calls 'business science'—and working with Freddy and Eleni on Elethea's finances.

She hasn't told the company's staff about Jake yet, but she has informed the board. The reaction was more understanding than she could have hoped for, a generosity she attributes to two factors: the looming acquisition and the fact that they interviewed and vetted Jake as well. The one person she hasn't told about Jake is her mother.

. . .

She's impressed by the progress the team has made during her absence. Jerry and Layla have taken her rock-climbing epiphany—her hurried and almost forgotten voicemail message to use ESR directly on BFD150 to alter its folding, as well as on the lysosomes—and used it to extend the lives of the lab's nematode worms and fruit flies, with no toxic aftereffects.

Mice are the next test step in the evolutionary ladder, a mammal whose physiologies are much more similar to humans' than the lowly worms and flies. Part of this similarity is an extended life. While the lower species' lifespan is measured in weeks, mice live two to three years, sometimes more.

Which poses a fresh set of problems for Elethea. "It'll be a year before we get measurable results from the mice," says Jerry, who's sitting with Petra in Elethea's conference room. "And at least double that to see if there's any effect on their longevity. Which was fine when our schedule was for an IPO, however long it took, right? But it won't fly for our acquisition plans."

Petra nods. "I've been thinking about that and playing with my AI models. Here's what I suggest we do." She walks to the whiteboard and writes: Group 1 and Group 2. Under Group 1 she writes "Treat with BFD150 at infancy"; under Group 2, "Treat with BFD150 at 18 months old."

"We track both groups of treated mice, along with their comparable controls, simultaneously. I feed all the data into my AI models to get accurate projections of the treatment's effects, but in weeks rather than months or a couple of years."

"I see where you're going." As he thinks, Petra watches him, a smile on her face. "That could work. But how would you ..." He waves a hand in front of his face. "Forget I asked. I'm barely computer-literate. AI is way beyond my comprehension. I'll just trust you."

. . .

Three weeks later, Jerry, Layla, and Bao huddle in front of Petra's computer screen. Petra has loaded the baseline data on the mice into her newly optimized AI models, along with data on both sets of control and treated mice three weeks into their tests.

"I'm not sure what we're looking at," says Jerry.

"That's because there's not much to see yet. Which is to be expected, but the trends are there, and they're looking good. The AI model is able to pick up on minuscule changes in the effects of BFD150 in the mice, then project trends based on that data. Right now it's giving us projections with a wide range of probabilities. As we add in more data, that range will get tighter and tighter. Within weeks, if all goes well, we should have a reasonably accurate assessment of whether BFD150 is affecting longevity factors in the mice."

. . .

Eleni has dinner waiting when Petra comes in. Bustling about the kitchen, she doesn't notice Petra's mood. The transition from hospital to home has gone smoothly. At Petra's urging, Eleni has foregone the wig and is now wearing her hair short, with no attempt to hide the grey. She still applies makeup each morning, even if she isn't planning to leave the apartment. But after two weeks, she's going stir-crazy, and her walks around the neighborhood—the doctors have forbidden her to drive, due to the mystery surrounding her collapse—don't do the trick.

As a result, Petra finds that Eleni has an agenda for today's lunch, one that erases the topic of Jake from Petra's mind. "I'm going back to work next week," Eleni says, scooping the falafel balls she has prepared over a hearty salad. "And so are you. The company needs both of us, especially with all the acquisition activity."

Petra, about to take a sip of water, puts the glass down. "No way, Mom."

"Call me Eleni. This is a work discussion."

Petra almost smiles. "Then, no way, Eleni. I can work from here while monitoring your situation and working. Plus, I can keep doing my side work on your condition."

"Would you listen to yourself, honey?" She corrects herself. "I mean, Petra. You're trying to lead a startup through its most important phase, cure a disease that's stumped everyone, and be a full-time caretaker. Which I don't need, by the way."

"I think we'll let the doctors decide that last one."

"They already have," Eleni says. "I talked to Dr. Cummings this morning in preparation for this conversation. He told me that he not only wants me to go back to work—that sitting around obsessing about my condition is detrimental to my recovery—he wants me to go in five days a week, if I'm needed. Which I am, especially if we're opening our books to acquiring companies." She looks at Petra with fierce eyes. "I like being productive, honey. And if I've only got a little time left, I want it to be helping you and the company, not sitting home taking my vitals every three hours."

Petra starts to object, but Eleni is on a roll. "You can stay here and work on whatever, but you'll be here alone. I'm not staying here. It feels like a fallout shelter."

"Do I get a vote here?" Petra asks.

"No. It's my life. Here's my proposal. I plan to work until my condition makes that impossible. I know you won't tell me when that is, but Mona will. Or Freddy will. At that point, I'll retire to this nice shelter with a daytime caregiver. Who won't be you. And then I'll graduate to a nearby facility—and there are a number of good ones, I've checked—or hospice here."

She pauses, both to gather herself and to let the plan sink in for both of them. "But you are going back to work on Monday. As the CEO, not Chief Scientist. And I'm coming back as your Head of Finance."

53

Side Pot

"HOW LONG DO I HAVE TO ENDURE THIS RELATIONSHIP?" Jake asks.

"Endure? Such a harsh word." Perkins rolls his shoulders, as if letting the insult roll off him. "But to answer: As long as you're at Elethea. Or as long as your mom and dad are alive." He tries a friendly grin. "You should be honored, Jake. Normally I can find enough material to—I like the word 'persuade'—my spies within their own lives. But you, my friend, while you may not be a Boy Scout, have led a pretty pristine life. Which led me to your dad. But enough chit-chat. What do you have to report?"

It's been two weeks since Petra fired Jake, a confusing two weeks that has left him unmoored. He has no routine to fall back on. He can't go to The Ascent anymore. He has renewed his triathlon training, but found his heart isn't in it. And Perkins has him by the balls and is starting to squeeze.

The only positive is that his departure from Elethea is not common knowledge, even within the company. He was copied on an email from Mona, saying that he was taking personal leave to attend to a family matter back in Ohio, that the company wished him well. She asked the team to give him some space for the next week or two, not to call or email. He assumed from that message that Petra was keeping the news under wraps—perhaps telling only Jerry and Mona—as she tried to figure out how to tell the board and the rest of the company that one of her strategic hires turned out to be a spy for the competition.

"Let's be clear about something up front," Jake says, trying hard to come across as Perkins' equal in this conversation. The only advantage he has in this relationship, he realized as he prepared for this meeting, the first since Perkins showed him the file on his father, is that Perkins believes he's still at Elethea. "Sabotage, if and when I carry it out, will be a one-time deal, so we better make it good."

"Why just a one-time deal? If you're careful, I could see it being..."

"Forget it. First off, the actual science is so far beyond my capabilities that even when I get the lab guys to break it down for me, I barely understand it. I sure as hell wouldn't know how to go about sabotaging the solution."

"What about experiments, then? That's where I could see you doing some damage."

"That's the one area where they're vulnerable," Jake says. "Ever since you showed me the files on my dad, I've looked at the company through new eyes. The good news is, Elethea isn't Salvana, where access to most of the facilities are with a traceable key card. It's a very open environment, so it's a possibility. So for the past two weeks I've kept an eye out for vulnerabilities. And, to see what I could get away with, I made an alteration to one of the experiments, which did set things back a few days, until they caught and corrected it. But keep in mind that everything we do there is measurable, which means it's also traceable. If suddenly the company starts seeing mistakes and problems, even if they don't suspect sabotage, they'll put in systems that..."

"...that you'll have to learn how to navigate. I get it, Jake. It's not going to be easy, either practically or ethically. And I'm sorry about that, believe it or not. I really am."

"Then why the hell are you doing this?"

Perkins pauses, a moment that grows past the point of discomfort. Jake can't tell if Perkins is lost in thought, has checked out of the conversation, or is just fucking with him. Finally, Perkins seems to come back to the conversation. "Because I'm a patriot, and this is what my government has asked of me. My job right now is twofold. Keep an eye on the market in general and delay the development of any meaningful longevity solution. Right now, thanks to your Petra, Elethea is leading the pack. By a comfortable margin."

"What's the government's end game? To kill us all once the solution is complete? Or kidnap us and take us all to a deserted island? Or is it like the final scene from *Raiders of the Lost Ark*, where you buy us, swear us to secrecy, and then bury our work in one of their warehouses?"

"Nothing that draconian. We'd start with a meeting like this, telling them what was at stake. Then we'd offer them an attractive offer, more than what you can get from any biotech company. You'll all be rich, and the planet will be safer.

"Bottom line here, Jake, is that Elethea's solution could break the planet. Do the math. The world population has almost doubled in just my lifetime. And that's without your solution. We can't allow any longevity solution to be available to the general public. It's as simple as that."

"And what if Petra and the board hear your offer and still insist on going forward?"

"We've got files like the one I have on you on everyone in the longevity market. If that form of persuasion doesn't work, we can use the full powers of the government to ruin their lives. And if that still doesn't work, then we have no choice except to take them off the board. Which is just what it sounds like."

54

Filling In the Hand

"YOU NEED TO TALK TO YOUR MOM," Mona tells Petra.

Petra snaps to alert. "Why? What's happened?"

"She keeps asking me what's up with Jake. Maybe we should have gone with a different story than a crisis back at home. She wants to know his address to send flowers, wants to call him and see if there's anything she can do." She shrugs. "It's the mom gene kicking in. I'd be doing the same if I didn't know the truth."

"Okay. Thanks for the heads up. I'll tell her tonight, over dinner."

Within Elethea, only Mona and Jerry know about Jake. Both of them were shocked at the news. In the short time Jake had been with the company, he'd made friends and impressed the scientists with his probing questions and ability to translate what they were up to in terms their families could understand. Jerry's immediate focus upon receiving the news had been on the lab and the possibility of sabotage. Under the guise of preparing for an upcoming technical review with potential new investors, he had queried the team about recent work and double-checked their experiments and findings for alterations. He was convinced that, if Jake had joined as a saboteur, he hadn't had the chance yet to put his plan into effect.

Mona's concern was for Petra. She knew her boss was kicking herself for having been played, first in the climbing gym, then at the coffee sessions, and finally at work. For a poker pro like Petra, being played was the ultimate sin.

Telling the board had been humiliating. Petra waited until Jerry completed his audit and told her that he hadn't detected any sabotage before calling an emergency evening session. They met at Headwaters HQ, with Freddy providing dinner. Zac flew up from LA and Trina rode over with Keeley. Petra arrived with Jerry and Mona in tow.

By unspoken agreement, everyone chatted over drinks and dinner. It was clear that Petra wasn't herself and so, whatever the news or issues, they'd let her get to it in her own way, on her own schedule.

The board took the news of Jake being a spy better than Petra had. Reassured by Jerry's audit and the news that the solution was still on track, they sought to comfort Petra, saying that all of them had interviewed Jake, and all of them had been taken in.

"Thanks, but you each had an hour with him," Petra said. "I had over a year. The two are hardly comparable. I got taken. Big time."

Mona chose that moment to speak up. She'd been in board meetings before, primarily as a recorder, but also to update them on items such as facilities and budgets. So she wasn't intimidated by either her surroundings or her audience. "Can I say something?" Without waiting for permission, she plowed ahead. "I don't know Jake's motivations for doing what he did, but it seems to me that we came out ahead in all of this." She saw Petra start to object, so she held up a hand. "Let me finish. Let's say this guy was auditioning to join Elethea from the start." She looked at Petra. "Looking back, do you think that was the case?"

"I've thought about that," Petra answered. "A lot. I was the one who brought up the subject, who recruited him to join the company. But he could have been playing the long game."

"Agreed. But before you start kicking yourself again, think about how much knowledge and business skills you gained over the past year from what you called his *MBA tutoring*." Mona turned to Freddy. "I've certainly seen evidence of that tutoring. You?"

Freddy nodded. "I'd like to think it was due to my COO sessions, but a lot of what I brought up with you, you already knew."

Mona continued. "All I'm saying is that we—Elethea and especially you, Petra—came out on the plus side of your relationship with Jake." She cocked her head as she looked at Petra. "I can't see you divulging the crown jewels to anyone, especially in a coffeeshop or in a climbing gym. Now, if he'd been here long enough to learn our science and understand details of the solution, I'd have a different opinion. But from where I sit, you came out ahead in this relationship."

Petra reached over and patted Mona's hand. "I appreciate your positivity, Mona. But I still fucked up."

* * *

Petra waits until she and Eleni have cleared the table of the dinner dishes and are drinking espressos from the coffeemaker that Eleni has insisted on buying as her way of paying rent.

"Mamá, Mona tells me you've been asking about Jake. I need to tell you what's up on that front."

Eleni listens to Petra's self-flagellating account of Jake's treachery. At a couple of points she tries to interject, but Petra asks her to wait until she's done to respond. When she reaches the end, she opens both palms in a futile gesture. "I got played. If this were poker, that bastard would have all my money by now."

Eleni listens sympathetically, her face showing her pain over her daughter's plight. "Can I talk now? Because this is all starting to make sense."

Petra looks at her oddly, but motions for her to continue. Eleni stands up, walks over to the door, and takes an envelope out of her briefcase. "The day Jake joined Elethea, he came to me and asked me to do two things. The first was to hold this letter to you..." She passes the envelope to Petra. "The second was to open an Elethea account and directly deposit his paychecks into it. He said that any access to that account would require your sign-off. I was confused, but he said he'd explain later. But he told me if anything happened to him, if he left the company for any reason, or worse, I was to give you this letter. I'm surprised he didn't tell you about it."

Petra sighs. "He tried to. He told me to talk to you, but I was so angry, and you were just out of the hospital, so I blew him off."

She opens the envelope and takes out the single sheet of paper. "Let's see what the SOB has to say."

55

Check Raise

"WHAT'S YOUR TAKE ON THIS PERKINS GUY?" Max asks. "Is he a government lackey or a true believer?"

"Hard to say," Jake says. "At first I thought he was just an asshole, a retired cop who misses being able to bully people. But the way he talks about the government and his role, I now think he's a zealot, determined to either bring us down or keep us off track for as long as possible."

"Where do things stand now between you two?"

"That's the good news. He doesn't know I was fired, so I can feed him whatever information or results we want."

"The United States government," Trina says, letting those three words settle over the table. "That's an adversary to be taken seriously."

It's been two weeks since Jake has returned to the Elethea fold, with hugs all around. His relationship with Petra is a bit tense on both sides, she for his duplicity, he for the harshness of his firing. But they're back to weekly updates, sometimes with Lisa Carroll, sometimes just the two of them, preparing for the launch and its ramifications. And Jake has been invited to the latest BSD/Elethea board meeting, on the yacht.

Freddy stands up. Recognizing that his part of the meeting is concluding, Jake does the same. "Thanks for the update, Jake. And welcome back. You were missed." They shake hands, and

Freddy says, "Kerry has a crew member standing by to take you to shore."

With Jake gone, Keeley takes command of the meeting. "Before we go any further, let's make sure we're all on the same position regarding acquisition versus IPO. I know the Hydras are all in on acquisition. Petra? Jerry?"

"Both you and Freddy have done a good job of summing up the pros and cons of each. Neither of us got into this endeavor to ring the bell on Wall Street. Or to get rich. The goal for each of us is the discovery and creative process, not managing quarter-to-quarter results to satisfy the market. So yeah, we're in favor of acquisition."

"Great," Keeley says. "Zac will be running point on both finding the right companies and negotiating a favorable price. Any questions for him?"

"What about us?" Jerry asks. "Do they show us the door with some parting gifts and say thanks for playing?"

"Hardly," Vinod says. "You'll probably have what they call *velvet handcuffs*."

"What does that entail?" Petra asks.

"Handcuffs for founders are usually for two years," Freddy says. "They'll want Jerry to work with their team, merging Elethea science and solutions with their own. And they'll want you to be the face of longevity, to do a media and analyst tour that does everything from educating the analysts and media about the solution, to explaining how smoothly it fits into the acquiring company's science approach and tools."

"Will they integrate the team into the larger company or let us stay on our own?" Jerry asks.

"That's part of the negotiation," Zac says. "If it's important to you to keep your team together, then I'll make it a requirement. Same with location."

"Do we have any role in the negotiations?" Petra asks.

"Not in the direct negotiations, but I'll need your help up front to help me set the floor, the minimum of what we'll accept. I'll take it from there. There are basically three types of acquisition. The first is called an 'acquihire'. It's where the acquiring company just wants the talent, usually just the engineers—or scientists in this case. That's not what we're talking about here. But if it were the case, I'd probably set the price at four hundred million." He lets the number sink in. "Which is a tribute to the team you've hired and their impressive accomplishments to date."

Petra looks at Jerry when Zac quotes the asking price. Jerry tried to look nonchalant, but it's clear he's impressed. Zac doesn't notice as he looks down at his notes. "The second option," he says, "is if we had to sell today for some reason. We're in an enviable position: post-discovery, post-POC, with tests guided by AI projections and a solid management team. I haven't done a single outbound call, yet I've heard from three companies already. If we needed or wanted to sell right now, I'd work with Jake and Lisa Carroll to develop a whisper campaign that would drive up both interest in Elethea and the acquiring price. Perhaps way up."

"And why wouldn't we take that offer?" Jerry says. "It starts the two-year clock for Petra and me, and it makes the team immediately rich." He holds up a hand. "I'm not suggesting we go that route. Just asking."

"Two reasons," Zac says. "Number one, because I hate to leave money on the table. And number two, I'm not around Elethea the way Freddy is, but it seems to me like you and your team want to see your solution through to the point where it's working at the mammal level, even if that mammal is a mouse. And as quickly as your team works, that could be sooner rather than later. Which brings us back to reason number one, don't leave money on the table."

56

A Dead Hand

"CAN YOU JOIN US in the conference room for a few minutes?" Bao asks.

"Sure," Jerry says. He looks up from his monitor and then frowns. "I know that face. What's wrong?"

Bao has already turned towards the conference room, leaving Jerry to follow. When he gets there, Jerry finds five of his team sitting around the table. "Okay, guys. What's up?"

Josef speaks first. "At first we thought it was just some random anomaly, but…"

"But what? One more time: what's wrong?"

"We've got a mouse problem. To be specific, a dead mouse problem."

"Details, please," says Jerry.

Leslie speaks up. "As you know, part of my daily routine is to check on the mice every morning. Four days ago, I found one of the mice had died. I wasn't concerned, because these things happen, right?"

Jerry nods slowly.

"Then yesterday, there were two more."

"Why didn't you say something then?"

"We discussed it, and we did a thorough examination of the mouse enclosures, making sure there wasn't a problem with their water access, their bedding, or any other external factor."

"Was there any sign of what killed them?" Jerry asks.

"None at all," says Bao. "So we agreed we'd keep an eye on things to see if it happened again. But this morning, there were four more."

"They're all in the treated group," says Leslie. "And they're all males."

Jerry gets up and walks over to the mouse area of the lab. He examines the seven dead mice but has no idea what he's looking for. He shifts his examination to their enclosures but, like his team, finds nothing there. He walks back to the conference room. "Stay here. I've got to tell Petra about this. Then I'll return and we'll discuss our options."

He walks over to Petra's cube and waits for her to look up. She smiles, but then sees the look on Jerry's face.

"We've got an issue," he says. "A serious one."

"What's up?"

He relays the story of the dead mice, just as his team has outlined it to him. When he finishes, Petra says, "No clue what killed them?"

"None."

"It's only the treated mice, and only males?"

Jerry strokes his chin nervously. "I've shut everything down and brought the team together. We'll look at this from every angle. If you've got any thoughts on what might be up, come join us. Otherwise, I wanted to let you know in case we need to put the brakes on Zac's conversations with potential buyers."

"You've checked to see if there were any toxic aggregates building up in their cells, like the issue we had before, when we were doing ESR only on the lysosomes?"

"I haven't, but the team has. Everything looks fine at the cellular level."

"Then why? And why only the males? And if they're all get-ting the same food and treatment, why aren't they all dying at once?"

Petra looks up at Jerry, her mouth and chin tight. She swal-lows drily. "I didn't factor gender into my AI models. I can't imagine gender would be a determinative, but I'll factor it in tonight and let you know what I find." She looks at Jerry. "This is bad, Jer."

"I know."

"OK, I'm going to clear my schedule for the rest of the day and see if I can figure out what's going on here." She turns immediately to her AI monitor, already forgetting that Jerry's still there.

Two hours later she walks into the conference room, where Jerry and the team are looking at the problem. "I'm going home. I think better there. I'll call you if I find anything."

57

Narrowing the Field

"HONEY, I HOPE YOU TAKE THIS in the spirit it's given, but you look like crap," Mona says. "I can't believe Eleni let you leave this morning, looking like this."

"I left before she woke up, went to the gym to clear my head. But thanks for the critique."

"Well, somebody's got to tell you, especially if you're meeting with our possible new bosses." Mona's eyes narrow. "You *are* meeting with them this afternoon, aren't you?"

"No. I begged off, told them I had a stomach bug. I just came in to pick up a few reports, then I'm heading back home to try to figure out what's up with the mice. I was up all night, going over my past models, comparing them with what we're using now. I went line by line, then I challenged the starting assumptions. And even if I figure out why the mice are dying, we're only halfway home. We need to figure out why it's gender-specific, why only the males are dying."

Petra picks up the reports and puts them in her briefcase. She stands up and heads for the door without saying goodbye. Mona doesn't take it personally, just calls after her to take a nap when she gets home.

Petra waves without looking back and leaves.

Mona walks over to where Jerry is working with Nigel. She gets his attention and nods with her head at the conference room. "Keep an eye on our girl," she says to him. "She was up all night with this mice thing and she's looking more than a little frazzled."

"We all are. But you're right. She takes these things harder, beats herself up."

"Is this as serious as she says it is?"

"Yeah, it is. It could put the acquisition at risk. It will certainly delay it, at any rate. When you're talking about the numbers that Zac is getting—and we're still negotiating—tests on worms and flies don't count. Mice are the starting point, a species with the same basic physiology as humans. If we can't show flawless tests with the mice, the offer is off the table."

"What are the vets saying?"

"About what?" Jerry asks.

"About why they're dying." Mona leans back, appraises him, and rolls her eyes. "Put a couple of the dead soldiers in a bag and give it to me." She shakes her head. "Scientists."

* * *

"Do we keep potassium cyanide in the lab?" Mona asks when she returns, handing over the bag with the mice in it.

"No, it's highly toxic," Jerry says. "Why do you ask?"

"Because that's what's killing your mice."

"According to who?"

"According to Dr. Emilio Mendoza." Mona reaches into her purse and takes out a business card. "He's a veterinarian and professor in Stanford's Comparative Physiology department. And a running partner of Izaak's. Took him no time to determine that they'd been poisoned, then an hour of testing to determine what the poison was."

Jerry leans back against his chair, forgetting that it's on wheels. He almost topples, then rights himself. "We don't use potassium cyanide for anything. I won't allow it in the lab." He twists his ponytail for a few seconds. "This is purposeful poisoning. Sabotage. Which means..."

"It's one of us." Mona looks around the building, seeing everyone with fresh eyes. "Grab your keys," she says to Jerry. "Let's do this over at Petra's."

* * *

The next day, in the science briefing before lunch, Jerry announces that Petra has some good news. He turns the floor over to her.

"Thanks, Jer." She looks around the lab at the scientists, some standing, some leaning against their desks, some seated. Petra gives them an embarrassed smile. "I just want to apologize to you all for taking so long to figure out what was happening with our mice. I know how seriously you all took this setback, how you went over your own work, then did peer reviews of each other. But in the end it all came down to a flaw in my AI model. So my apologies to all of you. But we're back on track. I've told Zac to restart the negotiations."

58

Setting the Trap

PETRA IS BACK IN HER APARTMENT, PBS NewsHour on in the background, the volume low. She looks up now and again from her work to catch the headlines, then is back at it. There are two windows open on her large monitor. One is an online poker game with three hands open. She's is playing the three hands simultaneously, her fingers dancing back and forth across the keyboard. She mutters to herself at times, either questioning a play from an opponent or critiquing one of her own.

The other window is a live feed from a camera, showing a wide-angle shot of the Elethea lab. She's been monitoring the screen for the past two hours, as indicated by the count on her poker screen. When she needs to use the bathroom or dish out the take-in dinner, she switches the visual to her phone. Just in case.

A shift in lighting on the Elethea screen catches her eye. The front door has opened, with an angle of light suddenly illuminating the floor and part of the far wall. Petra sits up and leans closer to the screen. Then a figure comes into view. Though it's from the back, the long braid and the easy, athletic gait betray the identity of the visitor: Layla.

"The last one I would have suspected," Petra says. She grabs her laptop and car keys and heads for the door.

• • •

She kills the lights of her Subaru as she turns the corner and coasts to a stop just down from Elethea's front door. She grabs her briefcase from the passenger seat, locks the door, and mounts the steps to the front door. She opens it just as Layla is exiting, her hand on the handle.

To her credit, Layla shows no alarm. She smiles warmly. "Just making up for coming in late this morning. The northwest swell hit this morning. Solid six feet and glassy. I was out there for three hours, just couldn't bring myself to paddle in." She gestures around the office. "What are *you* doing here at this hour?"

"I thought I'd check on the mice, make sure the fix to our formula is holding. But it looks like you beat me to it."

"I didn't check on them. Once you said the error was fixed..."

Petra holds up her laptop. "Nice try. After the last batch of mice died, we did a necropsy and discovered the poison. Do you want to show me where you keep the potassium cyanide, or shall I show you where we put the camera?"

Layla starts to protest her innocence, but the look on Petra's face stops her. She's only seen two faces of Petra in her time at Elethea: the first friendly, the second focused to the point of ignoring her surroundings. But this third one is of barely restrained fury.

"Before I escort you out—don't worry, I'll let you pack your things—you want to tell me why you did it?"

Layla stares defiantly back. "I'm happy to, but not standing here. You really want to know, let's go back inside."

Petra pushes the door open and motions Layla inside. The two women head wordlessly down the hall to the conference room. Petra flips the lights on, and Layla turns to her, any sense of remorse or shame absent. "Have you done the math yet?"

"Excuse me?"

"The math. Your number. I'm assuming you have one. Your share of one billion. Of two. Of three."

"No, I haven't done the math," Petra says. "I'm not in it for the money. Never have been."

"Then you're the only one who hasn't. Maybe Jerry hasn't either, though I'll bet you Alice has."

"And if they have, so what? Everyone, you included, risked everything and worked incredibly hard to develop this solution. You all deserve to profit from your efforts."

"That's the key word here, isn't it? Profit. According to my math, both you and Jerry will make between three and five hundred million when you sell the company."

"It's Monopoly money you're talking about, Layla, most of which I'll give away. Same with Jerry, I'd imagine. I don't know a single one who's here for the money."

"Don't kid yourself, Petra. You're not out here in the lab every day, listening to these guys talk about what they're going to do with the money, comparing notes on what type of look-at-me car they're going to buy."

"Maybe you're right, but it's not why they came here. They came for the intellectual challenge and to do something that changes the world."

"Then let's talk about that world you're changing." Layla leans back against the conference table and shifts her feet, as if bracing for something.

"Remember in our interview, when you asked me how I spent my year off after Berkeley? Before joining Elethea? And I told you I surfed my way around the globe?"

"I remember. What's that got to do with sabotaging our work?"

"In Bali I met a retired Silicon Valley VC. I'm sure Freddy and Keeley know him. We got to talking, and it turns out he left the Valley and the rat race to pursue radical improvements in health care for all people. *All* people, Petra, not just the rich."

"Our solution is for everybody."

"Bullshit. You know how I know it's bullshit? Because I've seen your preso to investors, where you say life expectancy is, depending on the country, 75 to 80. Right?

"Yes. What's your point?"

"Those numbers, *your* numbers, are for first-world countries. Or developed countries, which is the politically correct term. That same number for developing countries is 30 years less. Who deserves your solution first, Petra? Who?"

"That will be for others to decide. We're scientists, not politicians or sociologists."

"That's where we differ. When we crack the code—and don't worry, it will be a different solution than yours, a better solution—we'll distribute it free to any developing country and their people."

"Admirable. And first-world and second-world people, or whatever the correct term is? What happens to them?"

"They get in line and wait their turn. We tell them they only move up once the longevity numbers for their third-world counterparts rise. Maybe *that* will motivate the first world to finally get off its ass and provide the drinking water and health care that it should have in the first place. And to start to undo all the damage we've done to their environment. As if we own the planet and they're squatters."

She stops, her face aglow. Petra regards her new adversary with a look that borders on admiration. "You make some good points, Layla. I'll give you that. And another time, another place, I'd probably be trying to join your company. But I've got obligations to the people who placed their faith in me. One of whom I thought was you. So find a box and pack up. I'll wait here and then show you out."

59

Showdown

THERE'S A KNOCK AT HER DOOR, which she rarely keeps closed. She doesn't acknowledge the knock. She knew he was coming and asked her assistant to be somewhere else. Now he must decide whether to wait in the hall or intrude. She knows it's petty, but it's what the SOB deserves.

Finally, he opens the door slightly and puts his head in. She pretends to be on the phone and motions him inside. He comes in but stops in front of her desk, unsure whether to take the chair in front of her or sit at the small conference table. She motions to the table as she wraps up the imaginary call.

Cheryl rises and crosses to the small table, which has three empty chairs once the two of them are seated. "Thanks for coming, Detective."

"Mike."

"I'll stay with 'Detective' for this meeting, if it's alright with you."

"Fine by me. I got to admit, I was a bit surprised to get your invitation. I normally don't see you except for our quarterly check-ins."

"Well, I thought the new developments on that front merited a meeting. Face to face. I didn't want any of this in email until we had a chance to meet."

He sits back slightly, eyeing her. "You've got my attention. What's the latest?"

"Before we get to that, let me bring in the other guests. I'll ask Tonya to show them in."

"She isn't at her desk."

"I think she's back by now." She presses a button on the speaker phone in the middle of the table. "Please send our guests in."

The door opens and Petra walks in, followed by Freddy. If Perkins is surprised, he doesn't show it. "You know Petra, of course," Cheryl says, in a saccharine voice, her mouth holding back a smile. "I don't know if you've ever met Freddy. Jason Fredericks."

"Met, no. But of course I know who he is." Perkins extends his hand, which Freddy takes. Then he turns to Cheryl. "Why does this feel like an ambush?"

"I prefer to think of it as an intervention. A chance for a fresh start."

"And why would I, why would we all, need a fresh start? Things are going so well. Here and, I believe, at Elethea." He looks at Petra. "Or am I misinformed?"

Petra smiles at him. "They're going better since your spy was identified and fired."

"Now it must be you who's misinformed. What spy are we talking about?"

Cheryl clicks the button again. "Tonya, please send in our other guest."

The door open and Jake enters. He nods at everyone and takes the last seat at the table.

"I think we all know each other," Cheryl begins, "though in different contexts. Detective, do you want to pretend otherwise?"

"Why should I? You and I both interviewed and hired our man Jake here and sent him out to research the world of longevity and the players in it."

"But you were the only one of the three of us who saw sabotage as being part of that job description," says Jake.

"Sabotage is a harsh word."

Freddy speaks for the first time. "What would you call it, then?"

Perkins ignores Freddy and turns to Cheryl. "Can you tell me the purpose of this meeting—sorry, this *intervention*? Otherwise, I'll have to take my leave of the four of you and your smug smiles."

"The purpose," Cheryl says, "is to update the different contracts at play here. Yours with Jake, yours with me, and yours with Salvana."

"And I would do that why?"

Freddy answers. "Because the last thing that you and your boss—and I'm talking about the government now, not Salvana—want is for news of your corporate espionage to get out."

Perkins almost snorts his reply. "Corporate espionage? In Silicon Valley? Between multibillion-dollar companies? Hold the presses."

"I agree that corporate espionage isn't usually front-page news," Freddy says, "but what about the government's plans for our technology? The way I understand it, there are two plans at work here. The first is to keep hindering, destroying even, the programs under development. That wouldn't play well in the press, your own government trying to limit our ability to lead a longer, more productive life."

"You don't have any..."

"But wait," Freddy says, a smile tickling the corners of his mouth. "As the late-night commercials say, there's more. What if I told you that your government, the one you pay all those taxes to, is planning to acquire this longevity solution, keep it for itself, and administer it only to the select few that it deems worthy of an extended life?"

"And you thought the uproar about Obama's death panels was something," Cheryl adds. "Your plan smells a bit of the Third Reich."

Perkins' face and overall demeanor have shifted now, from relaxed and smug to full alert. There's no panic there, but he's taking on the attributes of a cornered animal.

Petra speaks up for the first time. "I've asked our marketing team to put together a sample campaign for each of these two plans. The government's efforts to destroy innovation that could benefit millions of its citizens, and its intention to use this solution to play God, deciding who lives and dies based on the government's own definition of *value*." She slides a piece of paper across the table to Perkins.

He scans it briefly, then puts it face down on the table. "If you'll remember from our first meeting with Jake," he says to Cheryl, "as well as subsequent meetings, there's nothing in print about any parts of our arrangement. And the money we pay our man Jake here can't be traced. Where's your proof?"

"I think that's my cue," Jake says. He takes out his phone and places it on the table. He pushes a button and the detective's voice comes in. "...If you think the government is going to make this product available to the general public and then have to support this new generation of old farts, both financially and with health care, you're crazy. Governments pretend to care about their citizens, but what they really care about is power. Getting it and expanding it. From what I gather, the government's plans for a true longevity solution are twofold. The first is to administer it only to their best and brightest—the Einsteins, Edisons, and Steve Jobs. The second is to make it available selectively to the uber-rich, charging them exorbitantly and keeping those monies in dark, untraceable accounts to fund the kinds of activities that never make the news."

Jake's voice comes out of the phone. "What about the normal American?"

"I raised the same question to my bosses. Their answer was brief and to the point: 'Fuck 'em. This is not a medicine. It's a weapon. And we'll use it where and when we think appropriate.'"

. . .

Thirty minutes later, Perkins leaves. "Well, that was fun," Cheryl says.

"I didn't think we'd get a response today," Petra says. "That's the only surprise."

"Between Jake's tape and Petra's marketing plan, he wasn't really in a position to negotiate," says Freddy.

It had been a civil discussion. After Jake turned off his tape recorder, Perkins asked if he could step out and make a call. He came back 10 minutes later and sat down. "What do you want?" he asked in a pleasant voice. "I'm assuming you don't want this to get out, not while you're in the process of being acquired." Seeing the surprise on Petra's face, he smiled. "That came from another of my longevity spies, not our mutual friend, Jake. Again, what do you want?"

The Elethea terms were straightforward. Jake was to immediately end any employment or relationship with Perkins, Salvana, or the government. Perkins was to cease any activity related either to Elethea or its acquiring company. And Cheryl was resigning from Salvana with one year's salary and full benefits, with a second year of medical benefits guaranteed in case she hadn't found a job by that time.

Perkins had stepped out to make another call. This one lasted 15 minutes, but when he returned it was with a full agreement to all the Elethea terms. Perkins had then picked up his stuff and extended his hand to the nearest person, Jake, who shook his head slightly and kept his hands on the table. Perkins took the cue and left.

"That was too easy," Cheryl says. "We should have asked for new cars—or houses—while we were on a roll." She turns to Petra. "Thanks for the idea about extending the health benefits to two years, just in case I'm still unemployed."

"Based on your track record and what I've heard about you from Petra," Freddy said, "employment is the least of your worries. Hell, I've got three startups that could use your services today, two as COO, one as CEO."

"I'm not ready to be a CEO," Cheryl says.

"You think I was?" Petra says. "And I don't have a business bone in my body. Think of what Freddy could do with someone like you."

"Give it some thought," Freddy says, sliding one of his cards across the table.

"Thank you," Cheryl says, putting the card in her briefcase. "One last thing before we end this kumbaya session. I know we all got what we wanted just now, but I'll be damned if I know how we got here." She turns to Petra. "It started with me telling you about Jake, right?" Petra nods while Cheryl mouths a 'Sorry' to Jake. "And, unless you're a great actor, it was a total surprise to you." She motions for Petra to take up the story.

"And I storm back to Elethea and fire Jake, who doesn't exactly protest his innocence but tries to drag my mom into it. Which I thought was a real weasel move."

"What did Eleni have to do with it?" Cheryl asks.

"My thought exactly. I just thought he was playing me, knowing that my mom liked him. But I was afraid news of that sort would upset her, maybe even set back her recovery."

"So the firing was real, not faked?" Cheryl asks.

"Definitely real. And it stood that way for three weeks, until Jake's absence became too much of an issue, and I told Mom about firing him. That's when she told me about the account and the letter."

A confused Cheryl turns to Jake, who picks up the story. "When Perkins started blackmailing me, I knew I had to pretend to give in to him initially, to buy myself some time to figure things out. I needed to have a way to tell myself—and ultimately Elethea—that he didn't own me. Luckily, he thought he did, so he never questioned the authenticity of what I told and showed him. Which was fortunate for me, since most of it, while sounding real, was always one or two plumbs off from the truth."

"And the account and letter that Petra mentioned?"

"I didn't want to profit from my treachery, and I couldn't refuse Perkins's money, whether it came from Salvana or the government, without arousing suspicion. So I told Eleni to open up a separate Elethea account and direct deposit all my paychecks in there. If anything were to happen to me, all that money would go into a separate R&D fund to continue the lab's work. I also gave her a letter for Petra, explaining everything. Then I set about figuring out how to get out of my situation with Perkins and the government."

"All of which I screwed up by going to Petra," Cheryl says.

"Which I'm grateful for, because I had no idea how to extricate myself," says Jake. "You forced the issue."

Petra brings the story to its close. "When I read the letter and Mom told me about the shadow account, I called Jake up to apologize. We got together that evening to see where things stood with him and Perkins and what possible courses of action we might adopt."

"Nothing occurred to us initially," Jake says, "but we agreed I had to start recording all my meetings with Perkins. Once we had the recordings, the two of us went to Freddy, who agreed it was time to confront Perkins."

"He likes to be called *Mike*," Cheryl says.

60

Cards on the Table

"IT TOOK LESS THAN 30 MINUTES for the government to agree to all our conditions," Freddy tells the assembled team. "Summing it up: Layla's gone, Jake is back, and the acquisition is on track."

"What's going to happen to Layla?" Nigel asks. "Are we going to press charges?"

"We don't need the publicity, not in the middle of an acquisition. But we'll keep an eye on her." He turns to Petra. "Maybe we'll hire Mike Perkins."

As Petra starts to stand to address the company, Freddy interjects. "Sorry, one last thing. From the first day that we worked together, Petra has advocated for this group in a way that no other CEO in my experience…" He turns to Keeley, who nods, "and it looks like in Keeley's experience as well, ever has. Petra took less stock so that we could increase your guys' share. And when it comes to the company's future, she has asked us to be as open as possible with you." He motions for Petra that he's done.

Petra initially looks down at her feet, clearly embarrassed by Freddy's praise. She nods her thanks to him, then looks out at the crowded room "I know that Jerry or I have met with you all individually to keep you apprised of the IPO vs. acquisition discussions. It seems like everyone's comfortable with the decision to pursue an acquisition while we prepare to launch the company and product to the world. Which should also get the vesting clock started."

A hand goes up. It's Michael, the newest hire. "What's a vesting clock?"

Freddy steps in. "It's the schedule by which your shares vest and you can sell them on the open market. The standard vesting schedule is four years, which means that every month that you're here post-acquisition, you vest $1/48^{th}$ of your shares. As an example, if you had 48,000 shares of Elethea stock, you'd vest 1,000 of those shares every month that you're here."

"Can you tell us what companies you're talking to?" Nigel asks.

Petra and Jerry look at Zac. "I can't do that yet, but what Petra has insisted on—and again, this is a first time for us—is that we have a three-person team vetting the companies that make our short list. I'm the principal negotiator. My job is to get the highest possible price and the best terms for shareholders, which is everyone in this group. Jerry will handle the science side of things—how well will the teams and the science mesh. And Mona will handle the HR—culture, benefits, and the like. If you have questions or input in any of those three areas, come see any of us."

"What can we do to help while the negotiations are going on?" Maya, another recent hire, asks.

"Make sure all the tests you're running can stand up to the toughest examination so we can get the highest possible valuation," Zac says. "The mice results have to be bullet-proof, since that's what Petra feeds into her simulations to show the companies in question that BFD150 and its resulting solution will scale to the human level. It's your mice results coupled with Petra's AI models that are at the foundation of our talks, so both of them have to be able to pass even the toughest questions and scrutiny.

Especially since we won't have human trial results to point to in our negotiations."

"You Americans are such pansies," Bao says. "In China we'd already be a year into testing BFD150 on live prisoners." He looks at Josef. "Taking a page from Doctor Mengele's playbook."

Josef raises his can of diet Coke in recognition. "You're welcome."

"And on that cheery note," Freddy says, "let's all get back to work."

61

Fifth Street

LATER THAT DAY, as Petra is packing tonight's homework into her briefcase, her mother looks over her cubicle wall. "Got time for a quick walk and talk?"

"Is it something we can do at home? Or is it a Rodin Garden conversation?"

"I'd prefer to do it here, since it's work-related. We've done a pretty good job of not bringing work into your apartment. I'd like to keep it that way."

Petra looks over with a smile that is half curious and half condescending. "Well, with that setup, you've definitely got my interest. What's up?"

As they exit the building, Petra takes her mother's arm and turns left, toward downtown. But Eleni overrides her and steers them into the neighborhood. "Downtown's got too many distractions. I want your full attention on this one."

The smile on Petra's face is now fixed in place. She has no idea where her mom is going with this. "Okay, Mom. You're driving this bus. I'll just walk and listen."

Eleni ignores Petra's tone and starts right in: "In today's meeting, I know Bao and Josef were only joking about experimenting on humans. But I thought: Why not me?"

"Why not you what?"

They walk in silence for a moment, then Eleni waves her free hand at her face. "Look at me, *kardia mou*. I'm not fooling myself or anyone else with this makeup. I'm dying and it's a hopeless feeling. But that meeting just gave me the first ray of hope since the diagnosis."

"Well, I'm glad," Petra said. "But I'm not sure what we're talking about."

"Why not experiment on me? I know you're working on a cure, honey, but for tonight can we agree you might get there too late, that I'm probably terminal?" Off Petra's silence: "I'll take that as a *yes*. What have we—what have *I* got to lose?"

Petra stops walking, which brings Eleni to a halt as well. The two women face each other, each scrutinizing the other for a reaction. Petra looks at the grooves in her mother's cheeks, the sag in her neck, the straw-like quality of her hair. But she also sees determination.

"Then we'll go talk to Jerry together," she says, finally. She links her arm in Eleni's. "Let's head back. I've got some health news of my own to share with you along the way."

. . .

Back at Elethea, Petra waits in the conference room as Eleni fetches Jerry. When he arrives, they waste no time presenting him with their health updates and resulting joint proposal. Jerry takes the news about Petra's health in stride, as if it were something he'd suspected all along. He asks a number of procedural and science questions, some of which Petra has answers for, some of which they table for later discussion.

"We don't need to tell anyone about this—even our suitors—until we have some results," Petra says. "Worst case, you'll have a ton of new data to load into my AI system, which I need to train someone in, given my recent test numbers. Best case, it stalls the disease's progress and you're stuck with the two of us for a few more years." She pauses, then her eyes bore in on him. "What do you think?"

"I don't need to think about it," Jerry says. "As a friend, I'm sad, for both of you. But as a scientist, what you're proposing is huge. It completes the equation. Using Eleni's term, I've got two human guinea pigs with two different health profiles. The first has an advanced condition. It would have been great to track her blood from exposure up to today, but I've got the next best thing: a family member who is also a scientist and who has tracked her data regularly for the past two years."

"So you don't have a problem with it?" Petra asks.

"From a scientific standpoint, none at all. From a personal standpoint, knowing what you two are facing, it makes all the sense in the world. Count me in."

. . .

"Last chance, Mom. You're 100 percent sure you want to do this? None of us will think less of you if you decide not to."

"Are you having second thoughts, *kardia mou*?"

Petra shakes her head.

"Then neither am I. I'm sure, and I'm ready."

Eleni is sitting, half reclining, preparing for her first infusion of the BFD150 solution. The equipment is set up in a corner of the living room in Petra and Eleni's apartment, the safest place to stage this unsanctioned, unethical, and illegal experiment. The Elethea team has been sworn to secrecy. The only ones in attendance besides Eleni are Petra, Jerry, Josef, and Mona.

. . .

The infusion setup came courtesy of Mona, of course. "There's always inventory out there," she says with a shrug when Petra asks her how she managed it. "I heard about a local rheumatologist who was retiring, so I made an offer on his infusion equipment." A few days later, Petra and Josef stood in Petra's living room as Mona directed the delivery team on where to put everything, checking off the items on the packing slip—the semi-reclining chair, an infusion pump for precise control of the rate and duration of the infusion, IV bags to hold the solution, a stand to hold the IV bags, tubing, catheter hub, blood pressure cuff, pulse oximeter, thermometer, and various antiseptic and dressing supplies.

Now it's showtime. Josef, who originally pursued a medical career in Germany before deciding he'd be happier doing scientific research, handles all the equipment and preparation. He's clearly nervous, so Eleni puts a hand over his as he taps her arm, looking for a good vein.

"Relax, Josef. If I die, blame it on Petra. After all, it's her solution."

All eyes shift to Petra, who just nods at Eleni's attempt at lifting everyone's spirits. "And we're positive we've got the dosage dialed in correctly?" Petra asks. "I wouldn't mind one last set of eyes on this one."

"I checked it as well," Josef says. "We're good to go, if you and Eleni are ready. We're keeping this first treatment at the lowest end of our calculated dosage range, and for a shorter duration than subsequent infusions will last," he explains for the third time.

He has worked out the formula and dosage with a friend who runs clinical trials for an East Coast pharmaceutical company. Together the two men posed hypothetical questions for the different levels in the testing hierarchy—mouse, dog, monkey, human. Josef took all these questions and parameters to Petra, who fed them into her AI system.

The results were discussed at the daily lab update, with the team encouraged to pose all the tough questions and raise the right concerns in this setting. They were also given previews of the presentation that Zac and Petra are using for the potential acquisition companies, as well as Jerry's recap of experimental results to date and a demo of how, using Petra's AI simulations, those results can be scaled to the human level.

The one item they haven't shared with anyone, employees or possible suitors, is the actual human testing with Eleni and Petra.

Without any fanfare or drama, Josef primes the IV tubing by allowing the BFD150 solution to run through from the bag hanging above Eleni's head, removing all the air bubbles. He sterilizes the IV catheter hub and inserts its needle smoothly into Eleni's vein. The solution begins flowing into her body.

Everyone standing around goes quiet, watching Eleni intently for any reaction.

"You all look so serious. You're making me nervous," she says. "Go away."

"Do you feel anything?" asks Petra.

"Nothing at all. This chair is quite comfortable. I'm looking forward to watching my soaps from it."

The infusion pump turns off after 30 minutes and Josef frees Eleni from the catheter. She stands up, then wobbles. Her eyes flutter. Her knees start to give out. Mona rushes forward to catch her, then stops as she sees the grin on Eleni's face.

"*Skila*," Mona says, giving her a big hug.

Eleni smiles at the others. "I'm teaching her to swear in Greek. She just called me a bitch."

"How do you feel?" Josef asks.

"Comfortable. Relaxed."

"Okay," says Petra. "My turn."

Josef repeats the infusion process with Petra, then everyone gathers on the other side of the living room to talk. "What's next?" Eleni says to the group.

"Josef and I set up a schedule for increasing the dosage and infusion times," Jerry says. "If neither of you shows any negative reactions, we'll move ahead, cautiously but aggressively."

Eleni turns to Petra. "If this works, when should we start looking for changes in our symptoms?"

"We're shooting in the dark here, Mamá. But I wouldn't expect anything dramatic. If it works, our blood will tell us before any other physical changes."

Jerry pulls out a couple of syringes and vials. "Which reminds me, ladies. Give me your arms. I'll be delicate."

62

The Final Hand

"DOES EVERYONE HAVE A DRINK?" Freddy calls out. "Raise your hand if you still need something." Two hands go up, the last arrivals ferried in from the San Francisco dock. Two members of the yacht's crew take their orders and hurry off. Freddy's standing next to the dining room, which holds all of the Dicks, plus Keeley and Mona. The Elethea team, now 16 strong, is either seated in the lounge or standing, trying to look nonchalant amongst all the trappings.

"I know you've all been speculating on who was romancing us and what the final price would be. I'll let Zac and Mona update you on the terms, then turn things over for a final word from Petra."

When everyone has a drink in hand, Freddy raises his beer in salutation. "I know this journey has felt a little rocky at times, but I can assure you that it's gone smoother than almost any acquisition I've negotiated or been associated with. My first toast goes to all of you. You've achieved more in our two years of working together than any other startup I've been associated with. We, as a board, would like to toast all of you for your dedication and your innovation."

A few employees nod their thanks. A few glasses go up hesitantly, unsure whether they're supposed to toast themselves or not. Jerry raises his glass to them in encouragement, until all the arms are raised, drinks in hand.

"With that, let me turn it over to Zac and Mona, who handled all the negotiations, Zac on the final price and Mona on the terms.

Zac stands. "Let me cut right to the chase. The winner is Stanza with a price of $3.2 billion. I know you want to pull out your phones and either go to the Stanza website or calculate your share of three point two billion. But before you do that, any questions about the acquisition?"

"What's our vesting schedule?" Nick asks.

"Let me take that one," Mona says, cutting Zac off. "I need to tell you all that watching Zac negotiate with the three possible suitors was like a master class. He made each company feel like they had an inside track while at the same time using the other two competitors to raise the price. But the reason I wanted to speak up here is that he also negotiated on your behalf. Standard vesting, as I know from previous startups I've worked with, is four years. Zac negotiated that down to three years plus forward vesting in the case of Stanza being acquired. If you're not familiar with forward vesting, it means if Stanza is acquired, you will vest all your stock immediately."

"Where are they based, and will we have to move?" someone pipes up.

Zac responds. "Let me return the favor by bragging on my negotiating partner. She told all three companies that you all want to stay together in this space, to be a separate division within the company with your own managing director. They were all fine with her requests."

"What about Jerry and Petra? What are their roles?" Josef asks.

"Both of them are locked into advisory roles for two years. Jerry will focus on integrating the science into their architecture and product lines while Petra will work with the Stanza management team to develop their go-to-market strategy, starting with the announcement of the acquisition. She'll be the face of longevity, both from a science standpoint and with the media."

"Will someone from Stanza be taking over their roles?"

"Those were the final terms of the negotiation," Zac responds. "Many of you know Ed from your Salvana days. He'll be taking Jerry's role of running the lab. Cheryl Aynesworth, one of our top competitors, will be joining as Managing Director. And now, let me turn it over to Petra to wrap things up."

There is tentative applause, but it grows quickly until everyone is applauding, with a few whistles thrown into the mix. Petra is taken aback, but as the applause continues, her eyes fill. As the team keeps applauding, she walks over to Eleni, pulls her to her feet, then points at her with her free hand. The applause gets even louder, if possible.

63

The Nuts

"WHAT TIME WILL THEY BE HERE?" Zoe asks.

"Mona just texted," Jerry says. "They're on their way, though 101 is jammed—some kind of accident—so she's coming 280. Twenty minutes, she says."

The Speak Easy is almost dead, which makes sense since it's two on a Thursday afternoon. The gang is assembled to welcome Petra and Eleni back from their month-long sabbatical in Greece.

The final bid of $3.2 billion by Stanza, a biotech giant based in the Valley, was driven up almost a billion by the results from the first two months of Eleni and Petra's treatments with BFD150. By mutual agreement, the two companies have stayed dark as they work through the final details, legal and financial, and finalize their plans for the acquisition announcement and subsequent marketing campaign. Jake and Lisa, along with their Stanza counterparts, have spent the month developing the marketing rollout, with Petra and the Stanza CEO as the central players. The two, accompanied by Lisa, will travel to New York to meet with Wall Street and the analysts who cover their market, then use Zoom to meet with the mainstream and science outlets.

In an unexpected but appreciated move, Stanza gave the Elethea team two weeks of vacation, urging everyone to recharge before jumping back into the fray.

Knowing her constituency, Mona took the suggestion to heart, locking the building and refusing all entreaties to open it up. The only exception she made was for the technicians she hired to feed the remaining experimental animals.

Slipping into Grandma mode, Mona took her three youngest grandchildren to Disneyland, Legoland, and Sea World, keeping her phone on silent mode the entire trip. Jerry and Alice took their sons out of school and did a two-week tour of minor-league baseball parks, with two Phish concerts tossed into the mix. Zoe, who, along with Izaak and Alice, was the recipient of a generous 'consultant' stock package, took the same two weeks off, joining Spyder and two other climbers on a trip to Alaska.

The Dicks, cognizant of the media onslaught headed their way, have developed, with Lisa's help, a PR plan of their own. Zac and Trina will be the public faces for the launch with the investment community, discussing the risks and rewards of their 'all-in' strategy with a single player. For his part, Freddy plans to continue with the responsibilities and schedules of running Headwaters, though he will make time each afternoon for either a call or a quick meeting with Cheryl, conducting ongoing "CEO for Dummies" training.

• • •

The Speak Easy group has expanded for today to include Jake, as well as Ed and Cheryl, the two newest Elethea/Stanza employees. For Ed, reuniting with his old Salvana compatriots has been a joy, though replacing Jerry has been a delicate process, especially when Jerry is in the building. To that end, Mona has suggested to Jerry that he come in after lunch on those days that he's on-site, giving Ed a chance to run the daily briefs and develop his own management style. She's also suggested that Jerry spend two days a week at Stanza headquarters, which is up in Burlingame, near the airport.

Mona has also taken Cheryl under her wing. While Freddy continues to coach her in her new role as General Manager, Mona advises her on all things Elethea, from employee histories to the unspoken rules of company culture.

This week, with Petra and Eleni due back, she has a sit-down with Cheryl. "This is your company now, Cheryl. You're not replacing Petra, you're taking Elethea into its next phase. You're better equipped to do that than anyone, including Petra, given your management experience. Freddy will give you CEO training; I'll do the same with Elethea. Petra will defer to you in this new role, I'm sure. If she forgets, I'll remind her."

During the month Petra has been gone, Zoe has taken over as Jake's climbing coach, both at The Ascent and at Castle Rock. Combining business with possible pleasure, she put out her 'I'm-interested' vibe after one of their sessions, but the interest wasn't reciprocated. It's clear, as she tells Izaak, that the boy's got a case of the Petra blues. They both silently wish him luck.

* * *

"I can't wait to see how they look," Alice says. She turns to Jerry.

"Petra took the BFD solution with them, didn't she?" He nods. "Well, we'll see what a month on it can do, then."

As if on cue, the door to the bar opens, Mona shepherding Eleni and Petra before her. After the round of hugs, the group settles into pushed-together tables, with the late arrivals filling the empty chairs.

"At the risk of sounding like a kiss-ass," Zoe says, "you both look great. Is it the Greek sun or are my two favorite human guinea pigs now poster children for BFD150?" She turns to Jerry. "Still love that name. I hope Stanza keeps it."

"They like it, too," he says. "They say it gives an edge to their corporate personality that's been lacking."

After Eleni gives the group a 10-minute discourse on their Greek sojourn—a few days in Athens, a week in the Cyclades, the rest of the time in their family village in northern Greece—the group breaks down into a number of side conversations. Jerry leans in and says to Petra, "I know you took your test kit. What do the numbers say?"

"Mom's hit-and-hold. That's good news, given the alarming rate of decline before she started with the solution. If maintaining the status quo is as good as we get, given her advanced condition, we'll take it."

"How about you?"

"I would have been fine with hit-and-hold as well, but since I'm in an earlier stage than Mom, the solution seems to have taken hold more quickly." She tries to look nonchalant. "My numbers show an 8 percent improvement over the past month."

Jerry's smile is broad. "I'll take those numbers any day of the week. So will the folks at Stanza. If those numbers play out over other diseases, the price tag for acquiring us will look like a bargain. In my initial meetings with them, we've discussed having a small team—they call it a 'Tiger Squad'—look into your theory that the solution may apply to other diseases. Because they already have a running start with your and Eleni's data, they've made Werner and its variants their initial target. They're hoping you'll join the team, as well as serve as their guinea pig."

Zoe walks over to join the conversation. "Your mom's still on Cloud 9, regaling us with her stories about the village. How was it, visiting family you'd never met before?"

"It was great, though the language was initially a problem. I'm like most kids who grew up with a second language: I can understand better than I can speak. But since Mom was my guide for the first two weeks and only spoke Greek to anyone we met, by the time we got up north I could hold my own. Though when you're with Eleni, you don't have to do that much talking."

"Sounds like she was in her element."

"And then some. After we'd been there for a week and had a feel for the place, she sat down with the village elders and told them about her recent windfall, that it was found money as far as she was concerned, and that she wanted to use some of it to help the village. They assured her that she wouldn't be upsetting any cultural norm, that the government allocated most of its help to the places that tourists visited, so they could use the help.

"She worked with them to make a list and then went to work on it. She paid to upgrade the village clinic, structurally and with new equipment, and to dig a second well. She also worked with the local bank to establish two funds: an educational fund for the village children, both trade and university, and one for infrastructure, since so many of the buildings and houses are in bad shape. They couldn't have been more appreciative, and she couldn't have been happier."

She looks over at Jerry, taking in his latest T-shirt. "Speaking of newfound wealth, I'm glad to see that the money hasn't gone to your head. Or into your wardrobe. How are Alice and the boys dealing with it?"

"The boys have asked if we can get a place where they don't have to share a bathroom. That's about it. For now, at least."

"I'm surprised Alice doesn't want to buy and run her own minor league team."

Jerry puts his fingers to his lips and nods in Alice's direction. "Don't give her any ideas. So far, all she's done is throw out all our mismatched pots and pans and buy a new set of copper cookware. Plus, one of those things that let you hang your pans from the ceiling. I never thought of cookware as art."

"And you?"

"If you take a look in the parking lot, you'll see one of the first new VW vans, hot off the Wolfsburg assembly line. I'm already the envy of the Deadhead grapevine."

An hour later, as things are wrapping up, Jake holds the door for the departing troops. Petra is the last to leave, nodding her thanks to the wait staff, then at Jake, who follows her outside.

"Such a gentleman. So how was climbing with Zoe?"

"Challenging. She's not much on the coaching side of things, is she? Just takes off and expects you to learn by watching. Or following." He smiles. "Or falling."

"That's Zoe. Did she hit on you? She's pretty direct on that front as well."

"She did. Just once, but I told her thanks, but I'm already seeing someone else."

"You dog. I knew I should have kept my email on, regardless of what Mona said. Tell me about her. How did you guys meet?"

"It was a meet-cute, as they say in the movies."

"Where was this?"

Jake looks squarely at her, holding her eyes. "In a climbing gym."

Petra hesitates, losing a step, then regains her stride. "Huh." She slows her pace, letting the others get a bit further ahead. She tries a smile, but it's an uncertain one. "What would Mona say? You know her rules about in-house dating."

"You don't think I checked it out with her first?"

"And?"

"She said you were no longer my boss. Cheryl is. She said she doesn't even know if you're even an employee anymore."

Petra stops walking. "I hadn't thought of that." She looks at him and smiles. "Huh."

Acknowledgments

TH: This novel had its genesis in a dinner with Jim Goetz, a leading Venture Capitalist and a friend for over 30 years. Ever since I retired from Silicon Valley and started writing full-time, we'd talked about collaborating on a novel that would take the reader inside the world of Silicon Valley, both from the VC side of things and the startup/founder side.

Jim came to our first planning dinner armed with a number of technology topics that we could hang the novel around. The topics had two things in common: 1) they were fascinating by Silicon Valley standards, and 2) they would lose the general reader by page three. So we tabled the book talk for later and just got caught up.

Jim told me about a recent gathering he'd attended of fellow VCs and startup founders. Part of the meeting centered on developments in the field of biohacking, which is the desire to extend human life to its fullest extent and the willingness to be your own guinea pig in the effort. Each person at the table had their own biohacking coach, their own unique self-experiments, and some amazing stories about hacks gone wrong. And that's when I knew we had a book.

Since I wanted our protagonist to be a woman, so that we could also explore the sexism so rampant in the Valley, Jim suggested I contact Theresia Gouw, one of the most successful VCs in the Valley and someone who had just launched her own firm, populated over 50% by women. When I told Theresia that the novel was about longevity, she said I had to interview her best friend, Dr Sangeeta Bhatia, a PhD and MD (showoff), who runs a nanotechnology center at MIT that focuses on "developing novel platforms for understanding, diagnosing, and treating human disease."

I contacted Dr. Bhatia, and she invited me out to the lab where I could meet her team and get their ideas on how to create an imaginary cure for longevity that wouldn't embarrass them as scientists, or me, as a writer. Dr. Bhatia and her husband, Dr. Jagesh Shah, another slacker with multiple degrees who's a former professor at the Harvard Medical School and currently a principal at a stealth startup, invited me to their house for what turned out to be a long and enjoyable evening, where we threw ideas back and forth, both from a scientific standpoint (them), and a novelistic one (me). Dr. Bhatia then invited me to her lab, where I spent two days under the tutelage of Cathy Wang, who listened to my ideas, made suggestions, and gave me insights into what a longevity startup would need— people, equipment, schedules, tests—to be believable.

Once I started writing, I recruited my gang of usual suspects to review the early chapters. It became obvious that one of my early readers, Amanda Iles, not only had great ideas for the novel, but had experience in the biotech field. So we bumped up her status to 'co-author,' which has added immeasurably to the final project, as well as giving me someone to blame if this isn't a best-seller.

The team of early readers deserves a large amount of thanks, not just for reading each draft, but for making key suggestions that improved the final product. Thank you, Jim Decker, Larry and Cindy Loper, Linda Gruehl, Ron Terry, and Dick Schreiber. Special thanks to Sean Tippett and Dan Leary, who had a number of suggestions about the science of biohacking, and to Annie Duke, the Queen of Poker, who walked me through how she would advise my protagonist to play in a high-stakes cash poker game.

A special thanks to Asheem Chandna, one of Silicon Valley's leading VCs. Asheem has been a pal for the past two decades and has brought me into a number of fascinating start-ups. He also graciously took time to give us insights into the workings of a VC firm and the different stages of working with a startup.

I'd like to thank Liz and Steve Friar, both for their friendship and for hosting me during my visits to Silicon Valley. And Nick Zackoff and Sue Thornton, our next-door neighbors and good friends who host me whenever I go out to our lakeside cottage to get serious writing done.

Finally, to the three women who are not only the loves of my life but who expect/demand to be thanked in every book I write: my wife, Pamela Pearson, and our two daughters, Rachel and Maya.

● ● ●

AI: Tom has already explained how I became the co-author of this novel. But what he couldn't say, because (thankfully) he doesn't live inside my head, is how grateful I am for his trust and camaraderie through the whole writing process. Without puncturing his long-cultivated image as a cynical asshole, I want to say that working with Tom on this novel has been a joy.

In addition to echoing all the thank-you's Tom has given to the experts and early readers who helped shape this book, I'd like to expand the gratitude list a bit.

I've known Dr. Martin Smith, Professor of Anatomy & Neurobiology at the UC Irvine School of Medicine, since my long-ago stint as a lab assistant at UC San Diego. Martin provided valuable early guidance on how to make *The Forever Game*'s biotech science ring true—although any errors or misrepresentation of the science or lab operations are mine and Tom's alone. Dr. Charles Versaggi, for 35 years president of the highly respected Versaggi Biocommunications in Silicon Valley, added some helpful hints on balancing scientific realism with dramatic flair.

My brother, Alex Iles, has always been a fully committed supporter of me and my life. And vice versa. His amazing wife, Sandy Kipp Iles, only amplified that support. Sandy died in September 2023, after a decade-long battle with breast cancer, but not before both she and Alex became cheerleaders for this book.

Last, but definitely not least, I want to thank my husband, Jim Hatfield, for...well, really, for everything. As a fellow writer and author, he knows exactly why working on this novel has been such a big deal for me. Jim is my partner, my best friend, and the love of my life. We're a team, always. As we say, we're just a couple of kids (ignore any age associations with that word) hurtling through the universe together, with curiosity and a whole lot of laughing.

About the Authors

TOM HOGAN is the author of three novels—*The Empty Confessional*, *The Devil's Breath*, and *Left for Alive*—and co-author of *The Ultimate Startup Guide* (2017). He is also an award-winning screenwriter and has written on politics and history for *Newsweek*, *The Jerusalem Post*, and *The Bulwark*.

• • •

AMANDA ILES is a writer who creates dynamic narratives on behalf of Silicon Valley executives and companies, from Steve Jobs to the latest hot startups. Before writing professionally, she earned a biology degree and worked in a developmental neurobiology lab at UC San Diego. She also has a graduate degree from the prestigious science writing program at UC Santa Cruz.

Excerpts from previous Tom Hogan novels

Left For Alive

Chapter 1

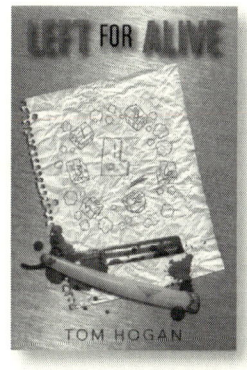

"IT'S LIKE I'M SITTING with the cast of *Deliverance*," the woman said, staring across the table at the three men. "All we're missing is the little guy with the banjo."

The men stared back at her, their faces hard and flat. The woman returned their stares, smoke braiding from the unfiltered cigarette held deep between her second and third fingers, snaking and then disappearing in the black air overhead. A burst of breeze slid through the bar's open door, pushing the smoke towards the men. When the one with the crooked nose frowned, the woman brought the cigarette down below table level, receiving a slight nod in return.

It was after closing time and The Gimp's was empty except for the four of them. The bar was dead dark, lit only by the dying fire at one end of the long room and the thin flicker of neon at the other. William and Lucky had stayed behind to help The Gimp close up. The woman was there uninvited.

The left side of her face slipped in and out of shadow in time with the neon, the whirring of the tape recorder the only sound. Her eyes moved to it. "Fine. We'll go off the record, if that'll make you boys more talkative." She jabbed her cigarette into the heavy glass ashtray and hit the Off switch.

She shook a fresh cigarette from the pack in front of her. None of the men made a move for the matches. She lit the cigarette herself and held the flaming match in front of her. "But let's get a few things straight, okay?" she said as the flame closed in on her fingers. "You don't want to help me, that's fine. Just don't insult my intelligence in the process."

The men's eyes moved from her face to the flame, which had reached her skin. She held the match a final beat, her eyes looking past the flame at the men, then shook it out with a single snap of her wrist. "For starters, lose the aw-shucks routine, okay? I mean, please. You guys are about as simple as calculus." She patted her notebook with her cigarette hand, dropping a touch of ash onto the cover. "According to my research I'm sitting across from a combined nine years of higher education and six years of prison time. So spare me the Gomer Pyle act, okay?"

The tall one broke the silence. "Since you asked so nicely, how can we help?"

The woman opened the notebook and took out two pieces of paper. Her fingers were long and yellow, the nails bitten just short of the point of pain. She pushed the papers across the table, the corner of one catching for a moment in the heavy grain.

The Gimp turned on a standing lamp with a ratty beige shade. The tall man read the two pages without touching them and without comment or expression. Then he pushed them over to The Gimp, who hummed tonelessly as his finger moved down the page. Lucky sidled to the back of the wheelchair and read over The Gimp's shoulder, his lips moving slightly as he kept pace.

"You write well," the tall one said, when the men had finished reading. "The first one—the Fairchild piece—grabs you from the opening paragraph."

"You're only saying that because you don't want me to write the second one."

"I'm saying that because the second one is lazy reporting. Your hypothesis is shaky, so you prop it up with a couple of sensational anecdotes and hope no one notices the lack of journalistic integrity."

"My, my. From hillbilly twang to full-scale erudition in six seconds." When he didn't return the smile, she dropped hers. "You miss it much, William? The teaching? I'll bet you were a hell of a professor." She pushed on. "The first one—the one you like so much—that's trodden ground. There's always a market for Donna Fairchild," she held up her fingers in quote marks— "'the J.D. Salinger of the left'—as long as she stays disappeared. So they'll publish it and I'll get to pay my rent, neither of which is a bad thing."

She nodded at the second piece of paper. "But this one. All the mystery surrounding your boy makes it more compelling. By far. And you know it. If I connect the dots the way I think I can…" She tapped the paper. "… I get the cover and a staff position. Especially if your pal Josh and Fairchild are connected. And I think they are. It all comes down to the dots."

"What kind of dots?" The Gimp pushed back from the table and wheeled his way among the tables, emptying the ashtrays into a plastic bar hanging from his armrest.

"Oh, I don't know," the woman said, mocking his nonchalant tone. "You mean, outside of his links to Fairchild and the Vasquez murder? Or why he's always the cops' first stop whenever there's a rape they can't solve? Or where he got the money to buy half this mountain?" She stubbed out the cigarette, picked up the notebook and tape recorder, and stood up. "Or where he goes when he disappears every six months?"

She smiled slightly as he stopped wheeling. "Didn't think I knew about the disappearances, did you?"

She walked to the door and stopped, her hand hovering over the knob. She turned and fixed her eyes on William. "Still don't think I'll write it, Will?"

"I think you'll try. I don't think you'll finish it, though."

Her hand tightened on the knob. "If you knew anything about reporters, you'd know the last thing you do is threaten us."

He nodded. "And if you knew anything about convicts, you'd know that if we were going to hurt you, the last thing we'd do would be to warn you first."

She started to say something, then stopped. She turned the knob and stepped out into the night.

The Devil's Breath

Prologue

HER FACE CARVED BY HUNGER AND PAIN, the woman hefted the gold ingot, her thumb partially covering the swastika in its center, and displayed it to the four men. Forehead pebbling from the furnace heat, she raised her voice above the harsh metallic chorus issuing from the adjoining room. "So this is it," she said, her voice half statement, half question. "The thing that could end your careers." Her eyes took in the three men in uniform. "And our lives." Her gesture took in herself and the fourth man, also clad in stripes.

She dabbed impatiently with her ragged sleeve at the sweat that had pooled at her eyebrows and snaked its way into her eyes before she gestured at the river of gold sluicing its way along the floor, disappearing beneath a heavy grey canvas curtain. "So let's explore, gentlemen. Let's trace this gorgeous river back to its source and see what we learn along the way."

The three stiff men—starched grey and black, lightning bolts on their collars—didn't return her gaze or acknowledge her at first. They weren't used to being talked to that way by a woman, much less a Jew. But they had no choice, at least for now. They would restore the balance and take their revenge after the woman and her partner had served their purpose.

As she turned from the soldiers, the woman chanced a quick gaze at her striped cohort. He was her age, mid-thirties, and as drained and beaten down physically as her. But his posture was almost as erect as those of the men in grey and black, and his eyes were alert. Catching his eye, the woman winked and saw him smile slightly before he dipped his head.

She placed the bar on the table with a deliberate thud, bringing the men's attention back to the item and her, and turned her eyes to the oldest and smallest of the three, the one with a bar and leaf next to his lightning bolt. "Herr Kommandant, if you would."

The Kommandant strode across the spotless cement floor, the harsh staccato of his heels cutting through the sweltering air, and led the group to a heavily polished steel door that mirrored the image of the approaching group in silver and grey tones. The group waited, eyes fixed on the door, until the Kommandant broke the silence. "I don't think it's going to open itself, Fritzsch."

As if slapped, the man to his right snapped to attention. Narrow faced with a grey complexion and deep-set eyes, he stepped forward crisply and placed one hand on the large, num-bered wheel, the other on the thick steel bar that bisected it. He turned the wheel twice to his left, listening for the click, then repeated the process in the opposite direction. At the second click, he pulled down on the bar.

The door opened silently on well-oiled hinges, the only sound the whispering of the rubbery seal at its bottom gliding along the floor. A blast of heat rushed out, causing the woman's short, butchered hair to stand to attention. The men blinked once collectively at the heat before their eyes tightened and focused on the room that emerged before them.

With the Kommandant again leading the way, the group

stepped into a large warehouse, its expanse cordoned off into separate areas by heavy canvas curtains that felt more like walls than dividers. The interior landscape was a study in grey: floors, curtains, walls, even the air.

A new wave of flamed air swamped the group, bringing a wet sparkle to their faces. As the Kommandant reached for his coat pocket, Fritzsch stepped forward with a handkerchief and moved to dry his glistening skin. But the Kommandant snatched the square cloth and dabbed at his own growing sweat. The other two SS stood silent and still, the sweat running down their temples, pooling along their jaws, and dropping to the floor. The striped pair put their sleeves to use, the thin cloth drying before they lowered their arms.

The first area contained two tables bowing under the weight of the ingots that were putting forth a dying heat as they congealed in their cooling forms. As the ingots neared their final state, a prisoner moved down the line, impressing a small swastika into the damp gold. When the group approached the table, the worker snatched off his striped cap and snapped to attention.

The Kommandant looked expectantly at Fritzsch, who again stepped forward. "Take your water break now," he ordered, "and don't return until we're gone." The man hastened off, his stride stiff from standing at his post for the past four hours.

The Kommandant walked to the table and picked up a still-warm ingot from a stack and examined it idly, turning it over in his hands. As if to regain his authority and control of the moment, he tossed the gold bar at the woman. Expecting the move, or something like it, she caught the brick cleanly with both hands and placed it back in its place on the stack.

Squaring his shoulders, the Kommandant took a deep breath and surveyed the small group. The two uniformed men, schooled in the Reich's ways, looked at him without meeting his eyes. The two prisoners, reflecting their new roles and the self-confidence that came with them, held his gaze, though there was nothing challenging in their eyes.

Letting his breath out slowly, the Kommandant looked first at the woman, then at her partner. "You're correct, my Jewess, both about my career and your lives. We have one week before Reichsführer Himmler and his accountant arrive for their audit and subsequent share of . . ." He motioned roughly at the table of gold. "Which brings us to our discrepancy. One that could prove fatal to all of us." He shook his head slightly, as if he couldn't believe it had come to this.

"These ingots," he continued, "are now regarded as a critical Reich asset, a major contributor to the war effort. So they are treated as such, meaning that we record and track them with diligence. There is one slight caveat. As creators and administrators of this prized asset—one that is unique to Auschwitz—both Reichsführer Himmler and I take a small portion as recompense for our initiative."

The man in stripes spoke for the first time. "I'm assuming, then, that this ingot has a twin. One without a stamp."

"Correct. At the end of each shift, the workers introduce a separate form, one that lacks the swastika. Those ingots, once cooled, are stored and counted separately from their swastika compatriots." He motioned to a separate area, partially hidden by a smaller canvas, behind which the group could see a small stack of ingots cooling on a metal table.

"Now a significant percentage of these ingots—to be clear, *my* ingots—have gone missing, along with the means of accounting for them. Finding those missing ingots and ledger, and the murderer who stole them, is your assignment. And as you correctly surmised," he said, nodding at the woman, "your only hope of survival."

The Kommandant led them alongside the sluice of gold until it disappeared under the canvas, a piece of which had been cut to allow the river's flow. Fritzsch parted the curtain and motioned the group forward.

The next area was dominated by a head-high cauldron of yet another shade of grey, this one the hard tone of a gun barrel. Its top issued a steady hissing sound, interrupted occasionally by the belch of dissolving gold. Haphazard wooden stairs in need of repair and additional support led up one side of the cauldron, culminating in a small platform, a precarious perch at the cauldron's lip with no railings. The workers up there strained against two objectives: emptying their wheelbarrows as quickly as possible and avoiding the ten-foot drop to the concrete, knowing that even a sprained ankle would be grounds for immediate replacement and subsequent execution.

A prisoner clad in only pants and heavy gloves stirred the liquid with a large oar-like object, his ropy muscles tensing and straining. In the gloom of the large room, he was a man of two colors, a fierce yellow on the front from the sweat and the ingredients of the cauldron and a dull grey on the back. On the far side of the room, a gradually escalating ramp made its way from the warehouse floor to the platform. The ramp was wide enough to contain two wheelbarrows, one ascending and the other descending. As the incoming wheelbarrow arrived, another worker stripped to the waist dug his shovel into the wheelbarrow bed and emptied its contents into the cauldron.

At the Kommandant's nod, the group moved as one to the next curtain, stopping to let the empty descending wheelbarrow pass. Fritzsch walked on ahead, put his hand on the curtain opening, and looked at the Kommandant, who shook his head, gesturing to keep the curtain closed.

"Last stop, the source of our gold," the Kommandant said. His eyes fastened on the prisoners. "And spare me your moral outrage, my Jews. As you'll see, the contributors of this gold are making no such objections." He nodded at Fritzsch, who parted the curtain.

This section of the warehouse was draped in darkness that was only interrupted by three high-intensity lamps, each of which hovered over a gleaming metal table. Halos illuminated the tables with harsh clarity, the strength of the light dimming with each meter away from the table and the body it held. It took a moment for the group's collective eyes to adjust to the dark and make out the pile of corpses stacked against the far wall. Two men, their arms and shoulders muscled, the rest of their bodies emaciated, hauled a corpse by the wrists and ankles to a waiting table where a striped worker opened the corpse's mouth, peered in, and then either shook his head—at which time the corpse was taken away—or went to work with his hammer and pliers, extracting the gold. Whatever he extracted, he dropped into the wheelbarrow next to his table, the sound of its landing softened by the teeth already harvested.

Then, with his right hand, which was clad in a thin surgical glove, he inserted a finger into the corpse's anus and felt around. If he discovered anything of interest, he reached for a large carving knife that sat on a stool next to him. Otherwise he motioned for the corpse to be taken away.

The woman held her face steady as she looked at the operation and the pile of teeth. She felt the eyes of the group, especially those of the Kommandant, on her. Her jaw tremored slightly, but she controlled it. Then she spoke. "I've seen what I needed."

The Kommandant nodded and turned to the striped man. "And you, my detective? Have you seen enough?"

"More than enough," the man said, his eyes fixed on the Kommandant. "It's an impressive operation that you and the

Reichsführer have built here. I'm sure history will be kind to you both."

Fritzsch took a step toward the man, but the Kommandant placed a single restraining finger on his chest. "I like your sense of irony, Jew. And your gallows humor." He smiled slightly. "Unless you and your wife would like to join that pile of corpses, you'll find me my killer, my ledger, and my gold. Now get the hell out of my sight."

The Empty Confessional

Prologue

Pittsburgh 2000

THE PRIEST WHISTLED TO HIMSELF a big band song from a bygone era. Slight of build and in his late thirties, he wore Dad jeans and a short-sleeved collared shirt with a Roman collar. His face, small-chinned and dominated by a hatchet nose, slid into a smile as he looked around the living room one last time.

The room still held the faintly fresh odor of the paint job one of the parish parents and his crew had completed in one busy day a month back. The IKEA furniture, an aging collection of ash and chrome—assembled by his fellow priests years ago in one beer-fueled and frustrating weekend—was arranged in a loose square, the center of which had been the focal point of that night's gathering. The coffee table had been pushed over to the far corner to free up the center, but his departing brethren had forgotten to put it back. Frowning, he walked over and, bending at the knee, pulled and shimmied the table to its proper position.

Trash bag in hand, he made one last circuit through the living room, gathering the remaining pizza boxes and napkins. He crossed to the front door and set the bag down, leaving it for the housekeeper who would be there in the morning. Nodding at the results of his efforts, he keyed in the security code and stepped out onto the covered porch.

It was as if the night couldn't make up its mind. When he had arrived at the cottage to set things up earlier that evening, it had been humid, the sky almost dripping. By the time the first guests arrived, the damp had turned to rain—not heavy but steady, enough to impel him to run out to the arriving cars with his umbrella. Now, with the evening concluded, the night air was crisp and the stars were out.

As the door clicked behind him, he stood for a moment and breathed in the crisp taste of the evening. Off in the distance he could hear a car with a bad muffler gargling its way down the street. He heard the neighborhood turning in: men picking up their beer cans from the stoop and shuffling inside; mothers gathering up the older kids, calling back inside to the younger ones; the odd whistles calling dogs home. The priest smiled to himself. Things felt right, in their place, as if he'd stepped back in time to a fifties sitcom.

His smile broadened as he thought back to the evening's events. It had been one of their most successful and enjoyable gatherings. The regulars had all played their roles, taking their places and joining in the activities without coaxing. The sole first-timer, a girl of seventeen with Botticelli looks, had stayed on the sideline at first, viewing the action with curiosity but unsure of where she fit in. But eventually, with the encouragement and coaching of one of the veterans, she joined in, at first cautiously, then enthusiastically. Those moments for the scrapbook made it all worthwhile.

The priest stepped lightly down the steps to the front walkway, which led to the driveway and the parish car, a late-model

Cutlass. With the faint porch light not extending beyond the front steps, he had to negotiate his way to the car in the semi-dark. But it was a calming dark, a warm gray that had the feel of a blanket at the end of a good day.

He took a shortcut across the lawn toward his car. His shoe moved from concrete to the soft reassurance of grass. As he felt it shift from grass to the gravel driveway, he stopped to let his eyes get accustomed to the dark, made heavier by an overgrown wall of shadow, high hedges, and ivy lining the far side of the driveway.

He took out his phone, flipped it open, dialed a number, and held the phone to his ear, his free hand reaching for the car keys. "Kevin? Jeff. Yeah, sorry about the last-minute notice. You know how it goes. With everyone so busy, you grab the moments when you can." He listened and nodded, moving around the back of the car and stopping at the driver's door. "We had the same thought about a schedule. From here on, it'll be the first Friday of every month." He listened some more. "Uh-huh. The regular crowd plus a newbie. Remember that girl who had the lead in *Grease* last fall? Yeah, that one. She was hesitant at first, but you know how Jerry is with rookies." He listened and chuckled. "Yeah, the 'teen whisperer.' Okay. See you next Friday then." He pocketed the phone.

He was still smiling to himself when a black-clad figure moving with stealth and purpose stepped silently from a hollow in the bushes lining the driveway that hadn't been there earlier. His left hand gripped the priest by the shoulder and spun him around. In a blur of flesh, bone, and motion, he drove three fingers into the space right above the Roman collar. The priest's throat spasmed once, a rhythmic flow of muscle and flesh, then collapsed, closing off speech and breath. The throat muscles spasmed once more before beginning to regain their shape, but the ability to speak was gone and breathing was only partially restored.

The priest's knees buckled, but before he could collapse, his assailant caught and dragged him into the hollow. It was dark and dense, with the feel of a cave. The two figures disappeared into it at the same time. Crossing his ankles, the figure in black slowly lowered himself and his cargo into a sitting position, a graceful motion that resembled an origami exercise. The assailant cradled the stricken priest in the crook of his arm and patted his cheek gently with that hand while the other rested lightly on the priest's throat, a gentle but powerful reminder of who was in charge.

The figure in black lowered his head until his mouth was right next to the priest's ear and said in a calming voice, "I know you can't speak, Father, so I'll say your confession for you. I'll try not to get anything wrong." His voice deepened slightly. "Bless me, Father, for I have sinned. My sins are: I have violated the trust and the bodies of children, damaging them for life. Including earlier tonight."

Disconcerted by the sudden violence followed by the gentle voice in his ear, the priest tried to gather himself and assess his situation. Realizing how close he was to both the street and the church, he let his shoulders slump, as if in defeat. At the same time, he gathered his muscles to scream and thrash. Anticipating the move, his attacker stifled the shout in his throat with a strong pinch of the thumb and middle finger to the priest's larynx. His other hand reached over and pinched the nerves next to the collarbone, sapping the strength the priest was marshalling in his knees to attempt to flee.

"And did you conclude the festivities by warning the kids that they and their families would go straight to hell if they told anyone about this evening, just like the other times?"

The priest's shout slid out as a silent rush of air, the last breath of a wounded animal. The futility of that sound, as much as the total control his assailant asserted with his fingers, caused him to surrender. His body went slack, the muscles softening.

His assailant nodded at the capitulation. "Wise move, Father. Now, as for your penance, I think we'd both agree that ten Hail Marys won't cut it. Not for the damage you've done, not just tonight, but in all those evenings in the past. Damage that will last for the rest of these kids' lives, through their adult lives and to the grave. Help me out here and put yourself in my place. What would you suggest for a crime of this magnitude?" He relaxed his control over the priest's vocal cords, but no response came.

"Didn't think so." He cradled the priest, one hand resting on his forehead, a move both comforting and restrictive. With the priest completely quiet, the man whispered into his ear, "You know how at the end of the Act of Contrition, that part where you promise to sin no more? I'm going to help you keep that promise by making it impossible for you to sin in this particular way ever again."

The priest's eyes widened, but all he could make out was a masked face that blended into the leafy darkness. His eyes closed as he felt the taut forearms tighten like a vise on his neck and then squeeze. As he felt himself collapse, the darkness closed over him.

Easing his way out from under the slack body, the black-clad figure knelt over the priest for a moment, taking a final assessment. Kneeling atop the unconscious man, he spread the priest's knees with his own until the upper legs were splayed and the groin was exposed. He flexed his hands once, then he tucked his thumbs and little fingers under, turning the remaining calloused fingers into hardened instruments. Calmly and methodically, he reared back and then pistoned his arms, driving his fingers into the priest's groin in three quick strikes.

He stood up for a moment and turned to leave but stopped, turned back, and repeated the attack. The only sounds disrupting the quiet night were the dull sound of the strikes finding their home and the whisper of the unconscious priest twitching reflexively at the pain.

Connect with the Author

Leave a Review on Amazon
Did you enjoy the journey? Your thoughts matter! Leaving a review on Amazon not only helps spread the word but also inspires more readers to dive into this story. *https://www.amazon.com/stores/Tom-Hogan/author/B078FH6K83?ref=sr_ntt_srch_lnk_1&qid=1740425308&sr=8-1&isDramIntegrated=true&shoppingPortalEnabled=true*

Visit the Author's Website
Want to go deeper into the story? Visit Tom''s official website for exclusive content, book updates, and a behind-the-scenes look at the creative process. *https://tom-hogan.com/*

Join the Author's Mailing List
Be the first to know about new releases, special deals, and more! Sign up for Tom's mailing list and never miss a moment of the magic. *https://mailchi.mp/aad207eeca50/ tom-hogan-author-website-subscription*

Made in United States
North Haven, CT
22 May 2025

68894213R00238